# THE DOOMSDAY SCENARIO

Jack Ramsay was born in Liverpool in 1961, to a sixteen year old girl who lived in a tiny house situated at the famous Wigan Pier. Against his mother's will, he was adopted at six weeks of age and brought up by new parents in the industrial West Riding of Yorkshire.

After studying for a degree in Industrial Design, he worked in the film and television industry, creating futuristic special effects for *Thunderbirds* producer Gerry Anderson and contributing to numerous television commercials and several feature films, including *Aliens* for *Terminator 2* director James Cameron. He has also run his own successful modelling company, where he was involved with advertising campaigns for many of Britain's leading industrial manufacturers.

Jack Ramsay has written for several newspapers and is the author and photographer of two previous non-fiction books about England. The first, *Made in Huddersfield* (NWP, 1989), was written at the height of the Eighties economic boom and is a powerful social commentary describing the ravaged industrial heartlands of Lancashire and Yorkshire. The book was found to be 'haunting and wonderfully photographed,' by the *Observer*, and the late Lindsay Anderson, who considered it to be a 'truly remarkable and poetic work,' recommended it in the *Spectator*'s best books selection of 1990.

The success of *Made in Huddersfield* led to the author being commissioned in 1991 to travel through England and write about what he found. Inspired by J. B. Priestley's historic English journey of the 1930s, the resulting book, *England, This England* (Sinclair-Stevenson, 1993) aroused some controversy and was serialized in six parts by BBC Radio.

Jack Ramsay recently made his way 'back to Wigan Pier', and was reunited with his natural mother after thirty-three years. He is married, has one son, and divides his time between his home in Lancashire and a cottage in Yorkshire.

*Author photograph by Gordon Peate*

JACK RAMSAY

# The Doomsday Scenario

*A story set in an imaginary Britain
of the present in the very near future,
whenever that may happen to be.*

PUBLISHING ASSOCIATES
LONDON

**THE DOOMSDAY SCENARIO**

First published in 1995 by The Publishing Associates
41-42 Berners Street, London W1P 3AA

The Publishing Associates is a division of
Berserk Entertainment Ltd
Registered Offices: London, England

A CIP catalogue record is available for
this book at the British Library

ISBN 1 899622 00 4

Set in Linotype Sabon by The Publishing Associates

Printed and bound in Great Britain by
HarperCollins Manufacturing, Glasgow
A division of HarperCollins Publishers

*for my mothers*

Watchman, what of the night?
ISAIAH 21:11

Michael Greenhalgh's head was throbbing and his stomach had started to hurt. He didn't know how he was managing to stand up, only that his limbs were so heavy and his muscles so fatigued that by now he should be falling; he should be crumpling to the floor.

He was aware that he was in an empty upstairs room, and that the room was intolerably cold. Coming from some-where close was the relentless thumping of reggae music, and the sporadic sound of gunshots muffled through flimsy walls. Beyond that he knew nothing except that he was naked, and that sometime earlier in his life, sometime long ago, he had registered very old wallpaper and noticed worn linoleum, flecked with a pattern of black and red and orange.

Three men were standing before him now and his six-foot-four-inch frame towered above them all. They were poking him and touching him; testing him, it seemed, for damage. He could not see their faces. Their faces were visible enough, of course, but he had no wish to linger over the details. For their faces must not matter. To see them would be to admit that they were real, and ever since his nightmare had begun he had not wanted to admit that they were real. To do so would be to acknowledge that these faces were going to kill him, and that would send him mad; it would mean the manimals had won.

One of the faces came close to him. Its mouth contorted

into a grimace and from between yellow-green teeth came a
string of filthy adjectives. The noises travelled on an air current embellished by what seemed to be a stink of faeces or
vomit, but which was the phenomenon called bad breath.
The noises Greenhalgh heard were meaningless, for his ears
refused to interpret the words and would not have done so
had he even tried.

A hand reached up and took him roughly by the chin. The
thick fingers shifted his face from side to side, each jerk to
the left making him aware of a patch of brilliant sunshine
stretched across the bare linoleum floor. The hand began
probing him elsewhere, and though he couldn't make out his
own words, he knew that he'd retaliated with a barrage of
distorted oaths. Instantly, a searing pain struck him in his
midriffs; a sort of muffled explosion sounded followed by
the flattening of his nose against the ice-cold floor. There
came a sensation of carbonated water to his nostrils, and
what he could have sworn was the crunch of his own breaking teeth.

Then he was filled with a loaded numbness; the patterns
of the linoleum were huge and very detailed; a dozen stinking cigarette ends fanned about his face.

*

Events were moving quickly now. The brittle blackness was
parting as though he were prising from beneath a heavy veil.
Greenhalgh knew there was a pain coming from his body
again. He was conscious that he was lying on a mattress;
that a dirty syringe was being held up; that a teardrop of
moisture was hanging tremulously from the end. There came
a needle prick and the hot liquid it released caused his
muscles to relax then almost immediately to contract. There
was a pressure, an expanding pressure, a liquid pressure
concentrated into a boiling sensation, active at the place of
entry near his abdomen, coursing through his body, drilling
into flesh.

*The liquid was pumping slowly into his arm, into his legs, into his entire body. The needle was plunging deep, horribly deep, but still no vision, only the cold less excruciating than it had been, the pain of warmth filling him up.*

*And now a heaviness, a wonderful expanding heaviness, almost sexual in intensity, very definitely sexual in intensity. His face being pressed suffocatingly into a pillow that smelt of cordite and oil. The hinges of his jawbone feeling like they were going to break as there came a vision of the three men clambering above him stuffing something into his mouth, a tangle of limbs receding into perspective, seeming to be naked as well, but probably not. Surely to God not, as he tasted blood and the cordite burned his throat.*

*And then the pain and the pillow again, coupled to a sensation that his body was being violated, horribly violated; fingers clawing at his face, hitting, smacking, swiping, stroking, sweaty hands clutching at his neck, followed by extended screams and a violent thump, like the cobbles had hit his face back in the alley after he'd been shot.*

\*

*Coming awake again, coming out into the light. Going off the ground, the weight of his body pulling agonizingly against his neck, being lifted from its duty upon the earth by his straining head. Verticals moving in crazy patterns, the old linoleum vanished, the light of day passed into night. Cold tarmac, broken glass, a cold night, a frosty night, a glimpse of inner-city pavement fading into black.*

\*

*Still going higher, up to the stretching lights of a distant city, up towards the stars. The feeling of being unable to breathe, an image of Francis Bacon's* The Screaming Man, *the mouth contorting, lunging, being replaced by the mouth of Michael Greenhalgh. By the big backbencher himself, surrounded by a bouquet of greedy microphones, jabbing his forefinger at a crowd, timing another cluster-bomb of words. The notorious Conservative Party MP for the West Midlands constituency of Ackebourne East, the papers always said. The fascist bastard who wanted to bring back hanging, the editors always said. But it had been a damned good speech, a brilliant speech, the speech of Prime Minister material according to* The Times. *The type of flagship speech that captures the mood of nations.*

*Now the maverick speaker was pirouetting on a fountain of glutinous bile. He was squealing like a terrified child. He'd become the frightened baby contained within all men suddenly released, screaming, crying, screaming, crying. Party and politics, the satisfying feeling of adulation before fawning subjects, the lust for power and prestige: each was taking on its true significance now and mattering not a damn.*

*The stem of a streetlamp going away into perspective as his life began to die. His feet beneath him at the end of naked hairy legs, the ankles like his wrists bound with sticky tape, his soles slashed with knives so the blood would fetch the dogs. Old stone flags catching an orange glow, the shadow of his lynching dangled in a puddle splashed against the night.*

\*

*Cold sweetish-smelling liquid suddenly running down his buttocks and thighs, then a pause, then a huge blinding flash, flames leaping all around. The weight of his body still pulling, but the curtains closing now, the struggle at an end.*

*Braided curtains, salubrious curtains. The most wonderful curtains he had ever known.*

# PART ONE

*Toward the New Social Order*

# One

The opening titles to ITN's *Early Evening News* were assembling on television screens throughout Britain.

Blue mirrored surfaces were turning smoothly on an invisible axis and becoming huge chromium-plated letters tumbling towards a vortex in the centre of the picture. At the same time a synthesized noise, somewhere between the roar of a hurricane and a volcanic explosion, was erupting as an overblown male voice announced the time of the bulletin and the name of its presenter. When the title of the programme had formed, the chrome letters assumed the consistency of molten metal and changed into an aerial view of the twenty-first-century London city skyline. Skyscrapers flashed past and there appeared the illuminated face of Big Ben. As it met the camera Big Ben exploded and the spinning shards were rearranged into the new ITN studios at Gray's Inn Road, emblazoned like a giant Wurlitzer against the night sky. Now there appeared so quickly the head and shoulders of Trevor McDonald it was a wonder the camera didn't knock him backwards off his chair, as it tore in atop the swish and flash and flare of a laser-bolt, and met him seated at a desk that seemed to be made from neon light.

Trevor McDonald was wearing a shiny mauve-coloured suit and tie and a cream silk shirt. He straightened a transparent pen between his fingers then assumed a sombre expression and a melodramatic tone.

'Hello,' he said.

'Britain could be on the verge of seeing the reintroduction of capital punishment, civil liberties groups were claiming this evening.

'The wave of moral outrage that has swept the country since the brutal murder two weeks ago of Tory MP Michael Greenhalgh is finally prompting ministers to act. Rumours abound that the controversial Crime and Punishment Bill may be brought in as Instant Legislation within a matter of days. Because of the vicious rioting that has gripped our inner cities, some observers believe that its entry onto the statute books is now inevitable. Although cameras have been barred from the debate, a scene of pandemonium is said to be reigning inside the Commons, with both sides locked over claims made by the Labour Party that secret ultra-modern "death chambers" have been commissioned in five of Britain's biggest prisons, and a revelation in the *Guardian* newspaper that an advanced "super drug" is being developed with which to carry out a punitive sentence.

'As if these allegations were not enough for the government to contend with, ITN can exclusively reveal that a number of top-level meetings have taken place at Chequers since early summer to discuss the new legislation. It is believed that senior Civil Servants and Police Chiefs were in attendance, along with prison officials from the United States and a representative from the European Court of Human Rights. Our sources indicate that the purpose of the talks has been to determine the most cost-effective way of carrying out a death sentence, hence the presence of advisors from America where the death penalty remains in force, and where different types of execution are practised across many states.

'Excited by these rumours, a huge crowd has gathered outside Parliament, where a gigantic videowall is currently playing a recording of Michael Greenhalgh's last public address as a tribute to the dead politician's popularity. Similar crowds have assembled in city centres across the country, leaving little doubt amongst political commentators tonight that capital punishment stands a greater chance of being reinstated than at any time since it was abolished nearly forty years ago.

'Meanwhile, *is* the Prime Minister likely to address calls to hold a referendum about the capital punishment issue, even though it is widely accepted that most of the population would unequivocally support the government's view? And if so, how soon might that referendum be?

'Live to our political editor now to find out.

'What's the atmosphere like with you at Westminster this evening, Richard?'

Various high-angle shots of the huge Westminster crowd had already been shown as Trevor McDonald was talking. Now the screen performed a clever optical trick and Richard Abraham's thin, bespectacled face was left filling the frame. Behind him, Michael Greenhalgh's silvery-haired features were animating furiously on the three-storey-high videowall, which looked like a cinema screen superimposed against the floodlit night. The booming voice was being relayed around the square by a series of enormous speakers, and clusters of coloured lights were hanging like bunches of fluorescent grapes above a multitude of tiny heads. Greenhalgh, who'd always looked too lopsided and large to fit comfortably into his own suits, but who'd been that rarest of creatures, a handsome politician, was ranting on about his pet subject of race relations. Whenever he generated a pause, the gargantuan face disappeared and was replaced by hundreds of miniature facsimiles, row upon tiny row, and each about the size of a domestic television screen. Then, almost as quickly, the videowall was filled with a single massive picture, but this time shown from a different camera angle, the fast-action editing working with the politician's words to generate a stream of acoustic energy relentlessly bombarding the night.

'It's very tense indeed, Trevor,' Richard Abraham was saying, in response to Trevor McDonald's prompting. 'As you can see, the entire population of London seems to have gathered here tonight, in anticipation of the new Bill passing successfully through its first reading. In memory of its larger-than-life author, a recording of Michael Greenhalgh's final public speech, which opened the Law and Order Debate at the Tory conference the day he was kidnapped, and undoubtedly his finest performance ever, is filling the videowall behind me.

'Standing here, I'm struck by the way this man's forceful political personality continues to make its extraordinary presence felt, captivating every face in this huge assembled crowd. Passionate, gregarious, a quite brilliant orator forever thumping clenched fists at the air, he seems to drag the words from his mouth and mould them in front of his face with his hands. He must be the only politician able to cause thousands of people to remain absolutely rivetted, merely by glowering at them in silence.'

There was another high-angle shot of the videowall and then Trevor McDonald was on the screen again. 'The way in which party speeches are co-ordinated nowadays seems to show how heavily politicians have come to depend on show-business techniques in the marketing of themselves, wouldn't you say, Richard?'

'It certainly does, Trevor. There can be little doubt that this new generation of videowalls suited the public persona of Michael Greenhalgh and the robust nature of his emotional language. But then, he was a performer and an astute exhibitionist who thrived on adulation. He was perhaps the quintessential example of a new breed of extravagant show-business politician, quite apart from being one of the most controversial.'

'We can see the truly enormous crowd behind you, but is the mood confrontational? Are we likely to see clashes between demonstrators and the police?'

'I think that's very unlikely. This rally has been skilfully orchestrated in a short space of time by the Tory Right, and it has one overriding aim—to manifest the intensity of public anger about the crime and punishment issue, in the capital city, outside the governing chamber, while perhaps the most contentious piece of legislation is being considered inside that chamber since the ending of the Second World War. The police are not here to provoke the demonstrators, but to protect them from a number of subversive left-wing groups that have been gathering at various open spaces in London since this afternoon.

'And that shows what a remarkable transformation has taken place in the social atmosphere of this country since I reported on a huge demonstration in Grosvenor Square a little over thirty years ago, and which was so reminiscent of the scene here this evening. Looking at the complexion of this crowd one begins to comprehend how the temper of our nation has changed, not by considering the political orientation of these people, which is far from being anti-Establishment, but by looking at how they are being policed. It was observed during the last war that the reason British servicemen did not practise the goose-step or wear the jackboot when they were on parade was because the ordinary people of this country would have laughed, and that continued to be true until very recently.

'But look behind me now,' he said, raising a gloved hand. 'We might not have arrived at the police state yet, but we *have* introduced the jackboot, and nobody has so much as sniggered. Our police force is in the process of becoming a paramilitary agency of law enforcement. National identity cards have finally arrived and were brought in under the jurisdiction of public opinion. And if it's long been said that a country gets the government it deserves, then I think it would be fair to say that the huge riot constables who are parading behind me, their faces blank and impassive behind the tinted night-visors of their helmets, their machineguns slung across their breasts, suggests that a country gets the police force it deserves as well. This, perhaps more than a popular desire to see capital punishment reinstated, reveals the subtle changes that are being worked deep within our society.'

To punctuate Richard Abraham's observations, there was a shot of several scowling riot policeman strutting before a jumble of digitized placards, jaws square, dark-blue padded leather glistening, heads-and-shoulders above the crowd and looking like low-budget rejects from an old *Terminator* film, but immeasurably more convincing because they were real.

Then back to Trevor McDonald at the studio.

'Richard, over the past few weeks we've seen rioting in Britain's inner cities, where a drugs culture has nurtured a generation of violent youngsters who seem to have no regard for human life whatsoever. We've seen what amounted to a General Strike by the ordinary people of Britain, in protest at the government's failure to crack down on crime. The Opposition Parties' Initiative 2000 was sent packing by voters in last year's local elections.

'Why do you think emotion in the country is running so high, and do you think our politicians are *seriously* discussing bringing back the death penalty today?'

Richard Abraham again.

'It is almost a part of parliamentary tradition for the Conservatives to present every couple of years a motion to the Commons to bring back the death penalty, but in the past it has always been defeated. The surge of moral outrage that has exploded across Britain these past few weeks, however, is quite unprecedented, though I think it would be difficult for any politician to deny that it is something which has been building for a very long time. Every so often, one of these horrific murders grabs the headlines and the whole country seems to respond. My colleagues would probably agree that the popular mood began to deteriorate after the murder in Liverpool some years ago of little James Bulger, when one Cardinal observed that Britain had suddenly caught sight of itself in a mirror and hadn't liked what it had seen. Since then, we've had a catalogue of such heinous high-profile crimes, including the Winchester student massacre, and the brutal killing of the policeman David Kowalski's wife and daughter in Manchester earlier this year.

Police and ambulance men are knifed or shot to death almost daily. It seems that human life is being reduced to the cheapest imaginable price. A state of emergency has been declared because of recent rioting. And now we have the truly horrific murder of Tory MP Michael Greenhalgh.'

Trevor McDonald had turned to face a holographic television screen that had assembled alongside him from a rush of glittering starburst, and which was floating ethereally above his chrome-plated desktop. 'Are you saying that there is a growing crisis in national morale, Richard?'

'Very much so, yes, and you only have to consider the feelings embodied by this crowd tonight to understand why. People feel desperately vulnerable. There seems to have risen to the surface a popular awareness that society really is on the slide, and that it might be about to start cracking around the edges.'

'People feel the law does not protect them any longer?'

'Yes. Crime figures have been rising to epidemic proportions throughout the past twenty years. Unemployment has reached almost five million—and that is only the official figure which many would dispute. There's a growing awareness that the crimewave is beginning to undermine the stability of our society, and that unless something radical is done soon—especially to combat the drugs problem—things may get out of hand.'

'Why, then, the significance of the Michael Greenhalgh killing?'

'I think his death could prove to be the final straw. He had the ability—and this is so very rare in politics nowadays—to give voice to the aspirations and frustrations of millions. He was critical of our social and economic structure, whilst his blunt comments regarding immigration control had gained him something of a new Powellian notoriety, although recent riots have very much vindicated his claims. Indeed, he was saying things publicly during the closing months of his life that only a few years ago would have been considered so politically incorrect as to be unthinkable in the extreme, even coming from the mouth of a right-wing Conservative such as him. Here was a man who put the question of Law and Order at the very top of the political agenda, as the country now seems to feel that we must. As a consequence, he was *hugely* popular with voters of all political persuasions. The fact that he tabled a motion to bring back hanging but was then abducted by a criminal gang and was raped and murdered and left hanging from a streetlamp in Manchester has, I think, been interpreted by the British people as a snub by the forces of lawlessness, against a popular desire to see capital punishment reinstated.'

As if to underline these words, the crowd cheered in response to a particularly poignant observation Greenhalgh had just made about the leniency still being shown towards convicted murderers. Although it had been forming a background noise to Richard Abraham's commentary, the dead politician's voice was achieving an almost evangelical intensity now, and anyone watching could see why it was being said that British political gatherings were becoming more Americanized every year. The thunderous rounds of applause that were accompanying the impassioned performance were so perfectly timed one could have believed there was a floor manager down at the front, prompting the audience when it had to clap. The idea behind the writing of the original speech had been to turn it into a piece of dynamic live entertainment; to heighten the impact of party doctrine by using key phrases that had become as mentally recognizable to the electorate as the pack-shots at the end of television commercials. And even though this was a video recording of a speech that had gained international notoriety, because of the audiovisual amplification, it was crackling like a fireworks display across the bitter-cold Westminster air with as much passion as when it had first been uttered.

When the applause began to subside, the ITN vision mixer cut to Trevor McDonald touching his earpiece back at the studio. 'We have a live report coming up from the Prime Minister's Nottinghamshire constituency, Richard, so we'll come back to you a little later in the programme. But before we go, do you think there's likely to be a referendum, and are we living through what could prove to be a turning point in British social history, if the new Bill achieves the Royal Assent?'

Richard Abraham commanded the screen again. The roar of the crowd had died away enough for him to speak, though his voice now had to contend with the pounding of rotor-blades high overhead.

'There's a belief in Westminster this evening that the vote on Greenhalgh's Bill is likely to be a very close-run thing, but that the government will probably win the day. As for a referendum, unlike the European *débâcle* some years back, I think this is one occasion where the government could be sure of unanimous public support, which would certainly strengthen the party's image. The problem for the Prime Minister is that, while the outcome would be assured, a referendum would slow down the political process—which, as you've said, is likely to go the Instant Legislation route anyway—and guarantee a resurgence in party fortunes that has already begun with the current debate.'

Trevor McDonald again.

'In other words, with a General Election looming, the government's priority is to get the Bill through its various stages before its term of office runs out?'

'Absolutely. Which is why, with the popularity of the Conservatives running at an all-time high, and with the reintroduction of the death penalty not being put to the Commons as a Free Vote, the government is bound to be accused by the Opposition of taking political advantage, particularly if it uses its powers of veto should the Bill be blocked by the Lords.

'It is worth remembering, too, Trevor, that various European conventions on human rights suggest that the death penalty will never be allowed to become a reality in Britain again. Nevertheless, I think that if the politicians were to ignore the will of the people this time—'

An enormous blinding flash suddenly filled the night sky behind Richard Abraham, briefly swelling up the sand-blasted façade of the Houses of Parliament and obliterating most of Michael Greenhalgh's massive face. A fraction of a second later came the noise of an explosion, surprisingly dull and unspectacular, with none of the stylish sound effects as portrayed in the popular films. At the same time there was a tremendous shattering of glass and the sound of rubble crashing to the ground. Richard Abraham was already dropping wide-eyed out of the frame and the cameraman was falling over backwards, leaving the screen filled with nothing but a starlit sky. Everything then went black because the video camera's automatic exposure had been fooled by the brightness of the blast, causing a fierce yellow streak to become smeared across the lens like a hot-spot of light superimposed upon an eyeball.

The camera quickly corrected itself to show figures stampeding into the upper part of the frame, several of them gesticulating and on fire. Clothes were rustling against Richard Abraham's microphone and his broken voice was sounding across the airwaves, augmented by a garble of words coming from a young female voice, the rhythm of which was rather obscene.

'Are you still there, Richard?'

'Yes, I'm still here.'

Richard Abraham clambered back up into shot, looking dishevelled and devoid of his spectacles. 'This is appalling, Trevor,' he said shakily, stumbling over his tongue as he tried to get his mouth to work and took in the tumultuous sequence of events. 'A bomb appears to have gone off at Westminster only yards from where I'm standing. There are flames licking against the night sky behind me. Young people have been turned into human torches on the ground. Never in all my years as a political correspondent have I experienced anything quite like this.' A chorus of sirens began to overlay his words as he looked nervously past his shoulder and a helicopter searchlight swept the crowd. 'I have actually been present at a live broadcast during what appears to be a terrorist explosion, at the Houses of Parliament. I felt the fillings in my teeth jump—'

There was another blinding flash, this time from the summit of Big Ben, in the left-hand corner of the frame, and beneath a little red panel saying ITN LIVE, which had emblazoned upon it the name of the equities consortium that had recently purchased the news company. The explosion was so powerful that for a moment there was a sound overload, the automatic exposure was fooled for a second time, and everything flared and went dark. Then—though he was to remain unharmed by what was taking place at Westminster—as everything started to come back into focus, Richard Abraham barked and fell out of the frame again.

The camera juddered to the lawn, then the screen was filled with another high-angle view of the surging crowd. But the scene was so harrowing that the vision mixer cut straight back to Richard Abraham, where the camera operator was managing to regain control, and was steadying the lens to show, firstly, an immense mushroom of fire and smoke billowing into the night sky, then the top of Big Ben exploding, beginning to peel, and collapsing down onto Bridge Street on one side and through the roof of the adjoining Ministers' rooms on the other. A moment later came a distorted basso-profunda carillon as the clock's huge bells departed from the main structure, tumbled invisibly through the air, clattered to the ground as though falling down heaven's distant stairs, and exploded into a hundred-thousand useless pieces of spent cast-iron.

Throughout it all, Michael Greenhalgh's face flashed above the carnage, his shrieking voice and more especially his hands—those big clenched hands, forever pummelling as fists at the air—amplified to enormous proportions, vying with the bangs and screams, but falling now on deaf ears. Just at the point when the high-angle camera fastened onto the videowall again he straightened, slammed his hands down, and braced himself against the lectern so forcefully that for a moment it looked as though he were going to wrench it free then toss it from the screen out into the rampaging crowd.

'*This government has been attacked for its criticism of the permissive attitudes that side with the morally-degraded mind of the criminal,*' he was saying, before punctuating the night air with another of his carefully calculated pauses. '*But there is never any mention of the individual's responsibility to society from those ignorant trendies who leap up and down triumphantly on court house steps when convicted murderers are released from prison!*

'*Never any reference to a shared morality from those who excuse bad behaviour on account of the social forces they claim have produced crime!*

'*That, ladies and gentlemen, is the double-minded hypocrisy that has lain at the root of our national decline for so many years, dragging our great country down into the quagmire, infiltrating our schools, destroying core educational values, inculcating the minds of our youngsters with a deviant sexual immorality. I ask every one of you assembled here—I ask the people of Great Britain, as we contemplate the approaching General Election and acclimatize ourselves to a new millennium—to consider our "criminogenic" society. I ask you to wonder about the morally reprehensible forces that have produced that society, and to ask what kind of a nation it is that we truly desire!*'

The original audience could be heard erupting into applause again, which brought a strangely surrealistic note to the explosive proceedings playing out before the huge screen tonight. It was almost as though the crowd were extolling the detonation of the bombs.

The ITN controllers decided to let the images ride, the flames now lighting up the night sky above Westminster's silhouetted spires grimly portentous of the fact that law and order really was breaking down in the violent social maelstrom that was becoming post-industrial urban Britain. There was a constant wail of sirens and a strobing of helicopter searchlights. There was the screeching of tyres and the crash of metal and glass drowned out by another furore of screams. Then came another explosion from the Houses of Parliament, then another, then another.

And then, almost as if the moment had arrived with a film director's sense of timing, there seemed to be a deeply ominous pause when Greenhalgh had finished speaking while the face upon the huge screen leaned towards the cluster of microphones straining to reach its mouth . . . there was the flash and whiz of an approaching rocket-launcher shell . . . and the videowall finally exploded. The screen shattered, seemed to bulge outwards from the centre, then ruptured as a million pieces of glass came at the TV cameras simultaneously, the bigger pieces carrying Greenhalgh's face with them for a short time as independently-moving fragments that separated into smaller pieces as they travelled through the air—some teeth, part of a nose, bits of grey hair, a hideous staring eyeball—each becoming more elliptical as it twisted closer to the lens. Everything blasting as though blown from a jet exhaust; as if moving in slow motion; as though time itself had been suspended, coupled to a tremendous crash that merged to a scream as the particles rained upon the panicking crowd.

There was a succession of cuts between an impeccable Trevor McDonald and the confused darkness at Westminster, during which time he apologized to viewers for the quality of the transmission and said they would get back to Richard Abraham just as soon as they could.

Then he started running through a bundle of international socio-economic misfortunes that comprised the other headlines, for Monday the 5th of November.

# Two

One of the millions of television sets upon which these dramatic events were unfolding was standing in the corner of a small, typically-furnished lounge on a modern residential housing estate at Droylsden in Greater Manchester.

Throughout the previous several minutes, a piece of soggy, translucent matter had been sliding down the screen, leaving a channel of red viscera behind it rather as a slug leaves its trail of slime upon a path. At the moment when Trevor McDonald started talking about the growth in armed vigilante groups being hired by the British middle classes for protection at night, the piece of matter began speeding up under its own weight, then plopped onto the biscuit-coloured carpet.

A few inches from the place where it landed, and almost touching the gory remains of a headless dead black dog, lay the end of a polished stainless-steel silencer. The silencer was screwed to a high-velocity Shueze automatic pistol, which was now standard issue for the Greater Manchester Airborne Police. It was a very capable method of soundproofing, prompting many constables to say that the explosion caused by the bullet leaving the firing chamber was a noise so quiet it was imagined rather than felt.

A largish square hand with noticeably well-bitten fingernails was holding the pistol. Though it was dead, the body to which the hand and arm were attached was still warm and wearing a dark-blue riot policeman's uniform. The complicated mixture of padded body-armour, luminescent-green perspex epaulettes, and dented metal shoulder-plates made it look like an outfit that might be worn by a soldier fighting some crazy war of the future, not somebody whose job it had been merely to uphold British civilian law.

There was not much left of the head that used to be attached to the shoulders. Only the bottom jaw was recognizably human. It was lying obscenely twisted against the scratched metal breastplate, being still attached to some flesh that had joined it to the man's throat. Lodged between two of the remaining front teeth was a tiny sliver of bacon fat; a legacy of the sandwich that had been masticated by the jaw against the upper skull not long before the body died. The rest of the skull had gone, having instantly disintegrated when a high-velocity exploding bullet entered through its mouth and struck against its tonsils, at the point during the carnage at Westminster when Big Ben's bells began their descent into oblivion.

Much of what had been contained inside the head was splattered across the artificial plastic stones glued randomly across the chimney-breast, behind where the body had fallen. Some of it was dripping from the ceiling. One sizeable curved portion of the skull, replete with skin and a patch of butter-coloured hair, was lying like a piece of discarded orange peel on the black-tiled hearth, next to a piece of the dead dog's snout and half a human ear. Though the room was furnished with the usual conflicting jumble of aesthetic tastes that characterizes any period, the small gas fire that was embedded into the hearth was the very latest in mass-market Modernist Revival styling. It was comprised simply of a chrome triangle set against a circle of powder-coated black metal, with the flames contained in a movable remote-controlled compartment running along the bottom. Its design was echoed by the silver motifs floating on a gold fretwork that formed the background to the cherry-red wallpaper, and also by the pink and orange scatter cushions strewn across the sofa.

On the mantelpiece above the fire was a framed colour photograph of a smiling mother and daughter, both bright with summer clothes. Between them was the rather surprised-looking dog, its head still intact, its pointed features clearly a hybrid of several different pedigrees. The woman was plump and holding an ice-cream cornet in one hand and clutching the dog by the collar in the other. She had thick black hair, high cheekbones, and pale, intense-looking eyes. The little girl's features were less marked, but her hair was the same colour as that growing from the piece of skull lying on the hearth, while the smallness of her milk-teeth emphasised the terrible frailty of her age, despite the odd feminine maturity of her grin. This made the rest of her face look older than it really was, as often seems to be the case when little girls are captured in close-up by happy parents on still photographs.

Back at the television set, having run through his list of headlines, and with chaos still reigning at Westminster, Trevor McDonald was filling-in by introducing the edited highlights of a slum society in holocaust, recorded during the latest round of riots several evenings previously. Bodies were lined up along pavements with blotchy sheets draped over their damaged parts. Intercut were jerky telephoto scenes showing leather-clad teenagers standing atop overturned police Land Rovers, mirrored sunglasses reflecting flames, bandoliers of 9mm ammunition wrapped around their chests, oversized machineguns slung from their shoulders on pneumatic steadipods. Thunder and lighting blazed from chunky customized muzzles, until another shot appeared which showed bandanna-clad youngsters rampaging down a burning street, shouting into cellular telephones and spraying gunfire at rows of blue-uniformed figures scuttling behind numerous bulletproof shields. Behind them helicopter searchlights clove paths through a burning darkness reminiscent of the London Blitz, superimposed above which was the furious bleat of police sirens and the constant pounding of rotor-blades.

Not since the outbreak of the Gulf War had the TV networks been so disrupted as when anarchy exploded onto the streets of post-industrial Britain, Trevor McDonald was saying. It was the ability of rival drugs gangs to pull together in the face of adversity that had taken the authorities by surprise, while our inner cities were becoming lawless ghettoes that rivalled the old South African townships for sheer, mindless brutality.

As if to underscore his words, the scene changed to show policemen engaged in hand-to-hand combat with machete-wielding rioters in Bristol. Then a helicopter gunship was hovering above a burning shopping precinct, just as a tall streetlamp toppled sparking onto an adjacent carriageway. There was a screeching of tyres, a cut to another angle, and an open-top Mercedez packed with jeering faces skidded into view, collided with the spent streetlamp, sent it spiralling like a leaden boomerang. The car seemed to be travelling at about a hundred miles an hour and was heading straight for a police cordon, the helicopter evidently trying to prevent it from reaching its target. Tracer fire flashed, bullets gouged at asphalt, chewed into steel, popped windscreens, blew out shop windows, pulverized flesh. There was a noise that sounded not so much like heavy machinegun-fire as the sound of automatic impact. Street furniture danced and clattered. But still the car tore onwards, until suddenly it hit the central reservation, played a sort of raucous xylophone tune as it ploughed through the metal railings, levered up in the air with its engine revving like a pole vaulter being released by his stick, performed an impossibly-fast cartwheel out of all proportion to its weight, assumed the texture of crumpled paper and came apart so quickly it was reduced to a chassis in moments, before it erupted in a gigantic fireball. It was like a chase sequence from a violent Hollywood film, which was where these workless youngsters generally sought inspiration, seeing as industry didn't require them to nurture a practical intelligence any longer, but they still felt obliged to relieve the monotony of their lives by gravitating towards high excitement.

There was a report from Birmingham, where rioters had just shot down a police helicopter with an ex-Soviet rocket-launcher. It was a fluke they'd managed to hit it, a journalist was saying, chewing adrenalin as something was shovelled into a shiny black bag behind him.

Cut to a pile of burning wreckage from which poked a single bent rotor-blade. Camera shift, just as the tangle of metal exploded again, followed by another slow pan across burning deck tenements and the detritus of looted homes scattered across wrecked streets. Splintered furniture. Burnt settees. Tyreless cars crashed at mad angles. Finishing in big close-up on the inevitable cuddly toy scorched and abandoned against a background of wet cobbles, pulling at a nation's heartstrings, empty window sockets behind a sad bear's button eyes, beyond which was silhouetted a forest of remote tower blocks waving flames against the night.

Then another pre-recorded report from Manchester, where Joan Thirkettle was standing in front of the camera wearing a riot helmet and uniform and glancing past her shoulder at a vast cauldron of light boiling behind her. A young riot policeman appeared in full battledress alongside her, holding a double-barrelled machinegun. Joan Thirkettle introduced him as Sergeant David Kowalski, who she said would be recognizable to the majority of ITN viewers.

She asked him to comment on the violence being enacted on the streets of Britain that evening. David Kowalski pushed a tinted visor away from his grimy brow. Speaking quickly between the sounds of gunfire and explosions, he said he thought it was unfortunate that the gradual descent of the inner cities into lawlessness seemed not to have mattered, so long as it was contained and posed no threat to the wider community. That had been our fatal mistake, he said, making the comparisons between these latest disturbances and the Los Angeles riots of the early '90s justifiable. The teenage gangsters engaged in running street battles with the police were the terrible consequence of an unemployed video generation having been brought up under an atmosphere of self-gratification and envy. In his opinion, that culture was epitomized by posturing designer-delinquents masquerading as heroes in the films, helping desensitize an emotionally immature male underclass and providing it with dangerous rôle models. The brainpower of these youngsters had been cruelly exploited rather than put to a constructive use and many were no longer integrated into their communities as they would once have been. Instead they sought social standing through illegal narcotics distribution, through violent exhibitionism, through racketeering and crime. That was why a sort of pressure was building just beneath the surface of society. That live ammunition was being used against rioting civilians on the streets of peacetime Britain showed how much of a strain this pressure was creating and that a shift was taking place within the national psyche. For our preoccupation with speculating about the social causes of criminal behaviour, rather than coming to terms with the reality of it, was pushing the tolerance of ordinary people to the limits as crime became the dominating factor threatening our way of life.

Then Kowalski and Joan Thirkettle ducked as a burning police Range Rover suddenly slewed across the road. It crashed through a shop window and exploded amidst an avalanche of Molotov cocktails and a babble of cheering delinquency silhouetted against the coiling flames. Kowalski excused himself and touched his radio mouthpiece, then was absorbed with instructions being relayed from a hovering helicopter into his ear.

Trevor McDonald used the break in the conversation as an opportunity to say that ITN had at last resumed contact with Richard Abraham. But before the recording disappeared from the screen, there was a moment when David Kowalski was standing more obliquely to the camera, and light was refracted against the chrome personal ID number DK0706 affixed to the shoulder of his tunic. The same number was printed on the shoulder of the bloody tunic on the corpse on the carpet in this Droylsden lounge now. As the door to the lounge burst open and the feet of half-a-dozen policemen strode about the body bringing in the smell of frosty weather and the night, as blasphemies were uttered when hardened eyes took in the terrible scene, and nostrils inhaled what one voice described as the godawful smell that emerges from a human head when it is cracked wide open, it could be seen that the face of the same David Kowalski was present in this Droylsden room tonight.

It had been immortalized on another photograph, standing between the black-haired woman and the smiling little girl. It was part of a bouquet of human happiness snapped after a police presentation award for bravery, hanging with fragments of the real face, now spread with its brains across a blood-stained North Mancunian wall.

# *Three*

Chief Constable Derek Driscoll was in uniform and seated inside the personal computer bay adjoining his office, at the top of Central Police Headquarters in Manchester. He'd just asked Central Computer to play back a videodisc recording of the kidnapping of Michael Greenhalgh, and was reclining in his padded black leather contour seat while the authorization code was cleared. The Greater Manchester Police were most fortunate in that the incident had been captured live by several closed-circuit colour television cameras, which had included in their field of vision that part of the Chester Road where the politician's car had been attacked, though as yet this hadn't been made public knowledge.

The computer acknowledged the request and there came up onto the screen a high-angle view of an inner-city pavement drenched in autumn sunshine. There was a modern telephone box situated midway up the picture, its distorted perspective tapering away from the camera, its shadow brutally dividing the pavement that occupied most of the frame. As the action was joined, Greenhalgh's dark-blue Jaguar was drawing to a halt alongside the phonebox, its nearside front wheel clearly punctured, the metal rim grinding against the surface of the road.

When the car had stopped, the driver's door opened and Greenhalgh's chauffeur George stood up wearing a pale-grey uniform and grey leather boots. He removed his sunglasses and squinted at the sunshine, then pushed back his peaked cap and wiped his brow and came round to the kerb to examine the burst tyre. Though neither George nor Greenhalgh were to have known it at the time, the tyre had been blown out by a sniper, moments before the Jaguar entered the field of view covered by the CCTV. The gunman had been hidden in some derelict tenements and had tracked the car telescopically with a silencered automatic rifle, leaving George to assume the puncture had been caused by the broken glass he'd driven over several minutes back down the road.

Driscoll watched intently as George straightened and glanced uneasily at the street. The chauffeur had been cursing the fact that the roadworks they'd encountered on the nearby Queen Elizabeth Way had diverted them into Normanshaw, one of the most dangerous and deprived areas of inner Manchester. So dangerous that, in line with other major British cities, the street signs directing drivers towards it were now coloured red, showing that it had been designated a hazardous quarter and the meeting of insurance claims couldn't be guaranteed. As George walked along the car and said something to Greenhalgh through the window, a leather-bomber-jacketed West Indian young man emerged from the phonebox and left the picture by the bottom right-hand corner, taking his shadow with him. Though the CCTV recorded sound as well as vision, the voices of the chauffeur and the politician had been too muffled from that distance to be amplified even by police audio-forensic. Nevertheless, enough of Greenhalgh's grey-haired features were visible animating through the back window to be enlarged photographically, and his moving lips interpreted as saying: *But Jaguar tyres are not supposed to blow out nowadays, George! They're like a fucking Roller's!*

The computer played a digitized simulation of those words for Driscoll now, then superimposed them letter by letter across the bottom of the screen.

George frowned and walked back round the front of the car, his shadow leading the way. He paused while an articulated lorry thundered past, only its wheels visible as they sliced through the top left-hand corner of the frame. Then suddenly he stiffened when he heard the whine of a high-velocity bullet coming straight towards him. In the split-second it took him to register the noise, his head had already exploded, his body had been thrown violently sideways, and his peaked cap had flown up and assumed enormous proportions as it hurtled towards the camera, then flipped out of the corner of the frame before it hit the lens. A moment later it came back into view, huge and blurred as it rebounded from the brickwork, then fell to a part of the pavement not being monitored by the CCTV.

As George crashed onto the bonnet amidst a spray of bloody viscera, Greenhalgh could be seen dropping his news-paper and flinging himself to the cream-coloured leather upholstery in the back of the car. At this point Driscoll paused the action and ran his fingers across the computer keypad. There was a liquid-sounding squeal as the laser scanned the disc, then the camera angle on the screen changed and the action moved ahead several minutes. In the new view the telephone box had moved from the right- to the left-hand side of the frame, and Greenhalgh was scram-bling on all-fours across the pavement, away from the open rear door of the Jaguar. He was swiping at his newspaper, which had fallen out of the car with him and was fluttering madly about his face, before it separated into a dozen broadsheets, was grabbed by the wind, and swirled along the street.

Fist-sized holes were appearing in the roof of the Jaguar now. Glass fragments were scattering across the pavement as the windows were shot out and popped like exploding light-bulbs. Muted female screams could be heard coming from off-camera and the paving slabs were being pock-marked by a series of small craters as the bullets gouged at the concrete. Greenhalgh's big ex-miner's hands were flying up to his face, some loose change was tumbling from his trouser pockets, and he could be heard grunting muffled obscenities. Then most of the telephone box exploded amidst a shower of glass and electrical sparks and he was on his feet and running from the frame, the scene having about it the curiously imprecise, almost badly-staged quality, which real incidents of violence often have.

Now Driscoll tapped at the computer keypad and the camera angle changed again. This time there materialized a view from the opposite side of the carriageway, in time to catch the politician stumbling into a cobbled alley running between the walled back yards of terraced houses, tripping over some rotting bin-liners full of rubbish, then disappearing from view.

It could be seen that the Jaguar had pulled up outside a row of battered Victorian shops fronting onto the main road; a bit of nineteenth-century brickwork lingering in a ferro-concrete ghetto. Sunk into the pavement were chunky metal bollards, designed to stop the ram-raiders getting at the windows. Everywhere complex patterns of graffiti, sprayed with luminescent paints, stood out against the grey monotony, while the two silver CCTVs that had recorded the footage already shown were clearly visible, glinting high upon their brackets near the guttering, beneath the tatty rooftops and an oblong of cloudless blue sky.

Driscoll told the computer to jump forward again, and, still watching from the other side of the carriageway, picked up the action where it showed several shell-suited, drugs-gang-type gunmen striding menacingly along the pavement, blasting at the shop windows randomly with shotguns. Though the gunmen were disguised by red protective masks of the type worn by ice hockey players, beneath these they were wearing black balaclava hoods. High-pitched female screams came from inside the shops as the windows fractured and blew inwards. One of the gang picked up an empty pram parked outside a doorway and threw it into the road. Then the sniper who'd been shooting at Greenhalgh suddenly ran out from behind a parked yellow transit van. Unlike the other three gunmen, he was devoid of a red plastic mask because it had accidentally fallen from his face, dropping over the edge of the balcony from which he'd been firing as the Jaguar approached the shops. He wore only a balaclava hood, black skin clearly visible around his eye sockets and at the wrists above his skin-tight red leather gloves. He shouted something into a cellular telephone, swapped his silencered automatic rifle for a pump-action shotgun held out by one of the other gunmen, aimed at the petrol tank of the Jaguar, and wrenched off several rounds. With the second or third shot, the back end of the car exploded in a gigantic mushroom of flame as the fuel ignited, though the posturing gunman didn't so much as flinch when fire erupted before him, and the bloody corpse of the dead chauffeur was nudged by the blast further along the pavement, its legs catching alight.

Then a signal seemed to be exchanged between the gang members and they followed Greenhalgh into the alley, out of sight of the cameras now, but where it was known that the politician had been bundled into a vehicle waiting at the other end.

Still Driscoll watched intently, the computer screen reflected as two tiny distorted squares upon the surfaces of his eyeballs. He asked the computer to hold and rewind. The gunman who'd emerged from behind the parked van shouting into the portable phone took several steps away from the ball of fire, as it appeared to suck itself back into the rear of the car as the image rewound, and he handed the pump-action shotgun back to the other hoodlum. Then he pranced in reverse along the pavement and disappeared to the place at the foot of the derelict tenements from where he'd come. When he was obscured by the van, Driscoll switched back to the first camera angle, looking down onto the pavement and the silver roof of the telephone box. This showed the gunman entering the bottom left-hand corner of the frame carrying his telescopic rifle, but slightly distorted because of the vignetting at the edge of the lens.

Here Driscoll paused the action and moved the cursor

across the screen until it was flashing above the frozen gunman's head. He depressed the mouse and the white outline of a box appeared. He kept on pressing, each time causing the box to throb a generation larger. When he was satisfied that what was contained in the box was sufficient for his purposes, he depressed the mouse again and the outlines of everything on the screen, including the perspective lines running between the paving slabs, throbbed luminously like thin neon tubes, as they were scanned by the computer. A series of concentric circles pulsated, then the image melted away, leaving behind the white outlines. The outlines twirled into a helix, then untwirled at once into a computer-graphics simulation showing the gunman running towards an imaginary ground-level camera position. At first the simulation consisted of the white outlines only, so that it looked like an architect's drawing. There was a pause, then the image rapidly began to colour itself in, the digitized resolution being nearly photographic in its quality. What was appearing on the screen hadn't been recorded by any of the video cameras. It had been generated artificially by the computer scanning the visual information supplied by the three CCTVs, and rearranging it in its memory bank.

Driscoll allowed the action to progress a fraction at a time, until the rifle-toting gunman was standing alongside the van, shouting into his phone. At that point Driscoll suspended the image again and asked the computer to assess the distance between the driver's window of the van and the balaclava'd head of the gunman. (All the windows of the van were covered by chrome foil, like the lenses of mirrored sunglasses.) When the computer established that the distance was precisely two metres, Driscoll cleared the screen and folded his arms. After a few moments of thought he asked the computer to assess the probability of anybody who was seated inside the van being able to see the features of the gunman clearly enough to provide the police with a description. The computer explained that it did not possess enough information to reach a logical conclusion. But it was prepared to speculate that, because the gunman had been so heavily disguised, a description by a witness being sufficient to result in a conviction was unlikely, even if the scene were to be recalled under hypnosis.

Driscoll let out some breath. He'd never been convinced by all this computer technology replacing the observational powers of human beings. And what Central Computer had just told him, and what he knew was concealed behind those mirrored windows on the screen, convinced him even more. He switched off the system, then walked through to stand behind the big glass desk that dominated his office, fifteen storeys above the teeming Manchester streets. The desk was positioned at right-angles to the large tinted outer window, and, though in theory transparent, many-coloured swirls could be seen subtly permeating the different slabs of glass, like the coloured pigments that are sometimes mixed into a clear-resin paperweight. He watched sheets of rain pounding the adjacent tower blocks, and ruminated briefly while a helijet approached the nearby Piccadilly Heliport, its clumsy conical-shaped V-TOL engines shifting from the horizontal to the vertical position as it whined into its final descent.

Then his attention switched to the twelve TV screens that were embedded into the scratchproof black perspex wall to the right of the window, one of which was tuned perma-nently into daytime television. A news bulletin was in pro-gress, but the image was mute, the sound turned down. He lifted a remote-control handset and brought up the volume as the screen switched to show a mob of journalists sur-rounding Driscoll himself, as he'd ducked into the back of a police car on a modern housing estate out at Droylsden, late the previous evening.

'A formal statement will be made tomorrow morning at ten o'clock,' he heard himself saying amidst a flurry of shouts and photo-flashes. 'I cannot answer any questions until then.' The car door was pulled shut and the journalists parted as the vehicle bulldozed them aside and drove away.

The screen changed to show a full black body-bag being

carried on a stretcher out of a neat new house and loaded into the back of an ambulance. A sombre voiceover mumbled as the doors banged closed, while a helicopter searchlight swept from somewhere above the scene, played with the fog swirling between adjacent gables, flared into camera, picked out frosty asphalt and misty windscreens, showed the perimeter defence wall ringing the houses in the background like the fortress of concrete that holds back a prison.

Then a photograph of David Kowalski flashed up. Nicholas Witchell said that the BBC's Home Affairs Correspondent was now going to look back over the life of Sergeant Kowalski, whose domestic tragedy had so captured the imagination of the British people earlier that year, and whose death hot on the heels of the killing of Michael Greenhalgh was in danger of sending an already badly deteriorating social atmosphere finally to the brink.

Driscoll frowned and sent the volume away. He snapped his fingers and a holographic clock appeared, extrapolating itself from the right-hand corner of his desk. It indicated the time to be seventeen-minutes-to-ten.

He snapped his fingers again and the clock disappeared.

Then he reached for a cordless telephone receiver, had second thoughts before he stabbed at the rubber buttons, clipped it back onto his communications console, straightened his tie, and walked out of the room.

# Four

'Something definitely stinks, Vanessa,' Blake Hunter said, wiping the condensation from the front window of the car and peering out at the wet Mancunian streets. Though it was nearly ten o'clock in the morning, the city was more or less deserted because of the torrential rain. 'For David Kowalski to commit suicide is too coincidental, what with him heading the investigation into the Michael Greenhalgh killing, and the row that's erupted over the death penalty.' He snorted derisively. 'Just think how the story will go. A young police hero, whose domestic tragedy touched the hearts of millions, finally throws in the towel because the brutal murdering of his family becomes too much to live with. As a consequence of which, the crisis in national morale deepens still further, and people start baying for underclass blood even louder.' He ran his fingers through his thick dark hair and snorted again. 'I'm telling you, love, it couldn't have been better timed.'

His producer Vanessa Aysgarth was driving him from the Great Northern Hotel, where they were staying while on assignment in Manchester filming a documentary for the BBC's new *Crime in Britain* series, down to Central Police Headquarters, where the press conference was due to be staged at ten to officially announce Sergeant Kowalski's death. Blake had interviewed Kowalski earlier in the year for *Panorama,* after the policeman's wife and child had been killed when they were caught between a shop window and an approaching stolen van at a retail park on the outskirts of Salford. A new interview had been scheduled for *Crime in Britain* later that week, except that now Kowalski was dead, and Blake was suspicious, as he had been since the story broke late the previous evening.

'I must admit it does seem rather convenient,' Vanessa said, hooking her platinum-blonde hair behind her ear, 'especially now that the country's on such a bloody knife-edge about the vote in the Commons.' She drew their black Volvo estate to a halt and waited for a tram to clear the road. 'I thought you said David was managing to get over losing Lucy and Melinda, anyway? It must be getting on for nearly a year since it happened.'

'It's about eight months, actually,' Blake said, stroking several days' growth of stubble while he marshalled his thoughts. 'He never implied to me that he'd come to terms with what happened, because I don't suppose you can ever get over having had your family wiped out like that. But he didn't strike me as being the sort of chap who'd brood over it so badly that he'd eventually go and kill himself, just because he couldn't cope.'

He was remembering Kowalski's tone the last time they'd spoken on the phone. He'd sounded withdrawn, almost vocally emaciated. That substantiated his apparent suicide, of course, but Blake couldn't escape the conviction that the man had been frightened.

Vanessa checked her mirror and touched the accelerator pedal. 'I wouldn't be too sure about that. It's the intelligent types who commit suicide because they're cynical enough to reason everything out.'

'I know, but David was too committed to police work. In fact, it was his commitment to his work that seemed to have helped him pull through. He was very methodical in his thinking. He wouldn't have taken his own life because he'd have felt as though he were copping out of a responsibility to society. *And* he was against hanging, which is something the forces of reaction didn't bother to publicize when they milked his life story last spring. He wouldn't have killed himself if he thought it would increase the likelihood of capital punishment being reintroduced, not even if he'd wanted to die. I didn't know him that well, but I knew him well enough.'

Vanessa knew Blake well enough, too, to have got used to his curious, at times rather irritating, habit of keeping information to himself until he was certain about his facts. She sensed there was something that he wasn't letting on about this morning, and that whatever it was must be of enormous importance.

'And I know you, darling,' she said sharply. The lenses of her rimless round spectacles reflected the lights of a passing shop window and cancelled her lovely pale-blue eyes, so that for a moment he saw only a pair of luminous white discs. 'You don't just think something stinks, there's something you aren't telling me either. You shouldn't be going to the news conference this morning, as it is. Lucky for you the shoot was cancelled because of the rain.' Her eyes had appeared again at some traffic lights and were sparkling as a prelude to a smile. 'Why don't you tell me what's bothering you? One of these days you'll keep something to yourself too long and end up dead.'

Blake smiled too, then automatically put his hand on her slender thigh, ran a thumb down the cableweave groove forming the outer seam of her black stirrup-corduroys, and watched a black Cuban-heeled leather ankle-boot at the bottom of her leg lift from the clutch pedal as the lights changed to green. Then he took his hand away and raised his eyebrows, not in anticipation of formulating an answer to her question, but because he'd just registered the marvellous way her hair was layered like the feathers of a bird's wing, where it draped onto her mauve-coloured coat, and had found himself vaguely desiring her again.

The feeling instantly disconcerted him. At forty-one, Vanessa was ten years his senior, and his closest and most trusted friend. Though they'd never been to bed together, or even so much as kissed erotically, they enjoyed an emotional intimacy that was rare amongst men and women outside the sheets of the same bed. If people didn't assume they were brother and sister, or even, occasionally, mother and son, then it was because they generally took them to be lovers. Blake was convinced that if it hadn't been for her support during the darkest days of his divorce, especially when a cruel court ruling favoured his ex-wife Victoria with custody of their two small daughters, even though she'd been the adulterous party, then he would probably have gone insane. More tears had flowed out of him during these last six months than at any time since he was a child, and it had been Vanessa's shoulder he'd cried onto, quite literally. He couldn't deny that he'd wondered sometimes if anything would develop between them sexually. But he'd usually dismissed the thought as dangerous and absurd, not least because she was married and showed no sexual interest in him whatsoever, and he would no more have expected to want to end up in bed with her than to want to end up in bed with his own mother. That was why he was unnerved now, trying to pass off the way he'd found himself looking at her a few moments ago as being a symptom of the fact that he'd come to depend on her for emotional support, whenever he was worried.

Her suspicion that he was keeping something to himself about Kowalski's suicide was not unfounded, however, and he decided to partially break his silence about it when they were turning onto Deansgate.

'Okay, Vanessa, when I phoned David the other evening to run through the rough shape of the interview, he said that something didn't quite fit about the Michael Greenhalgh killing.' He was squinting up at the huge Chinese Embassy that straddled the road and was in the process of engulfing the car. Though it resembled an immense brutally-stylized pagoda, it seemed to be made from glass and nothing else, so that all the ducting and cables were visible like a mess of multicoloured arteries, running throughout the building.

'And?'

'He said that since he'd interviewed one of the witnesses, he sensed he was on the verge of turning over a stone and wasn't going to like what he found underneath.'

Vanessa was silent until they came out into daylight again. 'I'm sure most policemen feel like that when they're investigating a high-profile case, love. Stick to the film-making assignment at hand, or you'll end up burning your fingers.'

They were splashing through puddles and driving up the slip road from Deansgate towards the police compound. Vanessa pulled up at the barrier, sent down the electric window, and handed their identity cards to the security officer. He put down his machinegun and slotted the cards into the computer, waited for the clearance beep to sound, then passed them back. The steel barrier folded out of the way, bending in three places like a mechanical representation of a human finger, so that it formed a three-sided square; then Vanessa eased the Volvo across the wet tarmac and rolled it down the ramp into the car park beneath Central Police Headquarters.

Blake was still chewing over his thoughts, but as she reversed the car into a space, he let out some breath and picked up the tail-end of her previous remark as if there hadn't been a silence.

'All right, there's something else too. David phoned me yesterday afternoon, asked me to go over to his house tonight, and said that he'd explain what was bothering him then. He admitted that he shouldn't be talking about it to an investigative TV journalist.'

He generated a silence.

'And?'

Vanessa knew Blake's silences.

'He also said that he was ringing from a phonebox out on that derelict industrial estate where we were filming the other day off the Oldham Road, so that his call couldn't be traced. Does that sound to you like normal behaviour for a policeman?'

Vanessa's brow furrowed while she switched off the engine, released her seat-belt, removed the bunch of keys from the ignition, and placed them onto the dashboard. 'No, it doesn't,' she said. 'And now he's suddenly become a dead policeman.' She looked very old for a moment, then changed the tune of her voice. 'There's always the possibility that the killing of Greenhalgh could have brought up unpleasant memories. It was a nasty murder, and David's unit did discover what was left of the corpse.'

Blake shook his head.

'When I interviewed him for *Panorama,* he was adamant about how hardened he'd become to the job, what with the Airborne Police getting the riots and all the drugs-related stuff. No, either he turned his stone over and was frightened to death, or somebody traced his call.'

A graphite-coloured Vauxhall Frontera crawled past them looking for a space and briefly blocked out some light. It reversed a short way and squeezed nose-first into a space diagonal to where the Volvo was parked, its rear end seeming to consist only of a tyre parcelled up in bright-blue leather, with a slit of glass winking over the top.

'I've never been convinced about servicemen saying they become hardened to the job,' Vanessa said, taking off her spectacles and using them to frame the pile of keys on top of the dashboard. 'It's complete bullshit. A steady exposure to violent crime is bound to have a detrimental effect upon their psychology. I think we could make a programme about it sometime. The stresses and strains of being a policeman at the beginning of the twenty-first century, now that they're armed, and all that.'

'I'd already spoken to Kowalski about it,' Blake said, watching several locks of her hair follow each other away from her shoulder and finding that, for the first time he could remember, he couldn't hold her eyes. He frowned and cleared his throat, then picked up his cellular telephone and his Newton memorizer from between his feet.

'What're you going to do about what Kowalski told you?'

'There's not a lot I can do yet. I'll see if anything's said at the conference, and take it from there.'

He was about to thank her for driving him down from the hotel, when he heard the heavy slam of a car door followed by the stylish clumping of stacked female heels, echoing dully within the concrete confines of the compound. He looked up and was struck so cold that Vanessa thought she heard him moan.

'What's the matter?' she asked, checking the direction of his eyes.

Coming away from the Frontera was an attractive, slim-built woman, aged about thirty, with dark shoulder-length hair. She was executively dressed in a satin-like material that was the same colour as the Frontera, and had paused to slip into a lightweight silver swing coat. The stylish ensemble was finished off with gunmetal-coloured ankle-boots and ultra-sheer stockings that would have been described by the manufacturer as vaguely-black, but which seemed to give her legs a deep, almost ochrous lustre, bringing out the richness of the flesh. She flicked her hair back with a jerk of her head, slotted a copy of the *Independent* beneath her arm, stabbed at her keyring to put the Frontera into defence-mode, then joined several male journalists who were waiting for the lift. She didn't seem to notice that Blake and Vanessa were watching her as she walked past.

Vanessa hooked her spectacles back onto her face and was amused to see how the journalists parted as the woman came up to them, like peasants making way for royalty. 'Nice, Blake,' she said, bringing her eyes back to his, 'very nice. But don't tell me that you just thought you saw somebody you knew but were mistaken, because it won't do I'm afraid.'

She'd noticed how straight the woman was holding herself. Blake was usually attracted to assertive, rather domi-nant women. That was why he got on so well with her, and was able to cope professionally with her extrovert, if at times almost masculine, personality, where so many lesser men couldn't. 'I saw the way you looked at her just then,' she went on. 'The expression that flashed across your face was one of pure unadulterated hunger.' She paused for effect. 'No, it wasn't hunger, it was greed. Pure unadulterated greed.' She took hold of his hand and interlocked their fingers, noting that he started squeezing rather tightly, though his eyes hadn't yet come back to hers. At the same time she crossed her long legs, wrapping one right around the other, pulled her knees up beneath the steering wheel, and revealed a sliver of bare flesh above one of her ankle-boots. 'You like your women to be female, don't you? You're an old-fashioned type, really. I'd swear there's a ruthless Tory streak buried in you somewhere.'

'Don't talk rubbish, Vanessa.'

'Who is she, then? It's not like you to notice a woman with more than just your eyes after what you've been through.'

He kept his eyes on the woman while he spoke.

'When I was coming up to the Tory conference here a few weeks back, I noticed her looking at me in the lounge at Heathrow, before we set off. She lingered behind me when we walked across to the aircraft, but no matter how much I slowed I couldn't fall in alongside her. I'm convinced she was making sure I went up the steps first, so that she could manoeuvre herself into a better position when she came aboard. She was also on the helijet from Manchester Airport across into Piccadilly.' His face wrinkled affectionately. 'During both trips she eyed me up, but very discreetly. It's funny, but somewhere along the line I must have dropped one of my gloves. She picked it up without me seeing it, then used it as an excuse to generate a few words when we got to the barrier. I think you could say I was taken.'

'She's very beautiful, and she's strong and sophisticated. Look at the way she holds herself. Those men next to her feel about three inches tall. But she's also one of us. She isn't ex-Oxbridge.'

Blake found his eyes coming back to Vanessa. Her own

eyes were already waiting to meet him, and he saw that her pale lips had become rather moist, that the hair which she'd earlier hooked behind her ear was tumbling slowly over one eye again, and that she wasn't bothering to move it out of the way. He was conscious, too, of how reassured he felt by her warm lavender-like smell, and by the crow's feet scoring the flesh around her eyes, when he eventually said: 'I doubt if I'd have given the incident much thought, were it not for the fact that as we went through the barrier we both seemed to be drifting in the direction of the lounge, when she noticed a young guy standing with his arms folded just inside the entrance doors. He was obviously waiting to meet her, but I got the impression that she hadn't expected him to be there. He picked up his case when he saw her, and it was as though she just switched off and veered away from me. She followed him into the back of a taxi and vanished into the traffic without so much as a backward glance. I tried not to read too much into it, but I *knew* I'd seen her somewhere before.

'Then I remembered she was in Manchester the afternoon that Greenhalgh made his big speech before he was kidnapped, except that her hair was tied up, which was why I hadn't recognized her straightaway. I've seen her in Birmingham as well.' He frowned again, and had to swallow. 'What I can't understand is that when she was flirting with me at the heliport, it was as if we'd known each other for years and we were somehow picking up from where we'd left off. And yet when I saw her at the back of the conference hall the next morning, and I started heading towards her, she turned and walked away.'

'She probably wanted you to chase after her.'

'No she didn't. She's too intelligent to waste time doing puerile things like that. She was a genuine person, and she opened the conversational innings, not me.'

Vanessa assumed a wry smile.

'I've seen her before, too.'

'Where?'

He was incredulous.

'At the news conference the other day after the Canary Wharf bombing. I saw her sitting in the audience when I was watching *Channel 4 News*.'

'Why the hell didn't you tell me?'

'Blake, she's only been in the car park with us for a few minutes.' She paused, then her face brightened and her tongue went to her cheek. 'This is why you've been at such a loose end recently, isn't it?'

'You're very intuitive, Vanessa.'

'That's because I know you, darling, but also because I love you. And I know that you're afraid to go after her because you're still grieving about what Vicky did.'

Blake didn't need to say anything, but watched through the window instead and kept hold of Vanessa's hands with both of his own. The underground car park was no longer a utilitarian environment fabricated from grubby concrete panels and rumbling with the generators that were feeding the huge chrome-plated building piled above it. It had suddenly become a rather beautiful place where even the conduit piping stapled to the walls was a detail that needed to be savoured, like the fine down embellishing the skin of a woman's face.

The dark-haired woman had turned to face the Volvo, while the journalists had lost interest in the computerized display above the lift and had become fascinated by their own feet. She tilted her head back and began scrutinizing the concrete beams dividing the low ceiling of the compound. Vanessa could have sworn that her eyes were glinting, even from that distance. Then the woman looked at the Volvo and appeared to catch her breath when she saw Blake sitting there.

The realization prompted her to turn sharply away.

'See what I mean?'

'But she knows you're here,' Vanessa said, squeezing his hand again and putting her spectacles back onto the dashboard. 'And you know that she's reacting like that because

she wants you. She's obviously here because of the conference, so go after her. You've an awful lot of love to give.
You're here because of the ending of David Kowalski's life.
Let yourself go again. Stop worrying about the state of the
world and use this morning to salvage something from your
own life instead.' Her voice seemed to have grown a little
hoarse, and both her hands were squeezing both of his,
when she said: 'Seize what's there for the taking. A woman
turns away like that when she knows she's going to end up
falling in love.'

Blake turned to look at Vanessa again, except that now
she was in the process of turning away from him, and for a
horrifying moment he wondered if she were being turned-on
by the dark-haired woman as well. Then he realized, with an
overwhelming feeling of gratitude, that she wasn't gloating
over the other woman but was trying to help coax him back
out into the light. Withdrawing from a long and committed
relationship had left him so badly damaged that he'd remained celibate since the separation, the thought of having
to ease himself into another emotional routine seeming so
unpalatable that he'd doubted sometimes if he would ever be
possessed of the urge to find a mate again. He hadn't really
taken his occasional cloudy feelings of desire towards Vanessa very seriously because the value he placed on their
friendship always stood in the way. This morning he was
quite clear in his mind why he'd had to wait so long for his
body to start working again.

He let go of her hands when he saw the lift arrive and the
woman followed the journalists into the cubicle. When the
steel doors had sealed them in, he brought his eyes back to
Vanessa and was relieved to find that he no longer had any
difficulty keeping them there. 'I wish I'd said something to
you about her before.'

'What on earth for?'

'Because now that I have done, I feel as if a tension's been
released in me.'

She smiled. 'Why don't you make sure that you apprehend

her when you get upstairs?' Though the smile intensified, it seemed to Blake to be a little thin. It wasn't so much that she was showing more of her very good teeth, but that the flesh at the bottom of her face was somehow starting to contract. 'I want to see you happy again, love.'

He opened the car door.

'I'll make my own way back up to New Central Square,' he said, feeling guilty for thinking the words, much less for uttering them. He kissed her on the cheek, but before he got out she felt for his hand again.

'I worry about you sometimes,' she said. 'I worry about you an awful lot.'

Blake compressed his lips. 'I know you do, and if it hadn't been for you, I would have given up when I lost Hayley and Jennifer.' He let out some breath. 'Hell, it frustrates me sometimes.'

'What does?'

'I really don't know.' He frowned at a point in space and let out some more breath, surprised at his irritation and his loss for words. 'This probably sounds stupid, but sometimes I feel that I can't seem to express how much I value you, not as a woman, but simply as a human being. It's the same as when you lose your sense of taste. You know there's something there, something that you want to try and reach. And yet . . .'

'What, Blake?'

He frowned at the point in space again. 'The only way I can define it is to say that you make me feel incredibly secure. And I'm afraid of losing that security, more than I was ever afraid of losing Victoria. Do you understand what I'm trying to say, or does it sound ridiculous coming from a man?' He noticed that his heart was beginning to pick up speed and he was becoming a little breathless.

'No, it doesn't sound ridiculous. You're honest enough to admit it because you respect women, you never try to dominate them. You're very easy to be with, you know. Not many men are so at ease with their emotions'—her eyebrows raised, the mouth contracted again, and she laughed—'not when they are in the presence of women such as me, anyway.'

She looked lonely for a moment, almost crestfallen; then she squeezed his hands between both of her own. Blake looked at the pile of hands on his knee. His were rather square, matted on the back with dark hairs and raked with blue veins. Hers seemed small and rather frail, despite the long tapering fingers, despite the upright posture of the body to which they belonged, which, when it was on its feet, issued a self-assured female TV producer's voice; a voice which, inside this car on this wet Tuesday morning in this big city in the north, had become passive, almost frightened, and had assumed a tone he'd never heard before. He had a compunction to kiss Vanessa's hands. But before he could raise them to his face, he looked across at the lift doors and experienced a feeling of mental disorientation that could only be described as an emotional equivalent of going into a skid at the wheel of a fast car, on a greasy road late at night, then regaining control, just before he hit the verge.

'What is it that you're so afraid of, Blake?'

'I don't know.' The car was becoming claustrophobic now, he wanted to get away.

'But you aren't ever going to lose me. You spend more time with me than anybody else you know.'

'I know, Vanessa,' he said. 'Believe me, I know.'

He stood up quickly from the car and slammed the door, but found that he had to fight to stop his eyes from watering. Wondering what the hell had just happened, he fastened his coat, threw his scarf over his shoulder, and walked away, but found that he had to fight, too, to prevent himself from looking back; and that he used the staircase as an excuse not to have to linger in front of the lift.

Vanessa watched him disappear. She remained curiously impassive, the deep rumble that was filling the deserted compound filling the background to her thoughts with an equal degree of monotony.

After a few moments she finally hooked her hair back behind her ear, hooked her spectacles back onto her face, and snapped her seat-belt into position. When she came to pick up the bunch of keys from the dashboard, however, she found that her hand was shaking so much it took her all her time to find the ignition; and then she put the car into reverse by mistake.

# *Five*

Chief Constable Driscoll had descended from his rooftop eyrie and was seated behind the moulded plastic counter growing from the floor at the front of the conference room. The big embossed chrome emblem of the Greater Manchester Police Authority was shining like the Star of David on the wall above his head. To his left was a stocky grey-haired plain-clothes policeman who Blake hadn't seen before. To his right was a well-built red-haired man he thought he'd once interviewed when he'd been making a *Panorama* programme at New Scotland Yard. A young black secretary in blue shirt-sleeves, and wearing translucent-pink harlequin spectacles, was typing the names of the policemen into the computer keypad at the end of the counter. Driscoll's name came up sideways into the little electric window in front of where he was seated, bright-green lettering burning against black. The unknown policeman's name flashed up, misspelt to begin with, then quickly altered after an amused cough from somebody in the crowd: Detective Sergeant Wakern. And finally, the name of the red-haired thug: Detective Superintendent Stoneham.

When Blake took his position amongst the journalists and cameramen and a smell of wet clothes at the back, the conference was only a couple of minutes from starting. He looked past the bobbing heads and was relieved to see the dark-haired woman seated two or three rows from the front, looking at her tightly-folded copy of the *Independent*.

Stoneham looked at Blake once and seemed not to recognize him standing near the door. But when his eyes came back a moment later, his brow furrowed, and he looked to be muttering something to Driscoll under his breath without altering the position of his head.

There was a formal cough from Driscoll and a hush descended over the room. 'Good morning ladies and gentlemen. The Police Press Office thought it would be better to call a conference to announce our present line of inquiry, so if you don't mind, I'll now declare it open.

'As you already know, Sergeant David Kowalski of the Manchester Airborne Police tragically committed suicide last evening. The death of a policeman is always an unpleasant affair. Bearing in mind that David came to public prominence for a time earlier this year, and bearing in mind that one or two mildly improper news reports have already circulated, we are anxious to alleviate speculation about the circumstances of his death. We are living through an unusually sensitive time, what with important matters being debated in Parliament, and we would not wish to add further fuel to the fire.

'Meanwhile, we shall endeavour to answer your questions as thoroughly as we possibly can.'

After some additional formalities, during which time he introduced his two colleagues, and it turned out that Stoneham was with Special Branch and had indeed travelled up from New Scotland Yard, Driscoll generated a pause and opened the questioning. A flurry of voices and photo-flashes erupted from the crowd. Driscoll raised a hand then pointed to an overweight man with a squeaky Mancunian accent seated near the front.

'Andrew Leonard, *Manchester Evening News*. Was it not David Kowalski who'd been heading the police investigation into the killing of Michael Greenhalgh?'

'Yes it was,' Driscoll replied. 'He was working with Detective Superintendent Stoneham here.'

Stoneham's watery eyes scanned the room and lingered

again in the direction of the door. Driscoll pointed at somebody else.

'Carol Cruickshank, *Northwest Tonight*. You say that Sergeant Kowalski committed suicide. Prior to his death had there been any indication that he might have been emotionally disturbed?' Her voice was deeper than that of the squeaky Mancunian male who'd just preceded her.

'He certainly showed no indication to myself or to any of his colleagues,' Driscoll said. 'But then, it was probably true to say that David was not a man who was prone to revealing his feelings very easily. The possibility shall have to be considered that he might have been bottling things up.'

'You mean that he might still have been grieving about the murder of his wife and daughter?'

The voice was still that of Carol Cruickshank.

'He might have been grieving inwardly about the deaths, Ms Cruickshank, yes. He lived alone, he rarely socialized, and he was totally committed to his work. He was an experienced, capable officer who would have gone far. He was admired for his strength of will. If he managed to conceal his emotional fatigue, then that was because it was necessary in order to retain the morale of his unit of men. And this he managed extremely well.'

Irritated at how near he was to the back wall, Blake strained to look past a video camera in front of his face. Then the cameraman came away from the tripod and Blake had a clear view down to the front. He saw the dark-haired woman touch her nose with a handkerchief. Then she wrote something down, ran her fingers through her hair, and flicked it back with that jerk of her head that shook him to his foundations with desire.

Driscoll pointed. Another male voice announced itself and threw a question from the crowd. 'Was there a reason why David Kowalski was heading the inquiry into the Michael Greenhalgh killing? I understand that with incidents of a sensitive political nature, it is normal practice for Special Branch to assume control of the case.'

Stoneham straightened on his chair and spoke. His voice was unusually articulate, more so than Blake remembered. It was difficult to believe it could have been a product of the same biological forces that had fabricated the podgy body in which it was contained. 'Special Branch doesn't necessarily take control of the case,' he said. 'While it always becomes involved, Sergeant Kowalski discovered the body of Michael Greenhalgh and requested that he took charge of the investigation. An area sergeant can remain the senior investigating officer if he wishes to do so.'

'Do you think that Sergeant Kowalski might have been adversely affected by the circumstances of the politician's death? After all, it was a brutal murder, and it might have awakened memories of his own domestic tragedy earlier in the year.'

The voice belonged to a young Asian woman.

Stoneham looked to Driscoll for assistance and Driscoll promptly steepled his hands. 'Again, you are asking us to speculate, young lady. It would be unwise for us to make rash assumptions at this stage.'

'Are there any suspicious circumstances surrounding the alleged suicide?'

'Not so far as we have been able to ascertain,' Driscoll replied. 'It appears to have been a simple case of a man deciding to take his own life. It is only a matter of hours since the body was discovered, of course, but we expect forensic evidence to indicate that there are no suspicious circumstances.'

'Chief Constable, are you prepared to state the method by which the sergeant took his life?'

Driscoll unsteepled his hands. 'Not at this stage, no. A formal statement will be issued once our forensic examinations have been completed.'

'Who discovered the body at the scene of the crime?'

The question this time was a trick offering from a tabloid vulture who Blake recognized as having flown up from London overnight. Driscoll spotted it immediately. 'Technically we are not discussing a "crime" here, young man. Sergeant Kowalski was found dead at his house by police colleagues who were alerted by neighbours, and who found the body in the living room.'

There was a frantic scribble of pencils when the living room detail was revealed.

The questions and answers went round in circles for a short while, during which time Blake was left wondering whether the policemen seemed uneasy at being asked who'd discovered the body. Then Driscoll pointed in the direction of the door again, and Blake's thinking was cut short when he had the distinct impression that an accusing finger was being aimed directly at him. It wasn't. An elegant forty-something-year-old woman with short blonde hair, seated a few feet to the right of where Blake was standing, dropped her hand. He recognized her from once having tried to pick him up after a news conference in London.

'Julia Hall, the *London Evening Telegraph*. Sir, did not Sergeant Kowalski possess a dog? There were photographs of it in the papers with him earlier this year.'

'Yes, madam, he did possess a dog.'

Driscoll deliberately clipped the sentence short, and the photo-flashes started going off again. Seizing on the sentimental angle offered to the story by the prospect of generating concern about an abandoned domestic animal, a dozen hands rose into the air and the policemen were bombarded with a garble of questions.

Driscoll seemed relieved and raised a hand as though he were a warden holding back traffic. Somehow Julia Hall managed to retain the initiative, her second question forcing its way between the babble of the crowd. 'Are the police prepared to confirm whether the dog is alive or dead?'

'Not at this stage of the inquiry, no,' Driscoll shouted. His thin colourless lips straightened contentedly, gouged a counterfeit split across the bony surface of his rather youthful middle-aged face, as the hubbub subsided in anticipation of his response and he stretched out the tension. 'Again, a

formal statement will be issued when it is considered appropriate.'

Blake knew what Driscoll was doing. He was deliberately
playing the card of the dog, being vague about what had
happened to it because he knew the media would jump. He
was trying to keep the questioning away from a dangerous
corner. Blake was probably the only person in the room
who suspected where the dangerous corner might be. Not
knowing if he were being galvanized by his professional
instincts, or by a desire to draw the attention of the dark-
haired woman, he decided to risk making his move. He
raised his hand several times, but was consistently ignored.
Then Driscoll looked at him, saw that there were no more
hands in the air anywhere near, seemed to realize that if he
failed to respond it might look obvious, shifted heavily in his
seat, and said, surprisingly reluctantly: 'Yes, Mr Hunter?'

'Do you think there has been a pattern between any of
these recent killings?'

'I do not understand what you mean, Mr Hunter.'

More photo-flashes blasted the shadows from his face.

'I mean, do you think there is any connection between the
killing of Messrs Greenhalgh and Kowalski, in the detonation of urban-terrorist bombs at the Houses of Parliament,
and the fact that a national state of emergency has been declared since the Doomsday riots broke out?'

Driscoll did not meet Blake's eye but instead directed his
answer as though it were a formal statement for the benefit
of the crowd.

'I see no pattern except the familiar pattern of lawlessness.
I see no pattern except that of a vicious underworld brutality undermining the conduct of the civilized as they go about
their business. There has been no connection between any of
these crimes. And before you all begin writing it down, it
should be stressed—and I repeat—that the taking of his own
life by David Kowalski is *not* being investigated as a crime.
If there has been any coincidence at all, it is that, when
judged in the mass, these incidents serve to remind us of the

organized forces of evil that are beginning to wreak havoc amongst all our lives.'

'Going back to what you said earlier about David Kowalski,' Blake continued, 'you claim that he was the senior officer assigned to the investigation of the Michael Greenhalgh killing, because he requested it. But wasn't the sergeant in Yorkshire on an area exchange with Bradford at the time of the politician's disappearance? And was he not brought back to take over the case on the Greater Manchester Police Authority's orders?'

Blake had neglected to mention this to Vanessa, and was aware of it only because Kowalski had told him when they first ran through the shape of the interview, a week before he died.

Driscoll and Stoneham both perceptibly stiffened, then Driscoll cleared his throat and smoothed his hand beneath his chin. 'No, Mr Hunter, he was not. I do not know from where you have obtained such information, but I can assure you that it is quite without foundation.'

Half the audience had turned to look at Blake, including the dark-haired woman. Most of the journalists were frowning, not at Blake, but at the nature of the insinuation that had just drifted into the room. 'Clearly, I must have been mistaken,' Blake said nonchalantly. For a moment the dark-haired woman held his eyes inquisitively; then she looked away.

'Yes, clearly you must.'

Detective Sergeant Wakern, who had still said nothing, had recently steepled his hands. He now unsteepled them and examined his fingernails and Stoneham steepled his. The posture seemed as if it were being passed between the policemen like a game of pass the parcel.

Before anybody else could speak Blake returned to the attack. 'Do you not agree, Mister Driscoll, now that this story has made the headlines, now that it has been revealed that a sort of national folk hero has committed suicide, ostensibly through pressures of work which can be sourced to the crimewave, there will be yet more moral outrage expressed by the general public?'

Driscoll looked perturbed as he tried to work out the direction of Blake's questioning through the confusion of blue flashes. He dribbled his words from his mouth as though he were thinking aloud, then corrected himself mid-sentence and speeded things up. 'That would probably be the outcome, irrespective of whether we were discussing a suicide or a straightforward homicide. My priority is to report the facts as accurately as possible, not to speculate about how such an incident is likely to affect the national mood.'

Still Blake persisted, bolstered by the knowledge that the exchange would probably be going out on the *Early Evening News*. He did not have to fight for verbal pole position any longer because now everybody in the room was listening to him, and Julia Hall's long fingers were on her sheer-stockinged thigh and her large green eyes were on his face.

'But surely you agree that by holding a news conference so quickly, the media is bound to begin speculating about the reasons why David Kowalski should have decided to'—he checked his notepad theatrically—'er, take his own life?'

'I repeat, Mr Hunter,' Driscoll retorted forcefully, yet maintaining an icy professional calm, 'it is not my job to gauge how the public is likely to respond. It is my job to explain the facts as they are available to me at this stage.' He searched quickly for a raised arm elsewhere in the audience, but none was available.

Blake was still in control and when he pressed home his advantage the photo-flashes started going crazy.

'And is it not a well established fact, Chief Constable Driscoll, that you have been at the forefront of the Police Federation's lobbying of ministers for the reintroduction of capital punishment? Do you not see these recent high-profile killings as doing nothing but strengthening the Federation's case? Is that not the real reason behind this news conference being organized so quickly, to capitalize on the wave of national hysteria and a popular desire to "see the bastards hanged"?'

Then he looked beyond Julia Hall, whose fingers were now drifting discreetly yet deliberately across her crotch, and met the eyes of the dark-haired woman again. To his astonishment she was looking straight at him and very slowly and covertly shaking her head. The movement was barely noticeable, but the effort needed to transmit it, without making it obvious to anybody in the room, was draining the colour from her face. At the same time she was silently mouthing to him: *No, Blake, no.* Stymied, Blake lost his verbal footing and more or less forgot what he'd just asked.

Driscoll grabbed his opportunity.

'I shall say this once, and once only Mr Hunter. The allegations you have just made bear no relevance whatsoever to the subject of this news conference. Should you wish to ask any additional questions we shall answer them as clearly as we can. But any more remarks of the kind you have just uttered and I shall have you removed from the room. You are wasting police time, and also that of your colleagues.'

'That won't be necessary, Chief Constable. The relevant questions have been asked, as I'm sure a good number of my colleagues here will agree.'

Blake ignored Julia Hall and met the eyes of the dark-haired woman instead. He was about to raise his eyebrows ironically, but before his facial muscles could lift up the flesh she'd already turned away.

When Driscoll declared the conference closed Blake made sure he was one of the first people out of the door. He lingered in the foyer, watching the bodies file out and ruminating over the fact that, until recently, everybody would have had a visitors' pass fastened to their lapel showing their name at these hastily-put-together news meetings. But because every British citizen now had to carry a personal identity card by law, visitors' badges had become more or less obsolete. Instead, your styrene identity card was fed into a computer at the reception desk or security barrier whenever you arrived anywhere. The information on the barcode and your holographic photograph were then matched by the wonders of fibre-optics to the personal details held about you, along with your fingerprints, blood type, National Insurance number, and income tax code, at Central Matrix in Glasgow. Had it not been for the influence of bureaucracy and technology, Blake reflected, he might have been able to see the name of the dark-haired woman on her person. On the other hand, a list of names would have been churned out by the laser-printer after everyone came in, so there was a chance he might be able to get hold of that.

The mob of journalists took several minutes to emerge, but as yet there was no sign of the woman. Blake tried to look as if he were waiting to meet someone, and leaned contemplatively against the reception desk, being surprised that nobody challenged him about what he'd said during the conference. Then, beyond the scrum of figures congesting the entrance to the conference room, he saw her stand up. She'd been seated at the end of a row furthest from the door and was waiting for the people in front of her to file out of the way because the other direction was blocked by a couple of television cameramen, who were rolling up cables and putting equipment into aluminium cases.

Blake pulled a copy of the previous day's *Guardian* from his pocket and started turning roughly through the pages. By swinging the paper around and pretending to keep his eyes on the upper corners he was able to see into the conference room beyond. He saw the woman come out through the door. She looked across but made no indication that she'd seen he was there, probably because he was hidden by the newspaper. Then, rather than turning left towards the main entrance, she turned right and slipped through a pair of doors leading in the opposite direction. A couple of journalists followed her through. Trying to remain casual, Blake refolded his newspaper and followed the two journalists. As he pushed open the doors he saw them disappearing into the Gents, and caught sight of the woman's silver swing coat disappearing into the Ladies.

He also went into the Gents, raised his eyebrows at the journalists, one of whom he vaguely recognized, splashed his face with cold water, then pretended to wash his hands, exhaling theatrically as he stood in front of the dryer to stretch everything out. The journalists urinated; then, for what seemed like an eternity, lingered over the fastening of their flies and the washing of their hands. The dryer stopped blowing, but before it came on again, Blake heard a cistern flushing muffled through the wall. When the dryer switched off again, he stood in front of the mirrors and pretended to remove some dirt from his eye, thanking God when at last the two journalists disappeared. He followed them out, lingering in the vestibule and waiting for the sound of the woman's heels to give him his cue. Instead, he heard the clobbering of boots and a stocky riot policeman in blue shirt-sleeves, with his face dirtied like an SAS commando made up for a nocturnal reconnaissance, barged into the toilets and said, 'Hey up, then,' as he nearly pushed the door in Blake's face.

There was nothing for it but for him to go out into the empty corridor. He nodded pointlessly as he squeezed past the policeman, praying that he was going to do his ablutions and not just to have a pee. Outside he bent down and began fumbling with his black monk shoes. The shoes were kept tight by a piece of leather shaped like the flap of an envelope, folded from the inside towards the outside of the foot, and secured by velcro. He played with the velcro so that he had something to do with his hands; then there was a clack of stylish female heels from the Ladies, and the dark-haired woman came out into the corridor.

Blake rose to face her and both of them froze.

Close up to her he could see that she was not just as tall as he remembered. Her slender legs were encased in stockings that were so sheer there hardly looked to be a nylon membrane encasing them at all, and they were so perfectly proportioned that from a distance they made her look longer and more graceful than she actually was.

He stepped up to her and looked into her wonderfully tranquil dark-brown eyes, which were so moving they were almost painful to contemplate. 'Where on earth did you get such amazing eyes?' he heard himself saying, shaking his head incredulously as he took them in.

Looking into them again, he saw that each pupil had running around the edge a thin band the colour of sand; something he realized he'd noticed that night at the heliport but had forgotten until now. The sandy colour bled towards the centre of each eye like the blending of watercolour paint. This made the pupils seem to be imbued with a luminosity, the dark centres framed by tiny borders so that they appeared to be lit up. That in turn had the effect of marvellously exaggerating her eye movements and gave her a curiously attentive, rather staring quality that almost verged on the severe. As they considered each other, he wondered if she were able to sense the frightening emotional impact she was having upon him. If she was, she was managing to conceal it.

'Why are you following me, Mr Hunter?'

Her surprisingly husky voice sounded like his: eloquent, articulate, but without the plum-stones cluttering up the mouth. He'd already taken that to be indicative of a sound mental order; of a lively assertiveness needing to express itself clearly and precisely. Her words were not animal noises used to create a veneer of clever sophistication. They were not designed to prop up a shallow intellect, like those artificial flavourings that give a false sensation of taste to synthetic food.

'Because you've been leading me on then avoiding me, and I know that you're not the kind of person who'd take a delight in doing such a thing. You also tried to warn me about something inside that news conference and I want to know what it was.'

The woman tensed as though she were going to push past, but Blake slapped his hand against the wall so that his arm created a barrier. The flesh lifted above the collar of her metallic-grey blouse while she swallowed, then settled down nervously behind it again.

'Please go away, Mr Hunter.'

'It's no use, love,' he said, looking into her eyes, 'that isn't you speaking.' He noticed that her pupils were slightly dilated, but already he could feel his control of the situation slipping away. He lowered his arm and she stepped past and started walking towards the doors that led back to reception. Blake came alongside her, amused to think they could have been friends leaving for lunch.

'Please, Mr Hunter—'

'You get about quite a bit, don't you, but for whom? Which paper is it? Is it radio? Is it regional TV?'

They'd arrived at the doors leading to the foyer, so he slipped in front of her and brought his back up against the handles to form another barrier. The only way she could get past was by pulling him out of the way. Then she was reaching inside her handbag, deliberately preventing her eyes from meeting his. As she opened the bag he felt the curious combination of fatherly affection, and of having invaded someone's privacy, that he always felt when he saw inside a woman's handbag. He was relieved to see that there were no cigarette packets inside, either, though he knew intuitively that she didn't smoke. He also sensed an opportunity to find out who she was when he saw her identity card, noting that the holograph of her face was just as naturally ravishing on the picture as the person whose real hand was searching alongside it now.

'Where are you from?' he was asking. 'You were at the Greenhalgh speech the other week, you were at the press conference after the Canary Wharf bombing the other day, and now you're back up in Manchester at a news conference held to announce the supposed "suicide" of a policeman. I've never seen you before, yet suddenly you are present at key media gatherings following a number of high-profile incidents.' He saw her hand come away from the bag and realized that her Christian name only had been revealed on her identity card. The surname was obscured by something else. 'Who are you? Why did you signal to me'—he felt immensely happy as he read, then heard himself repeat, the name—'Abigail?'

She snapped her handbag closed, but not before the trembling hand had produced the small black plastic device resembling a torch that it had gone to retrieve in the first place. It was a microstunner, the hi-tech successor to the old-fashioned rape alarm; a small device that many women carried which packed a painful electric shock when brought into contact with the human body.

'You know what this is,' she said. The eyes really did look as if they were lit up from inside. 'If you don't move out of the way I shall touch you with it and your nervous system will be immobilized for the next quarter of an hour.'

'And if you do, I shall sue you for assault. That way I'll find out your name because there'll be plenty of witnesses, seeing as we're in a police station. So go ahead and strike me. I'm prepared to take it because it means that in court I can stand up and tell everybody that I think I'm going to end up falling in love with you.'

At this she seemed to shudder, though Blake meant the words to sound like humorous badinage rather than for them to come out with the air of seriousness they somehow managed to adopt. There was a silence, and then the stocky policeman came out from the toilets, his face bright and podgy and clean. He was rubbing his hands up and down his shirt front, looked guilty when he realized that he had an audience, then stiffened as he assessed the situation.

'Officer, this man is molesting me,' the woman said, her eyes still refusing to meet Blake's.

The policeman started walking towards them, and Blake said under his breath, with an intensity that surprised even him: 'All right then, you can turn up your nose and you can walk out of this building now, but you know perfectly well that I won't stop until I reach you and find out what the *hell* it is that you're up to.'

The woman managed to bring her eyes to meet his. Her nostrils seemed to flare, as though she were struggling to prevent a ball of energy from blowing the lid off her emotions. Though she remained inscrutable, he sensed that she was only managing to do so under extreme duress. The eyes were not the same eyes that had frowned at him when she'd asked him to please go away several minutes ago.

He took the microstunner from her and she gasped softly. Smiling now, he held her hand, but she didn't pull it away. 'It sounds stupid, doesn't it?' he said, lightly stroking her fingers, which were warm and moist and definitely trembling. The policeman was almost upon them. 'Here I am, a fully grown man carrying on like some illiterate love-struck teenager.'

He let the hand drop and stepped aside. But before she pulled open the door, the eyes turned to him again, and the husky voice croaked: 'No, it doesn't sound stupid'—the words barely articulate noises rather than a cluster of consonants coupled to vowels. The dropped hand lifted as if it were about to return his touch; then she seemed to have second thoughts, pushed her way through to the crowded foyer, and was gone. Before the door closed again, Blake saw Driscoll emerge from the conference room, frowning in his direction.

Then the stocky policeman was coming alongside.

'It's okay, officer,' he said hoarsely, 'I wasn't molesting her.' He laughed, but found that the laugh faltered because of a sticky substance clogging the back of his mouth that could best be described as glue. He cleared his throat and looked at Abigail's microstunner, which was still in his hand. It smelt vaguely of powder and scent. It was her smell: it was the smell of roses.

Far from looking malevolent the policeman appeared embarrassed and rather confused. The door had closed again, shutting out the hubbub of Reception and obliterating Driscoll's staring face.

'I must admit,' the policeman said, squinting through the slit of glass, 'I wouldn't exactly blame you if you had been. She's bloody gorgeous.'

'Is there any chance of me getting hold of a printout of the list of guests from the news conference when everybody came in? Professional enquiries and all that?'

The policeman grinned and held open the door.

'I don't mind giving you a caution, but if you make any more requests like that I'll have to ask you to accompany me to the station'—he paused for effect—'as they used to say in the films. Besides, half the fun of going after women is supposed to be in the chasing of 'em, isn't it pal?'

He winked once.

'Point taken,' Blake said, and stepped through the door.

Most of the media people had cleared. A few cameramen were carrying metal cases out through the automatic doors, which, because of the relentless toing and froing of bodies, were sliding open then closed confusedly, filling the doorway with blasts of hot and cold air.

Blake made his way outside and stood on the herringbone setts just in front of the building. It had stopped raining. It was a bleak late-autumn morning, but the huge tower blocks piled all around were lit up so brightly it could have been the end of a miserable afternoon. Vehicles were filing out from the car park underneath police headquarters, their tyres swishing against wet tarmac as they lined up at the security barrier surrounded by a cloud of blue fumes. A moment later, he heard the sound of the engine for which he'd been waiting and the Frontera lurched over the top of the ramp, assumed the horizontal, then joined the queue of vehicles down at the lodge.

Blake stayed where he was, his hands thrust deep in his coat pockets and surrounded by a cloud of his own steam. There was a moment when the Frontera was perpendicular to the entrance of the building, as it curved round with the departing vehicles and waited for the barrier to fold out of the way. Because of her position, and because the Frontera was taller than the cars behind it, he knew that Abigail would be able to see him standing in her rearview mirror. He could only make out her head and shoulders dimly in the poor light, but he knew that she would be watching. It was like the melodramatic final scene to a film, with the heroine rather than the hero driving away into the sunset, or rather the dull Mancunian weather.

Then the Frontera was through the barrier, hemmed in by high brick walls as it accelerated down the slip road to join Deansgate at the bottom. It slowed as it came to the white dotted lines, splashed through puddles, swerved out into the traffic, and was away.

Blake couldn't help thinking that it looked as though the Frontera were being driven by somebody who'd become unusually clumsy at the wheel. He knew why, of course, and the fact that he knew why only enhanced his growing sense of euphoria. Though he'd no idea who this woman was, though she might conceivably be up to no good, he couldn't escape the feeling that his whole life had been leading up to this moment. No cryptic analysis was required, either, when he had a premonition that the domestic misery of the past several months was finally on the verge of being tidied away. For he knew that Abigail would be trembling with anticipation just as much as he. She'd struggled to conceal her feelings back in the corridor, and he had to admire the composed, professional manner by which she'd nearly pulled it off. But what he knew deep down must be her integrity, her essential decency, the simple uncomplicated goodness that generated the power behind those extraordinary eyes, had surfaced and had its way. She was on the verge of falling in love with him, but as yet was keeping her distance for reasons best known to herself. Something of enormous importance had come between them since they'd spoken that night at the heliport. But he was not going to force her hand. He knew that when they eventually got together their relationship wouldn't require a period of breaking-in; that their chemistries were so unique it would automatically begin on full power. He knew, too, that she would come to him when she was ready, just as surely as he knew that they were going to find themselves in one another's company again very, very soon.

Blake's assessment of everything that had taken place so far was correct, of course. He wasn't the only party excited to wonder if a predetermined pair of destinies were being brought together at last. When Abigail saw him framed in her rearview mirror she was overcome with desire herself; something which was having upon her body a quite extraordinary erotic effect. But Blake couldn't have known that the way he'd challenged Driscoll about the 'alleged' suicide of David Kowalski back in the news conference, implying that he knew something everybody else didn't, had set the alarm bells ringing in her mind. That was why she knew, too, they would be back in one another's company again very, very soon. It was because of this, and because of her feelings for him, that she feared for Blake's safety and why now suddenly she was afraid.

Indeed, as she accelerated up a slip road past giant stainless-steel stilts, joined the twelve-lane Queen Elizabeth Way slicing majestically through the sky, and headed out past the slums from the southern edge of the city, she realized that she was so afraid she felt more isolated and unsure of what was going to happen next than at any other time in her life.

# *Six*

When Vanessa crossed to the new overflow car park that was being built behind the studios of BBC Manchester, later that day, the rain of the morning had gone and the evening had turned so cold there was snow in the air, making the ground treacherous beneath her feet.

Because the deserted compound was unfinished and an obstacle course of frozen puddles and piles of unlaid brick setts, a temporary security-light had been erected near the entrance of the kind that detects advancing body heat. She anticipated the familiar mechanical click when she turned off Oxford Road but felt only a little uneasy when the beam didn't come on. Normally she wouldn't have risked walking out to her car unaccompanied like this, especially since she'd left her microstunner in her hotel room that morning and tried never to go anywhere unarmed. But like many people who find themselves in such situations, while one half of her mind was urging her to get away, her legs were carrying her body forward, so that by the time she'd found the Volvo the thought that she might have been striding headlong into disaster had evaporated, and she was feeling for her seat-belt and slotting the key into the ignition.

Because she hadn't seen Blake since she'd dropped him at the news conference, before she drove away she took out her cellular phone and decided to give him a call to find out what time he wanted to eat. The phone had been switched off all afternoon and she'd been working on her own in an editing suite since lunchtime, leaving instructions at the switchboard that she mustn't be disturbed. She'd already checked her message box and found it empty, but no sooner had the liquid-crystals pulsed to signify that the portable had been turned back on, than it was trilling and she was lifting it to her ear assuming it was Blake.

It wasn't, it was her husband Max, calling from the darkened offices of his Public Relations company in the Regent's Park district of London. He was seated at his desk, having just lit a cigarette and put his phone into the hands-off mode whilst he'd been connected. His short red hair was rim-lit by a spotlight behind him, but his face was lost in shadow, shielded by the headrest of his luxurious blue leather chair. Only the outline of his chrome spectacles showed against the blackness, along with the side of a pink, smoothly-shaven, forty-something face.

'Why hasn't your portable been switched on, you stupid bitch?' he snapped. 'I've been trying to contact you all afternoon. I phoned that useless assistant of yours and she said you weren't answering in the editing suite, either. What the hell have you been playing at?'

It might have seemed that Max's hostile attitude was a reaction against him being relieved to find that his wife was safe. Far from it, and when she realized who was speaking to her, Vanessa felt a weariness come over her and had literally to drag the words from her mouth.

'I knew it would annoy you,' she said, gripping the steering wheel with her free hand so tightly the knuckles turned white. She was a strong woman who could wrap most men around her little finger, but nothing in the world made her feel more subordinate than the sound of her husband's cold, calculating voice.

'You're pushing your luck, Vanessa.'

'I don't care any more. I really do not give a damn.'

'You don't either, do you? Which is a silly thing to admit to me at such a crucial stage in the miserable sequence of events that constitutes our matrimonial saga, darling. A very silly thing indeed. Anybody would think you were trying to avoid your husband.'

'What do you want, Max? I'm tired, I've just cut some very unpleasant riot footage, and I want to get back to the hotel.'

'Poor Vanessa,' he said, stretching the words into a hideous sentimental drawl, sucking at his cigarette again, then reaching to tap it on the rim of an absurdly oversized glass ashtray. 'You sound so dreadfully forlorn.' The hand that returned the cigarette to his mouth was manicured, while both the shirt cuff and the suit cuff had a curious metallic sheen, making the attached arm look as though it were encased in brushed aluminium foil. 'You know, it never ceases to amaze me how you automatically assume a subservient tone when you talk to me, and yet you're such an assertive female with everybody else. My God! To think that you once punched a leading American film director in the face and broke his jaw for groping at your lovely arse. The mind boggles at your latent schizophrenia.' He tittered from the shadows. 'Oh, I like that. That's very funny. I shall quote myself there.' He tittered again, though menace was creeping into his voice now. 'You do, incidentally, adopt the same servile attitude when you're with our dear Blake, though obviously you're not aware of it. And neither, I think, is he.'

'If you don't tell me what the fuck you want, Max, I'll cut you off and I'll put the phone under the wheel of the car and drive over it right now.'

'Do that, and you'll be as good as driving over your own skull. As it happens, I just wanted to let you know that I'm flying to the States for a few days, that's all. Important research, as they say. But because I enjoy toying with your emotions, I wanted to remind you that I know where you are, and that I shall be monitoring your every move.'

The inside of the car was beginning to steam up now. Vanessa let go of the wheel and wiped her forearm once across her window. Outside, a train was ambling across a viaduct, its lights sending a stroboscopic glare across the compound, picking out frosty windscreens and sending elongated shadows fanning like giant spokes across the huddled cars. She had a sharp eye, born of the film-person's habit of walking around and forever seeing the world through a mental viewfinder, and before everything went dark again, as if prompted by Max's words, she wondered if she saw a figure moving between the piles of new setts, several yards from the vehicle. She squinted as she started speaking and activated the internal locking, just in case.

'You're enjoying this aren't you, you rotten bastard? Every moment do you savour.'

'Funnily enough, yes. I used to be decent and idealistic, and still considered myself so when I met you. But as a frame of mind, decency outlived its usefulness when I was sensible enough to realize that you have to get what you can out of this misbegotten world.' He put the cigarette to his mouth again, tilted back his head, and shot out some smoke. A blue pother was building above him now, while somewhere outside there was the muffled thud of a huge explosion, though he didn't so much as flinch at the sound. 'Where is Blake, anyway? I take it from the way you're talking to me that he isn't exactly sitting next to you.'

'I'm not sure where he is. The shoot was cancelled because of rain, so I gave the crew the day off. I dropped him at the news conference this morning that was held to announce David Kowalski's untimely departure from the world.'

She had a vision of Blake and wondered how he could remain oblivious to the lack of affection between Max and herself nowadays, even if she had no choice but to keep up a front. Then again, on the occasions when he wasn't conveniently called away on business, Max had mastered the art of not remaining in the same room if anybody was at their Hampstead house. Whenever Blake stayed—which, since his divorce, was quite often—Max was always putting a small distance between himself and her, moving about the kitchen rattling crockery, going up to his office to make phone calls. Such oblique behaviour suited his restless personality, and he worked hard to keep up appearances—much harder than she did, which was where she had the upper hand—though how much longer it could carry on she wasn't prepared to speculate.

Max had lifted his feet onto his desk, while the explosion outside had blended with the chatter of machinegun-fire and seemed to have alerted every police siren in London. 'If you gave the crew the day off, that means you've had plenty of time to seduce Blake. Have you screwed him yet, darling? I do hope that you haven't, though it goes without saying that the moment you do I shall know about it. And then you'll be outside that car, bending down and placing your head before a nice low-profile tyre, your queer assistant no doubt kneeling up behind you and rolling back your trousers, her eyes gloating having stuck something into herself first . . .'

Vanessa winced. 'Quite apart from being a rotten bastard, you do have a way with words, Max. And your timing is brilliant, I have to give you that.'

Cigarette to mouth followed by another chuckle.

'You know, Vanessa, that's very true, and I also have a most sophisticated imagination, hence the large number of design awards hanging on the walls of this prestigious public relations tower in which I'm sitting. Speaking of which, we devised this Virtual Reality thing the other day, and it made me think of you and Blake. Not shagging each other, of course, but your wretched politics. There was this futuristic scenario—let's call it the *Doomsday Scenario,* shall we?—all derelict backstreets, overgrown slums, and piles of burnt-out cars. A bit like the way things are already, but without the gypsies salvaging all the scrap.

'Anyway, I plugged myself in and galloped about on a horse in a red huntsman's tunic. There was a pack of hounds and some more riders, and do you know what we were all chasing? That's right, three manimals. One black, one white, and one a mongrel in between. Pretty symbolic really, I suppose. And beyond were these bloody mile-high glass tower blocks. You could see right through them, right up the skirts of the tarts sitting at the computer terminals in the offices, right inside their vaginas if you wanted to, the sides whizzing past like the walls of a cave. And there we were outside, chasing these underclass scum bags just like they were so many terrified foxes. When I aimed my plasma pistol, I felt the kids' heads explode, like that scene in *The Day of the Jackal* where Edward Fox was shooting at that water melon on a French hillside. Bang! Three worthless skulls splattered all in a row. It felt wonderful. We've even added a scene where there's a bulldozer pushing a big pile of underclass bodies into a hole in the ground, post-Holocaust style, which is the place where you go to tot up your score. That's where we'll be back to again, by about the year 2095, of course, quite apart from the fact that I've always believed that it wouldn't take much of a change in outlook to start hunting people instead of foxes. And slaughtering all that inner-city shit we'd be performing much the same sort of duty really, stopping them breeding like AIDS-infested rabbits. They say you'll be able to have it off with Marilyn Monroe with these Virtual Reality suits soon, by the way. I pity the memory of dead actors who've since been revealed to be gay, though.'

This was typical of Max, she thought. His conversation was forever flitting from one subject to another without bothering to start a new paragraph. That was why he'd been so successful at his job. It occurred to her then that he could keep so many different projects going inside his head simultaneously, and could switch effortlessly from one to the other without a moment's thought, because he'd never needed more than a few hours sleep each night, whereas she needed more than most. Not that she'd been getting it just lately.

'Can I ask you something, Max?'

'Fire away.'

'Why did I marry you? How in the name of God did I end up betrothing myself to such an ignorant fascist shit?'

'A couple of reasons, Vanessa. One is that you were not nearly as politicized as you are now, and neither was I. The other is because you were stupid, and I mean that in the nicest possible way. You've since found that you like to dominate your men, but I'm one of the few men you could never hope to dominate. You get your kicks by lying on top of men; you like to lick men between their naked buttocks, so as to speak, which is why you've started to go for the younger variety, who you find so much easier to mother. You aren't fucked up, but it's what turns you on. You didn't realize it when we met, that's all, though I don't think you should read too much into it. Twelve years is a long time, darling, and we all need time to grow. Especially if we're creative. We all have our kinky secrets, our little oddball erotic urges. Just think yourself lucky that you haven't discovered you're a dyke.

'Meanwhile, on a serious and altogether more important note, has my dear wife heard the latest from Parliament?'

'No, she hasn't.'

The tears were running down her face now, finding their way into the grooves scored from her nose to the corners of her mouth, hesitating beneath her chin, forming little dark spots on her lapels.

'The *Guardian* reckons it's hypnotized one of these secret "death chamber" contractors and managed to assemble a computerized simulation of what they think the new gallows will look like. They claim it's all stainless-steel, computerized technology, and hydraulic-operated trapdoors. Pretty amazing, really. They're going to publish the pictures on Thursday, but the PM's furious because the media's getting too close for comfort now. What neither the PM nor the media realize is that they're being *allowed* to get that close!' The titter had become so mechanical it was being used to punctuate the drawing of breath and the sucking of smoke now, nothing more. 'How do you guarantee that public opinion remains on your side over such a controversial issue as bringing back capital punishment? Why, you instigate a little PR leak like this and it keeps the country's sense of wonder going. And the liberals flock to it like flies to a sodding dung heap. It's so obvious. But then all PR work is obvious. That's why I've been so successful. To be a good politician you not only need to be a simpleton, you need to be a good PR man. And to be a good PR man you need to be a good politician, but you certainly do not need to be a simpleton. Put that into your little film, if you dare.' He dropped his feet from the desk, reached to stub his cigarette, and adopted a cheery note of finality.

'Anyway, Vanessa, I've finished my smoke and I have to fly, quite literally, within the hour. In the meantime, why don't you go back to the hotel and smarten yourself up? Put on some make-up and a short skirt. It would do you the world of good because you could look so much better than you do. Perhaps in another life you might have been a truly beautiful woman. But you haven't got another life, have you? You've always been marooned in this one. I wonder how much longer it's likely to last.' A pause. 'Still, there is always masturbation.' Another pause, cheeriness gone, voice as cold as ice now. 'And just remember this whilst I'm away, bitch. Make one move in Blake's direction. So much as plonk your hand on his fucking leg, and I'll be down on you like a ton of bricks. I shall personally screw a silencer onto a Sheuze automatic pistol and stick it inside your mouth. Having pulled out all your teeth with a pair of pliers first so that I can fit the damned thing in. Just remember. My eyes are everywhere, you useless, frustrated slut. *Everywhere!*'

He started to snigger through his nostrils but hung up before the sound could mature into a fully-fledged laugh.

When Vanessa cancelled the phone she could hear a ringing in her ears. She unhooked her spectacles and wiped her eyes, then felt panic-stricken for a moment as silence resumed and she caught sight of herself in the rearview mirror. 'How much longer . . .' she croaked, her lovely face almost white beneath the glow of the vanity light. 'How much bloody longer . . .'

All she wanted was for somebody to hold her again.

But if she'd been too afraid to cut Max off when they

were talking, then it was a measure of her resolve that, far from descending into self-pity at the prospect of her continuing isolation, her desire to drag herself out of it fuelled her determination to cope with it all the more. Meanwhile, it was necessary to rid herself of something that she'd been meaning to rid herself of for some time. She turned the ignition key so that the dashboard electrics came to life and sent down her window. Then calmly, coolly, she slipped off her wedding ring, stuck out her other hand, and threw the ring away into the night. There was a faint metallic ping as it hit something solid in the darkness, then a sharp crack as it came to rest on the surface of a frozen puddle, several yards from the plastic front bumper of the car.

It was a small triumph, rather puerile its way, but it had the effect of clearing her mind and giving her the confidence to get through the rest of the evening. Then she remembered the skulking figure that she thought she'd seen earlier, quickly closed the window, and wiped the windscreen with a cloth. She hooked her hair behind her ear, switched on the engine, heard an old Pet Shop Boys track called *A different point of view* come on full blast on the CD, realized the album it was taken from was still one of the best she'd ever heard, turned up the volume even louder, then drove across the car park at about twice the necessary speed, feeling at that moment that she wanted nothing more than to dance naked to the music until she dropped.

As she went, the front nearside wheel crashed through the frozen puddle upon which the wedding ring had come to rest, cleaved it down the middle, sliced it clean in two. The ice fractured as though it were a pane of glass. A pool of water welled between the cracks and engulfed the golden ring.

After a few moments, the figure that had been watching Vanessa emerged from behind the setts and contemplated the disappearing car. Silhouetted before the glare of office windows stacked above surrounding rooftops, it lit a cigarette, then bent and plunged a hand into the freezing puddle.

Short, thick fingers searched through the water, tossed the pieces of spent ice aside. Then the figure straightened and lifted the wedding ring to its black button eyes, clouds of breath and smoke puffing about its face.

By now, Vanessa had made it to the compound entrance and had paused before turning out onto the road, the music muffled and booming, the right indicator flashing orange against a brick retaining wall rising sheer against the night. A couple of cars swished past, there was a brief squeal of tyres, then the Volvo was gone, its exhaust fumes lingering beneath a lonely streetlamp.

When the engine had receded and the background rumble of the city resumed, the figure pulled out a cellular telephone and started stabbing at rubber buttons. A curiously high-pitched voice muttered something unintelligible when the connection was made. Then the part-smoked cigarette was dropped into the swirling puddle and the stocky body headed back to the street, its cloud of drifting breath mingling with a few snowflakes fluttering in the bitter air.

# *Seven*

Three hours later, when Manchester had succumbed to another night of rioting and the snow had turned back to rain, Chief Constable Driscoll was standing in his office aiming a remote-control handset at one of the TV screens embedded in the wall facing his desk.

Since the state of emergency had been declared he'd taken to staying at Central Police Headquarters till the early hours, monitoring operations from his leather chair if he wasn't down in the control centre, or scrutinizing the riot discussion programmes that were being broadcast nightly on the major network and satellite channels. As the senior police officer in a region that had seen some of the worst street fighting so far, it was necessary for him to keep informed about civil disorder right across the northwest, and these TV debates were still the best way—even if the intellectual content had gone downhill lately and they'd started to take on a dreary monotony. He could also link up to a number of video cameras that were attached to helicopter gunships currently patrolling Manchester, or to CCTVs outside this very building. One of these was panning across the station slip road leading to Deansgate, and showed a plump little security guard bending to a car that had pulled up at the barrier.

Prompted by a message from the control room warning him that a serious allegation was about to be made against the Greater Manchester Police on TV, Driscoll was bringing up the volume of *State of the Nation,* just as scenes of live rioting were resuming that showed a young Air Constable crawling in a burning Mancunian backstreet, dragging a shattered leg behind him as machinegun-fire hammered all around, and blood streamed down his pale, nearly adolescent face.

A female voice was explaining that the stranded officer's tracer-signal had been missed because of radar interference, and that his helicopter was powerless to help him. The aircraft could be seen hovering above burning rooftops, visible only as a cluster of navigation lights flashing against the blackness, its rotor-blades pounding, the beam of its searchlight sweeping frantically at great coiling flames. The onboard gunner had already blasted the rioters with rubber bullets, the voiceover added solemnly, so that the unit could try to swoop back to attempt another rescue. But the gangs seemed oblivious to the gattling-gun and were descending like a pack of rabid wolves, falling over themselves to get at the body squirming in the middle of the road. If the helicopter opened fire with live ammunition, the safety of the rescue team would be jeopardized and the constable would almost certainly be killed. Driscoll folded his arms and wondered if being accidentally shot dead by his colleagues might have proved a more merciful end for the policeman than what was about to happen to him now.

There was a horrifying moment when there seemed only to be kicking limbs silhouetted against the blazing darkness, as the constable disappeared beneath squabbling humanity and his bloodied hands clawed at a frenzy of stamping feet. When he realized the helicopter had abandoned him he began to scream hysterically. It was a really nauseous, high-pitched squalling that set Driscoll's teeth on edge. It reminded him of the stories his grandfather used to tell him when he was a boy about petrified deserters during the First World War, and how crazed they became when they were stood blindfolded in front of their own firing squads. There was a hideous telephoto close-up of the constable's deformed, pink mouth, followed by a wider shot showing the rioters deliberately dragging him by his wounded leg across to the pavement, rifle-butts jabbing at him all the way, his discarded helmet spinning until somebody kicked it like a football out of the gutter. Then an outrageously-spoilered white sports car wrapped in black-tinted windows screeched up, blue smoke puffing from skidding fat tyres. The cameras were really feasting now; saw doors flung open and masked figures piling onto the tarmac; zoomed in on machetes flashing silver against the light. But instead of hacking at the terrified figure on the ground, the rioters pulled a length of rope from the boot of the car, tied it around the constable's neck, and threw it over the arm of a streetlamp. They made obscene two-fingered gestures and briefly performed a bizarre ritual dance for the benefit of the watching nation, defying it to bring back hanging as viewers anticipated what they were about to do next.

Then, like ugly choirboys ganging up to ring a church bell, half-a-dozen of them grabbed the end of the rope and hoisted the policeman up with a ferocity that was truly horrible to contemplate.

When the uniformed body was kicking pathetically on the end of the cable and the other rioters began pumping their shotguns, the report was killed. Driscoll briefly saw the studio panel back at *State of the Nation* comprising several newspaper editors, right-wing politicians, and socialist academics, surly faces turning very pale, chroma-keyed flames burning behind them as the magic of technology brought the conflagration to the heart of the debate. Before anybody could speak, one of the academics got up and walked off the set putting a handkerchief to his mouth; an action that prompted the vision mixer to cut to another live report. But she accidentally pressed the wrong button and filled British TV screens with the lynching of the young policeman again, who'd quickly been reduced to more or less a limbless trunk wrapped in a bit of tatty blue material. (This was what the academic had seen on the studio monitor, and the mood of the watching nation was never to be quite the same again.) The picture performed a clever starburst trick and wiped to show a burning electric train, sprawled down an embankment crackling with blue special-effects sparks.

There followed scenes that wouldn't have looked out of place edited into a film about the Blitz, except that they were in high-resolution colour—many viewers being treated to the spectacle of civil disorder in widescreen prologic, cinema surround sound—which made them look like outtakes from the East European wars.

Then a bespectacled black community leader was on the screen, telling the flak-jacketed female reporter that the constable had been deliberately shot in the leg by another policeman, moments before the rioters spotted him. He saw a uniformed figure lifting a telescopic rifle to his shoulder, he said with some distress, just as the constable was about to be hoisted to safety. The video camera followed him into an alley running behind a row of burning shops, several hundred yards from the fighting. The community leader pointed and the camera steadied on the operator's shoulder; saw shiny herringbone setts receding to a dark vanishing point. There was a car burning at the end, and a helicopter searchlight was feeling its way across black roof timbers shivering with fire. But there was definitely nobody there, and no way of establishing, short of a forensic examination, if anybody had been there, though the camera stared suspiciously at a manhole cover before it cut away.

As the female reporter adjusted her visor and turned to hand back to the studio, she adopted a sceptical tone when she referred to Chief Constable Driscoll of the Greater Manchester Police. She wondered aloud if he could defend the force against another allegation of the type levelled by the community leader of Bensham Green. Of course, now that the ability of the drugs gangs to stand up to the forces of law and order was going to their heads, she said, the anger felt by Chief Constables everywhere was perfectly understandable. Profits that ran to millions were being invested by a minority of clever narcotics barons into legitimate business concerns, so that an expanding Mafia-style criminal empire was getting a foothold in the commercial infrastructure of British towns and cities. But this innocent bystander, who was known for his honesty, claimed to have seen a policeman shot by one of his colleagues in order to incite the rioters into murdering him in front of the nation's TV cameras. This was the third such allegation in as many weeks, she added melodramatically, flames playing with the curves of her helmet as strikingly as they would have played with one or two other noticeable curves, had she been encased in shiny clothing.

Was society on the verge of descending into a dreadful Hobbesian nightmare, she asked, losing the common power that kept wise men in awe?

Were the police adopting clandestine methods now that we lived under the continual fear of danger and violent death; where covenants without the gun were but words and of no strength to secure a manimal at all?

How much longer before a Home Affairs Select Committee was forced to ask some very serious questions pertaining to police accountability, despite our living under that condition where every man was against every man, if not in body then in spirit?

She used these lyrical observations to link to a comment made by the community leader about the convenient timing of Michael Greenhalgh's killing, but Driscoll was already frowning and sending the volume away. Though he regretted the loss of the Air Constable, and was fed up with hearing these spurious allegations, he found it more pertinent to note that the reporter hadn't once condemned what that drugs-infested filth had done to one of his men. A hundred policemen had been murdered in the northwest alone since the riots began, and all the social explanations in the world couldn't explain away that single, irrefutable fact. The inner cities were collapsing. Yet she was more interested in speculating about whether a murdered constable had been shot in the leg by another policeman first. The media was always ready to question the killing of rioters by the police in self-defence, but generally remained silent when it was the other way around. And that just about summed up the media's hypocritical attitude, he reflected bitterly. When there used to be such things as World Wars it was common practice for an army to point its collective gun at an enemy, if it threatened the defending nation and perpetrated crimes against humanity. But if armed policemen did the same when they clashed with the enemy in their own society—an enemy who wished to harm innocent civilians as surely as a marauding army during times of war—then paramilitary action was condemned as morally reprehensible by a tribe of liberal sentimentalists, whose comfortable political stance was really a product of the hierarchical social structure they professed to oppose. As far as Driscoll was concerned, one's duty to one's country was the same whether the forces of evil attacked from without using heavy artillery, or whether they rose from within brandishing black-market firearms, bad language, and knives.

He saw the female reporter replaced by the studio panel at *State of the Nation;* imagined a brief stunned silence after the din of rioting before the accusations began to fly; then stepped across to the picture window that offered such a commanding view of his beloved city while its inner suburbs burned. In the middle distance amberoid smoke showed against the belly of the night sky, radiating from the slums where the Air Constable had died, rising above a million streetlamps flung across nocturnal Lancashire. Driscoll found something curiously reassuring about the flicker of conflagration just then, refracting across hundreds of mirror-finished windows stacked in the foreground, even if the whole of Manchester seemed to be catching alight, which was not exactly an agreeable prospect. What always struck him as powerfully surrealistic at this time of day was how the sound of gunfire was never discernible from up here, when the riots were in full swing. There was not even the thud of explosions, and a kind of loaded silence hung over the dim-lit room. As with most tall buildings in the area, the office had been soundproofed to deaden the noise of helijets flying to and from the adjacent Piccadilly Heliport, and acoustically it was cut off from the outside world.

He returned to his desk and to David Kowalski's report into the killing of Michael Greenhalgh, which he'd been considering before the message came through warning him about the *State of the Nation* report. He winced when he saw several colour photographs of a charred corpse dangling by its neck from a streetlamp. It was all that was left of Greenhalgh, whose badly-mutilated remains Kowalski's Airborne patrol had found at an abandoned industrial estate on the outskirts of Manchester. One of the pictures showed the slaughtered wild dogs the unit had gunned down to get at the body. They were sprawled across a frosty cobbled backstreet, hot intestines steaming where they'd been exposed to the bitter morning air. It was a popular sport amongst the underclass to torture people with wild dogs, of course, and whoever strung Greenhalgh up had followed convention and slashed his feet so that the blood would attract every hungry animal roaming Newton Heath. But what had struck Kowalski as odd was that the killers must have known that the most agile pit-bull in the world couldn't have leapt high enough to reach the politician's legs. Forensic had also established that he was dead before the dogs came anywhere near, which was well after the corpse had been set on fire. In Kowalski's opinion, the animals had probably been enticed for dramatic effect.

It wasn't until he'd shredded the report and was entering his personal computer bay that it occurred to Driscoll that he hadn't recognized the face of the Air Constable he'd watched being lynched on TV. He hadn't rummaged once through his memory to search for a name, yet he would have interviewed the young man as a new recruit, and examined him several times on parade. But then, some things were more important in the general scheme of things than worrying about the death of a few foot-soldiers in front of the gloating news cameras of the world. No war had ever been fought without casualties. No change for the common good was achieved without pain. The female reporter had plagiarized Hobbes, and a passage she'd avoided quoting from *Leviathan* came back to him as he sat down in front of the computer and switched on the screen—the one about force and fraud being the two cardinal virtues in war. He'd tried to imply this during a row with David Kowalski several evenings ago, now that urban warfare was a reality in post-industrial Britain. A witness to the Michael Greenhalgh kidnapping—a newsagent called Frank Wardle—alleged to have seen something at the scene of the crime that Driscoll had been unofficially ordered by the Home Office to keep out of the public domain because of the tenuousness of the national situation. Kowalski had accused his commanding officer of suppressing evidence. Driscoll had retorted that he was doing no such thing. He was merely following orders and trusted those orders had been issued because Whitehall believed them to be in the public interest. He'd reminded the sergeant that they had a duty to their government, that Britain was living through one of the most crucial phases in its history, and that if the new Crime and Punishment Bill received the Royal Assent it would have a massive impact on police and public morale.

That was why, as a Chief Constable, he had to consider most carefully how he used the powers vested in him when deciding what to release to the meddlesome media. He'd suggested to Kowalski that the newsagent's allegation was so difficult to support they might as well try to prove that Greenhalgh had been abducted by an unidentified flying object. But David Kowalski, who'd been motivated by a strong sense of duty, as were most of his colleagues in the British police force, had stood his ground. Facts about a high-profile murder shouldn't be manipulated because the government was fighting for its political life and wanted to bend the outrage prompted by that murder to its electoral advantage. It was corrupting the use of power, he'd asserted, seeming strained with the burden of his knowledge and looking a little too big and clumsy to fit properly onto his chair. If it wasn't for the Home Office intervention, he'd doubted if his position with the Greater Manchester Police could remain tenable. And then, as if to drive the point home, David Kowalski had died.

Sometimes it was necessary to be economical with the truth if the long-term stability of society was in question, Driscoll reasoned, while reflecting on the dead sergeant's personal story, which had become a minor national tragedy in itself. That was why, as he slipped a CD into the console, cupped the mouse beneath his palm, and prepared to erase David Kowalski's version of events from Central Computer and to substitute it with a fabrication of his own, he found that it was already becoming an effort to acknowledge whether the Air Sergeant, not to mention the lynched Air Constable, had ever existed.

# *Eight*

The following morning, Blake was standing in crisp sunshine beneath a cloudless blue sky, halfway along the cobbled back alley where Michael Greenhalgh had been kidnapped after he'd scrambled from his car.

The alley had since been scraped clean of the rubbish and the filth and the black plastic bags amongst which Greenhalgh and his assailants had become entangled. Every last morsel of grass growing from between the stone cobbles, every last scrap of evidence, had been removed by the police for forensic examination to help piece together the minutes leading up to, and pertaining to, the politician's brutal killing.

Busying itself a few yards away was a television camera crew, gearing up for a take. Blake was checking through the script and acclimatizing himself to a number of revisions that he'd recently written. The cameraman was squinting into the video viewfinder of the steadicam that was harnessed to his shoulders and chest. The sound recordist was adjusting his earphones and stroking what appeared to be a small fluffy animal attached to the end of his boom. Behind him, Vanessa was hooking her platinum-blonde hair over her ear and running through a list of continuity directions with her young Sloane-inspired assistant, Sarah. Two armed private security guards were stationed one at either entrance to the alley, the man at the Chester Road end keeping watch over the film crew's Volvo estate car, parked a hundred yards away in a square of sunshine. These days Norman-shaw was much too dangerous a place for important-looking strangers to go gallivanting about unattended, least of all TV camera crews, which became natural targets for anybody and his rabid dog.

Because Blake's director had been taken ill with food poisoning a few days previously, Vanessa was now acting as replacement. She finished speaking to Sarah, then lifted her radiophone to her ear. In response to her words, a youth of about twenty-one years, who was on industrial release from the city film school got out of the Volvo, emptied the steaming contents of a polystyrene cup into his mouth, crumpled the cup into a ball, flicked it into the air and headed it into a concrete wastebin, then came jogging along the alley carrying the electronic clapperboard. He was obviously excited because he was participating in real programme making, and the naïve seriousness with which he was taking himself was imprinted on his pasty face. As the youth stood and cupped his hands to light a cigarette, Blake was fascinated by his blonde crew-cut: it had a smooth, suede-like texture reminiscent of the realistic hair on an old Action Man doll that he'd bought from a jumble sale back in Leicester, when he was a boy.

With her back to the youth, Vanessa pulled a face in response to his exaggerated galloping, then stepped between the crew and said: 'Okay Blake, we're nearly ready.' She muttered something else into the radiophone, and the figure at the opposite end of the alley from the Volvo gave the thumbs up sign and stepped out of sight, so as not to be visible behind Blake's head and shoulders once filming was under way.

Blake adjusted his collar and tie, then suddenly felt constricted and began loosening the tie from his throat. 'No, I'm not wearing a tie,' he said. 'I'm sick of wearing bloody ties.' He pulled it angrily away and stuffed it inside his coat pocket, but left the top button of his shirt fastened.

'You haven't shaved for a few days either, Blake,' Vanessa

said. Her manner suggested that she'd been wanting to draw attention to this for some time, but had sensed she'd better tread carefully.

'No, I haven't shaved, but I *have* washed my hair, and I've washed behind my ears, and I've deodorized my armpits, and I've put on a clean change of underwear.'

Not wanting to get into an argument, Vanessa clipped her response short and turned away. She'd noticed a tension in Blake throughout much of the past twenty-four hours. Over dinner the previous evening, he had, in fact, been nothing short of distracted. He hadn't said anything about whether or not he'd managed to speak to the beautiful dark-haired woman after the news conference, mainly because they'd not had chance really to speak to each other on their own since then. She certainly had no intention of prying, but she wondered whether or not his tetchiness this morning might mean that he hadn't succeeded. On the other hand, his stubbled ruggedness, while out of keeping with what was considered acceptable presentation for this kind of television documentary, seemed appropriate to the fetid inner-city environment in which they were standing, and also to the disturbing subject matter of the film. The vigorousness of his little outburst, while he stood there frowning in his thick black overcoat, with a wedge of bright sunshine slanting over the dirty brick terraces behind him, only added to his sex appeal. As well as that, the soul-searching that was taking place in the public consciousness of Great Britain at the moment meant that conventional social parameters had become rather soiled, much to the chagrin of earnest Tory editorials. People were so concerned about the crimewave, that if unshaven young television presenters stood in front of cameras during serious documentary programmes, looking like they'd just been out for a night on the town, it somehow didn't matter. It emphasised the deteriorating social situation and reflected the insecurity affecting the national mood. Creatively this appealed to Vanessa, so she decided to let things be.

Blake composed himself and looked at Vanessa huddled girlishly in her mint-coloured leather blouson, black stirrup corduroys, and black leather ankle-boots, her large breasts occasionally getting in the way of her own elbows. He felt a wave of affection, and said feebly: 'Sorry, love. I'm a bit ratty this morning,'—realizing that his previous response had sounded abnormally petulant.

After the incident with Abigail at the police station yesterday, when he'd got back to the hotel and mapped out the new scenes they were about to shoot and revised his script, as the afternoon had worn on he'd been consumed by a sort of angry sense of futility. The only way he could describe it was that by suddenly having come into contact with Abigail, by being unable to escape the conviction that he'd been working up to this moment for much of his life, his political passions had become deflated.

Normally he walked around relating everything that he saw and heard and felt and thought to the socio-economic factors suspended over everybody's lives. And no one could grapple with what was happening to society and be anything but pessimistic, unless they were so lost in the depths of their own conceit they lived in a different universe entirely. But now that his attention had become focused on this woman with whom he knew he was going to build up a love things seemed to have shifted into a different perspective. Even the horror he'd felt just lately, when he wondered how it was that Victoria had managed so effortlessly to cancel her feelings, switch her emotional allegiance to somebody else, then become so thoroughly hostile to him simply as a human being, didn't anger him as much as it usually did. Nor, for that matter, did the air of sniggering superiority infecting some of the remote opinion-formers that sensible people such as himself came up against in the columns and reviews. The world did not seem quite such a frightful place, and he wondered whether or not the trauma of his divorce might have played a big part in shaping his recent perceptions. He assumed that when he finally got into contact with

Abigail, his professional composure would somehow pull itself back into focus and everything would come back to normal.

Meanwhile, he'd been consumed by a mood of self-doubt that had left him on edge. He didn't need to be told why, of course. Anyone in his position and possessed of only a modicum of worldly wisdom would be able to work out the reason why.

He felt the tension ease when the crow's feet cracked the flesh around Vanessa's eyes, and she smiled at him and said: 'Okay, time to stiffen up please.'

Sarah stepped forward and briefly touched Blake's hair, dabbed some powder onto his face to take away the shininess of the skin, and smoothed his lapels.

'Are you ready, Blake?' Vanessa asked.

'Ready.' He handed his script to Sarah and took the clapperboard from the stubble-haired youth. 'I still can't believe this film will be transmitted, though. The subject matter is much too dangerous.'

'Because you're too sexy, more like,' Vanessa said. She winked and Blake was surprised to see that Sarah coloured a little before she turned away.

They all braced themselves and the cameraman started looking at the tiny videoscreen attached to the top of the steadicam. The youth noisily blew out a mouthful of smoke, to emphasise his disappointment at not being allowed to hold the clapperboard in front of the camera, then trod on his cigarette.

Vanessa looked at her watch.

'As I say, it's a longish take if we do it in one, Blake. If you find you want to cut it in half, just stop.' She paused. 'Okay turn over, Chris. Whenever you like, Blake.'

Blake held the clapperboard up to the camera and spoke the title of the programme as Chris started to film: 'Toward the New Social Order,' he said. 'Scene twenty-seven, of which this is the only take I intend to do.'

He handed the clapperboard back to the youth, winked at

everyone, and started walking slowly towards the camera, lecturing with his hands.

'In a parliamentary democracy such as that which is possessed by Great Britain, it has been said that crime is the product of a number of conflicting socio-economic factors. Looking at how there was an explosion of crime after the collapse of Communism in the former Soviet Union, for instance, some observers have claimed that it is one of the prices that must be paid to retain the freedoms that we take for granted in a libertarian society.

'Before the collapse of Communism, because of the repressive nature of the totalitarian regime, crime statistics in the Soviet Union were generally low. Law and order was maintained, not because it was a special characteristic of the Russian people, but because the threat of secret police and labour camps tended to keep insurrectionist behaviour in check. Fear was largely the key. Doors were kicked down and dissenters simply disappeared. This did not prevent corruption taking place in the higher echelons of power, of course. But it went a long way to stop crime from either subverting the authority of the government, or from undermining the stability of society at large.

'In a free democracy such as ours the police are not empowered with the authority to kick down front doors. Criminals, and for that matter social dissidents of whatever kind, cannot be rounded up and caused simply to disappear'—he paused for effect—'at least, not officially anyway. Rules of law have got to be obeyed. Incriminating evidence must be obtained. Witnesses must be found. Every criminal captured in Great Britain today must be subjected to the judicial procedure and tried democratically in a court of law, before being convicted.'

Everyone had shuffled a little way along the alley, back in the direction of the car. Blake looked at the ground and allowed the cloud of breath surrounding his head to rise and clear the frame.

'But Britain has arrived at something of a crossroads. As

the new Criminal Justice Bill enters its final reading in Parliament, as a nation we face a growing moral dilemma. We are being subjected to a crimewave that is so grave it is beginning to undermine our comprehension of democratic freedom, and to affect the perceived stability of our society. At the same time our economy is undergoing a substantial shift of emphasis. In the face of massive competition from the developing countries of the East, it is radically altering in its basic shape. As capital has diverted into the growing financial, futures, and information markets, this has had the effect of shedding several million manual and low-skilled jobs from the labour market. Many workers have found that their jobs have simply become obsolete. Because the criminal fraternity is drawn largely from this same class of people who have been becoming disenfranchised economically for many years, the question must be asked whether or not the wave of crime spreading through Britain is really a by-product of the capitalist economic system.

'Now that the heavy factory and labour-intensive industries have all but disappeared, we must ask whether or not the growth in crime is really a symptom of the restructuring of the economy that has been taking place over the past fifteen or twenty years. For it can be seen that the massive increase in crime has been concurrent with the breaking down of the industrial base, and of the deterioration of the British economy in general.'

He looked away, then brought his eyes back to the camera. 'But for it to function adequately, and if one looks again at the Soviet experience, our economic system requires a substantial degree of liberty. To facilitate free competition and a free exchange of people and goods, it requires an absence of the authoritarian atmosphere inherent to central control, and to the oppressive nature of what the world has so far experienced as the Communist ideal.' He paused again and assumed a mild expression of surprised scepticism. 'On the other hand, it is that very lack of political oppression which *enables* the proliferation of crime.

'So, with the prospect of capital punishment rearing its ugly head again, as the nation demands retribution against those who behave as they do largely because of the socio-economic circumstances that have produced them, could it not be said that the bringing back of the death penalty is a means by which prejudice seeks to contain a body of people who are denied a reasonable stake in society? People who would once have been absorbed into productive industrial life, but who have been abandoned by an ever contracting economy?'

Blake allowed another serious pause. He had come up so that only his head and shoulders were framed in the camera-man's viewfinder. He then imbued his gravelly voice with such a calm intensity of passion that the tears began to prickle Vanessa's eyes.

'If that is so, then we have to ask why there has been a shift in a more authoritarian direction. For by denying the underclass a stake in society, by reacting with justifiable horror at the brutalizing behaviour that a steady drip-feed of disadvantage and corrosive boredom has produced, are we not refusing to understand the economic forces that have produced that underclass, because those forces are linked to the prosperity enjoyed by ourselves?'

Now there came the closing lengthy pause, suitably down-beat in implication and on which the film would freeze-frame as a run-in to the end credits.

'Are we really admitting that the "underclass" no longer serves a useful economic purpose? And if so, would it not be to society's advantage that, as the Bow Group unofficially believes, its less desirable elements should be systematically eradicated?

'Are we saying, in other words, that there is no longer any need for these people even to remain *alive?*'

Blake looked seriously at the camera, then turned on his heels and took several steps along the cobbled alley, his hands thrust deep into his overcoat pockets, his back to the lens. Then he stopped and relaxed.

'Cut,' Vanessa said. 'Excellent Blake, excellent.'

Blake turned round and started walking back towards the crew. 'I don't think we should show me gloomily walking off into the sunset like that. I think we should freeze-frame as I turn away from the lens, so that you get the side of my head streaked and blurred while my face is sort of half-aimed at the ground.' He was back in front of Vanessa, surrounded by a cloud of exhaled steam, rubbing his gloved hands together in the bitter cold. 'Push the film during processing, and it'll give a rugged, grainy finality to the closing shot.'

'It might end up looking like a pop video,' Vanessa said.

'It doesn't matter. It's the informality that will emphasise the seriousness of what I'm saying. As will this'—he scraped his gloved fingers across the stubbled chin and smirked.

'You should be directing, love.'

'I will when the time's right,' he replied, noticing again that the alley beneath his feet was so clean one could have believed that the police had mopped and hoovered the cobbles to finish the job off. 'Do we need to go with any of it again?'

Vanessa turned to the cameraman.

'Is the gate clean, Chris?'

Chris closed the back of the camera. 'Clean,' he said.

Vanessa brought her eyes back to Blake. 'I don't think we can keep the bit about the police not officially kicking down front doors. That isn't in my copy of the script.'

'Sorry.'

'Other than that, it's fine. We'll use the first half at the beginning of the programme, and then work in the closing comments around what this bloody criminologist no doubt has to say when we interview him this afternoon.'

'Right.'

He pecked her on the cheek and headed back to the car.

# Nine

While the crew was packing up, Blake and Vanessa ran through the rest of the day's schedule with Sarah alongside the Volvo.

Blake stood with his arms folded and his back against the car, but he was only half-listening to the conversation, most of which was being conducted between the others with only occasional reference to him. He was too busy trying to picture the violence that had been enacted where they were standing, and down in that sun-drenched cobbled alley, when Michael Greenhalgh had been attacked.

His eyes panned across the row of old shops, up onto the corroding steel balconies wrapped around the adjacent tenements, from where the gunman had fired his opening shots; across a bricked-up cotton mill; then back down to the wide pavement next to where they were parked. He noticed the little video cameras bolted high up to the walls, out of reach of ladders (there was a black market even for closed-circuit security equipment), following the handfuls of pasty-faced figures trickling along the street. The shop windows that had been shot through by the other gunmen had been boarded over, but commercial life was filtering as normal in and out of the little doorways. Blake wondered why the shop owners hadn't covered their smashed windows with the aluminium roller-shutters, putting it down to some cryptic clause of the insurance firms. They would now be doing their level best to avoid paying out claims, classifying the carnage as being the result of a terrorist attack—or an act of God for which the financial system of which they were a part held no responsibility whatsoever—and thus underlining the legalized fraud around which he sometimes felt the industry was based. Only the butcher's shop frontage remained intact. Even from where he was standing, he was touched to see the little borders of plastic leaves running around the aluminium trays, finished off by a striding ceramic bull, bringing a dose of fertile innocence into this misbegotten place. A whiff of that long lost world of warm beer and evening shadows stretched across cricket greens, slipped in amongst scuffed platters piled with ground-up pigs guts dumped in bloody heaps in a dusty window; the bull staring at a street raked only with the shadows of its own darkening soul.

A few yards away, the telephone box that had been shot to pieces as the hapless politician clambered from his Jaguar was wrapped neatly in a green plastic tarpaulin, secured with padlocks and chains. Chris had artily filmed it as an establishment shot for the documentary, draped in stripy shadow, when they arrived. The shadows had since disappeared and the boldness of the image had faded away, like the heart and soul of the suburb its significance completely lost. Even the concrete paving stones that had been struck by bullets had been dug up and the sockets crudely filled in with little patches of fresh tarmac, like chewing-gum pressed beneath a dining-table by a mischievous child. There was no indication of where Greenhalgh's chauffeur George had stained the gutter with his brains. Everything had been rigorously scrubbed away; the pieces of bloody viscera scooped up and placed into little plastic bags; the lab technologists somewhere piecing together the slaughtered driver's obliterated head.

There was only the vaguest of scorch-marks, and a few blobs of melted plastic, where the Jaguar had exploded when the shotgun blew away its petrol tank. As far as the traffic sidling past was concerned, as far as the scattering of people drifting somnambulantly along the pavements were concerned, nothing untoward had happened here, and probably never would. Blake often felt these places were not as bad as some people made out, even if the concrete surfaces spattered with machinegun-fire did put in him mind of the blocks of flats he'd seen gouged by shrapnel blasts, when he'd been on assignment in Bosnia. But there was no doubt this environment had been driven down to the very bottom of the pile, the burnt-out cars heaped along sidestreets so ancient and weed-infested they were rusting into weirdly surrealistic sculptures. Some years previously an attempt had been made to humanize the late-Sixties maisonettes that formed the general backdrop. The top storeys had been removed and replaced with pitched roofs and the windows swapped for maintenance-free uPVC, whilst down on the ground, multicoloured brick paver setts had been laid around contrived flowerbeds in trendy geometric motifs, to try and introduce a bit of pattern between the buildings. But this had been a mere tinkering with cosmetics in comparison to the social problems festering beneath. All it had done was stave off a social implosion for a few more years, and many of the homes had since been abandoned. The Modernist Revival, which had arrived with such a rush of forward-looking optimism, had made little impact here. That was because the movement was really a reaction against deteriorating moral standards being linked by the public to the economic failures of the '80s—failures which had been born of an idealization of the past, and which had, ironically, hastened the demise of poor areas such as these. Even the Modernist Revival's bold usage of red was said to be a subconscious response to the growing brutality of the age, and that because it borrowed on forward-looking movements from yesteryear, it was really a retrospective attitude born of an essential pessimism.

This decaying inner-city place had been too aware of the inevitability of its miserable social destiny to care about any of this, Blake reasoned. When populist outlook swung away from a nineteenth-century nostalgia, Normanshaw had still been coming to terms with being a hangover from the last time the future had failed, never mind noticing anything out of the ordinary when a few shattered bodies had thrown a mess of blood and guts across one of its tatty streets.

His eyes came back along the shops and read the hand-painted legend that had been daubed onto the chipboard bolted across the front of Frank Wardle's newsagent's. On a whim, and remembering the things David Kowalski had said on the phone before he died, he decided he needed to speak to Wardle himself because he knew that he'd been a key witness to the Greenhalgh kidnapping. Kowalski had indicated that something didn't fit about the politician's death. Blake couldn't put his finger on what it was, and was none the wiser since the news conference the day before. But the fact that such a well-liked politician should have been murdered, and what had since happened to Kowalski himself, seemed less like mere coincidence the more that he thought about it.

'I'm just going to get a bar of chocolate,' he said to Vanessa, squeezing her affectionately by the shoulders. She seemed irritated. 'I won't be long.'

He was shocked at the fortification inside the shop. It was hard to believe the building had been witness to the coming and going of the generations. Both its commercial intestines and its social life had slowly rotted away. Only a tatty brick shell remained, stamped dry even of its aesthetic dignity as the streets around it ticked relentlessly towards the time-bomb of their own destruction, life draining through the little plastic door reinforced with steel plate through which he was passing now. That door—or at any rate, the aperture cut out of the brickwork into which it was slotted—had been built to frame the passage of industrial workers over a hundred years ago. Now a new and ever expanding breed of clientele had emerged who had to be kept at bay; who wanted to point guns and blast away the shop's unassuming heart. The memory of the original workers who first settled here, huddled in their hovels as Frederick Engels trudged through the stinking pig-sty of their lives, had all but disappeared; as had any semblance of the industry that brought their class to life. Only their brutalized descendants were left, scattered in mouldery concrete cages, eking out the remnants of a wretched existence as their class was slowly murdered.

For what was left was this.

A counter running the length of the interior, from the window to the partition wall at the back. Administering the space from floor to ceiling, slicing the shop clean in two, a gauze metal screen. No way of getting behind the screen except through a heavily-padlocked gate. The customer-side segregated from the part of the shop containing the goods and money. Nothing—not a single object, not a wastebin or a chair, or heaven forbid, a plastic guide-dog appealing for a bit of generosity to the blind—occupying the chamber in which the customers stood when they came in. The floor made from shiny terracotta-coloured ceramic tiles rising to dado height up the walls. Above that, the walls rendered with textured masonry paint, of a kind that would produce a nasty gash if somebody's head happened to be thrown against it. No pictures on these walls. No public notices. No announcements of animals lost or found, suggesting a community knitting together beyond.

Only the acrid smell of disinfectant, a fluorescent tube hanging over the stench on the customer-side of the shop, housed inside a casing of toughened aluminium gauze, bright and bold as it shone with its single thankless task upon a weary world.

About halfway along the dividing screen a hole about twelve inches square cut into the gauze. This was the place where cash and goods were exchanged between proprietor and customer. Now that he was close up to it, Blake could see that backing up the cage was a thick sheet of reinforced—no doubt bulletproof—glass, lifting to a couple of feet above average human height. The glass was clear to facilitate an examination of the goods that were on display. And what was cordoned off was effectively a normal news-agent's shop. There were tiered racks of confectionery and jars of cough mixtures and boiled sweets. A row of soft cuddly toys were dangled by their ears on plastic pegs, still trying to cast their alluring sentimental spell, but through a creeping network of prison bars fortifying society against the growing internal siege. On the counter immediately behind the screen, arranged in neat rows, was a variety of popular newspapers and magazines. Bloated tabloid headlines screamed up at Blake's eyes, braying for somebody else's blood, while simultaneously they profited from the misery that had thrust the knife deep into society's guts and spilled that blood across its floor.

Frank Wardle was standing behind the confectionery rack, scooping handfuls of a popular wafer-fingered biscuit from a wholesaler's box, and dropping them amongst the display. He was a bald, red-faced little Yorkshireman with a nest of broken veins on each cheek. He didn't lift his eyes because they'd already examined the closed-circuit television monitor concealed behind the counter when Blake paused outside the building. The wafer-biscuits were one of Britain's oldest and most famous popular brand names, part of its collective heritage. They had been on sale in the neighbourhood sur-rounding this shop since the time when front doors were supposedly left unlocked at every hour of the day, and children poked fireworks instead of shotguns through the letterbox.

'Don't look so shocked, lad,' Wardle said, 'the screen does its bloody job.'

'It's pathetic,' Blake said.

He knew these places existed, knew that they'd been around since the early Nineties in Glasgow; but he had never yet been into one in England. Noisily he drained himself of breath, rubbing the toe of his shoe against the ceramic floor tiles, the rasping sound working with the sterility of the space to emphasise how it felt as though it were a piece of the outside that had been brought in and dumped indoors.

'The reason for the tiles,' Wardle said, 'is that the shiny surface unnerves people.' He finished unloading the biscuits and threw the empty box onto a pile at the back of the shop. 'According to the shopfitters, people don't feel comfortable walking about on a ceramic floor, if they've got their shoes on. But if you're a robber, you need to move quickly. So the idea is that, if anybody comes in to case the place over, they feel unbalanced and it helps to put them off.' He pulled a face. 'Of course, they're also easy to keep clean. You know what I mean. If some of the customers get mugged while they're in here, and I need to hose away the dried blood when I've shut up shop.'

'You're joking, of course,' Blake said, irritated at having just been taken for a short ride. 'I suppose the glass is bullet-proof too.'

The newsagent smiled. 'No, but it's thick enough to be as much. Besides, nobbut an idiot fires a gun point-blank at a thick glass partition, unless he wants to end up looking like a colander.' Wardle had come across to stand behind the screen. Blake saw the man's eyes moving in and out of the diamond-shaped segments of the gauze, which crisscrossed his face and seemed to emboss it with a fishnet pattern of deep black scars.

'So what can I do for you, Mr Hunter?'

'You know my name?'

'I've seen you on television. And I've watched you filming outside this morning. I wondered when you'd be coming in to ask me some questions.'

'Actually, we hadn't planned to do that.'

'Good, because I've been grilled by the police two or three times already, and that's enough talk about it all for me.'

'You were interviewed by Sergeant Kowalski, I believe?'

'The dead policeman? Yes.' He sniffed. 'I thought you weren't going to ask me any questions.'

Blake smiled. 'David was a sort of friend of mine. And

anyway, these are not really questions. I'm only making conversation while I buy one of those old-time biscuits that you just put out on the rack.'

Wardle retrieved one of the biscuits and laid it squarely on the counter, a few inches behind the little hole cut into the screen, then rested on his fists. 'It seems a bit funny to me that he should go and shoot himself like that, even if he was still pissed off about losing his wife and kid. That's what they're saying on the news, isn't it?'

'I must admit,' Blake conceded, 'it's beginning to sound a bit funny to me.'

It had been revealed by the police that Kowalski had done the proverbial, and shot himself and the dog in the head. The public's response had been one of predictable outrage, though whether the sentiment was for the benefit of the man or the animal was not entirely clear. Blake suddenly changed his tack. 'Nevertheless, although I'm not here to ask you any questions, and though I've read about what you saw in the papers, Mr Wardle, I'd be interested to hear again about how much you saw that morning when the gang kidnapped Michael Greenhalgh.'

Wardle narrowed his eyes, chewed the inside of his lip, unclenched his fists, patted out a brief tune on the edge of the counter, and said, rather reluctantly: 'I was pulling up in my van when the gang chased the politician into that back alley over there.' He nodded at the wooden absence of daylight representing the window.

'What were they like?'

'They were all black, and they were all masked up. They'd got balaclava hoods on, and those red plastic things that ice-hockey players wear over their faces. They seemed to come from nowhere, shot the Jaguar and the shops to bits, strutted about all macho-like, then shoved the MP into a getaway car and buggered off. It was over in a few minutes.'

There was a silence, as if he'd nearly stumbled into saying something he shouldn't, then had stopped himself mid-paragraph before getting carried away.

Blake sensed it immediately.

'What else?'

Wardle shook his head. 'Come on, Mr Hunter, you're a journalist. You know how witnesses are threatened with injunctions and told not to talk to the media. They're warned about *sub judice,* that kind of thing.'

'Yes I know. But the *sub judice* rule applies to witnesses who are going to appear in court. You aren't going to appear in court because the gang hasn't been captured yet, never mind been brought to trial.'

Wardle's brow became corrugated and Blake wondered if the man had mentioned *sub judice* without understanding what it meant. Or, something which seemed altogether more sinister, because somebody else had spoken to him about it, knowing that he wouldn't understand what it meant.

'Look,' Wardle went on, 'I don't want any trouble. The police have told me that I haven't to talk about the kidnapping to anybody because they suspect urban terrorists, and it's important nobody gets scuppered.'

'Terrorists?'

Wardle touched the biscuit nervously, checking that it was still lined up with the edge of the counter. 'They also said the media are being prevented from saying too much and began talking cryptically about the Official Secrets Act. It seems the order came from the Home Office, because a right snotty little bugger came in here last week and showed me an injunction which has been taken out preventing the TV and the newspapers from reporting it, until the police have completed their investigations. A separate piece of paper had my name typed on it.'

'To prevent the media from reporting what?' Blake knew nothing about any injunction, though Wardle seemed not to have heard his question.

'It was implied that the gang might decide to come back and shut me up if I started spouting off to journalists.'

Though Wardle came across as rather overplaying the part of the dour Yorkshireman and sounded to be on the verge of digging himself verbally into a hole, Blake decided that he was probably far shrewder than he looked, that he wanted to talk, but that he was going to need some prompting.

'I understand, Mr Wardle. But you seem to be implying that you've told the police something they'd rather nobody else knew about. If you tell me, I can assure you that it won't go beyond the walls of this shop.'

Wardle snickered. 'Aye, I bet you say that to everybody. For all I know, you might be working for the police. Putting on a front to try and catch me out.'

'Do you really believe that?'

'No, I don't suppose that I do. You haven't tried to fool me with talk about bloody "*sub judice*" for a start.'

The newsagent was beginning to give.

'*Is* there something else which you haven't told me about?'

Wardle took in some breath and pursed his lips. 'I must be a fool for standing here and even thinking about talking to you,' he said. 'But do you know why I'm probably going to?'

'Why?'

'Because you haven't offered me any money. A bribe's never entered your head, has it?' He smirked and Blake sensed a feeling of camaraderie pass briefly between them. Wardle certainly was shrewder than he looked. 'Okay, there *is* something else. It's nothing much, and it's probably more than my life's worth to worry about it now. Just promise me that you won't say anything to that bloody film camera you were talking into, or that good-looking blonde bird you're obviously thick with outside.'

'You have my word.'

Wardle swallowed. 'Like I said, the gang members came from nowhere, they were all black and they were all masked up.' He paused for effect now that he was back in control of the conversation. 'Except for the one with the light-coloured eyes.'

'Light-coloured eyes?'

'Aye. There was a biggish chap who only had a balaclava hood on. He seemed as if he was the leader.'

Blake's brow had pulled itself into a frown as he tried to imagine the scene and wondered why he hadn't heard about the light-coloured eyes through the grapevine. 'The detail about the eyes hasn't been mentioned in the news.'

'Course it hasn't. The only people I've talked to about it so far are the police. Why do you think I'm so uneasy about mentioning it to you now?'

Blake thought for a moment, coupling the information to the memory of David Kowalski's strained voice speaking on the phone before he died, while at the same time a sense of fear began nagging at the edges of his mind. 'How on earth could you manage to see the colour of the gunman's eyes?'

Wardle sighed uneasily, as though still wondering if he was doing the right thing by talking. 'I was just about to get out of my van, when the guy who'd lost his mask stopped to shout some abuse right alongside my door. I saw that he had lightish eyes.' He shrugged. 'Funnily enough, I didn't remember until I was interviewed the second time by that Kowalski bloke. He struck me as being a pretty decent lad, you know. He didn't have that sense of reticence policemen usually have.'

Blake's alarm bells were definitely ringing now.

'Did he see you?'

'Who?'

'The man with the lighter-coloured eyes.'

'No, none of the gang did. I haven't had the van long. It still has some of that one-way mirror stuff stuck to the back of the windows. Looks like a bloody mobile glacier mint. The black guy came up right next to my window, but he couldn't see me. I'm convinced that if he had, I wouldn't be standing here now, thinking that maybe you don't strike me as being such a bad fellah, and that I might well let you take this old-time biscuit here out of the shop for nothing.' The biscuit became his focus again, its jolly packaging bringing a terrible note of pathos into the concrete bunker of the shop. Wardle frowned once and sniffed. The poor man was not only desperate to confide in someone about what he knew, he was pining for social intercourse not split in half by a metal screen; for conversation not conducted with its back against a wall.

'You know the gang was black because you could see the black skin around their eyes and wrists, right?'

'Right. You'll know so from the papers, Mr Hunter.'

'What about the one alongside your van; the one who'd lost his mask?'

'Aye, he was black too. In fact, because he wasn't wearing his plastic mask, he was showing even more. The black skin around his eye sockets was shining as plain as day.' He drew a circle round one of his own eye sockets with a forefinger, to indicate how large the holes had been around the eyes of the gunman's balaclava.

Blake thought for a moment.

'The police have been going over Normanshaw with a fine-toothed comb trying to find the mask, haven't they? The one it was reckoned came from the guy who came up alongside your van?'

'Aye, but they've got it now.'

'Oh? That hasn't been in the news either.'

'It probably will be tonight, though I've told the police I don't want any more publicity.'

'What do you mean?'

'One of the little bastards across the road had it.' He frowned again and touched his forehead wistfully. 'No, no, he's not a little bastard. None of 'em are really. The kid's mother brought it in last night because she'd heard them talking about it on TV. Said she found it in his bedroom and didn't want the police crawling all over her flat. I suppose the kid must have got it from underneath the balcony where the gunman had been shooting from.' He jerked his thumb in the general direction of the tenements outside. 'I suppose they see the gang as heroes, Christ knows why.' He touched his forehead guiltily again and his two chins became three. 'Aye. Christ's probably the only one who does know why, because the politicians and the police certainly bloody don't.'

'You mean to say that the mask has actually been *in here*?'

'Aye.'

'And then you called the police?'

'Aye.'

'What did you tell them?'

'I told them that somebody had pushed it anonymously through the door.'

'Did they believe you?'

'I don't know. They only seemed bothered that they'd got hold of it at last.'

'In other words, it's gone?'

Wardle nodded. 'They came round and took it straight-away.'

Blake's heart sank at the same time as his mind started racing and a coldness descended from the top to the very bottom of his body. For a moment he'd thought that he was going to get hold of a key piece of forensic evidence. Then, remembering a *Rough Justice* documentary he'd once presented, he thought of something else. It was a long shot, but it was worth a try.

'Where did you keep the mask until they arrived?'

'Why?'

'Please. Where did you keep it?'

'Here, behind the counter.'

'Whereabouts behind the counter?'

Wardle gestured with some irritation behind the racks of sweets. 'On the counter here. Why?'

'Could I come round and take a look?'

'Now there's a funny thing.'

'What?'

'That's just what the police forensic scientist said he wanted to do.'

Blake's eyes widened. 'You mean they've already been?'

'No.' Wardle looked at his watch. 'He's supposed to be coming at lunchtime today. Said he'd need about half-an-hour.'

'Please can I come round the counter, Mr Wardle? This is terribly important.'

Wardle let out some breath.

'That depends.'

'On what?'

'On whether or not you actually came into my shop this morning and made conversation while you bought your biscuit, because I can see the way your mind's working.' His eyes went down to the biscuit, scrutinized it for a moment, then came back up to Blake.

'I haven't been into your shop this morning.'

'No, I didn't think so. Just as I must have been imagining things when that young lad's mother came in with the mask last night.' Wardle walked along the counter, pulled out a bunch of keys, and unlocked the gate in the partition screen at the back of the shop.

'Thanks,' Blake said stepping through, the prison sensation intensifying. 'Have you got some cellotape?'

Wardle took a roll from a drawer.

Blake went to the place where the mask had been laid under the counter. He had to squat to get at it, but he could see there was some dust, some flakes of powder, and a few hairs accumulated on the shelf. Working across the surface a furrow at a time, he tore off strips of the cellotape, laid them over the residue, and lifted everything up. Then he found a magazine-sized piece of styrene, wiped it with his sleeve, and pressed the lengths of cellotape lightly against it to keep them straight. When he'd finished he asked for some old newspaper. Wardle tried to offer a plastic carrier-bag, but Blake said that it could make the evidence sweat. The evidence being the microscopic flakes of human skin, dandruff, or hairs he was hoping had been deposited by the mask onto the shelf. He hid the styrene inside a folded edition of that day's *Guardian*, to deter any questions from Vanessa or the crew, then told Wardle to wipe the counter with a damp cloth and tell the forensic scientist that somebody had accidentally cleaned it since they'd spoken.

'Or better still,' he said, 'direct him to a different part of the shop altogether.'

'You're forgetting something, Mr Hunter,' Frank Wardle said when Blake had been let back into the customer side of the shop, and the padlocked gate had been resecured. He pushed the wafer-biscuit through the opening in the gauze, out onto a shelf that protruded a few inches from the hole. Blake picked it up. Now that he saw it close up he realized what had been bothering him about it for the past several minutes. Since last he'd bought one the packaging had changed. The graphic design was the same, but the tin foil and the paper wrapper had disappeared. Instead the biscuit was vacuum-packed in shiny plastic. He remembered how he used to labour over the opening of the original wrapper when he was a boy. The slow removal of the paper sleeve, the running of your fingers down the grooves of tin foil between the chocolate sticks, then the lifting of the foil like the bonnet of a car, was an activity you savoured. Going back even further, he could remember his grandfather twisting the tin foils around the end of his forefinger, flattening out the ends, then turning them into little goblets which he lined up like trophies on the mantelpiece. He used to do the same thing with the gold foil from inside his cigarette packets. Even the original paper sleeve offered the possibility of being folded into a paper dart, just as the tin foil convinced you, because of its thinness, that you really could fold it into a square more than eight times. The new wrapper was made from that plastic paper which tore easily but instantly unwrapped when you screwed it into a ball. It was simple, it was quick, it was more hygienic; but the sense of exploration that was once part of the enjoyment of eating one of these biscuits, just as much as the taste, had disappeared.

Frank Wardle seemed to be hearing Blake's thoughts. 'I've lamented the passing of the foil-and-paper wrappers, as well,' he said sombrously. 'Sales have gone down, too. I told the wholesalers they would, but nobody wanted to know.'

'Where two machines were necessary, now is only one,' Blake said cynically, bringing the biscuit to his face. 'Productivity and profitability go up, efficiency is improved, but with it another clutch of jobs is shaken out by the relentless contraction; by the draining of the human spirit by the will of the machine.' He had a vision of himself sitting astride the wall of the school playground when he was a boy and thought he saw why the character was being gradually drained from modern life. But the image was already spiralling away before the conclusion was fully formed.

'You can apply the same laws of market-fed efficiency to the rest of the economy,' he added drily, looking at the miserable walls. 'And the fuse burns a little nearer the powder-keg, the result being the interiors of shops such as this, everybody fighting to take a bite from an ever-decreasing cake, the noose being brought back to string the working class up by its bollocks.'

Blake began fumbling in his pocket but the newsagent was already raising a hand, meaning that he must take the biscuit for free. 'Why did you let me behind the counter, Mr Wardle? You've interfered with what could amount to a major piece of evidence.'

'So have you.'

He smirked.

Blake thanked him and put the biscuit into his coat pocket and opened the door, letting in the noise of the street.

'You're going to get those bits of tape analysed to see if you can get a DNA profile made, aren't you?'

'I'm surprised you guessed.'

'Why? I watched you telling the country all about it on television once.'

'Has it ever occurred to you, Mr Wardle, that black people almost invariably have very dark eyes?'

Wardle held Blake's eyes.

'Now funnily enough it had, Mr Hunter, though not until

this morning.' Then as Blake was about to leave, he lamented: 'Like I say, it's a funny business about that policeman shooting himself.'

As Blake closed the door he noticed that Wardle looked puzzled by the insinuation contained in his own words, and that the redness which was a feature of his expression was going patchy as the colour began to leave his face.

# *Ten*

'I'm afraid that we lost him, Abigail,' Mark Halliday said, stepping into the darkened Elizabethan bedroom, sticking out a hand, and switching on a light. 'I don't suppose he knew that he was being watched, but he managed to give us the slip as if he did.'

Abigail was seated at an octagonal table working at her laptop computer. Through the window behind her stretched flat Cheshire countryside studded with elms, some sunset lingering above bare branches as the afternoon came to a close. Strewn across the four-poster bed alongside her, as incongruous against the richly-carved Jacobean furniture as the microchip technology, was a selection of popular newspapers, vulgarly demanding the return of institutionalized murder before the fabric of society broke apart.

The broadsheet that Mark threw onto the bed when she looked up was using a more generous quantity of polysyllables to make much the same request. She glanced at the furious headlines, which were really a testimony to the gazumping of human dignity by the ferocious buying and selling that was the driving force of the age. Old people murdered in fortified flats, bodies stripped naked for the few extra coppers fetched by their rags, teeth wrenched from their mouths to get at gold and mercury. Vigilantes torching ten-year-old car thieves or dragging them onto wasteground, pouring hairperm lotion over them, then watching them torn to pieces by wild dogs, which always went crazy for the smell. Black-market videos of such ritualized executions were doing a roaring trade, according to one correspondent. Not even the dead were safe, according to another. Grave-yards were being stripped of rotted corpses because ground-up bones and rancid flesh could be used to make fertilizer, or as a constituent of crude explosives. Not that long ago the editorial attitudes demanding retribution against such horrors would have been altogether more civilized, and it made Abigail's stomach churn to think how recent that time was.

'How could you lose him in broad daylight,' she said disapprovingly, clearing the computer screen, removing a CD, and popping it back into the storage box. 'And at such a crucial stage?'

Mark sat on the bed and ran his fingers through his thin-ning blonde hair.

'I'm sorry for cocking it up, but these things happen. I tried to phone to let you know, but they said you were with Sir Ian and mustn't be disturbed.'

'You were supposed to have become Hunter's shadow.'

'I know, but he just disappeared into thin air. The crew drove back to the hotel after they'd been filming outside the newsagent's, then went into the Futures Bistro at the other side of New Central Square. When they'd been in there for about an hour, Hunter went to the lavatory, but slipped out before we realized that he'd gone. We can't be everywhere at once, you know, especially not in a toilet which has several exits.'

'Where is he now?'

'He returned to the hotel about half-an-hour ago, carrying some bags from Kendals and a cuddly teddy bear, probably a present for his kids. Wherever he went this afternoon, he wasn't in a hurry to get back. The film crew left the hotel at three without him. No transmissions have been recorded passing between Hunter's and Vanessa Aysgarth's portable phones today, so whether he was supposed to have gone on the shoot is anybody's guess.'

'What about when they were outside Wardle's shop this morning?'

'Hunter entered shortly after midday and was in there for about fifteen minutes. During that time the crew was outside packing up. Aysgarth looked as if she were being chatted-up by her young female assistant, whose eyes were all over her, to be perfectly frank. Aysgarth looked uneasy and kept glancing at the shop while Hunter was gone. It's a pity we didn't have telescopic mikes instead of lenses. Anyway, when Hunter came out he was carrying a copy of the *Guardian* and eating a chocolate biscuit. Aysgarth went straight over to him and linked his arm. She obviously fancies him like crazy, you know.' Mark started rattling some loose change speculatively in his trouser pocket when he said this. 'You only have to see how her face changes to realize that she's in love with him. It's a curious thing, but she's the sort of woman who doesn't bother with make-up and hardly makes the effort to look female at all. Yet when she's near Hunter it's as if he brings out her natural beauty. You notice it a mile off. I'll swear she actually changes colour, loses her paleness. I feel sorry for her in a way, because I'm convinced he doesn't realize the effect he has on her. Or maybe he doesn't want to, which is probably putting her under some strain.'

'Just get to the point, Mark.'

The loose change had stopped rattling now, the hand having gone up to remove the spectacles from his face while the knuckles of the other rubbed surveillance fatigue from his eyes. 'Everybody got into the Volvo and then they drove back to the hotel. Cut to: Scene in bistro, crew eating Greek salad to canned music, chequered tablecloths, the jolly rattle of crockery coming from a kitchen, the crap on the front of those newspapers on the bed a mere figment of our degraded imaginations, some early Christmas trimmings, Aysgarth still being eyed-up by her assistant, and us losing Hunter when he goes for a pee.'

'Anything else?'

'No, except that it wouldn't surprise me if Wardle's property has been left without a police guard so that he can act as bait. Shall I put somebody onto Hunter at the hotel this evening, in case he decides to go back to Normanshaw?' The spectacles were back on his face, the fingers wandering across his bony chin.

'No.'

'Why? If he knows something, it could jeopardize the entire operation. And what's the point in telling me off for losing him this morning, if you don't want him watched now that I know where he is?'

'He doesn't know anything.'

'How can you say that after the fuss he made at the news conference yesterday?'

'I can just feel it. He doesn't know what's going on.'

'Feelings are definitely *not* what we're about, Abigail. And besides, if Hunter does know something, you know that he'll probably end up having to be killed.'

'Yes, I realize that.'

Abigail had begun to look rather strained. She took another CD from the box, slotted it into the computer, and brought Blake's identity card holograph onto the screen to open his personal file. The resolution of his face was so strikingly lifelike it was as though his deep-blue eyes were looking back at her from the monitor; the lines running from the nose to the corners of his mouth cut so deeply they could have been scored by a knife. Both the picture and the file had been lifted illicitly via modem from Central Matrix, even though Glasgow was supposed to be impenetrable to hacking. Such were the advantages of working with brilliant minds when matters of constitutional importance happened to be at stake.

Mark's eyes were on her face. 'Correct me if I'm wrong, but I detect that you might be developing a personal interest in Blake Hunter. If you are, you're on very dodgy ground.'

'Stand corrected immediately. I am not developing a personal interest.'

She was lying, of course, but being the stronger and more experienced personality, she was skilful enough to look Mark straight in the eye, causing him to turn away first so that she remained in the ascendency.

Since she'd spoken to Blake during the flight up to Manchester nearly a month ago, and her interest in him had first been aroused, she had, in fact, found out quite a lot about him. Through her sources at Central Matrix, it had been a straightforward procedure to get hold of his basic biographical details, and a copy of his identity card holograph, as soon as she'd returned to Copley Hall.

Following her little confrontation with him at Central Police Headquarters, however, when she'd found herself thinking about him with more than mere idle curiosity, she'd obtained a copy of his latest Psychometric Report. Though compiled mainly for employer purposes by offering an overview of general personality traits, it also gave a speculative assessment of emotional and behavioural characteristics. It was the easiest way she'd had of finding out what kind of a man Blake Hunter really was, not to mention learning something of his private life, too. Her hunches about his domestic situation had proved exact. She'd learnt that his marriage had been dissolved, and would not have allowed herself the remotest interest in him if it hadn't. And she knew that, despite him being close to Vanessa Aysgarth and frequently spending the night at her house in Hampstead, according to her sources at the BBC—and no matter what Mark had just implied—there was nothing sexual about their relationship whatsoever.

Abigail's dilemma was that, while she knew she was developing strong feelings for Blake, the observations he'd made at the news conference about the circumstances of David Kowalski's death implied that he might be aware of Project Doomsday. She'd told her superiors that she wanted the information about him lifting from Central Matrix and putting onto the database for purely professional reasons, which was why she would have to be absolutely sure of

what she was doing before making any potentially dangerous moves. That, if nothing else, was going to put her
allegiances to the test, though the quizzical nature of Mark's
observations suggested that she'd already been placed under
scrutiny.

Mark slid his hands back into his trouser pockets and
nodded at the computer.

'What have you managed to dig up about Hunter's background?'

'Nothing much that I didn't know already. He's lower
middle class like us, grew up in a prosperous suburb of
Leicester, has a younger sister called Elaine, and studied Political History at Sussex University. His mother is a college
librarian and his father is commercial director of a printer's.
He wasn't particularly distinguished at school, but when he
became interested in politics in his late teens, he seemed to
find his *modus operandi*. He's not at all like the run-of-the-
mill journalist, and has been described in one of the papers
that bothers to notice him as an eccentric American with an
English accent. He might almost have gone to art or drama
school, rather than to an academic university.

'Something that probably links to this, and which has
cropped up on his Psychometric Profile, is that he seems to
have encountered a certain amount of friction while working
with some of his older, more upper-middle-class colleagues
at the BBC. The men rather than the women find it difficult
to cope with his powerful emotional integrity, which according to what he's told his psychometric counsellor is probably a reflection of the fact that he hasn't been brought up
to suppress his feelings. They can't seem to handle the fact
that he's human enough to have been affected by grief more
than once in front of a camera, or that he seems to get on
so easily with women and prefers their company to men.'

The observations that were being made now were not so
much an indication that British social mores were changing,
as they were a reflection of the fact that a different kind of
person was getting a foothold in the world of TV journal-

ism. Those people had always been there, but the doors of opportunity had not always been easy to open. Now that so many programmes were being put out to tender, however, a different breed of journalist was emerging as the class-based Establishment hierarchies finally started to break down.

'He's also been badly affected by his divorce,' she went on. 'Told his counsellor that he probably married Victoria Carlton for all the wrong reasons, and can't believe that he was naïve enough to think that the innocence she possessed when he met her represented for him a kind of romantic social stability. She's ex-Rodean, ex-Cheltenham Ladies College, and comes from a family of merchant bankers. I suppose theirs was an odd social mix for a marriage, especially if you consider Blake's politics, of which her parents did not approve from the start. They were together for seven years and she's managed to retain custody of their two little girls on the grounds that they didn't see enough of their father, because he was always gallivanting about the country filming reports.'

'You mean that Carlton was the adulterous half?'

'Yes. And losing his children seems to have been the one aspect of the affair that really has cut him up.' She raised her eyebrows rather shrewdly. 'To compensate for this he says—and I'm quoting him here—that he's trying to view his years of marriage as "part of the pattern of self-development that intelligent people generally see superimposed upon their lives the older they become." ' The eyebrows went up again as she reviewed the recent history of her own personal circumstances. 'I think I know what he means there . . .'

'What does it say about his relationship with Vanessa Aysgarth? There's something about it that I can't put my finger on yet.'

Abigail scrolled to another page.

'Nothing really. Granted they're unusually close. He depends on her for emotional support quite heavily, and not surprisingly this seems to have intensified since his marriage broke down. But then it's fair to say that he doesn't conform to the average predatory male in the way he regards the female species, and definitely not in the way he treats Vanessa. He seems to look up to women and says that it's often struck him how the less sure a man is of himself emotionally—and here he claims a man's social class is irrelevant—the more likely he is to find it difficult to form satisfying relationships with women that are anything but sexually orientated. Blake isn't like that and he isn't interested in the culture of masculinity, which he says is just as prevalent in its own way amongst the Eton-Harrovian lot at the BBC as it is amongst his own. There's no question of a dominant mother complex or of repressed homosexual feelings, either. He's simply comfortable within himself and doesn't spend half his life trying to deny or justify his own psychology. Another reflection of his genuine nature is the fact that, far from expecting women to want to look at him because he's a confident, good-looking man, he's always surprised to find they should want to look at him at all.' She smiled to herself, and Mark thought he noticed a twinkle in her eye. 'A lot of men won't allow themselves to relate to women like that, of course. Certainly a lot of men can't handle the Vanessa Aysgarth type, nor can plenty of women, for that matter. Blake can, because he's strong enough to give them space to breathe.' Her eyes veered across to Mark. 'The only dubious thing I've been able to dig up about Vanessa is that her counsellor suspects something happened to her when she was a kid that was so unpleasant she refuses even to talk about it. As for Blake Hunter, I'd say he's a pretty decent human being and absolutely no danger to the operation.'

She crossed her brown-leather-trousered legs to punctuate her observations, but Mark had already heard a convoy of cars coming up the drive outside and was standing by the door reaching for the handle.

'See what you make of these then,' he said, throwing a red plastic envelope onto the bed. 'I guarantee they'll show you more than any computer analysis, and maybe prompt you to take some of the things this particular testosterite says a bit more seriously than you do.'

A sardonic smile tried to break out on his face, but the moment wasn't frivolous enough to support it and he left the room without saying another word. A second later his hand came back in and impishly flicked off the light, then his face appeared thumbing its nose, the flesh tinged bluish-grey from the computer on the table. 'And I think you're dropping a bollock, Abigail, by ordering me not to have Hunter watched at the hotel tonight. Whatever the computer says about Aysgarth, there's something fishy about her keeping her distance from him.' He paused, finding that he was watching her expression closely when he said this. 'Just a feeling I have, that's all.'

Abigail knew he was watching her too.

'You just told me that feelings are not what we're about, Mark.'

He grunted and closed the door again.

She rose smiling, switched on a lamp, and picked up the red envelope from the bed. Inside were a dozen colour photographs of Blake and Vanessa, mostly together on the same shot, and all taken with a telephoto lens. Something the psychometric counsellor had deduced about Blake which she hadn't read aloud to Mark—she was quoting it mentally to herself again now—was that 'Blake seems to gravitate towards strong women, and strong women tend to gravitate towards him.'

The observation brought another smile to her face when she looked at one of the shots, where Blake and Vanessa were fooling around and he was pretending to grope at her breasts. Mark had written PTO in the bottom corner of this picture. She turned it over. A large red heart had been scrawled childishly on the back, and a question mark drawn in the middle. She smiled again. Although the psychometric report said there wasn't any sex between Blake and Vanessa, even Mark could sense that it was only a matter of time before there was. The look on Vanessa's face said everything, suggesting she had a softer, more passive side that probably only Blake knew about. And some couples looked right together, she reflected. What worked about Vanessa and Blake visually were Vanessa's mature good looks, and the fact that she was tall and carried herself so well and was obviously older than him, seeming to balance his rugged intensity. But Vanessa was married and Abigail suspected for no reason she could define that it was unlikely she'd make a pass at Blake because of this; something which was enough to keep her conscience clear about wanting him for herself.

She put the photographs aside and rubbed her eyes, which had become strained from staring at the monitor for most of the afternoon, then winced at her carelessness when she saw the mascara smudged on the back of her hand. The pictures had distracted her more than she thought.

The sound of tyres running over gravel had grown louder and the glare of headlights was now swelling across the ceiling. She went to the window and peered out into the night. Doors slammed, a security-light came on and showed that three shiny black limousines had pulled up in front of the house, the infrared scanner instantly detecting body heat as it emerged from the rear of the cars. Voices trickled across frosty air, bellicose laughter boomed from down in the hall, dogs barked from the gatehouse at the bottom of the drive. Several Lords and at least one Lady were crunching the gravel now, clouds of breath puffing about stern faces; faces ready to begin Phase One debriefing; faces steadfast in their determination to keep Britain on the right and only course.

The security-light went out and Abigail closed the drapes, locked the bedroom door, slipped off her boots, unfastened her trousers, then took off all her clothes.

Crossing naked to her bathroom, those remarkable dark-brown eyes with their curious sandy-coloured rims—a biological accident, the opticians had always said—considered again the catalogue of human suffering sprawled across the bed. She could get into her Frontera and encounter most of it half-an-hour's drive away, in the drugs-infested slums of Manchester in one direction, or those of Stoke-on-Trent in the other. People stripped of dignity and feeling. Creatures described as human because they were flesh-covered bipeds that could articulate words in their throats, but where any other resemblance ended and the manimal in them began. It wasn't much further to the dangerous urban wastelands of Birmingham or Liverpool either, or to the nightmare that was becoming South London. And yet, social breakdown seemed so remote from this six-hundred-year-old room with its Renaissance motifs and carved caryatids, its Classical-style pilasters and tasselled velvet cushions, its wide polished floorboards and its scattering of Turkish rugs.

It was a long way, too, from the unopened packet of five-denier stockings she picked up from the clothes chest at the foot of the bed. On the front was a pair of elegant female legs, poking provocatively from between black satin. The retail price of those stockings would keep a member of the underclass alive for at least twenty-four hours, while she would simply wear the garments once and throw them away. Somewhere in a factory, large amounts of money had been invested in complex spinning machinery so that beautiful women could wear stockings that were so delicate they not only emphasised female sophistication, they laddered if you so much as caught them with your hand. She was aware of impending social catastrophe. She was aware that industrial civilization was dying a slow and painful death. But her standards remained high, and one of those was that she was pernickety enough to wear only the sheerest available stockings. Nothing less would do. And the way she regarded her legs was a by-product of capitalist culture. There was no evading the inevitable. As a woman she could no more suppress her natural urges to parade and display than she could fail to respond if she heard the squalling of a baby in the middle of the night.

It was going to be a long and difficult night tonight, she told herself uneasily, hearing laughter booming up again from the bottom of the stairs as she stepped into the shower. Just as it was going to be a long and difficult age.

# *Eleven*

'Where the hell were you, Blake?'

'I'll tell you soon, Vanessa,' he said.

'But it completely buggered up the afternoon. I had to do the interview myself.'

Though her voice was coming out of the telephone in his hotel room, it sounded unusually loud; almost loud enough for her to have been standing next to him. Vanessa was one of those people who spoke so close to the mouthpiece it sometimes distorted her words, so that she always sounded fussy and boisterous and concerned. It generally left her taste behind on the plastic when you came to use the telephone after her, as well; a taste which often reminded him of nicotine, although she didn't smoke.

'Look, I'm really sorry love,' he said, trying to placate her anger, then rubbing his eyes having just taken out his contact lenses. 'But I really didn't have any choice.'

'What was it about?'

'As I say, I'll tell you when I'm sure.'

'Sure about what, Blake?'

'I'm not saying anything this time. You know how super-stitious I am about revealing things too soon.'

'Does it relate to the film?'

'As I say, I'll tell you when I'm sure,' he repeated firmly, being careful to keep any semblance of irritation out of his voice.

He heard a weary exhalation of breath, the tone and

duration of which implied that the temperature behind it was now cooling down. 'Okay, if that's the way you want to play it. But I'll expect a full explanation about whatever it is.' She paused for effect. 'Over dinner, of course. At yours and not at the BBC's expense. At my choice of venue. And provided you escort me back to my room, then come in for a nightcap.'

'Over dinner,' he replied, not biting at the humour. 'But not tonight, because I won't have anything to tell you until at least tomorrow afternoon.' He changed the tune of his voice. 'How did the interview go with the criminologist?'

'We didn't do it. The sod wasn't there when we arrived.'

'Bloody hell, Vanessa, you just told me you had to interview him yourself, and made me feel guilty by telling me I buggered up the afternoon.'

She tittered.

'Knowing how cagey you were being, I had to try and squeeze out of you where you'd been somehow. Twisting the old arm and all that?'

'I wish you were younger than you are,' he added, picking up the thread of humour which he'd left dangling several sentences previously, 'and not quite so married to Max. Then I'd probably come downstairs and do something to you that I wouldn't especially regret afterwards.'

'Any time, young man,' she replied rather matronly, cringing at the innocent reference to her husband but noticing that Blake seemed to be in a better mood than he had been that morning, 'any time.' It was now her turn to change the tune of her voice. 'What shall we do about going through the schedule for tomorrow's shoot? Bishop has faxed up some amendments. We'd have done it this afternoon, of course, had you not pissed us all about.' She inhaled deeply, but the sound was more a gesture of depressed resignation than her body informing her lungs it wanted air. 'I'd rather we didn't leave it until tomorrow, love.'

'How long will it take?'

'About half-an-hour.'

'Okay, come up to my room in twenty minutes, and we'll do it here.'

'Have you eaten yet?'

'No, but I'm not particularly hungry tonight. I'll have some sandwiches sent up later.'

'It *must* have been exciting,' she was saying rather thickly. But she was already hanging up before he heard the final syllable.

Blake wasn't so much excited as deeply apprehensive; so much so that he'd been unsettled for the first couple of hours of the evening.

When they'd got back to the hotel after the Normanshaw shoot, under the pretext of going to do some shopping, after lunch he'd taken the pieces of cellotape out to the Independent Forensic Institute (IFI) at Prestwich. The *Rough Justice* documentary that he'd thought about when he was inside Frank Wardle's shop had been concerned with the farming out to the private sector of police forensic work, and the way this was alleged to be opening up the scope for collusion between private laboratories and insurance companies in their avoidance of paying out claims. It was while in the process of making the film that he'd got into contact again with Steve Hamer, an old friend with whom he'd been at university in Brighton, and who was now a scientist at the Manchester IFI.

During the process of interviewing Steve, he'd learned about the rudiments of DNA profiling and of the quite astonishing advances made in the science in recent years. The way it used to work, when it was still a very basic forensic technique, was that if a blood or semen sample could be obtained from the scene of a crime it could provide enough information for a DNA pattern—the molecule that forms the genetic material of all living organisms—to be assembled. Forensic scientists could use them to build up an idea of a subject's sex and blood type, and even go so far as to discern hair and eye colour. Comparisons could then be made with DNA profiles taken from police suspects and virtually foolproof convictions could be secured, because the chances of error in DNA profiling stand at some three billion to one against. All of which was fine, so long as suspects of the correct physical type were held in police custody, or were identifiable from police records.

In comparison to these fairly crude beginnings, the latest DNA profiling technology had become so sophisticated its potential was positively frightening. Not only could computerized scanners now build up a basic profile. They could extract such a minutiae of information from a blood, saliva, or microscopic skin flake sample, they could assemble what amounted to a recognizable photofit picture of the person from whom it had been obtained. The computer was linked to a laser-printer, enabling two-dimensional images of the person's face and body to be produced. The resolution of these images was still less than satisfactory, of course, even after computer-enhancement. They were rather like ghosts. They resembled very blurred photographs, similar to the extreme blow-ups of criminal suspects sometimes captured by security cameras in shopping malls. A major disadvantage with them was that, while the computer could generate a complicated human matrix from a single hair bulb, for instance, it couldn't determine the length of a person's hair or the style in which it had been cut. But provided it was known roughly what the person looked like who was being looked for, and if anyone profiled had unusual physical characteristics, which generally registered, the lasergraphs were in most cases recognizable.

More significantly, the technology was advancing so rapidly that it was only a matter of time before all DNA computer systems in the country were linked to a single database at Central Matrix in Glasgow, where basic forensic information was already held about every citizen of Great Britain. Each DNA profile that was generated produced its own unique set of recognizable binary digits, as individual as a fingerprint. The idea behind every profile system being plugged into Central Matrix was that, once a profile had been generated, a search could be made through the holographic image bank. Because the holograph reproduced on a person's identity card was also computer generated, when the information from a profile was fed into the same system, an instant comparison could be made between the two. In this way, profiles could be correlated to information already stored on the database at Glasgow. And because each DNA sample was so unique that the possibility for error remained so unlikely, the system would become almost infallible, with the computer-enhanced pictures generated at the forensic institutes providing a back-up guaranteeing the authenticity of the match.

Investigative journalists occasionally used forensic techniques in the making of current affairs television programmes. But the high cost tended to make them prohibitive. Latest-generation DNA profiling was one of the most expensive forms of forensic work there was, at several thousand pounds per profile. While Blake knew Steve Hamer, and Steve might once have undertaken the work for nothing if there were serious security implications, the activation of the DNA system was a complicated procedure that didn't go unrecorded. For the purposes of exchanging information quickly between departments and different institutes, many buildings had their internal computer networks linked to an electronic nerve centre, hence the advent of the phrase 'intelligent building'. Each time a profile was made, the institute had to pay a subscription fee to the Taiwanese company that had devised the expert system. A failure to do so—quite apart from the impossibility of avoiding detection—resulted in the programme being withdrawn from the institute, and the imposition of a heavy fine.

The cost of the profiling that Blake had proposed would have to come out of his monthly working budget from the BBC. But before anything above a hotel bill was undertaken, it was supposed to be authorized by the programme producer, which in his case meant Vanessa. He hadn't complied with basic Corporation regulations, and should he have wasted valuable resources in the pursuit of flimsy evidence, disciplinary proceedings would probably be severe.

But he'd decided it was simply too great a risk to inform anyone of what he was doing, even Vanessa whom he trusted more than anybody else he knew. The reason for her outrage on the phone was that Steve had been delayed in a meeting when he'd arrived at the institute. There was too much at stake for him to have gone back later, and by the time they'd finished and he'd got back to central Manchester, he'd missed an interview the crew was supposed to have filmed at the university. He'd not even explained to Steve from where he'd obtained the residue. He'd just asked him to see what he came up with, and would take it from there. For if the plastic mask *had* come from the gunman who'd shot at Michael Greenhalgh's car, if it *had* come from the same masked gunman that Frank Wardle had seen standing alongside his van, if the gunman *had*, as the newsagent claimed, been in possession of light-coloured eyes—if the gunman had been, as Blake now suspected, a male Caucasian disguised as a West Indian yardie—there was every possibility that the residue from the shelf in the shop would be good enough to produce a DNA profile, confirming the facts beyond doubt. And if an image came up on the computer screen of a white man, he would be in a position to blow the entire Michael Greenhalgh incident wide open, thereby exposing what he suspected might be a right-wing conspiracy at the root of it, bearing in mind the racist overtones.

He stood up from the bed when he heard Vanessa's knock. It seemed to have arrived well before the twenty minutes had elapsed that he'd requested to enable him to continue collecting his thoughts. He sighed and went over and lazily pulled open the door. At the same instant that he thought he was seeing things, and felt what could only be described as a rapid expansion then contraction of the matter housed inside his head, he understood why the knock had come so soon.

For it wasn't Vanessa who was standing there.

It was Abigail.

She stood against the heavy silence of the corridor and looked at him intently. After a few seconds, during which time their eyes examined each other with an intimacy they had never managed before, Blake stepped back from the door and asked her in.

'I knew you'd come,' he heard himself saying. He felt the inadequacy of the words, but they were all that he could muster. He closed the door and rested his back against the panels, inhaling the smell of roses and clean hair as she stepped past. 'I didn't expect to see you so soon, but I knew that you'd come.'

She turned and smiled, looking at him a little coquettishly from a few yards into the room. She was wearing an olive-green leather overcoat with batwing sleeves, a beige angora sweater, beige slacks, and light-brown ankle-boots. Her dark hair was flowing onto the collar of the coat and was lustrous beneath the glow of the lamp. He realized how wonderful it was to be able to look into those magnificent eyes without wondering if they were forever on the verge of pulling away; just as he knew that now they were never going to turn away like that again. Around her neck was a string of large handmade silk beads, of a similar colour to the coat but streaked with a swirly pattern, and of a kind he recognized as having once seen on sale at the Manchester Craft Village. Already his mouth had started to go dry and he was beginning to be affected by a very slight tremble.

'I couldn't stay away any longer,' she said quietly, her eyes warmly exploring his face.

There was still an uncomfortably large distance between them. It was a space each wanted desperately to cross, but neither could pluck up the courage to make the first move.

Then Blake remembered Vanessa.

'Oh God,' he said, 'I'm expecting my producer to come up to my room any minute now.' He moved away from the door and snatched the phone from the coffee-table. A soft trilling sound filled the room while he stabbed at the rubber buttons.

He was answered immediately.

'Vanessa?'

'Yes Blake?'

'Listen, something's just come up. Can we go through the production stuff tomorrow instead?'

She sensed the urgency in his voice. 'That's okay, love,' she said warmly. There was a pause. 'Are you all right?'

'Fine. It's, er, to do with where I went this afternoon. I've got to go out.' He hated having to lie.

'Is it because of the riots?'

'What do you mean?'

'All hell's broken loose tonight. I thought you'd have had your TV switched on.'

'No, I haven't, and it isn't. I'll explain to you what it's about in the morning. I'm really sorry I've messed you about today.'

'Don't worry. See you.'

He hung up, feeling the relief. When he put the receiver back down he noticed that it rattled nervously before his fingers managed to unclip themselves and let it go.

He stepped away from the coffee-table but was still compelled to keep his distance from Abigail, despite the immense wave of sexual excitement now taking hold of his body. 'Have you noticed,' he said, 'how thoroughly natural this all seems? It sounds stupid, but now that I really think about it, I've been expecting you all evening. That's why I've been so unsettled.'

He could hear the flutter of snowflakes touching the window behind him and the slash of wet tyres down in the street.

'Yes,' she said softly. She eased a little closer. The tranquil eyes seemed very large, the thin luminous rims around the big dark pupils shining against the beautiful background of her face. 'And stop saying that things always sound stupid.'

Blake held up his hand. It was shaking noticeably. 'Look,'

he said, genuinely incredulous, 'look at what you do to me.'
It was not so much that his heart was beating faster than it
had done before, but that it was beating more powerfully.
Each pulsation of blood shook him, shook him so much that
he could feel his jugular pumping, really pumping in his
neck, as though every scrap of muscular energy in his body
were being channelled behind each thrust of liquid as it
heaved through his veins. Even his eyeballs were affected.
The glow of the table-lamp in the corner of his vision was
pulsating slightly with successive beats of his heart.

'Look at what you do to me,' she said, narrowing the
space at last. She held up her own hand. It was shaking
nearly as much as his. 'The difference is, I've had to try and
drive here as well.' She smiled with her eyes, shocked at the
effect he was having on her now that she had him all to
herself.

He stepped up to meet her and took the trembling hand,
the contact instantly playing havoc with his loins. 'Your
eyes,' he whispered, bringing his fingers to her face and
gently stroking the fine down of her skin at last, 'I swear to
God I would die for those eyes.' The eyes were moist, and
he could see contact lenses skating about on the surfaces
when she blinked, now that she was closer to him than she
had ever been before.

She nuzzled his hand then pulled it down and pressed it
hard against her breast, allowing her handbag to drop to the
floor. She was wonderfully warm, nestled inside her big
green coat, the angora sweater gorgeously soft and feminine
beneath his palm. He could feel her beating heart, thump,
thump, thump, out of sequence for a moment with the banging tearing through his own body; then suddenly they were
beating together in perfect unison.

'Is it possible for two strangers to come together like this?'
he asked hoarsely, her eyes now only a few inches from his
own. The room felt deafeningly quiet.

'I think so,' she said softly. 'I've been having a dream for
years. In the dream I go into a large room that has a grand

mantelpiece, and there are no lights on. There are heavy curtains with rain behind them, and a lot of old furniture. It's very warm, there is the flicker of firelight playing against the ceiling, and there is always a dark man seated naked on the sofa, with his back to me as I come in through the door. Each time I've gone into the room and reached out to the man, he's started to turn round, but I've *always* woken up before I could see his face. I've been having that dream for a good fifteen years, for half of my life. But that night after I saw you at the heliport I had the dream again, and in it the man finally turned around, and it was you Blake, it was you.'

The tears ran down Blake's face, scoring grooves across the dry skin, so that she saw a pair of moist streaks reflecting a trickle of golden lamplight.

'There's something else I've always known about the man,' she went on. 'Because he's naked, each time I've approached him in the dream I've noticed a birthmark on his shoulder, about the size of a ten-pound coin. Somewhere about here'—she touched the back of Blake's left collarbone, and he gasped—'you do have one, don't you? Tell me that you do.'

'Yes,' he groaned with amazement, still managing to choke back the emotion. 'But how on earth could you . . . I just can't understand how . . .'

His eyes had filled up despite himself.

'Christ, I didn't realize I'd been so alone,' he said, genuinely surprised at his tears, feeling suddenly cold and hearing the self-pity but not caring a damn. He smiled at her, the emotion quickly subsiding in anticipation of what he knew was going to take place in this hotel room tonight. He smothered her face with kisses; worked his way round to her neck; combed his fingers through her hair; sensed that the pressures of the past six months were about to be cauterized from his body; knew that the pain and humiliation of what Vicky had done to him would at last be sent away.

He was almost drunk with desire when Abigail lifted his

face away and looked deep into his eyes. 'You've been hurt by somebody, my darling, you've been so terribly hurt. But you've been hurt only because you have so much love to give and nobody has been strong enough to take it from you.' She was cradling his face between her hands now, the tears charging down her own cheeks, the moisture bringing out the smell of roses more than ever. 'You have an ability to penetrate into somebody's soul and see what makes them tick. And it frightens you because it's always made you feel so alone; as though you were surrounded by people who are only half alive. But not any more, darling. You'll never be on your own again.'

Their lips came together lightly, getting to know one another first. Then she pulled away as though suddenly consumed by guilt, her head beginning to shake. 'I'm so sorry,' she said. 'I've wanted so desperately to come to you.'

'Why were you avoiding me?'

'Later,' she said. 'It's important, but not so important that it's going to spoil the beauty of this moment.'

The kisses moistened and the two of them became crushed together in a passionate embrace, both moaning with arousal, hyperventilating, hands greedy for one another's bodies now, clutching at hair and pulling at clothes. The erection in Blake's trousers was such an encumbrance it was getting in the way. She wriggled out of her coat and let it fall to the floor, slid her hands down inside the elasticated waistband of his trousers, peeled the trousers back exposing his naked thighs, locked the fingers together, then pulled him by his buttocks so savagely against her that it crushed the erection against her pelvic bone.

Then she went very heavy in his arms, and without further ado, he bent and scooped her up, the groom about to walk his bride over the threshold. He carried her across to the bed and very gently laid her down. His trembling was in anticipation of crossing a different type of threshold altogether now—trembling as he approached a threshold he had never crossed before, but had always known was there to be reached—trembling slightly beneath her weight at the point when he lowered her to the quilt.

He knelt at the side of the bed. Her hair had fanned onto the pale-blue pillow, her face was burning with anticipation, it was as though she were looking at him through a soft-focus filter and her eyes were glittering like stars. 'Take my boots off,' she gasped, her voice shaking, saliva clogging her throat. 'Pull them off . . .'

Blake walked on his knees to her feet and gently pulled the velcro loose. The heels of the boots were about two inches high, and he noticed that it was their wider triangular shape that gave her that unmistakable sound of expensive sophistication. Indeed, he was never to see her wear conventional slender high heels. She always wore shoes with this thickish triangular heel, so that she was pursued by a marvellously stylish *clump,* rather than a straightforward tartish *clack,* whenever she crossed a solid floor.

Beneath the boots were cotton socks a shade lighter in colour than the slacks, exuding the smell of warm leather and clean femininity. He dropped the boots to the floor, then, as he turned to walk on his knees back up her body, he suddenly sighed and plunged his face between her legs, inhaling the muskiness of her animal scent which was already seeping through the fabric of her clothes. She sighed too and arched up, then took hold of his head and dragged him up her body, pulling him by the hair towards her face.

A moment later he had her slacks off and was on the bed with his face buried in the generous dark tuft. At that moment he was aware of the true meaning of happiness for the first time in his thirty-one years. He began to perceive something of the frightening intensity with which one could come to desire another human being, if it happened to be the right one. Knew what it meant for two mammals to fuse as one flesh with not a single ounce of compromise. Knew that at last he could begin to give his each and every all. His body shook with frantic exultation as he explored her and her legs came up and locked into the scissor-position around his shoulders. He actually drank her juices, covered his face and his shaking hands with them, used them to lubricate both their fleshes as he skated up and down the hot wanting body, across it, around it, round onto the firm buttocks, spreading the moisture between the buttocks, up the small of her spine with his tongue, coming back round to her glistening thighs. He heard the sound of her fingernails clawing against the plastic headboard of the bed, then scrabbling briefly against the bedside cabinet followed by a thump as something dropped to the floor.

And all the time she contorted with pleasure, her gulping became a frantic whimpering, her eyes burned like those of a frightened cat as his tongue assumed control.

When the moment of consummation arrived a little over half-an-hour later, it was with a detonation of pleasure that consumed them at once in combination. The pleasure came with such an intensity that Blake felt the muscles throughout his body stiffen with a kind of cramp. He panicked, felt winded, smelt wet hair, saw her panicking too, locked against him soaking with the sheen of her own oils exhumed and gripped by a similar muscular contraction; until at last the agony subsided, sending them both into a deep, untroubled sleep. They didn't wake for several hours, but when they did it was Abigail who now took him, doing things with her fingers and tongue he could never have dreamt a woman would dare to do; spreadeagling him face down on the bed; savagely taking the dominant rôle; consuming him in another agony of animal ecstasy as he succumbed completely to her lack of inhibitions; to the bonding with this naked flesh.

And when, utterly exhausted, they collapsed into sleep for a second time, curled together beneath the soaking quilt in a natural foetal embrace, the huge Great Northern Hotel was pressed beneath its heavy nocturnal quiet. Even the rumbling of the city outside had died away. The room was disturbed only by the soft rhythm of their breathing, by the creaking of the building under its own weight and heat, by the sharp late-autumnal wind bringing another flutter of early snowflakes against the glass.

And from somewhere beyond the ring of tower blocks outside, burning brightly but shut down until the morning, there came the distant chatter of machinegun-fire, the intermittent thud of exploding rocket-launcher shells, followed soon by the remote scream of sirens, as a different type of nocturnal sound slipped itself into gear; playing its tune of havoc upon the fabric of the night.

# *Twelve*

Her name was Abigail Sanders. She was twenty-nine years
of age, and, to Blake's complete astonishment, was an electronics engineer by training, working now in an executive
capacity for one of Britain's few remaining big industrial
manufacturing companies. That explained her underlying air
of studiousness. It was a quality about her which had always
appealed to him, but one which he didn't really articulate
until they were sitting in bed eating breakfast together the
following morning.

Abigail did, in fact, possess something of a definite scholarly demeanour. It didn't overpower her natural physical
beauty, of course, but if it had been a fraction more pre-
dominant it would have quarrelled with her femininity.
Fortunately—and this was something he encountered rarely
in women—her good features only served to emphasise her
intelligence and her elegant sophistication. Straightaway, so
many minor observations he'd made about her clicked into
place—such as the way she wore her hair, the cut and style
of her clothes, even the shape of the heel that he'd noticed
the night before, when he'd removed the ankle-boots from
her excited body.

He could remember a number of similar such women,
with serious eyes backed up by a genuine intelligence, from
when he was at university. Unlike Abigail, they tended not
to take much pride in their womanhood. Even if they had
decent figures, they seemed incapable of shaping their hair

to the best advantage, or they would always wear the wrong clothes. They reeked of militant feminism in a way which was decidedly off-putting to the average healthy heterosexual male, who preferred his woman to look like a woman, not some miserable excuse for a man when viewed from more than three feet away. Skirts seemed alien to the sartorial outlook of such women. They retained a flat-shoed masculine demeanour, prompted by what appeared to be a deliberate suppression of their latent femininity. There was a girl on Blake's course at Brighton in the first year who had been rather that kind of person. By day she was as plain and square-faced as they came, and never of much interest to any of the boys. But at the university get-together that first Christmas, she astounded everybody when she came dressed up to the nines, devoid of her hideous spectacles, with a mane of hair that nobody had imagined she possessed because it was always smothered beneath banana clips, revealed the best pair of legs any of the lads had ever seen, and put all the other women to shame. It was as though she'd flowered into a different human being, like the beautiful butterfly at last breaking free of its pupa. Thereafter she sank back into a monotonous blandness, of course, though she was never regarded in quite the same way by any of the males again.

Abigail might have been that type of person once, he decided, before those vital features of hers had matured. Before those incredible eyes became capable of holding their own, reinforced by experience and intelligence to fly away into a life of fine tastes, delicate textures, stylish clothes. Before her exquisite femininity had been paraded to the world, accepting itself for what it was, acknowledging that here was a beautiful female organism designed not only to serve a practical purpose upon the surface of the earth, but one meant to be loved by men. And as he thought about this, he was overcome by the simple realization of how much he really loved women—something Vanessa had long told him that, in her experience, few men truly did.

Like him, Abigail had recently experienced the trauma of a divorce, though she had not yet had any children. According to her, the lack of children had helped make her separation more of an academic than an explosive emotional matter, and he heard himself heartily agree. He also discovered to his joy that, like himself, she was a product of the comprehensive and redbrick university educational system; just as she'd been rather surprised to learn the same about him, when she'd first read his file on her computer. Fooled by his articulateness, his thick hair, and his healthy good looks, she'd taken it for granted that someone of his physical stock would be private school and Oxbridge educated, bearing in mind his media profile and his job.

But it was when she decided to follow her instincts and explain to him why she was in Manchester, that Blake began to get some inkling of just what he'd been getting himself embroiled in. Then the significance of what he'd obtained from Frank Wardle's shop began to press down upon him all the more. Abigail's journalistic demeanour was a sham, of course. She was part of a secret group that had been assembled to try and gather evidence to incriminate a number of key public figures, who were implicated in what was believed to be some kind of a right-wing conspiracy connected to the current *débâcle* raging over the reintroduction of capital punishment. That seemed to connect with what he suspected might lie behind the killing of Michael Greenhalgh.

She explained that the gradual swing to the Right by the Conservative Party over recent decades had long concerned a small consortium of industrialists, judges, and, curiously, a number of ageing Tory grandees, who believed the privileged classes should use their position to act as a guiding force to ensure a general stability to society. She named several One Nation ex-Tory cabinet ministers and Lords who'd been considered so soaking wet they were sacked from government and hung out to dry long ago.

'You make it sound as though you're some kind of undercover agent,' Blake said, as he shook his head and straightened the breakfast tray on the bed between them.

She smiled, her teeth gleaming in the sunshine now pouring through the window.

'I admit it sounds a little bit that way, but I'm nothing of the kind. Half the time it's so unbelievably boring I wonder what the hell we're playing at. It means a lot of running around following people, watching where they go in the evenings, sitting in cars, blending into the background in cafés or restaurants. Sometimes I think we're just a bunch of bloody amateur detectives. There's a continual air of anticlimax hanging over everything that we do. Still, they always did say that real spy work was tedious and boring, didn't they?'

'You said we.'

'I'm up here with another chap, Mark Halliday he's called. He's an industrial chemist. He's been in Manchester for a while.'

'I suppose it was him you followed into the taxi that night at the heliport.'

'Yes. There are others like us scattered across the country, mostly with a background in manufacturing industry. You could say that we're the ground troops, put out into the field to gather incriminating evidence. We don't even exist as an official group. We meet occasionally at large houses in the country with our aged mentors, but that's about as far as it goes. It's all rather unreal.'

'But why? What's the purpose behind it all?' He passed her another round of buttered toast, his eyes wandering across her breasts, a slight tremor descending to his groin as he remembered how much joy those breasts had given him the previous evening.

'It's simple, really. The group has seen what's been happening since 1979. The shape of British society is changing. Wealth is flowing into the hands of a privileged and ever-decreasing minority, with a growing mass of people at the bottom being pressed down into barbarism by the gradual destruction of industry and the dismantling of the Welfare State.'

Blake raised his eyebrows and seemed to carry on speaking for her. 'That's why they're bringing back the death penalty, to encourage society to feel as though it's keeping that growing barbarous mass in check, now that an underclass has been created by the winding down of industry and now that these people serve no useful purpose to the workings of mainstream economic life.' He lifted the thermal cover from the cafetière, pushed down the plunger, and let out a great deal of weary breath. 'Toward the New Social Order,' he said ruminatively, deliberately speaking the title of the film he was making with Vanessa.

'What do you mean?'

'Isn't it funny how circumstances have a way of bringing people together? Or perhaps it's fate. I imagine you're doing what you're doing because you care about your country. I'm doing what I'm doing because I care about my country. And a small group of people somewhere are buggering up our country because they only care about themselves. As a result of which, I've just spent the most important and incredible night of my life in bed with you.'

'I still don't understand what you mean.'

'The film I'm working on is all about what you've just mentioned. You say that society is changing, and that's right. Though it's going to take us a while to get there yet, we're slowly reverting to something of the feudal structure that we had before the Industrial Revolution. But whereas before the Industrial Revolution the bulk of the nation's wealth was concentrated in the hands of a powerful controlling aristocracy based around land ownership, and the social order was governed by the rule of rank, by chivalry, and a commitment to the crown, this time it will be the new gods of knowledge and information who are pulling the strings. And, like then, there will be a largely illiterate, subservient population that has fewer and fewer democratic rights, while our rulers live a life of computerized luxury. Hence our deteriorating standard of living because we no longer produce enough. Hence the growing brutishness of modern society, which is taking on parallels with the Middle Ages. Hence the expanding underclass, because the financing of the Welfare State has become too much of a burden on the taxes of those still lucky enough to have a job.' He looked at a small jar of Baxters marmalade in his hand. 'The underclass is becoming the modern-day equivalent of that great mass of sixteenth-century peasants and serfs, who were pressed down into the gutter beneath a fear of disease and religion. Even the disease is coming back, what with AIDS starting to kill them off. AIDS—the modern black death wiping out the scum of the inner cities. No wonder we can't find a cure for such a marvellous form of population control.' He snorted in conjunction with a sharp pop from the marmalade jar as he snapped loose the lid. 'Thank God I'm not the only one who can see what's happening.'

'There are more people in what would be classed "establishment circles" who know what's going on than you might have imagined, Blake. In fact, it's much of the establishment old school who are worried. They've seen the way the Conservatives have been remodelled by a new type of republican right-winger, who's risen from the lower middle class like us, and whose patron saint when they were at college was Baroness Thatcher, with her contempt for the English upper classes. They worship power and money, they have no sense of duty, and they have absolutely no feeling for tradition. That's why Britain has slowly lost its patrician atmosphere, why the Royal Family has become a joke, and why the country is increasingly self-orientated and fascist.'

'I must admit,' he said, 'I'm highly amused to think that two or three doddering old-fashioned Tory "grandees", who've since come out of the closet and gone on record as saying that they knew all about the damage that was being done by Thatcher, should suddenly come to the aid of the ship now, as it finally starts to sink beneath the waves.' He snorted derisively. 'That's bloody typical, that is. They knew what damage was being done to the economy at the time, but they didn't stop the rot when they had the chance. They didn't want to risk bringing down the government. At the end of the day, party political affiliations meant more than the destiny of their own country.'

He snorted again.

'At least they're doing something now,' Abigail said. 'They probably had no idea at the time just how much damage was being inflicted. It's always easier to see things in hindsight, once you're away from the intensity of the moment. And a good number of industrial and legal people have long expressed similar concerns.'

He poured the coffee.

'So what's the incriminating evidence that's in the process of being gathered?'

'We believe that at the root of the current wave of crime hysteria are a number of powerful City institutions. So much of this country's wealth has been diverted away from industry into the financial and futures markets that the only way we're ever going to get to grips with our mounting social problems is if there is a major shift of economic policy, and a massive devaluation of the currency. But that will weaken the strength of the markets.'

'I suppose your people have seen it because you're involved with manufacturing industry.'

'Yes, and quite a few other people like us. But these City people are not nearly as stupid as some observers believe. They're clever enough to have seen how society has been deteriorating. They're clever enough to realize that it is the restructuring of the British economy and the decimation of industry since the early Eighties that is playing a major part in society's disintegration. But they're also ruthless. If the public is ever made to understand what lies at the root of our socio-economic problems, the new fiscal power base fears a swing back towards more egalitarian principles, which of course undermines its entire philosophy.

'So, gradually, they've been engineering a sort of wave of

hysteria about the crime problem. Pushing national sentiment along in a particular direction. To divert attention
from the economic causes, they've been rallying the nation
to thinking that the death penalty might provide an answer
to our problems. And if there's one thing that has always
bound this country together emotionally, it is a belief in the
virtue of capital punishment. It cuts right across the classes
and it doesn't matter who you vote for. If there was a
referendum tomorrow it would come straight back. It would
never have even been abolished. And look what happened
when Michael Greenhalgh submitted his Green Paper to the
Commons. The Opposition parties' standing sunk to an all-
time low and it's never recovered. Why do you think there
was so much media attention, week after week after week?
Because powerful forces ensured that the subject didn't go
out of the media spotlight. They wanted to get public opinion on their side. And with a General Election looming, they
*have* to.'

'In other words, the murdering of Greenhalgh—big public
figure heavily favoured by the people for his extreme views
on crime and punishment—gets the nation baying for
underclass blood even more?'

'That's it.'

The events of the previous evening seemed suddenly remote to Blake. As Abigail revealed more about what it was
she was involved with, a melancholy morning-after feeling
began to invade the airy confines of the room. He wondered
if he could ever recapture the simple feeling of happiness
that had consumed him when she'd stepped through that
door not ten feet from the bed not much more than ten
hours ago. The more deeply he was drawn into contemplating the truly terrifying changes that were being worked, not
only upon British society, but within the whole of Western
civilization, the more it seemed the events of the previous
evening had occurred in a different time and place. The
hotel room seemed such an innocent place, with its heavy
traditional furniture and its two lovers sitting up eating

together in bed, with the muffled sound of vacuum-cleaners moaning along the corridors and the vibration of lifts playing with the framework of the bed, with the hoot of trams and traffic warming up for the rush hour in the city outside, as everything got ready for another day.

'We know that a number of key public and media figures have connections with these City institutions,' she went on. She named a number of prominent Tories including a couple of cabinet ministers, several national newspaper editors and columnists, and at least one Labour MP whose political credentials were considered dubious to say the least.

'Christ,' Blake said, his voice muffled behind his hands, which ostensibly had come up to rub the sleep from his eyes, but which were really attempting to scrub away the nagging sense of fear drawing in once again, as he wondered whose DNA profile might come up onto the computer screen at the Manchester IFI.

'What has Manchester got to do with it?' he asked, lowering his hands and blinking back into daylight.

'Greenhalgh's murder took us by surprise. We'd assumed he was a big enough bastard that he was probably one of them himself. In fact, because of various professional connections of his, we were convinced of this. All we can assume is that he was such an important fish, he simply became expendable. A necessary sacrifice to forward the cause.' She paused. 'Did you know that Greenhalgh was a friend of Chief Constable Driscoll's?'

'No, but I'd a funny feeling Driscoll's name was going to crop up sooner or later.'

He was remembering what Wardle had said about the gunman having light-coloured eyes, and this being kept out of the news for supposed security reasons. That authorization would have involved Driscoll.

'Well, the two men knew each other extremely well. Driscoll is one of them. He's a non-executive director with one of the City institutions that are implicated, and has very intimate connections indeed with at least one broadsheet newspaper editor, if you understand what I mean. He's also a shareholder in Strangeways Prison.'

'But he can't be. The police are not allowed, least of all somebody with his public profile.'

'That's the theory, but you know how bent everything is Blake. Names can be devised, new identity cards can be generated when you have the right friends in the right places.' She looked cynical for a moment. 'Even my identity card has been played around with, so that I can get in and out of the various news conferences I've attended.'

'You *are* called Abigail Sanders, aren't you?'

There was genuine alarm in his voice.

'Of course I am. But the American news agency for whom my card says I work doesn't exist.' The cynical expression disappeared. 'Driscoll is one of a new breed of Chief Constables and one of only two who—behind his carefully affected slight Lancastrian accent—have an Oxbridge degree. He hasn't risen through the force from the old working-class or lower-middle-class channels, as used to be the case. At only forty-two he's one of the youngest Chief Constables ever to be appointed, despite the fact that he joined the police force quite late in life. Why do you think he's risen so quickly? Because he's got friends in high places who are working together in the move towards greater central control. We've even gone so far as to wonder whether Driscoll was a kind of sleeper, installed years ago, in anticipation of just such a historical moment as that which we're living through now. But it's so difficult to prove anything.' She let out some breath. 'The bastards have got everything so thoroughly stitched up.'

'That's why you were trying to warn me in the news conference the other day, isn' it?'

'Yes, and I've been frightened for your safety ever since. The insinuations you threw at Driscoll were spot on. David Kowalski must have been murdered to whip up more national hysteria, or else he found out something that he shouldn't, and it had to be knocked on the head.'

'Kowalski suspected. I can see it now. He phoned to talk to me about the interview and he was afraid.' Before Abigail could ask what he meant, Blake changed the direction of his voice. 'You didn't come to me last night just to warn me, did you?' There was alarm in his voice again, though not as strongly as before.

'Darling, I've wanted to come to you since I saw you that night at the heliport. I knew I was taking a risk by flirting with you, but it was a risk I had to take.' She lifted her eyebrows resignedly. 'You're a very attractive man, and I'm a healthy woman. Then I realized that you were probably on your way up to the Tory conference like me, and when I saw Mark frowning at me by the entrance I knew that by getting into contact with you I might have put you in danger and I might have jeopardized my cover. Especially now that you've upset Driscoll, who I've been watching like a hawk. That's why I've since been trying to avoid contact with you.' She reached out and stroked the side of his face. 'But you are a beautiful man, and I've been waiting for you for fifteen years, and I'm not a cold-blooded "secret agent" who is able to switch her emotions on and off like a tap. I'm just a normal human being with ordinary human needs, and like you I've been lonely *in here*.' She flattened her palm savagely against her breasts.

Blake took the hand and kissed it.

'I'm frightened,' he said. 'I'm frightened by the selfish bigotry of ruthless people, I'm frightened for my country and millions of its people, I'm frightened for your safety because of what you've been doing.' He paused. 'And I'm frightened now because of what I did yesterday.'

Abigail's brow furrowed and he explained to her about what Frank Wardle had said; how he'd obtained the residue from the shelf in the shop and had taken it out to the forensic institute to be profiled.

'That confirms it,' she said. She seemed to be shaking a little, and it was now her turn to rub her face with her hands. 'Oh Christ, Blake. If you can uncover any suggestion that Greenhalgh was deliberately murdered . . .' She changed the tune of her voice. 'I want you to come down to Berkshire with me on Friday and meet some rather important people. They might seem a little stuffy, but their hearts are in the right place.' She got out of bed, put the breakfast tray onto the coffee-table, picked up her handbag, and pulled out a bunch of keys. Blake was staggered at the slender proportions of her naked figure. 'Meanwhile, I have to attend an all-day meeting in Alderley Edge which starts at ten-thirty. Will you go downstairs and fetch my suit carrier and shoes from my car, while I go in the shower? I'm parked round by the library.'

'Suit carrier? You mean you went out last night armed with a clean change of clothes?'

She came over and knelt astride him on the bed, her face suddenly sly and seductive, her lips rather moist. 'It would not have been very respectable for a lady to arrive carrying her clean suit, just in case she ended up staying the night, now would it?'

He touched the hanging breasts in front of him and she closed her eyes and sighed.

'And there was I,' he said, crudely groping at the two generous lumps of flesh, 'all innocent in here last night, worrying about DNA profiles and media clampdowns, with no idea of what devious plans were being hatched as your Vauxhall Frontera made its way slowly across the city.' Her eyes opened and as he looked into them he suddenly frowned. 'When did you take your lenses out?'

'When you were asleep. You looked so beautiful laid there, you know, curled beneath the quilt. You were actually smiling.'

'Any man would fall asleep smiling after what you'd subjected him to. Christ. It never occurred to me to think that women might get turned-on doing that.'

She tittered. 'If you think that's kinky, wait until I've got you into some of my underwear.'

Blake's face remained serious. He was not amused.

'Hey . . . I'm only joking,' she said.

She lifted his chin. 'You're very deep, aren't you? You analyse everything. You're the kind of person who can step into a crowded restaurant and make an instant assessment of the mental credibility of everybody who's sitting in the room.' She moved over and sat next to him, suddenly affected by a slight tremor. 'It's early days yet, Blake. But I'm experienced, I'm a sensible, mature woman in complete control of her mental faculties. And I know I'm not rushing into things when I say that I know I'm going to end up falling in love with you, and that it will be the most natural thing in the world. And I want to fall in love with you, do you understand that? I want to drown in your affections and I don't ever want to come up for air again.'

He swallowed with some difficulty, then kissed her deeply, feeling her nipple harden beneath his palm. Abigail took her face away, having sensed a slight disturbance beneath the quilt.

He followed the direction of her eyes. 'As you might imagine I'm a bit tender this morning,' he said ruefully, his mind a little stale because of the political matters they'd been discussing. 'And I'm sorry if I seemed a bit moody just then, but I'm scared. I'm scared about what you've told me and about what it is that we're getting mixed up in. But, as stupid as it sounds, I'm also overjoyed that it's brought us both together.'

'There you go again.'

'What?'

'Saying that things sound stupid. It's your way of apologizing for your honesty and integrity. And you mustn't do that. You must never do that.'

She slipped her hand under the quilt and Blake gasped. Suddenly the ache between his legs was intensifying. Then it began to leave his body at a tremendous speed, as she moaned and asked him not to be afraid about what they had discussed. When he entered her, she asked him not to be afraid, either, about pushing her face beneath the waves and keeping it submerged forever. But by then, he was too over-come with happiness to fully comprehend her words. He knew only that he was going under the waves with her, find-ing that the pain that might have been the pressure of water filling his lungs was in reality the simple pain of ecstasy, causing him to cry out as it pumped explosively from his loins.

# *Thirteen*

Some rough-cut footage from the documentary that Blake and Vanessa were making was rewinding on one of the TV screens that were set into the wall of Chief Constable Driscoll's office. The film had been transferred to a video-disc and carried scenes recorded a few days previously at Boxton in central Liverpool. It showed the blitz-like after-math to some of the bloodiest riots in British history; riots that had gone on to flare across the country as surely as if they'd been ignited by a trail of fresh petrol running along the motorways.

Blake was wearing a blue flak-jacket over a black leather blouson and was standing between a number of smouldering cars that had been turned onto their roofs. He was speaking to the camera, his dark features bouncing from every shiny surface in Driscoll's black-and-chrome office, including the lenses of the rimless rectangular spectacles which the Chief Constable was in the process of clipping onto his face.

Driscoll leaned against his desk, lifted the remote-control handset, and thumbed the play button.

'Of course,' Blake was saying, 'the difference between the riots this time, and those that happened at the beginning of the 1980s, is that this time the young protagonists came armed with machineguns.

'During the historic street disturbances of Margaret That-cher's first administration, the rioters were armed with not much more than sticks and stones, and they were met by a police force whose strategy for responding to civil disorder remained somewhat antiquated, to say the least.

'Now there has emerged a generation that has at its disposal an arsenal of automatic firearms which has been filtering into the inner cities from the old Warsaw Pact countries, with the growth in drugs-trafficking since the collapse of Communism in 1989. It doesn't matter that hardly any of these youngsters can shoot straight, or that they are so high on crack-cocaine they are not conscious of what they are doing in the subjective sense of the term. When you have an UZI sub-machinegun clasped defiantly in either hand, when you are spraying leaden death indiscriminately at rows of policemen huddled behind shields and armoured cars, you do not need to be accurate in your marksmanship. Sooner or later, bullets will find their way between the gaps and encounter something important.

'Equally significant is that for the first time rioting has broken out that does not seem to have been a product of racial tension. This appears to have been a case of violence for the sake of violence, and it serves to remind us how much of a moral deterioration has been taking place within our inner cities.

'At its most extreme, it shows how today's working-class youth is in the process of becoming steadily depoliticized, as Britain enters its post-industrial phase and a workless generation has been jettisoned from playing an active rôle in the workings of mainstream society.

'It shows how a small but influential minority has forged a private world, where villainy has become the only way of obtaining the material rewards and social standing that used to be achieved through moving into a life of responsible, productive work.

'It graphically illustrates how, in a world of permanent mass unemployment, as the Western capitalist economic machinery begins to break down, millions of frustrated individuals have become so cruelly manipulated by the aggressive market values surrounding them, that communities are being fractured to the point of implosion, society is dividing up into a number of distinct social demarcations, and political solidarity has been replaced by the brutal cynicism of the gun.'

Blake paused while a lorry-load of rubble was shot noisily into a yellow skip. As he stepped through crisp winter sunshine towards the camera, wisps of blue smoke could be seen coiling from empty window sockets at either side of the frame, feeling their way up scorched brick walls. Fire engines cluttered a wide street lined with burnt-out shops. Numerous luminescent-green vested figures were shovelling and sweeping, paramedics were loading full body-bags into an ice trailer in the background, and the road was saturated with foam and water and was smeared with noticeably large patches of red.

When the clatter had subsided, Blake brought his eyes back to the camera and carried on.

'A number of social scientists predicted the degree of violence exercised during last evening's outbreak, and maintain that it has been an inevitable effect of economic decline. Others go further, and claim that our inner cities have been deliberately allowed to deteriorate. They allege that the fear of reprisals from the drugs gangs acts as a backhanded method of policing the disadvantaged. They believe that organized crime has been allowed to become a dominating feature of British life because it prevents the poor from questioning the economic reasons for the deprivation that has descended upon their lives. They believe this has been sanctioned from on high with the avowed aim of keeping the inner cities fragmented, and of avoiding the politicization of the unemployed.

'These same observers claim that the riots were an explosion that was waiting to happen; that it was only a matter of time before the underclass grew to such a size that it would not only prove an unbearable burden on public resources, but would begin to pose a serious threat to the economic stability of the wider community.

'The government has been under pressure for many years to bring violent offenders to book, and yet the social contract between the governors and governed is essential to the maintenance of law and order in a civilized society. Have these scenes of internecine warfare therefore set the stage for a popular prejudice to be fostered against the underclass? Are they an indication that the social contract might be showing signs of breaking down?

'The police have long feared such a social disintegration. They call it the Doomsday Scenario. The new Crime and Punishment Act currently being debated in Parliament is generally accepted as being designed to prevent the Doomsday Scenario from ever becoming a reality. It promises that capital punishment will be reintroduced before the next General Election. Michael Greenhalgh, the leading Conservative politician who tabled the motion, was recently kidnapped and murdered in Manchester by a gang of criminals whose violent behaviour the new Bill is intended to placate.

'Will the longest night in British history prove to be a turning point? Tonight on *Crime in Britain* we ask: Is the new Crime and Punishment Bill a response by a government desperate to appease the anger of the British people, for reasons of political expediency? Or is it really a sign that we are seeing the beginnings of an entirely new, increasingly repressive, social order?'

Blake's head and shoulders disappeared and the screen flashed white then was replaced by a length of black scribble which scrolled crazily through the top of the frame. A sequence of numbers counted down, then the footage ran out and was replaced by video snow as Driscoll cancelled the disc.

At the same time, the telephone started trilling on his desk. The screen that was part of the casing was flashing to indicate that a videocall was coming through. It remained blank after Driscoll's astonishingly hairy hand sliced through the umbrella of light surrounding his desk-lamp, then lifted the cordless receiver to his face.

'Chief Constable Driscoll speaking.' There was a pause: he had obviously been expecting the call. 'Yes, I've managed to get hold of a disc from the Oxford Road studios, and have just watched some of it through. It formed a nice little progressive postscript to the lynching I watched on the same screen up here the other evening, though to be honest I was able to imagine the general content before I started.' He murmured in the affirmative while he digested information being channelled into his ear. 'Yes, it was most convenient for the BBC that Blake Hunter should already have been in the north when the riots broke out. He is still in Manchester working on the same film-making assignment, and I have this morning taken the precaution of placing him under surveillance.'

He turned to squint at the little blank screen by the phone on the desk. A noise began at the back of his throat that might have been the start of a short laugh or simply the hawking clear from his windpipe of a gobbet of phlegm, but it was abandoned halfway. 'No, it isn't,' he continued, meaning the videoscreen wasn't switched on. 'Actually, very few people I know bother with them yet. They're so used to speaking without seeing that being obliged to keep your eyes fixed in the same position becomes rather irksome after a while. One of the idiosyncrasies of human nature the futurists never thought about, I suppose.' The noise started again at the back of his throat, but this time mutated into a short mechanical titter that segued to the words: 'A bit like the history of socialism really . . .'

The laugh ceased while he reached for a photograph of Blake that was laid on top of the desk. He frowned at the picture and laid it back down, then aimed his eyes instead towards the distant Cheshire Plain, visible between the tower blocks at the other side of the tinted window that formed the outer wall of his office.

'As for Frank Wardle,' he went on, 'and the slight conflict of evidence regarding what he claims to have seen during the kidnapping of Michael Greenhalgh, I think that for the moment we must assume he is not an intelligent enough human being to question what he thought he saw.' There was a pause. 'Have you really? I wouldn't have thought that was necessary.' There was a lengthy silence, during which time he muttered in the affirmative again before he cleared his throat conclusively, and said: 'Thank you. Please offer my regards to the Home Secretary, and remind him that I shall look forward to seeing him again at Chevening in a couple of weeks' time. Not at all, no, and a very good morning to you.'

His face dropped when he heard the line go dead at the other end. He replaced the handset, picked up the photograph of Blake again, then stepped across to the window and watched the distant traffic pouring into the city. He was just thinking how it was that standing with his hands knitted together behind his back was a posture for which he was renowned throughout the force, when his eyes shifted down to a several-thousands-strong procession of demonstrators carrying banners through the streets, and he smiled. Once, such crowds would have signified public sector pay disputes or anti-nuclear rallies. Now, huge numbers of respectable people were on the march instead, demanding a crackdown on crime. Even decent churchgoing Christians were saying to hell with the nonsense about forgiving those who trespass against them. Every day of every month of every year their personal spaces were being violated, and they wanted revenge. Those people down there were fed up with conducting their lives as though living under siege. They were fed up with the failings of the judicial system and of a useless tinkering with legislation. Emotion was at last being crystallized. Public opinion was making itself heard as never before. The momentum had begun.

He was pleased to see a show of public solidarity, here in his city on a bright autumn morning daubed with fluffy clouds. He was pleased, too, to see a civilian helijet wending its way in from Manchester Airport, the sun glinting against its silver fuselage as it banked into its final descent. The introduction of a fleet of first-generation Aeving helijets, and a half-hourly shuttle service in and out of central Manchester, had proved to be the council's most successful business initiative in recent years. It had boosted the city's international profile and was helping it finally to host the Olympic Games. It was why the Conservatives had moved their annual get-together to the huge conference centre that had been built in New Central Square. More notoriously, it had proved useful for ferrying journalists in and out when the riots exploded; when Manchester found itself the focus of media attention and experienced a level of civilian bloodshed not seen since the Peterloo Massacre.

As a sequence of chaser-lights flashed on around the rim of the heliport ready to receive the flight, it occurred to him how there was still a sense of scale to this place, although it was so big. It crackled, it sparkled, it had an identity all its own. He'd watched it change profoundly in recent years, of course. He'd seen the old industries die and new opportunities come along. But most important of all, he'd lived to see the new social order getting under way.

'It all began here,' he murmured eventually, glancing again at the banners far below. '*Everything* began here.'

There was a moment when he considered his mission in life and felt a pang of self-doubt pushing to the surface of his mind. Then, feeling strangely apprehensive when he caught sight of his reflection in the glass, he brought the photograph of Blake out from behind his back, looked at it disapprovingly, stepped across to his desk, and fed it into the shredder.

# *Fourteen*

The Independent Forensic Institute at Prestwich had been built just as the Modernist Revival started to influence architectural styles, and it looked incongruous surrounded by detached Victorian houses and tall trees.

While it retained something of the fussy brick-built quality of the late-Eighties, and the car park was a sea of pink herringbone setts, when seen from the outside, most of the windows appeared to have been made from mirror-finished copper plate. Framing the automatic entrance doors were two big chrome columns. These lifted the full height of the building's five storeys and were joined at the top by a giant stainless-steel knuckle that folded backwards and disappeared across the roof. Somewhere near the centre of the roof the knuckle split into three, spread out north, east, and west—with the arm at the front forming the southern epicentre—then went down each wall again so that the structure looked like a massive architectural parcel tied up with metal ribbon, holding itself against the ground for fear of floating away.

When Blake pulled up at the barrier on his way to see Steve Hamer about the DNA profiles, the slabs of metal ribbon were tinted blue with the sky and a latticework of black branches reached across them making patterns from the road. Along with the wind moving through the big trees and bringing a terrific rush of leaves scurrying across the pink setts, a feeling of unease came into the atmosphere of the moment that managed to find its way through the open window right inside Blake's very warm car.

The security guard came out of his little plastic booth and said there were no visitors' spaces remaining, and would he please mind parking out on the street. Blake could see several free spaces but did as he was asked, found a gap in the cars a couple of streets away, then crunched back along the wide avenues, which were absolutely smothered with distended foliage. It was a brilliant late-autumn morning, but curiously, the sunshine and the bright colours had the effect of emphasising the melancholic, rather dreamlike quality that had descended upon his thinking instead of washing it away. No doubt he was tired because of the amount of physical energy he'd exerted with Abigail the previous evening. Indeed, he felt sexually hungover in a way he hadn't done for a very long time. But all this talk about political conspiracies and people being murdered, to enable scheming financiers to ensure Britain remained on course toward a new social order (and despite him being driven to make similar conclusions coming out of Frank Wardle's shop the previous afternoon), seemed too fantastic to contemplate.

He was irritated that thoughts about dangerous conspiracies should have invaded his mind at all, for as he became acclimatized to the prospect of falling in love with Abigail, this should have been the happiest morning of his life. He was aware that the move toward a new social order was happening, of course, as the film he was involved with was attempting to show. But in a democracy such as the one possessed by Great Britain, in his opinion the flow of history was effected largely by accident. It moved in a particular direction, not, as Marxists tended to believe, through some predetermined pattern deviously thought out beforehand, but through an almost unconscious process of its own. And that process was largely a result of the muddle and disorganization which the democratic process enabled. It was the job of journalists such as himself to warn everybody, in the hope of making people realize the error of their ways and help pull things back onto a more even keel. Things would never be perfect. Human beings were not perfectible. There would always be scruffy streets of the kind he'd seen on his way out to the institute, interwoven with glittering super-stores and a mess of graffiti and corrugated industrial units staring blankly at the traffic. Theoretically, the people who were responsible for all that ugliness and bad planning could be cajoled, persuaded not to allow their emotional weaknesses to get the better of them or to make things unpleasant for everybody else. Conspiracy was a popular paranoiac method of explaining away their irresponsibility, from accusations by the homosexual industry that the media was homophobic, to whether or not some member of the Royal Family had engineered photographs of herself to be caught naked, to undermine the political philosophy of newspapers that fell into the trap of publishing the pictures. In all Blake's years as a political journalist, none of the so-called conspiracies that had been mooted from time to time in the left-wing press had ever amounted to anything much.

Steve was waiting in reception and strode towards him, white-smocked, and held out a large moist hand. As the automatic doors shut out the blustery air behind him, Blake wondered if the attractive middle-aged receptionist seated at the desk was trying to catch his eye, but passed it off as imaginary. Just as he might have wondered if his imagination were getting the better of him, had he tried to attach any significance to the fact that the woman reached for a phone as soon as the two men disappeared through a door.

'Thanks for turning the job around so quickly,' Blake said, when they stopped at the vending machine outside the laboratory. He said he wanted black coffee.

'You go back down south, soon, don't you?' Steve asked, making conversation while they listened to the trickle of hot water filling the cups.

'Tomorrow afternoon.'

'Rather you than me,' Steve said, lifting the vending

machine's little flap. 'I enjoyed being at college in Brighton, but the thought of staying down there permanently fills me with a curious sense of dread. Me, a Tunbridge Wellsie too. There's still space to move in the north. And the scenery is better, and the women are less priggish. I'm probably too sensitive for my own good, you understand.'

He squinted over the top of his red spectacles as he said this, and Blake wondered whether Steve appreciated the meaning of his own words. For he'd noticed that, though the conversation so far was not affected, it was contrived enough to suggest that mentally they'd started to drift apart. Except for the thick wedding ring adorning the fourth finger, creating a hot spot in the sunlight as it came up fitted to the hand offering a plastic cup, Steve seemed not to have changed since they were at Sussex University. Blake hadn't been as strongly aware of this quality the last time he'd been at the institute making the *Rough Justice* programme, but it had been there nevertheless. Now it was stronger than ever. Steve's chestnut-coloured hair was still long and tallocky, and the wide features had retained the look of rather youthful scepticism they had always had; the squareness making the head look as though it had been cut out roughly from a piece of wood and the edges finished off with a bit of sandpaper. He himself had put on over two stones in weight since university, but Steve was as lanky as he had ever been. His body, while almost effeminately narrow at the waist, was such an encumbrance that it seemed as if his physical movements trailed a second or two behind the brain impulses that generated them. He still habitually stooped beneath door frames. He had the same smell of carbolic soap hanging over him, and—remarkably—was still wearing the tan-coloured Chelsea boots that had always been his sartorial trademark.

As they walked through the laboratory and Blake shuffled these observations into a pack in his mind, as he listened to Steve reminiscing about university, he found himself curiously stiff and unresponsive. He put it down to the fact that sometimes he felt uncomfortably old, even stuffily conservative, for his age, and left it at that.

Steve sat at a tall wheeled stool and pushed one across to Blake, whereupon the makeshift atmosphere to the conversation seemed to disappear.

'Have you come up with anything?' Blake asked, lubricating his mouth with the chemical substance in the cup, which the liquid crystals on the vending machine had classified as a beverage called coffee.

'Yes,' Steve replied, leaving the word open-ended.

Blake didn't pick up the loose-end.

Instead his heart began to pick up speed.

There was a large table in front of them, cast in grey-green plastic, and seeming to be moulded to the pile of computer screens flickering on top. Like everything these days, like the building they were standing in, the table and its contents looked as if they were all growing out of the floor.

'The fully automatic, as opposed to the semi-automatic, scanner,' Steve said, nodding at the technology.

He touched a keypad and a small plastic tray emerged from the console, similar to that which emerges from a compact-disc player to accept the disc. He slotted a sample slide into position and watched the tray go back into the machine, then removed his spectacles, pressed his face to the eyepiece of an inverted periscope—this also appeared to have sprouted organically from the table—and adjusted the focus. 'You've got this stuff from a sweet shop, haven't you?' he said to fill up the silence.

'How did you know?'

Steve's face came away from the periscope, his eyes rather small now that the thick convex lenses had been removed. 'There were a lot of tiny sugar fragments mixed in with it, and some other identifiable particles.'

He punched in a command to the computer, his fingers dancing silently across the surface of the rubber keys. There was a pause and the sound of electronic activity; a sort of vague whirring and chattering, backed up by a hum of mechanical sophistication, which for some reason reminded Blake of a gaggle of rich women heard through the bedroom floor at a dinner party in a large country house. The big computer screen in front of them went blank, there was a rather severe beep, and then some boxes of figures appeared, playing with the even blue glow bouncing across the spectacles that had found their way back onto Steve's face.

Then the figures disappeared and an image came onto the screen. It was blurred. It was a little granular because it was computer generated. It hadn't yet been sharpened by its journey through the laser and its transformation into two dimensions on a piece of paper.

But its shape was unmistakable.

It was a mouse.

'A mouse,' Blake said dumbly.

He let out a gust of breath, and noticed that the breath was shaking. Suddenly he began to be irritated by the wheels beneath the base of his stool.

'The *mus musculus* to be precise,' Steve said with some amusement, his face in focus now that the eyes were back to their normal size. 'The common house mouse, length around three inches. The computer can provide a full body matrix, of course, right down to the relative elasticity of the rodent's anus.'

He swapped glass samples and repeated the activation procedure. There was nothing to be amused about this time. 'A small West Indian boy, aged nine years,' he said, unfolding an arm and stabbing once at the keypad. The image on the screen began to fill in, with the body materializing as a sequence of fine horizontal lines, until the feet appeared and the cursor jumped across and printed out a physical matrix in a box down the right-hand side.

'Height, approximate weight, blood type, teeth disorders, vitamin deficiency, probable shoe size, you name it, it's there. And it's all come from a few skin flakes.' Then he began apologizing for the quality of what was a quite brilliant resolution. 'Of course, these are still early days. But the technology is bound to get better.' He touched the keypad again. 'This is the bit I like best, though, Blake. This is what you're really paying for.'

Blake lubricated his mouth with the cup of liquid, noticing that the taste, or rather lack of it, no longer seemed to be of any importance.

There was a pause while the computer digested the new instructions. The screen blanked out and became blue again. Then it was filled with fine white lines running horizontally and vertically, like the longitudinal and latitudinal lines on a map of the world. A sequence of figures running along the bottom started to work furiously and the white lines began to lean backwards, then pointed away into perspective. Then they started to strobe, came apart into two panels and began to fold around themselves.

At the same time as they were folding, the two panels split into four, the four panels into eight, and so on, until the divergence reached the seemingly infinitesimal. By now the lines were assuming the outline of a human brain, beginning with the medulla oblongata that hangs underneath and comes up to meet the cerebellum, like the stem that comes up to form a bunch of broccoli florets. All the time the image was revolving, embellishing itself with more and more lines. The spaces between the lines got smaller and smaller and started to fill up with colour. The greyish outer brain became surrounded by a multiplicity of different coloured organs. Then there materialized a pair of eyes; two round, suspended, staring spheres. The skull began to build in sections over the brain, jerking into place a panel at a time. Now came the layers of tissue and the facial muscles, folding around the eyes so that the staring rounds became mild ovals. Then the face became visible, the jawbone and teeth still exposed as a ferocious grinning skeleton at the bottom. The computer bridged the mouth cavity with flesh and the hideous grin disappeared. It twisted the shape around, peeled away the skin, pushed it back into position, built up the eyebrows, shaped them with invisible fingers, printed out the ears, had second thoughts, erased part of an ear, then mapped it out again, moulding it from the pink duct going off into the centre of the head.

The assembly took a few minutes to form, after which there was revolving on the screen a realistic computer-graphics simulation of a complete human head. Although the resolution was still quite granular, the colours a little exaggerated, and the shape a smidgen too angular at the corners, the face would be recognizable to anyone who knew him. It was almost certainly the West Indian boy who had been in possession of the plastic mask.

Steve told the face to stop revolving then stepped over to the laser-printer, lifted a plastic flap, squinted inside, went back to the keypad, and activated the printing process. 'The best way to show how it works is to take a blood sample from the person who is having the profiling done,' he said. A hairline band of intense white light bled out through a split in the casing as the laser began to work and a high-pitched, almost liquid-sounding squeal interfered with the air. 'It's an expensive way of making a point, but I guarantee that you'd recognize yourself and would be able to judge how good the resolution really is.'

'Is this the only profile that you've managed to obtain?'

'No,' Steve said lightly.

He met the lasergraph of the West Indian boy as it emerged from the machine, held it up, then laid it on the desk when he realized that Blake wasn't interested. He went back across to the console, removed another slide from the rack, told the tray to come out of the machine to fetch it, sent it back into the bowels of the casing. 'Subject number two,' he added drily, avoiding Blake's eyes.

The computer started up again.

Blake could hardly bear to watch. The same sequence was repeated as before, except that Steve bypassed the first-generation body identification. Instead, he went straight to the revolving three-dimensional matrix of the head. When

Blake realized what was happening, when he realized that he would have to watch the image assemble from the white lines upwards, the tension was so unbearable he wondered if Steve was doing it on purpose and almost banged his fist down with anger. His eyes went once round the laboratory. Long tables filled with plastic casings. A few white-smocked figures hunched beneath the copper-plated windows, the glass of which, when seen from the inside looking out, was actually a coffee-coloured tint. Outside, a blank brick wall scrawled with the elongated patterns of nearly-naked tree branches. Somewhere above that, the roar of an aeroplane fleeing across the sky.

As he brought his eyes back to the screen and watched the flesh beginning to form, when he saw that the flesh was black, Blake's heart sank.

'Another West Indian male,' Steve said, still as drily as before. 'Aged twenty years. His body perforated by the effects of crack-cocaine.'

Blake drew in a lot of breath and felt his rib-cage expand, then let the breath back out slowly through his nostrils. No matter how sophisticated the technology, the black youth was of the correct physical type to be implicated as a member of the gang that had attacked Greenhalgh. The computer couldn't provide him with the benefit of the doubt. Then he heard Steve's voice breaking into his reverie and he wasn't quite so sure.

'There is one interesting detail about him. It would have been revealed had I shown you the body matrix first.'

'What's that?'

'He's an amputee. His left leg is missing from the knee down.'

Blake almost cried out.

'Is that everything?' His throat was so dry it felt as though his mouth had been stuffed full of sand and it had absorbed all the saliva.

'One more.'

'For Christ's sake, Steve.'

The speed with which oxygenated red liquid was entering via his pulmonary veins into his left atrium, was pumping through his aorta, then was being distributed throughout his body, started to speed up again.

'What's the matter?' Steve was saying. 'If you'd have asked me what I'd found when we came in, I would have told you that the computer had come up with a mouse, two West Indian males, and a single male Caucasian. But you didn't. You've just sat there as miserable as sin and been bloody impossible to talk to.'

'Sorry, Steve. I was up late last night.'

He felt a deep wave of affection for Steve, coupled with a sense of guilt for not having realized that the staleness of the conversation was a result of his own apprehensiveness and nothing more. Then came the needle stab in the belly when he realized he'd just heard the words *single male Caucasian*.

Steve lifted an eyebrow, cleared the screen, and set the sequence going again.

'Most of the residue from the third subject was made up of flakes of dried saliva, layered as they might be on a mask or a helmet.' The white lines leaned backwards and started to strobe. 'You never get much from saliva because it deteriorates in the atmosphere. But there was a single hair bulb.'

He grinned, stabbed at the keypad, and sat back to watch. Blake knew whose face was materializing before the flesh had finished forming over the skull. He knew because of the knitted brow and the way the jaw widened like a pear at the bottom. Or not so much like a pear as the jawbone of an ape, giving the skull something of a heavy neanderthal quality. As the closely-spaced grey-blue eyes came together and the head revolved, he was surprised at the accuracy of the depiction. Because the computer couldn't assess the length of a subject's hair it tended to begin by showing it cut very short. The operator was able to dip into the photofit memory bank and try out a variety of styles, if the matrix

were being used in police identification work. It was true
that the features coming together were rather blurred, as
though seen through eyes that were half closed. But they
were already filed so clearly in Blake's own memory bank,
because they'd stared at him so very recently, that it was
merely a question of bringing the two mentally together. As
it happened, the hair now colouring in on the cranium was
cropped as close to the scalp as it was on the real head in
real life. Of course, it was the brilliant red colour that had
the effect of negating the blurred quality of the features,
pulling the face into its own special kind of focus. Pulling
into focus the face of Detective Superintendent Stoneham,
the Special Branch thug who'd come up to Manchester from
New Scotland Yard.

'Male Caucasian aged thirty-eight years,' Steve was saying
from what sounded like the end of a very long corridor. He
touched the keypad and a boxful of words was superimposed over the face. 'Everything is there, including bone
fractures, of which this chap has quite a few. Judging by the
constituency of some of his enzymes, and a small amount of
stainless-steel that's been picked up by the scanner, I'd guess
that at least one of his limbs is held together with metal
pins. In fact, he has quite a few defects.'

'How do you mean, Steve?'

Blake was starting to feel sick.

'Well, the left arm has been broken in three places. And
I don't mean broken accidentally, but smashed. There's a
gunshot scar in his right leg, and various minor fractures
and abrasions throughout his body. He could be a criminal
or a mercenary or a stuntman, it's impossible to tell. Do you
want me to go on?'

'No. Just print him out completely, will you? A full body
matrix and half-a-dozen copies of the head should be
enough.'

Blake remained casual but swallowed with some difficulty,
his tongue now an enormous encumbrance trapped within
the sticky confines of his mouth; the room in which he was

standing an enormous space in which he was trapped. He'd told Steve the day before that the profiling was being used in connection with the crime documentary he was making for the BBC. Still possessed of a compunction to cover his tracks, knowing that it was vital he give no indication that anything was wrong, as Steve removed the sample slide from the plastic tray and shook it as though it were a thermometer he'd just pulled from somebody's mouth, he started congratulating the computer for its remarkable sophistication, smiled generously, levelled out his brow, and livened up his overall presentation.

As he did this, he noticed how the words coming out of his mouth were forming independently of the real thoughts fitting together inside his head, and he realized it was happening because he was frightened.

Eventually, he was aware that he was shuffling the lasergraphs together and sliding them into a yellow plastic envelope; was handing Steve his BBC debit card; was standing with Steve on the red marble floor in reception; was being assured by Steve that there was no possibility for error regarding the profiles; was glancing away from Steve and noticing that the middle-aged receptionist had been replaced by a young blonde girl wearing a skirt so short he wondered why she'd bothered putting it on; was shaking Steve's moist hand again; was telling Steve to keep the sample slides and the CD safe because he would probably need them later; was saying to Steve that, yes, he did still have the cottage in Upper Hanford; was having a vision of that cottage and the failed marriage that had been conducted beneath its sagging red-tiled roof in the shadow of the village church; was suddenly feeling a spasm of guilt when he realized the smiling faces of his two small daughters Hayley and Jennifer, who'd been conceived in that cottage, hadn't been conceived in his mind for at least twenty-four hours past; was conscious that the two smiling faces were already so well featured and well fed because they were well away from the rot, the pert little mouths already sending out aitches into the air; was walking across the red marble floor, then between the automatic doors that came away from the air; was glad of that bitter air; was noticing that since he'd arrived some clouds had come across the sky and begun to scrub out the sun.

# *Fifteen*

Foremost in Blake's mind as he emerged from the institute was the need to speak to Abigail. Not only to speak to her, but to curl up to her in front of a warm coal fire; to bury his head in her breast; to shut out the daylight; to forget that he'd been stupid enough to toy with the idea of lifting dangerous stones, taking a peep at dark secrets hidden underneath; secrets now turned into lasergraphs contained in the plastic envelope under his arm, holding the ability to put a gun against his head.

But he'd left his portable phone, along with the Newton into which Abigail had programmed her mobile number, in the glove compartment of his car. As he crossed the herringbone setts and walked away from the barrier the distance between himself and that car seemed unbearably irksome. Ever since Abigail had left his room that morning, and he'd waited a little while before going downstairs to Vanessa to discuss the production schedule put off since the previous evening, he'd found himself sinking into the conviction that his movements might be being monitored. Now, as he pulled up his collar and waded through the foliage carpeting the main avenue, the feeling that he was being watched was more powerful than ever. But the broad streets were unnaturally quiet and seemed to be drained of colour because of the lack of sun. There was nothing; nothing but wide pavements as deserted as they had been when he'd arrived. Nothing but rows of parked cars, big gateposts, big houses dumped at the top of gravel drives bending between the rhododendrons, the low rustle of dry foliage and, somewhere, the remote hum of traffic. But if there were so many parked cars, he found himself wondering obscurely and checking more than once over his shoulder, where were the lighted windows in the houses? Where were all the people? And why were there no twittering birds?

He began thinking about Detective Superintendent Stoneham. Even if it couldn't be proved that the fragments of residue from the mask had come from the scene of the Greenhalgh kidnapping, they *had* come from Stoneham, and those samples had been picked up with pieces of sticky tape from inside a newsagent's shop in Normanshaw. In conjunction with Wardle's evidence and a statement that could probably be secured from the black youngster who'd got hold of the mask, along with one from the boy's mother, he had enough proof to lay the incident wide open.

But who could he go to? Chief Constable Driscoll was almost certainly implicated and he was the number one policeman in Greater Manchester. If what Abigail had told him were to be believed, there might even be people implicated who were working within the BBC. That made the prospect of getting in touch with his newsroom suddenly seem foolish and dangerous. As he turned these thoughts over in his mind, he noticed that he couldn't see the surface of the pavement he was walking on. He could only see the thin concrete kerbstones describing the contour of the avenue, running along the edges and nosing beneath the piles of dead leaves. Then he was startled when hundreds of thousands of those dead leaves came scurrying towards him in a mass, the terrific rustling blanking out his hearing, acquiescing with his growing unease and making him feel suddenly exposed. The leaves settled down then angrily gathered momentum again. They chased in circles around his ankles as he hurried across the road. Then they changed direction and dived beneath the parked cars, accompanied by a great roar of wind rifling the trees, so that the air was active with a swirl of yellow fragments attacking windscreens and slapping against his face, tasting of earth and trying to find their way inside his thick coat.

Turning onto the avenue where he was parked, and feeling a sudden urge to surround himself with people, he was wondering whether to use public transport to get back into Manchester when he noticed a crew-cutted youth wearing a black leather jacket and green jeans, walking along the street up ahead and moving close against the cars. A hand reached out and thumbed a door stud quicker than an eye could blink, then flashed away when it found that the door was locked. The cars and the wide pavement swept away to the vanishing point very sharply, and Blake could see his own vehicle parked perhaps fifteen or twenty spaces along. He could see it because he hadn't parked it very well. It was a metallic-red Ford Mondeo two-litre injection, provided courtesy of the BBC for the duration of his time in Manchester. He could see it because the front offside wing was cocked a foot onto the pavement, the only bump breaking up the long perspective of glistening metal.

Suddenly the youth was alongside the Mondeo and aiming a shiny black compact at the door. It was an alarm immobilizer. There was a brief electronic squeal, and the indicators pulsed orange as the black box did its job. Then the youth held up what looked like a car shock-absorber attached to a pistol grip. It was actually a lock-rammer, a powerful device adapted from the pneumatic screwdrivers that punch a hole through the skull of a pig to knock it senseless in a slaughterhouse. Professional car thieves had started using them to punch the locks clean through the doors of cars, to minimize damage in order to break in.

The youth touched the gun against the lock and fired, yanked open the door, and bent to get inside. Blake was about to set off running to intervene when he suddenly found himself wondering: Why should he risk injury in the defence of property that was not his own? The youth was obviously a professional car thief, and probably armed. He'd already crouched in a gateway while he assessed the situation, so that he'd been out of sight when the youth glanced round before he blew away the lock. But in an odd way, the prospect of the car being stolen made him feel relieved. Throughout the morning he'd been trying to convince himself of the improbability of the vehicle having been 'bugged' while it stood in the compound beneath the hotel, before he'd driven out to Prestwich. If it had, if anybody was sitting in the next street waiting for him to drive away, so they could track his movements on a blue screen, then the youth stealing it would throw them awry.

Before Blake had put the full stop behind the thought as it finished in his mind, a grey-haired man wearing a black overcoat was running down the centre of the road. He was coming from the opposite end of the avenue, his head and shoulders bobbing above the roofs of the cars. He was shrieking and gesticulating madly, demanding that the leather-jacketed youth get out of the fucking car. Blake looked around the gatepost, wondering if the man was a vigilante, and saw the youth slam the door and hunch over to hot-wire the ignition.

Then the man running down the centre of the road appeared to trip and fall and dropped out of sight behind the cars. At the same instant that Blake recognized the brief squeal of the electronic ignition—as the hot-wire became live—his senses were being smacked between the eyes. The roof of the Mondeo was peeling back exactly like a freshly-opened tin, but one ripped apart by an old-fashioned can opener, leaving the edges all ragged and bent. The driver's door shot out sideways at an incredible speed, and smashed straight through the brick wall running alongside. There was a huge mushroom of fire and smoke expanding in all directions, overlaid with a terrific bang that seemed to jolt Blake's eyeballs in their sockets. Blended with the bang was a deep rending noise that could only be the sound of metal being ripped apart like paper; and then a gust of hot air came at him along the pavement. Instantly, a dozen car alarms screamed into life all down the avenue. At the same time there was the hideous clatter of glass breaking in the surrounding houses, some of it crashing down onto patios and drives.

Flying through the air now was a multitude of blackened objects, most of them dragging flames, and one of which looked uncomfortably like the arm of a leather jacket still containing the object it had been manufactured to fit. It twirled through the air like a boomerang, trailing a bit of soggy red, until it disappeared into the ball of smoke folding up through the trees and casting a big partition of shadow across the street. The last thing Blake saw before he obeyed his reflexes and pushed his body to the ground was the bonnet of the car parked immediately behind his own snap up, break away, and go cartwheeling across the road like a piece of spent cardboard.

Then it was all over, everything was clattering to the ground, the asphalt alongside his face was scattered with lumps of smoking debris, and there was a smell of petrol and burning plastic filling the air. Along the pavement now sweeping away from his eye in a massive perspective and raging with leaves disturbed by the blast, the remains of his car were blazing away, the flames leaping into the air being aggravated by the wind. The vehicle had been blown completely apart, leaving the roof bent back like the lid of a Jack-in-the-Box. Bits of distended metal pointed in all directions. He could see a vague shape slumped across the wheel, horribly distorted and with sections of it definitely missing, but still recognizably human, the flames encapsulating it a brighter colour than the rest, burning furiously in the centre of the inferno. A moment later the figure toppled under its own weight and fell out onto the pavement, a flutter of blue cinders instantly snatched by the air.

Blake lifted to his knees. Through the clearing smoke, he saw the grey-haired man staggering along the centre of the road, shimmering through the heat-haze, docking out a finger of fire trying to take hold of his arm. An automatic pistol was clearly visible in his hand, blood and oil and shock were spattering his face.

Then a silver Range Rover was screeching and careering into the avenue, coming alongside behind the drifting smoke. Then the man was running alongside the Range Rover, which slowed but didn't stop as a nearside door was flung open and hands grabbed hold of his lapels and hauled him inside. And then the door was slamming, an accelerator pedal was being stamped to a floor, there was a shrill complaint from four low-profile tyres, and the Range Rover was tearing past at the other side of the cars. Blake was already ducking back down, his breath rasping and gasping, particles of gravel embossed against his hands, some of it down the insides of his shoes. As the Range Rover shot past dragging a cloud of dead leaves, he saw the interior as though through a hand-held telephoto lens in a film. The grey-haired man was talking furiously into a cellular phone, the whites of his eyes showing as he blinked his senses back to life. Blake had never him before, and he couldn't make out the features of the third figure silhouetted behind him, either.

But the thickly-set features of the neanderthal face sat rigid behind the steering wheel—features blurred with fat beneath a flash of red hair, the piggy eyes obscured by mirrored-sunglasses, the muscular body seated upon a padded contour-seat bolted into fifty-thousand pounds' worth of thundering metal, speeding away atop four revolving rubber rings—those he had seen before.

A neat facsimile of their arrangement was depicted on the lasergraphic paper contained inside the yellow envelope, still clutched beneath his arm as he scrabbled backwards into a drive and dry twigs snatched at his hair now.

Blake was running. Already the police sirens were screaming through the trees behind him, blended with the chorus of panicking car alarms, the racket oscillating and surprisingly remote to say that he had run no more than two or three streets. To say that he had not run far from the bomb that had blown his car and a teenage thief into pieces, but was meant to have blown Blake Hunter into pieces; to silence him; to separate the limbs from the torso; to blow apart the head and the brain that only hours previously had begun formulating affection for a lovely human being called Abigail. The racket was oscillating and surprisingly remote, to say that Blake Hunter had not run far from the bomb that was meant to have prevented the brain that wanted to love the woman from blowing the lid off a barrel of rotten apples that probably went to the top, to the top, to the very very top.

Blake was stopping. The blood was pounding in his ears. Overlaying the pounding was a buzzing caused by the bang of the explosion, strong enough to replicate the effects of tinnitus. His throat was parched so much it hurt. He was breathing convulsively, the shock beginning to hit at last, a corrosive wheezing noise coming from his chest that would not go away. Still there was nobody about. Why was there nobody about? Why were there only cars, and who did they belong to? Parked cars, cars that were parked. So many cars crushed together because one side of each street was painted with double-yellow lines. Cars that had newspapers folded on back seats. Cars that had trinkets dangling from mirrors. Pairs of gloves on dashboards. Toys and teddy bears staring at the upholstery. The red glint of alarm-diodes guarding under oath. A few pretend dogs having a motionless conference with teddies and seals. A few real dogs, curled into balls and staring up white-eyed and dangerous. Then a few nodding plastic dogs covered in suede, miniature dogs back in fashion. Back from the past, hauled up to the future. The past brought forward again. Memories rewound and the play button thumbed. No blanks drawn. Nostalgia doing its trick. Erasing the truth. Neatening up history. Tidying up the past. Keeping the smokescreen in front of a future that could only mean the death of liberty; the obliteration by semtex of all parked cars.

Blake was walking. Managing to slow down. Breathing deeply, very deeply. Leaning against a powdery brick wall. Slowing down his heartbeat. Concentrating on stifling the pain expanding in his chest. Squinting into the sun which had shifted out from behind the clouds again. The tears pricking his vision. Blinking his contact lenses. Hurting. Smarting. A handful of the invisible sand that had sucked the saliva from his mouth back in the laboratory, now scooped out and flung in his eyes. He put his hand up to his head and heard the ticking of his watch alongside his ear, above the tinnitus song. Some traffic happening now, passing on the road at the end of the avenue, framed by glittering branches, by the colours of late-autumn coming to life. The heat of the star hanging ninety-three million miles away in space bringing them out, putting the shadows into focus, warming the strip of flesh above the collar at the back of his neck.

There was no doubt now, no doubt at all: Blake Hunter was a target. He was a dead man. His hunch that his movements were being observed had proved correct. It had started that morning when he'd bumped into a young French chambermaid outside his room when he'd left the hotel. She had bade him good morning with such a satisfying *au fait* precision, he'd wondered whether she was an actress employed for strategic reasons to play the part. She had held his eyes in such a way as to suggest that she either genuinely fancied him, or she was trying to pretend that she fancied him so as to disguise the fact that she was not a chambermaid at all, that she didn't fancy him, but was really some dangerous female removal person with a knife hidden up her sleeve.

The first proper thought that surfaced as the confusion of the preceding minutes requested that it be put into some kind of order, was the overwhelming desire to know when the bomb had been planted beneath his car. He wanted to know with an intensity that bordered on the absurd. Had it been fixed in position the night before, the vehicle tampered

with in the hotel car park, and not primed until his pursuers
could see where he went this morning? Or had it been fitted
into place while he'd been inside the institute? The streets
were quiet and the electrified walls high enough to have
made it easy. And how had they followed him out to the
institute? He'd watched his rearview mirror religiously all
the way to Prestwich, deliberately travelling via an awkward
circuitous route, going up and down terraced backstreets,
winding his way through industrial estates; but he'd seen
nothing untoward. Nothing but receding tower blocks piled
behind him, the glint of sunlight against reflective surfaces,
and the blueness of the sky filling in the gaps.

He'd avoided communicating with Steve on a telephone.
Did that mean his car *had* been bugged, traced on a little
radar as spies used to do in the films? Or was it somebody
at the institute? Was it Steve? Was it the attractive middle-
aged receptionist who'd caught his eye when he arrived, but
who'd disappeared by the time he left?

Now that he really thought about it, she seemed to catch
his eye when he'd taken the tape samples to the institute the
previous afternoon. But the glance might not have been a
signal to let him know that she wished to become impreg-
nated with his semen. It might have been a malignant stare
identifying his features, making sure they matched a description already passed to her, enabling her to report so that the
authorization could be granted to have the meddling bastard
killed.

He found himself standing at the head of a narrow lane
running between the fenced back yards of large houses. He
seemed to have entered a residential student district. There
were fire-escapes dog-legging up and down high walls. That
meant the houses had probably been divided into flats. A
young man was hunched over a draughtsman's table high up
in a studio window, being gazed at by the sun. Here at last
were some birds, flitting between ornate gables. There were
industrial-sized green wheelie-dustbins, bicycles chained to
drainpipes, authentic stone flags running into cobbles, all

bound together by yellow leaves and the deep Mancunian brick mottled in the sunlight. Here was picturesque late-autumn innocence, with the sound of people and shops and cars and roads manned by street furniture drawing closer by the minute. From somewhere came the natter of a yardful of playing school children, trickling through the trees. Everything seemed so unassuming in its timeless air of solitude that he barely noticed the sirens now. It was impossible to believe that these salubrious nineteenth-century streets were part of a society that was generally accepted as having gone on the slide. Impossible to take seriously the prospect of car bombs and murder and bent policemen and corrupt politicians and people being bumped off with the intention of rousing public indignation; all to ensure that the reintroduction of capital punishment proceeded through Parliament, reached its Royal Assent, and the new social order got under way.

Surely to goodness not, he kept trying to convince himself for the umpteenth time that morning, the shock of almost-death-tinnitus still ringing in his ears. Not death here. Not with a scene coming together before him of the kind there was now, where shards of daylight were piercing slanting shadows, and an abundance of dying leaves were making late-autumnal manoeuvres upon the musty air. Surely not death on this earth soon bursting with happy people and warm houses and cosy coal fires coming together for another twelve days; and somewhere lost amongst it, a warm-hearted investigative journalist and a beautiful electronics engineer, curling up amidst the tinsel and toffee, looking forward to a life of falling in love.

Abigail.

Blake saw his distorted features reflected in the shiny paintwork of a Vauxhall Frontera. Not *her* Frontera, but it was enough to bring the desperate need to speak to her careering back into his mind.

Enough to drag with it, too, the realization that he'd lost his cellular phone and his Newton in the exploding of the bomb. He couldn't contact Abigail and she couldn't contact him. He couldn't remember where she was staying because she'd programmed her address and number into his Newton and he'd only half-read them. He'd been too preoccupied with embracing her when she'd come to leave. He'd been too interested in acknowledging how stunning she looked when she'd dressed in the two-piece peach-coloured suit he'd fetched from her car. He'd been too mesmerized by her beauty when she'd tied up her hair, put on the shiny sheer legs, stood upon the stylish *clump clump* heels, exuded womanhood, painted her face, prepared her sexual plumage for its naked display to the world for the day. He knew she was staying at a country house belonging to one of her aged industrialist mentors, somewhere in Cheshire.

But he couldn't remember the name. He couldn't remember where it was. He didn't know where he was going or what he was doing. He was stranded. He was lost. He was alone. Theoretically he was dead. And if he knew he was still alive at that sun-speckled moment, blinking salty sweat and registering the crumbly texture of a long brick wall as it stretched away into the light, he might be dead for real later that afternoon, tomorrow, the day after, next month, next year, next life. Whenever they managed to catch up with him and strap the semtex against his skull and blow it apart for real.

Though the shops suggested that the clientele of the district was a couple of cuts above the rest, the main road at the bottom of the lane had none of the sense of unchanged Edwardian continuity exuded by the big detached houses and cobbles running down to meet it.

When he came to the bottom, Blake found that his contact lenses were bothering him terribly. He might have lost his most important means of communicating instantly with his world; he might be utterly cut off from someone who'd suddenly become the most important person in that world; but he did still have his spectacles inside his coat pocket. He'd nearly forgotten them that morning when he'd left the hotel, so preoccupied had he been with getting Abigail away from his room without being seen, for reasons neither could adequately explain.

Now he could explain, and he thanked the fates that he'd gone back to fetch his spectacles, just as he thanked the fates—reluctantly at first, because of the predicament into which they'd pushed him—when he considered how close he'd come to being blown up in his own car. He was consumed by the urge to disguise himself, to blend into the background and lose himself amongst the crowd so that he could try to collect his thoughts. Though his was not a popular public face, and even though he was only an occasional presenter of current affairs television programmes which did not attract large ratings, he was still recognizable. That might be so in a district such as this, which probably held a smattering of intelligent people who would be more selective about what they chose to watch on TV.

The application by Blake of his spectacles had the curious effect of totally altering his appearance. So while there was still nobody about he stepped back into the cobbled lane and removed his contact lenses, put them between a piece of notepaper, and folded it carefully back into his pocket. With his spectacles in place he felt calmer, less exposed, more able to work out a strategy to get through the rest of the day. He straightened his scarf and wiped his face with his handkerchief, then stepped out onto the main road and kept close against the wall. A few hundred yards further along, in a movement that was somewhere between a slow run and a generous stride, he joined the end of a queue of figures, and jumped onto a departing brown-and-orange bus glowing vivid in a wedge of sunshine. As he slumped into his seat the sirens tore into his mind again, fire engines tearing past the window on their way to put out the flames; to douse the crumpled bit of metal that was all that remained of his car. He didn't bother to wipe away the patch of condensation forming on the glass. He felt that it would help obscure his features from the outside world, would help erase the scene building in his mind of the men in white overalls who would soon have taped off the avenue and the lump of smouldering car.

Just as they would soon be searching through the leaves with tweezers and tongs; picking up pieces of cooked meat and depositing them into labelled plastic bags; shovelling the distorted remains of a real human trunk into a black bin-liner; taking away the little pile of mutilated remnants that might so easily have been his own.

# *Sixteen*

Late that afternoon, when the sun was dropping behind the Manchester city skyline and sending the tower blocks into a dense black silhouette, Chief Constable Driscoll was ascending in the lift to his office at Central Police Headquarters. He was in uniform, he was holding his black attaché case, he was staring up at the computerized panel flicking away the pile of floors, and he was noting agreeably that the trajectory of the pneumatic capsule was so effortlessly smooth it was impossible to tell whether it was actually moving, let alone when it started or stopped.

When he walked out into the reception area that fronted onto his office he was surprised to see his secretary Jean was still present, holding a cordless telephone receiver, and looking relieved to see that it was him. She usually went home early on Wednesday afternoons. But the way she was coated-up ready to leave, and obviously a little flustered, indicated that she'd been trying to get away for some time but hadn't yet managed to succeed.

'Yes, it was him,' she said to the phone, meaning she'd been waiting to see who emerged from the lift. 'Just a moment please, and I'll put you through.' She stabbed at a button on the console and put down the handset. Apart from the fiery glow of the sunset refracting dramatically through the big windows, the only source of illumination in the room was the spotlight sunk into the ceiling panel above her head. It was playing with the luminous surface of her bronze coat, and it put the shadows back into the cracks and crevasses of her face as she came upright. 'There's a man on the line wanting to speak to you, Derek. He's rung four times in the past hour and says that he's not prepared to talk to anybody but the Chief Constable.'

Driscoll's brow raised while he digested the information and Jean started pulling on a pair of skin-tight black leather gloves. He observed that the gloves emphasised the boniness of her fingers as obscenely as the black leather trousers brought out the shapelessness of her skinny legs.

'Thank you Jean,' he said coming across, putting down his case and hat, and taking the handset from the desk. At the same time he adjusted the bottom part of his face so that it resembled a human expression generally described as a smile. He didn't press the button that would bring the caller back on line. 'You can go now, and thanks for hanging on. Come in at ten tomorrow, if you like.'

Jean picked up her umbrella and handbag, smiled and said goodbye, then half-ran into the lift. When the lift doors had closed, Driscoll instantly erased the smile from his face. He didn't go through to his office but swung round onto Jean's warm leather chair and switched on a lamp. Before he took the call he swivelled to face the communications console growing from the right-hand wing of the desk. He ran a forefinger down a column of illuminated red rubber squares, until the manicured fingernail stopped at the window that was flashing, the red glow turning the flesh at the end a bright translucent pink. Superimposed across the glow was the legend LINE 2. He touched another button, then spoke to midair. 'Scramble incoming call on line two, please. Voice authorization D. G. Driscoll.'

There was a pause and a computerized beep, then another red panel lit up and flashed the words CALL SCRAMBLED three times around the office. Driscoll pivoted back to face the proper way, put the receiver to his face, and took the call. 'Chief Constable Driscoll speaking,' he said, assuming an air of polite calm. 'Sorry to have kept you waiting.'

The voice at the other end was that of Steve Hamer. He was devoid of his white smock and was sitting at a desk in a darkened office at the IFI, holding a clear perspex telephone. Behind him, the patterns of a venetian blind sprawled across the wall and blended with the shadows. There was a note of distress in his voice and he spoke rather too quickly, hunching over the desk when he realized that at last he'd got through to the Chief Constable. 'I'm ringing in connection with the killing of Blake Hunter. He was a friend of mine. I wanted to ask whether or not you knew that he'd been out to the—'

'To who am I speaking, please?' Driscoll interrupted, his eyes jerking away from the brilliant sunset filling the gaps between the tower blocks outside. How the hell had the voice at the other end of the line got to know about the supposed murder of Hunter, when they'd put a news blackout into force since the explosion?

'Sorry,' Steve said, letting out a lot of breath to slow himself down. 'My name is Dr Steven Hamer. I work at the Independent Forensic Institute at Prestwich. I wanted to speak to you about the killing today of the television journalist Blake Hunter. I'm absolutely devast—'

'Do you have access to a videophone, Dr Hamer?'

'I'm sorry, no. We haven't had them installed yet.'

'I see. You were saying that you have some information regarding the killing of Blake Hunter.'

'Yes. I don't know if this has anything to do with the bombing, but were you aware that Blake had been out to Prestwich to visit the Independent Forensic Institute, shortly before his car was blown up?'

Driscoll knew because he'd authorized the planting of the bomb, but of course he had to lie. 'We had no idea at all, Dr Hamer. As yet we are only at the beginning of our investigations. Though we have contacted some of Mr Hunter's colleagues, nobody seemed to know the precise nature of his whereabouts this morning.'

'Well, he'd been out to the IFI to see me.'

Driscoll looked at the framed 3D photograph of Jean's fifteen year old daughter Ruislip, standing on the corner of the desk, hands on hips, big teeth beaming in the glow of the lamp. She looked like a miniature version of her mother, except that she had much bigger breasts. He dragged the photograph across, laid it down, and ran a forefinger in a circular motion around the girl's two fine, upstanding protuberances. Then he inspected the tip of the finger for dust, and brought it rather sensuously against his tongue.

'Dr Hamer, it is almost six hours since the explosion. Why has it taken you until now to telephone the police with information regarding Blake Hunter's movements earlier today?'

Steve leaned back in his chair, the reflection from a lighted angle-poise somewhere to his left stretching two elongated yellow squares across the lenses of his spectacles. Immediately he became defensive, which was precisely what Driscoll wanted. 'I didn't know it was Blake's car that had been blown up! We all heard the bang and the sirens, but we just assumed it was another drugs-related killing. I'm devastated, for God's sake, and I've been rather frightened.' Like all people who inhabit white smocks during the day, now that he'd assumed a civilian pallor as he prepared to go home, Steve looked withdrawn, almost naked.

'Of course, Dr Hamer, and I do apologize. But what is it that is so important it has given you cause to be afraid?'

'Well, I can't help thinking that the bombing of the car has something to do with the fact that Blake brought some samples of human residue out to the institute, to have them DNA profiled.'

Driscoll's face dropped. Though they knew Blake had been out to the IFI, they had absolutely no idea why. They'd merely chosen to eliminate him there. Now, as he listened to Hamer, he found the cordial tone that he'd assumed was becoming less authentic by the minute; that it was rather more difficult to keep his voice entirely neutral. 'Human residue? Could you explain precisely what you mean, Dr Hamer.'

'He'd brought some skin flake samples, hair bulbs, and so forth for analysis here yesterday afternoon. They appeared to have come from a sweet shop, or perhaps a newsagent's.'

'A newsagent's, you say?' Driscoll cleared his throat. 'Please go on.'

'It's not so much to do with where the samples might have come from, but Blake's attitude to them before he left. He seemed very reticent. He asked me to keep the samples and the disc safe, and that under no circumstances must I mention to anybody the fact that he'd been out to the institute to get the profiling done. That seemed to me to be an odd thing to say. It was as if he didn't realize he'd said it. I've known Blake for a very long time, Mr Driscoll. Unless I'm mistaken, I'd say that he was shocked at what came up on the computer screen, but was doing his level best to conceal it. I would even go so far as to say that he was frightened. I didn't think anything about it until our receptionist told me that she'd heard the police talking about it being Blake Hunter who'd been killed, when she came back from her lunch break.'

Driscoll had a vision of Francine, the middle-aged IFI receptionist, writhing beneath him a few evenings ago. The picture quickly evaporated, for since the mention of a newsagent's, his face seemed actually to be growing in size, his eyebrows coming together so savagely the movement was distorting most of the flesh on his face. He ran his tongue across his lips and cleared his throat again, still determined to keep his tone casual. 'Do you have any idea what significance these DNA profiles might have?'

The way Steve answered the question would probably make the difference between whether he lived or died.

'None at all. Blake said something about them being used to make a point in a television documentary he was filming.'

'He said nothing else?'

'Nothing.'

Occupying the professional position, and a certain social stratification, that he did, Driscoll was not supposed to be the kind of person prone to showing his emotions very easily. But the adrenalin was beginning to be released even into his bloodstream now: now that he risked the question: 'And just what did these profiles reveal?'

'Only a mouse, a couple of young West Indian males, and a single male Caucasian.'

*Damn you to bloody hell, Hunter,* a voice said inside Driscoll's head when it heard the final three words of Steve's answer. But still the real voice coming from between the thin colourless lips managed to remain calm.

'Were there any distinguishing characteristics about any of these males?' He knew that to avoid implicating himself in any way, he had to keep a general interest in the three subjects; must not emphasise the one about whom he wanted to hear.

'Not especially, no.'

'What, no distinguishing characteristics at all?'

'Apart from the fact that the older black youth had part of a leg missing, and the white man had ginger hair, and seemed to have broken quite a few bones in the past, nothing much out of the ordinary, no.'

Driscoll paused for effect, visualizing a scene where he was putting a gun against Blake's head. 'Did Mr Hunter take anything away with him after you'd generated the profiles?'

'Yes. He took a set of computer-enhanced lasergraphs of each subject, but obviously they will have been destroyed along with the car. I could let you have similar disclosures, of course.'

The little scene involving a gun and Blake was still in Driscoll's mind. Now he was personally pulling the trigger. 'That would be most helpful, Dr Hamer, most helpful indeed.' Driscoll clasped his brow between his forefinger and thumb, closed his eyes very tightly, then opened them again. He seemed to suck in a lot of breath and let a great deal back out, but there wasn't any sound. He thought quickly, the only course of action open being to hold up a candle in the general direction of the Devil. 'I find it difficult to believe there could be a connection between what you have just explained, and the murder of Mr Hunter. However, if there *is* a connection, it occurs to me that there could be implications of national security. If Blake Hunter had indeed obtained the profiles for use in a television film, as you say, then he might only have been telling you the things that you needed to know. The film might well have involved particularly sensitive subject matter. You may be aware that several terrorist groups recently threatened to target a number of journalists, who in the past have produced TV programmes incriminating their regimes.'

'Actually no, I wasn't aware that—'

'Where are these samples and forensic records now?'

'They're at the institute.'

'And where are you?'

'At the institute. I was just getting ready to go home.'

Driscoll's face slackened.

'Please remain where you are, Dr Hamer, until we arrive. Do you have a family?'

'Yes, but my wife and children are away.' A sudden note of hysteria entered Steve's voice. That was precisely what Driscoll wanted. 'You don't think there's any likelihood that I might become some kind of *target* do you?'

'No, no. You should be perfectly safe.' Driscoll smiled. 'Somebody will be with you soon.' He placed the splayed tips of the two forefingers of his left hand over each breast on the photograph of Jean's daughter, then slid it out of the way. 'Thank you very much indeed for this new information, Dr Hamer. There is one final point I do need to stress, however. I must ask that you do *not* discuss the things that you have said to me with anybody else, until we have obtained a full statement from you, and our investigations have been completed. That is a normal police formality under these circumstances. I could request an official authorization to obtain your co-operation, but we rarely find that it is necessary.'

'I understand, and it won't be necessary now,' Steve said, sounding rather relieved. 'How quickly can you get here?'

'Detective Superintendent Stoneham will be with you as soon as he can.' To keep Steve's thinking moving in a part-icular direction, to stop it pausing in front of dangerous corners, Driscoll brought a note of sentiment into the closing moments of the conversation, to authenticate his personal detachment from the matter. 'You said that you were an old friend of Blake Hunter's?'

'Yes. We go back a long way. We were at university together in Brighton.'

Again Driscoll paused for effect. 'Most unfortunate. You have my condolences, Dr Hamer. Thank you for your call, and good afternoon.'

'Goodbye.'

Driscoll banged down the phone and let the big gust of breath out again, but this time spliced together with the proper sound effects. He uttered a crude expletive pertaining to bodily waste and drummed his fingers against the desk, then saw the blue light come on above the doors to the lift. It would be Stoneham, on his way up to the office for their four-thirty rendezvous. He reclined in the leather chair, flicked a switch on the desk that activated another spotlight in front of the lift, and mulled over a frown. During the time that the digital counter went crazy above the door, he was able to register the smell of female that was still orbit-ing the desk, and allowed his eyes to trace the outline once of a big lump of coral sitting in a recess in the office wall, touched by the glow of a tiny light hidden inside the casing. Then the blue panel above the lift doors changed to green, the doors parted, and Stoneham stepped into the room. He was noisily removing the cellophane from a packet of Mar-lboro King Size.

'Have you managed to find out what Hunter was up to when he visited the newsagent's, after he'd been filming in that back alley the other day?' Driscoll asked, before the stainless-steel doors had finished closing.

Sensing the tension, Stoneham frowned. 'Not as yet, no. Surveillance didn't come up with anything.'

'Well, I'll tell you what he'd been up to. He got hold of some skin flake samples and a hair bulb that had fallen away from *your* fucking missing mask.'

'Jesus Christ.'

Stoneham had inserted a cigarette into his mouth and was patting his body, searching for a lighter. The cigarette bobbed up and down while the distorted blasphemy came out from behind it, then assumed a perfect horizontal.

'Yes, Jesus Christ, because Hunter then took the samples out to the forensic lab at Prestwich, and had them DNA profiled.'

Stoneham took the unlighted cigarette from his mouth. 'Has he got the lasergraphs?'

'Yes, he's got the sodding lasergraphs.'

Stoneham's lips seemed to turn to rubber while he let out some loose breath. 'Hell. He must be onto us. How the fuck could he have got any bits of residue?'

'Obviously, the newsagent let him see the mask before we got to it, or else he showed him where it had stood inside the shop.'

'I'm still not happy about that newsagent,' Stoneham said, making a second attempt at inserting the cigarette. 'He's the key witness to the whole thing and he's still alive. Trying to frighten him with talk about Official Secrets and injunctions was a waste of time. We should've got rid of him straightaway, like we did Kowalski.'

'Our orders were to keep him alive, dammit! And we can't carry on bumping people off who are connected with Greenhalgh's killing, certainly not Frank bloody Wardle. That nosy black bitch from the *Observer* who exposed the Tory paedophile ring has already been onto the press office, referring to the row I had with Hunter in the news conference the other day.' He steepled his hands, let out another round of breath, then brought a clenched fist down onto the desktop so hard the photograph of Jean's daughter jumped sideways, the three-dimensional breasts seeming visibly to bounce along with it. 'The chances of something like this happening, the chances of somebody getting hold of a single hair bulb from that mask, then having it profiled, must have been billions to one against. I can't believe we came that close'—he held up a narrow space between a forefinger and thumb—'*that close*—to getting rid of Hunter.'

'It would have looked fishy if Hunter *had* been blown up in his car. And what about who the newsagent got the mask from? If it comes out that Hunter got hold of some residue, then had it DNA profiled—'

'Then we'll have to hope that whoever picked up the mask after silly bugger you lost it will start shitting bricks, thinking that maybe something of theirs might have been left behind on it, too.'

Stoneham had succeeded in removing a chrome lighter from his pocket and had lit the cigarette. The cloud of smoke surrounding his face was being attracted up towards the spotlight directly overhead. For a moment he looked as though he was smouldering, and might be about to spontaneously combust. Then he frowned and said: 'How did you find out about the profiling anyway?'

'A scientist-friend of Hunter's called Hamer just rang in from the IFI at Prestwich. He says Hunter took the samples out to him yesterday to have them profiled.'

'What are we going to do with him?'

'We can't do anything with him. We'll just have to carry on bullshitting. As long as he thinks Hunter is dead, he shouldn't be dangerous.'

Stoneham looked at the cigarette in his hand. 'Supposing Hunter goes to him.'

'Then we'll nail Hunter, because I've implied to Hamer that he might be in danger from the "terrorists" who blew up the car. We'll post a guard outside his house to keep him happy, monitor his phones, and effectively quarantine him from the outside world until we've located Hunter. Hamer's out at the forensic institute now. Hunter probably won't go back there, and won't even phone in if he thinks we were watching him this morning. But if he does, Francine will have him. Get over there now with Addison and see what Hamer's got to say, but don't twist his arm. You're CID making routine enquiries.'

'I can't go, can I?'

'Why not?' Driscoll was genuinely indignant.

'If he's produced a fucking DNA profile from something of mine, then he might recognize me, mightn't he?'

'Shit.' Driscoll stood up, the movement as much an attempt to cover his embarrassment as it was a reaction against Steve's call. 'All right, send Addison with somebody else.'

Stoneham tilted back his head and blew out a twin column of smoke from between his nostrils. The way that he held the cigarette was strangely effeminate, considering the stocky masculine body bulging from beneath the grey leather overcoat. 'I don't like the idea of that doctor having seen a computer-profile of my features, Derek, even if it is probably a bit blurred. All he has to do is recognize me in the papers, or see me on TV at a news conference, and'—he snapped his fingers. 'And what happens when Forensic realizes that the body of the kid isn't Hunter's?'

'I've already ordered the department into silence. Meanwhile, we release it to the media in an hour or two that it *was* Hunter who was blown up in the car. Any awkward questions and we say the security clampdown was put in place because of Special Branch's—because of *your*—continuing investigation, and there being a possible link between the explosion and the Michael Greenhalgh killing.'

Stoneham absorbed another lungful of smoke. 'Hunter could be anywhere. He could've made it to London by now, for all we know.'

'I don't think so. No car hire or public transport tickets of any kind have been registered to his ID card in the British Isles this afternoon.'

Driscoll was right. One of the major advantages to police

work of Central Matrix was that it enabled nationwide monitoring of a person's movements when they were travelling. Only minor roads and old trunk roads were free of tolls and bureaucracy now.

'He could have hitched,' Stoneham said.

Driscoll narrowed his eyes and picked up the phone again. 'He could have, provided he didn't use the motorways, but I doubt it.' He thought for a moment then changed the tune of his voice. 'What about that good-looking bitch who he encountered downstairs after the news conference the other day?'

Stoneham shook his head. 'Nothing, I don't think. We've scrutinized the video, but she appears to have been somebody he tried to chat up and who more or less told him to get stuffed. Anderson was coming out of the bogs and saw it all. Says she just gave Hunter the cold-shoulder and that as a consequence he looked thoroughly pissed off. I don't think we can read much into that.'

'And what about Vanessa Aysgarth?'

Stoneham fished in his coat pocket and pulled out something tiny. He placed it on Driscoll's desk. It was Vanessa's wedding ring, as retrieved by himself from the puddle in the car park the other night.

Driscoll raised an eyebrow and brought the ring up to his face. 'Hers?'

Stoneham nodded. 'She just tossed it out the car window after talking with her husband on the phone in the car park at the BBC. I thought she'd seen me at one point.'

Driscoll narrowed his eyes. 'So, it seems that we were right to keep the illustrious Mrs Aysgarth under observation. But I wonder if this means that she's reached the end of her matrimonial tether and has elected to transfer herself at last to young Mr Hunter's bed.' He paused. 'Where is she now?'

'Surveillance has been watching her and the film crew all day. They went out to interview somebody at the university after lunch, and now they're back at the studios down Oxford Road. Every phone into that building, along with every portable, is being monitored. We'll do the same when they go back to the hotel.' He blew out some more smoke. 'No doubt Aysgarth is wondering what's happened to old lover boy.'

'I'll bet she is. Assuming that she doesn't already know where he is, of course.'

Driscoll lowered his buttocks to the edge of the desk and nibbled his bottom lip. 'Hunter's got us by the bollocks, but there must be a reason why he hasn't rung a news agency to tell them that an attempt has been made against his life. I suppose that if he suspects the people behind the killings go as high as us, if he's seen your DNA profile, he'll not know who the hell he can trust and will bide his time until he can come up with something big. But there must be somebody.'

He pondered for another few beats, then added ruminatively: 'I wonder . . .'

# Seventeen

As Driscoll stopped wondering and pressed a sequence of buttons on the telephone in his hand, a mile across the city Vanessa was just starting to wonder about her assistant Sarah, who was becoming very affectionate in the back of the Volvo as Chris drove them through the early evening traffic back to the hotel.

She was in a bad enough mood as it was. After they'd interviewed the criminologist he'd taken them out to some dilapidated tenements, to demonstrate how a social hierarchy existed in the felonious pillaging of inner-city homes. It was a dangerous place to have gone into without a security escort, and they'd had to wait until it was nearly dark before making their way up through a stinking service entrance in a sidestreet off the Stockport Road, where they'd been met by a semi-derelict tenant whose face Vanessa never saw properly throughout the time she was there. What nobody had expected to stumble across, as they'd moved along a balcony in the gathering dusk, was the bloody aftermath to an old man murdered in his flat, a hammer having obliterated the aged skull with a single savage blow. The corpse had been sprawled naked in the middle of the lounge, a feeble ray of late-afternoon sun filtering through the window throwing a dim orange rectangle across sagging, emaciated buttocks. The sight of the pathetic white body and the smell of the Rorschach splurge spreading from its head had been difficult to stomach. But what had been driven home to

Vanessa—something which highlighted the criminologist's view—was that everything that had a resaleable value had been stripped from the flat, leaving nothing but an empty shell. It went without saying that the furniture and electrical appliances had been taken by the original gang of killers. But then another group of scavengers had moved in. They'd unscrewed the internal doors, removed the plumbing from the kitchen and bathroom, prised away the plastic architraves, skirtings, and central-heating louvres, then unclipped plug-sockets, light-switches, and the handles from the windows. Throughout the flat, the plasterboard had been pulled from the partition walls and the drained copper pipes wrenched from behind them—an activity which the criminologist said was the speciality of children. There were tiny pyramids of copper dust where the pipes had been cut with a hacksaw into more manageable lengths. Even the vinyl tiles had been peeled from the concrete floor, detergent stains spilled where the bitumen had been scoured away. Vanessa knew that such plundering had been a fact of inner-city life for many years. But standing in the freezing darkness, telling Chris to lower the camera from his shoulder because she couldn't bear the thought of exploiting the old man for the sake of a film, she'd been horrified to think that minds which could so savagely defile a human being could ransack a home with such attention to detail. It displayed a weird kind of sensitivity; showed what potential the manimals might have had in a society that wasn't organized economically as a brutish free-for-all. The thought of such waste, and the senseless killing it spawned, turned her stomach so much that by the time they'd reported the murder to the police she'd been left feeling absolutely sick.

Sarah had stayed at the criminologist's office while the crew had gone across to the tenements and hadn't been affected by what the others had seen. And despite the air of melancholy as they'd got back into the car, she'd not only linked Vanessa's arm, but had gently stroked her hair all the way back into Manchester. Now, to cap it all, as Chris sent the Volvo down the ramp into the car park beneath the Great Northern Hotel, Vanessa was having to contend with the fact that Sarah's hand was coming dangerously close to one of her breasts, and feeling not so much uneasy as downright infuriated.

Though Sarah wasn't the kind of person who came over as being gay, Vanessa had had her suspicions since she'd taken her on several weeks previously. From the start she'd linked her arm, and always seemed to manage copious yet discreet amounts of touching. This was harmless enough in its way, of course, the arm-linking being something which many women did. But just lately, Sarah's eyes had been feasting over hers almost constantly. In the evenings her skirts had been getting shorter. She was always slipping off her shoe and rubbing her foot up and down her legs under the dining-table, if the crew were eating together after a shoot. She was also the only person who'd noticed that the wedding ring had gone from her left hand. This angered Vanessa nearly as much as the obscene words she heard whispered into her ear, when Sarah described what she wanted them to do to each other that night—but more especially, what she had back in her room with which they could do it—just before they got out of the car.

Because she hadn't wanted to draw attention to what was taking place on the back seat, and hadn't pushed Sarah's hand away when she should, Vanessa wondered afterwards if being shaken by what she'd seen out at Ardwick had left her quieter than normal, and that she'd been sending out all the wrong signals. Whatever the reasons, she was still so distracted by her thoughts when she stepped out of the lift on the way up to her room that Sarah had appeared alongside her, and was making a pass outside her door, before she realized what was happening. She pushed Vanessa against the richly-papered wall and tried to kiss her, saying that she'd been building up to this moment for a month, and that she'd go crazy if she didn't come soon. With a speed that defied description, Vanessa took hold of Sarah's wrists, shoved her away, then slapped her across the face as hard as she could. She stood at least four inches above Sarah in her ankle-boots. But if she was surprised at herself for briefly enjoying the sensation of physical superiority, she wasn't surprised at what she'd just done, and she certainly wasn't shocked at how angrily she did it. For she knew perfectly well that it was a build up of her innermost frustrations that had caused her finally to snap, and she began to get an inkling of why she hadn't done the decent thing and put Sarah in her place back in the car. It was because she'd been looking for a confrontation, and as she clawed her hair from her eyes and made ready to attack, she realized it was unfortunate that it was her assistant who happened to be getting in the way.

Sarah was so surprised by Vanessa's reaction that she lost her balance and stumbled, her eyes seeming to open to about twice the normal size as the slap rang out and she reeled against the opposite wall. She'd genuinely believed that Vanessa was interested in her, and this noble aspect of her otherwise inexperienced personality caused her to stand her ground. Clutching her face she started justifying her actions to hide her embarrassment, and Vanessa had to admire the intellectual tenacity with which she did it. This was what had appealed to her when she'd taken her on. Though she was still only twenty-three and possessed of a rather naïve earnestness, she was a strong girl and when she matured she would go far. Unfortunately, her reaction in the heat of the moment was to think that Vanessa had been leading her on, and when emotion took over and she accused her producer of having a sexual hang-up about women, it aggravated the situation all the more. Sarah was grabbed by the scruff of the neck and slammed against the wall.

'No, Sarah, but no,' Vanessa snarled, feeling she could have laced into her with feet as well as fists. 'There may be things about myself which I still don't understand, but of that I'm absolutely sure. I've never had your inclinations and I can assure you that I never will. Do you hear me? *Never!*'

She banged her against the wall again as if to underscore the observation, then saw a button pop away from the collar of the girl's black silk blouse beneath her red leather jacket.

'That's what you think,' Sarah spluttered. There was the bright-red outline of a hand appearing on her left cheek now, complementing the red jacket and red jeans, and her straight dark hair had fallen girlishly across one eye. 'We can always tell, you know. I didn't know I was like this until a few years ago. And don't tell me that you never want to fuck a pretty woman when you see her! You're an artist, you're aesthetically motivated, you register beauty. I accept that and let my body show its appreciation, that's all. I still have boyfriends, so now I get the best of both worlds.' She cleared the hair from her eye, and Vanessa felt disgusted when she sensed that Sarah was enjoying the way she was being roughly handled, her otherwise nondescript voice having turned rather husky. 'You ought to at least give it a try, Vanessa. You might find that you like it, though that's what frightens you, isn't it? It scares the hell out of you to think that you might fancy laying another *woman*.'

Working in her profession, of course, the opportunity for Vanessa to go to bed with members of her own sex presented itself often enough, with a recent survey concluding that more than half of all creative staff were gay, bisexual, or something in between. She was tolerant of alternative sexualities and wasn't prejudiced against homosexuals in any way. She was aware that she was tall and noticeable, was broadshouldered and walked straightbacked with a strutting upright posture, and that feminine lesbians did seem to find her attractive. But more than any of these things, she was aware that she'd never been remotely interested in experimenting sexually with women, and what Sarah had just said had been said to her so many times before it really struck a nerve. She wanted to blurt out that what bothered *her* was that people like Sarah often assumed that other people were suppressing subconscious sexual urges, if they made it clear they were absolutely straight. But she didn't blurt it out.

Instead, and with an odd feeling of futility, she suddenly comprehended the enormity of the twenty-year difference between them, decided that she didn't want a scene in the corridor, took control of her hands, and felt the best thing to do was to try and turn away and forget the incident had happened.

She pulled out her keycard, slipped it into the handle, heard the lock release, then banged open the plastic door, feeling that if she'd turned to face her assistant, she could have hit her to the other end of the corridor with a single blow. She went into the darkness of her room and shut the door without looking back, but found that her heart was bounding in her chest and she was shaking so violently that she had to steady herself against a chair. If it wasn't for the fact that Sarah's clumsy pass had aroused memories of something unpleasant that happened to her a very long time ago—something she honestly thought she'd forgotten—she might have wondered if the way her body was responding was because she'd wanted to make love to the girl, and these after-effects were a manifestation of repressed carnal desire.

But they weren't.

Of that she was absolutely sure.

For several moments she stood in the centre of the room and stared at her dithering hands, the air alive with the sound of her own breathing and the oddly reassuring rumble of traffic down in the square. She seemed to calm after about a minute, and her first reaction was to go back out and apologize to Sarah for reacting so aggressively, even though she felt that the girl ought to be apologizing to her. They would have to face each other later and it would be better to make it up now, nipping resentment in the bud. But when she opened the door and looked out, the lift doors had just finished closing at the end of the corridor, then the computerized display began counting down the floors and Sarah was gone.

Vanessa was frightened to think how close she'd come to hurting Sarah, as she closed the door again and leaned with her back against the panels. She pulled off her spectacles and fixed her attention on the blurred red numbers of the digital clock flashing on the table next to the bed. She knew that she was under tremendous stress, not only because of what Max was doing to her, but because she was trying to come to terms with her feelings for Blake, which she was powerless to do anything about. She was a highly intelligent lady and usually very good at analysing her motives and working out why she behaved how she did at any given time. But, though she'd sensed recently that something was going to have to give soon, she hadn't realized how close to the edge she'd come until now. And that unnerved her. For it was bitterly ironical that, while she was preoccupied with her own sexual confusions and the uneasy realization that she was finding it virtually impossible to relate any more to men of her own age, she should remain powerfully attractive to a young lesbian woman. In a curious way, she almost wished she'd been brave enough to allow her assistant to seduce her. Not to thumb her nose at her husband, or because she wanted desperately to hold another naked body, but because she needed a naked body to relate to in an intimate, personable way. The trouble was that she'd never been able to generate a sexual interest in anybody unless she'd felt an emotional attachment to them first. Sexual pleasure for her evolved from being mentally stimulated, from really getting to know somebody and talking through ideas, and not, as so many of the self-centred people she encountered still seemed able to do, from isolating sex as a purely physical phenomenon, reducing it to a crude animal act, to the mere emptying of bodily fluids into a hole between a pair of legs. If she'd been shallow enough to regard sex like that, if she'd been the kind of person who took but never gave, she might not have been so damned lonely for so long.

When her cellular phone trilled inside her coat pocket she was so relieved that she felt the tension instantly begin to lift. She had an idea who it would be and it had come at exactly the right moment. In the few minutes that she'd been standing against the door, wondering what the hell had happened to Blake that day, she'd decided to let herself go. As she reached to switch on the light, she realized that she'd taken about as much as she could stand. She'd bottled up her anger for long enough. Now she was going to make her move and damn the consequences. That way she might start to clear her mind if nothing else.

She pulled out the phone and spoke very softly.

'Blake. Wherever you are, can you come to my room now, love? I desperately need to be with you—'

'Sorry, darling,' said a jeering voice in her ear. 'But it's little old me calling from the big old US of A. How's your goddamn libido this evening?'

Vanessa snapped.

A single piercing shriek.

The phone hurled against the bedroom wall.

It smashed to smithereens, some of the lumps of yellow plastic flying back at her so fast she had to cover her face and heard them spatter against the furniture. Her head rolled loosely upon its shoulders and she let the weight of her body slide down the door until she was sitting on the carpet. Her clothes had rucked right up, exposing her bare belly, but she didn't care. A minute later the phone next to the bed started trilling. She'd seemed to see it as a big close-up while she'd counted down the seconds and waited for the sound, picturing Max jabbing angrily at buttons, imagining a pulse of light travelling down transatlantic cables, hearing the telephonist answering in the hotel, making the connection to her room.

But there was still a chance that it might be Blake.

She hooked her spectacles back on and crawled across to the bed, reached for the cordless receiver, lifted it to her ear.

The voice she heard was literally spluttering with rage.

'Now just you listen here, you stupid fucking—'

'You're going to have to get rid of me, Max,' she interrupted calmly, drawing up her knees. A strange neutrality seemed to have entered her voice and she was staring at a point in space. 'You're going to have to kill me now, do you understand? And do you know what else? It will be a merciful release, you spineless, murderous little shit, because first I really am going to reveal to the world the corruptness of your affairs.'

She yanked the wire from the wall, threw the receiver into a corner, and rolled face-down onto the grey carpet, a clenched fist banging up and down, silvery hair fanned about her beautiful face. Her whole body started juddering rhythmically as the horrific images of the day and several from her life all ganged up; until there came a vision of Sarah thrusting on top of her, grinding her into the bed, blending to somebody else thrusting on top of her when she'd lost her virginity on a disused-railway embankment at age fifteen. She saw herself growing up again in that same countryside near Harrogate; remembered an attic bedroom which should have been a little girl's private space but wasn't. She thought of the loneliness and desolation that had gradually consumed her since she'd matured into this strong woman who could always answer men back; this assertive woman whose ordinary female needs were assumed to have taken a back seat for much of the past forty years.

When she curled into a foetal position and her voice finally broke and she let it all come out, there was a moment when it seemed as if she might actually be laughing.

# *Eighteen*

Tall blocks of flats were coming into view again now, que-
uing up amongst naked branches rising from a world that
seemed to be quilted with a frustrated geometry of shapeless
rooftops.

The flats were shifting round now, poking their silhouetted fangs at the setting sun, looming alongside the bus.
Shadows losing themselves to the golden hem of the day; to
a final cantilever of gilt burning between this labyrinthine
mess and an ever-decreasing plenty, as the big night stretched ever nearer. The big night darkening a ragged sky rolling
in to envelope nocturnal thieves who would soon be prowl-
ing the streets, their souls rheumatic with a desire to rob in
order that they may live. Minds made sordid by a wound
that never heals, he thought. Minds trained by values which
expect the barbarity they have spawned and the liberty they
deny to knuckle under and conform, he thought; so that an
orgy of self-celebration can proceed untroubled and unhin-
dered.

Blake had been travelling through the suburbs for a very
long time now. From one bus to two, from two buses to
three, hands thrust deep into overcoat pockets, body half-
submerged in the smelly seat, an endless succession of old
industrial streets. Draped chunks of a crumbling northern
vastness, rows of little houses still skewered strong to
attention, but the spirit of which had long since been defiled.
Tiny havens abandoned by a fractured faith, clawed back to

the greedy iniquity of time from which had sprung the discriminating boot of a greedy demon, to stamp flat the tortured carcass of this brick and stone eternity, as it stamped flat manmade cliffs that long ago ploughed the landscape with dormitory lives.

Blake saw sad figures mesmerized by their lack of purpose sliding past the window, treetop traceries flitting above their bowed heads, chimneys and gables as thick with the blackness of impending night as the roof slates sloped before them were freezing over with a layer of cold-season-white. Sad ghosts drifting before perished architectural façades, shadows of former selves meandering crookedly between the bent street furniture and underpasses gulping fumes and traffic. Faces stupefied by the buying and selling of brutality in a flat and ignorant landscape upon a fat and ignorant world. Faces resigned to the suffocating internment of their aimlessness. Faces shovelled aside. Faces staring from piled flats grafted to boarded-up shops, old homes sealed with breeze-block, pavements confetti'd with shards of glittering glass, the fate of streets sealed with the creeping cement of prejudice and hate as the pointed teeth and the car bombs and the atom bombs slowly grew.

Something else grew before him now, rose up from the tatty upholstery. The little pale face of a female toddler, already spending itself of energy despite the earnestness of its years. The face was bent over the back of the next seat, stubby fingers leaving greasy stains upon chrome. Mother's dark hair hung matted and shineless alongside, strands as black as the metal cage sealing the driver into his compartment up ahead. The young features grinned and showed their teeth and smiled at Blake with their eyes. A smile cracked his face too, then a lump moved in to occupy his throat, as moistures weaned by a soul devoid of malice or ill-will lanced corners of his face. He saw the child and, of course, his brow became concertina'd and he saw Hayley and Jennifer. He saw the cottage at Upper Hanford, twin village to Lower Hanford, echoing the two distant Slaughters, another pair not many miles apart. Ancient pastures cleaved by a motorway pointing the way to Cambridge, two smudges of stone kept at bay by traffic nine miles from Hertford. Accent on folksy country sentimentality at the heart of the rural dream. Little end-terrace at the foot of the main street. South-facing gable built in the Dutch-style. Rendered walls. Small bay window facing onto the village green. Tiny red slates artistically disarranged. Old photograph of Thirties' motorer framed above bulging wooden door. Climbing roses, neatly-cropped hedge, brass fittings, pub laughter filtering through close evensong, wooden spire of Medieval church throwing morning shadow across unadopted lanes. He heard again the peal of bells from that spire on sad spring Sundays. Heard the sombre twitter of birdsong through open windows, ushered in with a smell of night-scented stock on warm summer's eve. Heard the clatter of electronic shutters disturbing attached façades first thing in dewy morning, last thing at frosty night; the metal eyelids from inner-city shops at last seeped out into rural life. No clinking of milk bottles or the whistle of happy postmen now not with the dawning of the post-industrial siege.

He heard these sounds blend with the shrieking of Victoria when he came home a day early from assignment; found the space at his side of the bed occupied by another erect penis, foraging amongst the spaces between his wife's legs. Strategic memories flinging themselves upon the muddied canvas of his mind. Reading Little Bear stories to two excited little girls. *Daddy we love you.* The smell of scent and soap and cleaned linen living the big pot-pourri fib, despite the semen stains that had violated the ancient house supporting its crooked roof and crooked wife and life. *Daddy we love you.* He saw the open staircase, descended it again with his fingers on the shiny bannister, to the cosy lounge billeted with a clutch of original Art Deco fittings and flow'ry cushions; innocent infants now sleeping soundly above, foreheads kissed, expectant features shut down until the morning. Lamps shining upon open coals flickering across waxed pine, witness now to denials and automated hate, despite the concrete truth and the cast-iron stench of Mummy's big lie. *Daddy we love you.* And I love you too, my sweets, but Mummy hates me because she is committed only to herself, and her doting on you is an excuse merely to suffocate deeper upon her own conceit.

Children are so helpless and innocent, he thought, looking at the toddler's discoloured teeth unzipping again above the seat in front of him now. And I need you, Abigail, he also thought, tears at last beginning to run, not born of self-pity or sentimentality but of the fear that he had nearly died. I need you now, Abigail. My little girls need you. We all three need you. We need your strength to pull us through, to crash us beneath the waves and bind us all together, to tie the bow in a big ribbon which this time will never come undone. We need your dignity and your strength stronger than any woman's I have ever known. We need your eyes to show us the way with their wonderful incandescent pupils. *I swear to God I would die for those eyes,* I whispered when you came to my room to commence our love. But twelve hours later I nearly died for another reason instead, and I'm terrified. I'm on the run, and I think that if it wasn't for the prospect of getting to know you, Abigail, when I contemplate the misery and futility of the past year, I'd probably stay on the run forever. I would assume some new identity, change my appearance, forget my self-indulgent career, blend into the background, merge with the shadows, move anonymously through the England of the streets.

But I can't because I want you, Abigail. My fists are crushing together and showing white knuckles now; my nails are gouging crescents in my palms, because my passion for you is so strong. I'm probably fatigued and suffering from the after-effects of shock, but I feel sick, physically sick with need. I can't phone you now, I can't contact you, and for Christ's sake I don't even know where you are. But I'm coming to you at the hotel at seven this evening as arranged.

Of course, they'll be waiting for me in the shadows with their guns and semtex and their heads full of hate. But if I have to scale the outside of the building and break through panes of glass with my bare hands, I am going to be there.

The buses have been cruising the streets, starting and stopping in front of bent shelters all afternoon. Though I've worked in this city regularly I don't really know where I am, especially now that it is almost dark and full of streetlamps and a chiaroscuro of constantly-shifting lights. The bus I jumped onto at Prestwich eventually came alongside a grassy embankment, leading to a great Victorian public park. The stone battlements hiding behind the trees at the top seemed to offer a sanctuary of sorts; offered a chance to check the images of the exploding car and the spiralling limb that refuse to segregate themselves from my mind. So I alighted into the bitter cold, the air smoky with a hint of dusk as the afternoon looked to the possibility of draining itself of the day. I ran through clouds of my own steam between ornate pillars standing sentinel over a sombre deserted promenade, flaming with the fires of autumn. There was an antique tramway still used for pleasure trips, its rails mingling with the cobbles and the spent leaves, but sad and silent and shut down for the winter, the original nineteenth-century shed garaging the cars fortified with metal plates, with gauze, with barbed-wire and broken promises and broken glass and alarms. Have you noticed, Abigail, how these days windows are being *painted* on the walls of isolated public buildings, because they cannot sensibly be glazed with real panes any longer?

The park was immense and undulating, broken up by oases that were a mixture of rhododendron bushes, silver birch, and crooning crows. I made my way through the still desolation from one side to the other, past a lake that was frozen over and scattered with very depressed-looking water fowl, heads tucked sadly beneath folded wings. There was not a soul about, not even any wild dogs or stray squatters' pigs. But about halfway across I came upon a number of burnt-out cars, trophies from the previous evening's joy-riding smouldering serenely in the chill gloom. The gentle mound across which they were arranged was abstracted by a strangely appealing pattern of black skidmarks, scored savagely against the green. Some bullnecked gypsy scrappers were dragging the wrecks onto the back of a low-loader with a crane. A bulging mechanical claw was grappling with the spent black carcasses and crumpling the roofs, dangling them through the air and banging them down, chains lashing the clattering mass into a precarious heap of dead metal, ready for the journey to a bit of profit back at the yard. The gypsies stared at me and I looked at them and I saw the pump-action shotgun on the dashboard of the lorry. But once our stares had been exchanged we went our separate ways, and I came out at the other side of the park; out onto a wide residential avenue, so similar to the one I had left behind a mile or two ago that I wondered if I had walked in a huge circle.

Here I boarded a vehicle that was hardly a bus, but more a glorified transit van with windows. It was packed full of old-age pensioners seated upon tatty, urine-smelling red-and-black upholstery, all gabbling noisily as if they were members of the same exclusive club. Some of the younger ones (if that is the correct term for people much older than yourself) were wearing noticeably poorer quality clothing than the others. Some were actually devoid of teeth, part of that lost generation being seriously affected by the dismantling of the NHS. It looked to me as though the vehicle was filled to at least a third beyond its legal capacity, the driver no doubt hungry for his commission, so that he at least might evade the flames of the gathering fire. The bus jerked up and down narrow streets crammed with parked cars, pushed on beneath the cloudless sky into the busying suburbs, until the shabby shops wrapped in metal cages, the cameras keeping watch over the traffic bunched amidst a fury of ancient graffiti, and the mess upon the earth, all began again.

Where the vehicle juddered past tall flats striving to sing their heavenly rhythm, where particles of glass glittering far and wide were being breathed at by the frost, a sunken-cheeked young woman got on brandishing a screaming half-caste baby, and everybody went quiet, heads surreptitiously began to shake. The baby's frantic tantrum pierced all our eardrums in that tiny confined space. The whites of the driver's eyes showed in his rearview mirror, safe behind the gauze netting and the bulletproof glass, sealed with graph-paper patterns thrown across his red face inside his little cockpit.

Further on, when the bus fell beneath the glow of caged windows, the young woman suddenly got off and started smashing the baby's head with her hand when she arrived at the pavement. She dangled the child cruelly by one arm, began punchbagging it in the kidneys, screamed abuse from her toothless face of a ferocity that you wouldn't expect a member of the underclass to spray at the pair of dogs that were mating greedily outside a pawnbroker's shop, a few yards further along. Then she broke down and began weeping, clutched furiously at her hair and bawled with the tiny writhing mass now rolling away into the gutter, its pink mouth contorted, little legs flailing against disinterested passing faces, the two dogs surprised now, yelping as their contracted genitalia ripped themselves apart. The racket was drowned out by the tinny revving of the bus's cross little engine, which didn't seem powerful enough to drive it between the decaying streets, let alone propel its gawping cargo away from the concrete kerbstones ruled before that turgid little scene.

*How could you beat up your baby?* I wanted desperately to ask her, as we were finally hauled free and I tried to conceal the tears that were tumbling down my face.

But of course I knew the answer. When I alighted from that wretched little bus and watched my shadow stretch before me across more corroded working-class properties (they could not have looked more like sodden cardboard boxes if they'd had OPEN OTHER END stencilled across their walls), I knew that behind the social breakdown going on all around us, behind the internecine warfare a growing chunk of the underclass is waging against itself, behind the inability of my spoilt ex-wife to understand the snobbish outlook programmed into her by her social conditioning since birth, lay an explanation for aberrant human behaviour that is inseparable from the economic forces governing all our lives.

As I pulled up my collar and hurried between clouds of my breath away into the night, I wondered if I were deliberately concentrating on negativity, being pushed down into pessimism by the monumentally dangerous sequence of events in which I had become embroiled. But I am an investigative journalist, Abigail. An exposé of the seedier side of modern life has been my stomping ground for the past ten years. I am motivated by a desire to fight against tyranny and injustice; to bring to light the truth, the whole truth, and nothing but the truth. It is an awareness that has burned away in me from as far back as I can remember, ever since I was an infant at school and I was wrongly accused by a sadistic teacher of striking another boy. But I love my country, Abigail, I do not hate it. I do not want to annihilate my culture, I want it to improve and to endure. I want the productive genius of our people to be released again; to shine its light across the world; to foster a spirit of community instead of confrontation. I am a moderate. I believe that the mixture of social democracy and private enterprise that has given our society the most prosperous and stable period in its history is probably the only realistic hope that we have got, if we *are* to endure.

But if you are genuinely aware, how can you help but organize yourself mentally around a number of negative forces that daily affect society; that dictate the way you relate to your environment in this overcrowded, twelve-lane automated age in which we live? If you cannot leave your personal belongings unattended any longer, if you cannot retain peace-of-mind unless they are protected by steel shutters and alarms, how can it be denied that society is changing, and changing for the worse?

Do you know that for seven years of my life I lived in a quiet country village, smack bang in the supposed heart of rural England, and that if, early on a summer's morning, you stood at the old stone cross where the main road forked, you saw before you two streets where every door and window was shuttered by winking steel against the sleeping world? A picturesque village, the chocolate-box literature proclaims in its naïve innocence. Some roofs still thatched. An unpretentious example of good regional building. An idyllic rural backwater gathered cosily around a church housing fine Medieval carvings. But by night, the place is steel-shuttered against inner-city thieves stored twenty minutes away down the M10! It has to live with one eye glowering forever over its shoulder, watching for those who want to creep up and knife it in the back!

And do you know that great pains have been taken to blend the casings containing the shutters, when they are rolled up above the knobbly façades, so as not to spoil the ambience of the rural daylight scene? And can you believe, my love, that there is a little engraved plaque on each of the shutters declaring that they were 'specially manufactured in China' for a company called Heritage Security Systems (1997) Ltd?

How *can* you avoid thinking about the economic forces influencing our lives, when you are brought up against such grotesque sentimental madness?

The magic of exchange rates, the workings of global economics enabling some clever importer to undercut the productive spirit of his countrymen from behind his perimeter defence wall. Dickens's *Hard Times* slums remodelled in concrete and barbed-wire, barefooted waifs replaced by hitech delinquents blasting one another dead with shotguns. The clever importer then has the audacity to demand retribution when these barbarians threaten to undermine his lifestyle, simply because, like him, their 'human nature' drives them to seek privilege and prestige through cunning and opportunism, but on the wrong side of what a prescribed set of values deems to be the law!

The pursuit of the feudal dream has to persist, even when it fosters the corroding climate of brutality now affecting everybody's lives, as our factory workforces are finally sent to the knacker's yard, as the jettisoned barbarians build beyond the walls, as the looming of the noose stretches its shadow across the land.

To come to terms with why this is happening, Abigail, you have to step back and view contemporary history in a broad perspective. You have to appreciate that the pattern to human history is dictated by a constantly-shifting sequence of economic cycles, the most important of which began here in Manchester; here in this dirtied northwestern place so symbolic of changing Britain. You need to observe that the social pattern is in a continual state of flux, but that it is difficult to quantify because of the relative briefness of our lives in human generational terms. The direction in which the present changes are leading can be seen if one understands that a vast economic contraction is taking place, closely linked to advances in technology and the rising of the East. Look at this network of backstreets through which I am walking now, Abigail; now that I've got away from that little toddler who was seated before me on the bus, who grinned when she saw me rising to touch the bell and told me—forming the words as best she could so young—to 'go and fuck off, then'.

These stagnant inner-city warrens, these dreary suburbs and estates shoved up against the bases of the tower blocks, are the truth for about a third of the British population. When you understand why, the present economic cycle takes on a deeper historical significance. Such areas once formed the corpus of industrial cities everywhere. Despite booms and busts and poverty and world wars, they remained stable because their complex factory culture was necessary to the generation of the nation's wealth. Much of the old architecture has long since disappeared, of course, and been replaced with boxes and towers. But the basic social pattern remains the same. The people stockpiled here are essentially a product of the huge increase in population that took place when migrant workers were absorbed into the factories, onto the railways, down the mines, as the Industrial Revolution intensified onwards of nearly two centuries ago.

To get some grasp of why the urban communities endured you have to appreciate that the busy years of industrialization brought a period of relative social harmony. What all this muddle and sprawl represents historically is a period where the scale of industry enabled the democratization of wealth; spread it more evenly amongst the mass of the population. Society adopted a specific shape because the economic machinery could not function properly in any other way. As industrial democracy became more sophisticated, as the emancipation of workers gradually improved, standards of living rose for almost everybody. This did not happen because there was a benevolent desire on the part of the capitalist class to ameliorate the conditions of ordinary people. It happened because automated heavy manufacture had become part of a wealth-creating process that depended on the musclepower, and to a large extent on the *brainpower,* of an enormous body of skilled working-class artisans, and an intelligent service and managerial class. The dominance of the genuine landed aristocracy receded, and new centres of social and political power materialized. Though this social order was always fraught with difficulties, was dogged by economic disruptions, belligerent Trades Unions, and, ultimately, the collectivisation of politics during the years following the Second World War, the working classes benefitted from, indeed demanded access to, the commodities they were employed to produce. A social stability was maintained because capital had to cater for the expectations and desires of a complicated network of organized human labour.

But look what happened with the dawning of the micro-chip era, when an economic metamorphosis started that resulted in growing quantities of that labour being shaken out by industry. Future historians will look back to Britain's great industrial age and conclude that the social stability that lasted up to about 1980 was linked directly to the state of mechanical technology. As long as it remained at the level where it was crude enough to require large numbers of people to supervise its operation, the working class was of use to capital.

The present condition of the dim-lit brick-and-concrete streets through which I am passing represents the breaking down of that contract. These environments are part of the historical fallout period of Britain's first Industrial Revolution. The light that shone briefly upon the greatest period of our trading history is finally dissolving, just as the remnants of a sunset are fading from the sky above me now, ushering in a thick freezing-fog that shows the potential for rubbing out most of the satellite dishes and chimney-pots. As I scuff through sombre puddles of light thrown beneath the chipped lamps (illuminated plastic casings at the top wrapped in metal gauze, to hold back the raining stones), though the fog is suffusing everything with an uneasy silence, it is possible to perceive that a semblance of community life still goes on here, albeit one that is bumping along the bottom of despair. There are still laughing television sets behind closed curtains here, still the happy sounds of children splashing in bath-rooms there. Now there are a few ambling figures snatching at a bit of conversation by a burnt-out car across the street. Now there are clinking glasses and the rhythmic bump of music, my nostrils and ears playing with the smell of hops and the sound of desultory chatter, trickling through the openings leading to and from a pub.

But as our heavy industrial cycle expiates itself, physical science has advanced to the stage where it can replace the people housed behind these shabby façades, on a grand enough scale to cause a haemorrhaging of their prospects and living standards. Capital was never happy with the consensus politics and welfare ideals that developed during the years following 1945, because they threatened to spread too democratically the wealth that was produced by industry, just as they became preoccupied with its distribution instead of with its generation. So as the traditional factory culture has been eroded, the economy has reordered itself around the exchange of knowledge and information, of dealings in land-based and financial-orientated commodities, all much less dependant on a large, potentially troublesome workforce.

These neglected inner-city areas are a result of that process; of what is happening as our manual production lines are slowly transferred to the East. The big walls, the alarms, the shutters, the padlocks, the metal cages, the mental cages, the big computerized gates—these are the building-blocks of the confrontational atmosphere that will underpin the flavour of post-industrial life. This is the dawning of a new era in the way Britain's money works. You are quite right, Abigail, when you say that wealth is starting to be concentrated in fewer hands again, and that this will have the potential to influence the literacy of a growing chunk of the population. The piles of unemployed here are subsidising the new capitalist elites of the East, who in turn are overseeing an economic machine now being exploited by the capitalist elites of the West. We are reverting to a quasi pre-industrial social structure; discovering again the brutal state of nature that was one of the defining characteristics of Medieval life. Look at the security systems guarding our properties. I've forgotten the number of burglar-alarms I've seen winking red against the darkness now, because I've started to notice that the Housing Associations are copying the shops and my quaint village, covering glazed apertures with steel-shutters and cages instead. I pass a butcher's shop shutting up for the day, the armour-plating rattling noisily into position. I pass an off-licence and hear laughter exchanged between smiling faces through the opening steel-reinforced uPVC door, but from either side of a gauze Frank-Wardle-metal-screen. Occasionally my feet kick aside a tinkling nest of spent bullet cartridges, or a cluster of hypodermic syringes. I glance along a cobbled alley and see several silhouetted figures lacing into another squirming victim, feet kicking, fists smashing, pockets rifled, some grunting, some savage blasts of breath, then a lump of concrete being raised above extended arms. Like a coward I hurry away, sickened by the proximity of the violence; telling myself, as I hear a dull thud and a gurgling scream, that I must be a fool to move like this through one of Britain's dangerous places.

I wonder, too, if ultimately, in their desire to keep at bay the teeming hordes of the inner cities, villages like the one in Hertfordshire where I maintain my home will erect walls and machinegun towers to protect themselves; will take on the fortified characteristics of Medieval settlements in the pursuit of the rural ideal.

The greatest social problem facing our time is what society must do with a mass of people who are now superfluous to economic requirements, but who have been reared in a culture that has conditioned them to take material desire for granted. Because we can find neither the conscience nor the capital to support them, because the Welfare State cannot take the strain, the idea behind the bringing back of the death penalty is to keep the lower orders in check. By killing off the dangerous elements, by gradually exterminating the waste, we hope to offset some of the more unpleasant side-effects prompted by our economic contraction, and the moral atmosphere of society is bracing itself as a result. That is why there are politicians amongst us who justify it as a price worth paying that millions of our people be systematically desensitized and deskilled, then complain when the same aspects of 'human nature', which they celebrate as a virtue when it suits the requirements of their political propaganda, forces blunted sensibilities to start kicking against the pricks. Some of the same politicians talk naïvely about regaining the stable moral values of the early postwar years; of getting back to the basics of the past. But the antecedents of the youngsters who now effect a crisis in national morale used to be guided via disciplines forged through being absorbed into a life of productive work! Their moral principles evolved from them developing their intelligence and nurturing practical skills! As a consequence they were bound to the wider community, not set jealously against it. They retained a sense of civic responsibility because the will of the nation respected democratic principles; was not dominated by an atmosphere of avaricious, market-led self-interest.

I cannot escape the feeling that at the root of our anger about the crimewave lies an arrogant desire to force the behavioural patterns of the underclass to conform to those of the prosperous, but not to have to make any adjustments within ourselves. We are not prepared to accept that these people have become a liability to the workings of commerce, or that inadvertently this can effect their mental development by denying them a stake in civilized society.

Whatever reasons are brought forward to justify the virtue of market forces, whatever advantages they bring to the regulation of human behaviour, they still represent a system that is based around covetous desire and orderly tyranny. The brutishness of the underclass is merely the lowest manifestation of these common denominators, once they are devoid of the veneer of gentlemanly sophistication that obscures them higher up the social pile. The backstreet thugs who kick down some of the front doors past which I am walking now, then empty homes of their wretched contents, are motivated by precisely the same economic instinct as the City gent and the clever importer setting up his cheap production line in the East. In a world where everything, but everything, has been reduced to a price, the thugs conform to a set of mental guidelines their economic system has taught them to live up to—they attempt to usurp the advantage of the next man, to ensure their own survival in the only way they know how.

Surely stable moral values will begin to reassert themselves when we have the courage to face this; when we invest in minds that ought to represent our future and do not condemn them to the lingering death of our past.

I lower myself to a yellow plastic seat in a squalid American-styled café. I peer through a caged window at vacant faces passing through the puddle of fluorescent light thrown out onto the street. I lift a polystyrene cup of tasteless hot liquid to my lips. I dissolve a couple of sugar cubes to give the liquid some taste, then ponder a slab of stale cake. I try to shift my chair but find that it is bolted with the table to the grimy floor. I look at a television set fastened with steel straps and padlocks to the wall, nattering away with the day's news above the pair of stars-and-striped teenagers handing out the slop from behind the gauze screen. I see a camera moving between steel-reinforced doors during last night's riots, past huddled infants, past innocent bystanders caught up in the death of an industrial culture. I see black faces, white faces, whimpering faces lining a grubby community hall. I see an elderly West Indian man with a kindly face and curly grey hair crying in a corner, staring at a bloody skidmark on the blue linoleum at his feet. There are cheap tables on the screen now, drab colours, long windows covered in metal gauze, cups of steaming liquid being passed between tiny hands, a framed photograph of Prince Charles snipping a piece of ribbon on a sunny day back in 1999, and everywhere blank expressions daubed against the dreary walls.

Then a black hand is cupping over the lens and shoving the camera away, there is a change of scene, and I see that a number of public demonstrations have been held across the country today, supporting the reinstatement of capital punishment. The biggest was held in Trafalgar Square, and the size of the crowd is reminiscent of those garnered by the Pope; the mood of the gathering evocative of the Nuremberg Rally.

I'm relieved, however, to hear that Martyn Lewis is making no reference to who has been killed in the car-bomb
explosion in Manchester. It is not even being said in which
part of the city it happened. I am relieved because not only
would you be devastated by the news, Abigail, you almost
certainly wouldn't go to the hotel, and that is my only hope
of contacting you at the present time. Driscoll's bastards
have put a news blackout into force because they are trying
to flush me into the open; will be monitoring phone lines
and watching Vanessa and my crew. Of course, there are
dozens of journalists and friends I could contact by phone.
They must be aware of this; they must know that they cannot monitor everybody, not even with their insidious new
technology. They'll be waiting, too, to see if I withdraw any
money from a cashpoint, so that Central Matrix can put out
a trace. I don't know who I can trust any longer, not even
within my own organization. But I want to see what happens; some instinct which I cannot define is advising that I
should stay low.

As I drain the plastic cup, my love, as I prepare to journey
to you at the hotel to face whatever I may, some words of
Yeats's come back to me that have been slipping in and out
of my consciousness all afternoon. *The ceremony of innocence is drowned,* the poet said. *The best lack all conviction
while the worst Are full of passionate intensity.*

The words are at least partly apt. With our moral infrastructure so depleted, with a social atmosphere receptive to
the idea of institutionalized murder being put back onto the
statute books, with human suffering already such a highly
profitable commodity, it occurs to me that the brief two-
hundred-year ceremony of innocence that was our industrial
prosperity is coming to an end. In its place there promises to
rear again the mighty edifice of a feudal power base, reass-
erting its influence and its bloody reactionary authority.

I step back amongst frosty pavements, pass between shuffling figures and sidling traffic, disappear into the night. In
the distance police helicopters are circling, aiming fingers of

light at the huddled rooftops and towers swirling through the fog. Only when you are out here, mingling with the 'lowest of the low', can you discern the first stirring of the Doomsday Scenario; of the complete breakdown in law and order that the police have for so long feared. Out here bullets hurt, throats are routinely cut, skulls are flattened beneath lumps of concrete down rat-infested alleyways. A human life can be worth no more than the price a stolen TV set will fetch at a car boot sale to pay for the next fix, or tomorrow's loaf of bread. Journalists are blown up if they threaten to expose the workings of institutionalized corruption, commerce, and crime.

As I drop some coins into an armour-plated receptacle at the front of another bus before another caged driver, I consider how my present film-making assignment has brought me up against the realization that much of the Western world is on the verge of decaying into a new and dangerous age.

And though I try once more to stop the tears from lancing my eyes as I slump upon another urine-smelling seat, I fail. For I have become embroiled, I have smelt the blood, I have sensed the death of my land.

# Nineteen

In spite of her good spirits when she crossed the blue marble floor of the Great Northern reception hall, just before seven that evening, Abigail was trying not to attach any significance to the fact that she hadn't spoken to Blake since she'd left his room that morning.

She'd been trying to ring him throughout the day and was surprised that he hadn't contacted her. She'd called him on his portable at lunchtime, and also several times since she'd emerged from the meeting back at Copley Hall, shortly before five. But on each occasion a computerized voice had come onto the line suggesting that the number she was dialling was out of range or the phone was switched off. He hadn't answered, either, when she'd telephoned his room at the Great Northern, before she drove into Manchester. As she stepped up to the lifts, she sought solace in the knowledge that he'd said that if he couldn't phone after he'd been out to the forensic institute that morning—or if he got delayed interviewing the criminologist at the university in the afternoon—she hadn't to worry. He would see her at his hotel room at about seven that evening, as arranged.

While she was watching the computerized floor counter demolish the numbers, and a couple of lifts descended to meet her, she was thinking how she'd always found something reassuring about such solid English hotels as the Great Northern in Manchester, how they were as much a part of the flavour of this country as the full English breakfasts she never ate when she stayed in them, when the concierge appeared alongside her and took her by the arm.

'Excuse me madam,' he said, 'but would you mind stepping across to the reception counter for a moment, please? The manager would like a word with you.'

The young man was smaller than she was, and his shoulders were definitely narrower than her own; but the strength with which he gripped her arm emphasised the urgency of his request. Immediately she went cold and a premonitory feeling that unpleasant news awaited ran through her, as she came up to the big mahogany counter.

The manager showed a dazzling crescent of neat teeth that worked with the whiteness of his shirt to emphasise the starched subservience of his personality. 'Sorry to trouble you, madam, but could I enquire as to the nature of your business here this evening?'

Abigail frowned but remained casual, noticing that tiny beads of oil were standing out on the orange-peel surface of the man's bulbous little nose. She wondered how it was that, like Blake, she had the ability to make an instant assessment of someone's emotional credibility; was forever awarding them marks on a mental scale of one-to-ten. 'I'm here to see an acquaintance of mine,' she said. Her husky voice sounded intellectually refined in the face of this greasy little man, who, like many men she encountered, was being subservient not because it was part of his professional composure, but because his masculinity felt undermined in the presence of a beautiful, assertive woman.

'And might I enquire as to the acquaintance's name?'

Abigail's frown deepened, not because of her irritation at having been waylaid, or because nobody had so much as batted an eyelid when she'd stood at the same reception counter the previous evening and asked for Blake's room number. Her facial muscles were distorting because she knew that something was wrong.

'His name is Blake Hunter. Room three-hundred-and-twenty-two.'

The manager's shrew-like eyes scanned a computer screen behind the counter. 'Ah yes, of course,' he said. 'Blake Hunter, the BBC journalist.'

'Is anything the matter?' Abigail asked.

The manager ignored the question. 'Could I see your identity card please?'

She took the card from her handbag and snapped it face down onto the counter. The manager's manicured fingers fastened onto it and slotted it into the computer. While he scrutinized the screen a flickering blue glow was thrown across the white teeth and shirt, as he scrolled through the information contained on the barcode.

When he'd finished, he handed back the card and broadened his subservient smile. 'I am very sorry to have inconvenienced you, Mrs Sanders. There have been a number of unauthorized entries here recently, and the concierge saw that you were not a resident guest. You will appreciate that the democratic atmosphere of a hotel makes it easy for almost anybody to walk in unobserved from the street.'

Abigail replaced the card and relaxed, the sense of relief cancelling the observation that was forming about how acutely perceptive the concierge must have been, to notice her amongst the steady flow of coated figures passing to and from the dining rooms.

'Have you seen Mr Hunter this evening?' she added nonchalantly, hooking her handbag back onto her shoulder and watching the eyes of the manager and the concierge very closely.

'Yes,' the manager said. 'He went up to his room only a few minutes ago.'

The feeling of relief that had come over her blended to one born of a contented, even an excited, thrill of anticipation.

When she knocked at Blake's door she felt vulnerable standing alone in the muffled silence of the corridor. There was an altogether different atmosphere pervading the space than when she'd stood in the same position on the same thick blue carpet a little under twenty-four hours ago. The sense of unease that had surfaced when she'd accompanied the concierge up to the reception counter downstairs came back again, as her eyes traced a tiny imperfection on the pale-green acrylic skin that coloured the Victorian-styled uPVC door.

She was preparing to inform Blake that she'd told her superiors she'd made contact with him, and that they'd agreed he was an essential candidate to be drawn into the group, when she realized an uncomfortable length of time had passed since her knuckles had first abraded the plastic, and nothing had happened. Nervously she ran her fingers through her hair, knocked again, and looked once up and down the empty corridor. Still there was no response. It was foolish to expect the door to be unlocked, of course, bearing in mind that it was operated by an electronic keycard; but her hand was reaching out towards the brass handle nevertheless. To her astonishment the door cricked open, but this only had the effect of heightening her growing feeling of unease. Through the gap she could see a wedge of light sloping from the bathroom into the bedroom and immediately she felt relieved. Then the door was being yanked open and she was being dragged through it at a terrific speed, the wedge of light sloping from the bathroom was going out, the door was closing behind her and shutting out the light from the corridor, she was pinned with her back against the wall amongst darkness, she was noticing a glow flickering across the ceiling, she was inhaling the bacon-like aroma of male sweat and the faecal-like stench of bad breath, and she was struggling against a thick forearm that was wedged across her throat.

'All right Colin, let her go,' a familiar voice said tiresomely from out of the darkness. A lamp came on and Abigail was horrified to see that it was Detective Superintendent Stoneham who was pinning her to the wall, and Chief Constable Driscoll was stepping out of the shadows behind

him, wearing a shiny deep-emerald coloured suit with metallic lapels that were shimmering in the light. 'You must
excuse Detective Superintendent Stoneham, Mrs Sanders.
The lower orders are always more physical in the way they
express themselves, and Colin here really does not have
much experience of handling the fairer sex, poor lad.'

'Not funny, Derek,' Stoneham snapped, releasing Abigail
and pulling out his packet of Marlboro King Size. 'You
know damned well I'd no intention of hurting her.'

Abigail stayed with her back against the wall, confused as
much by the tension between the two men as by the speed
with which everything had just happened. Then her eyes
went to the wall opposite the bathroom door and identified
the source of the flickering glow. There was a man wearing
cordless headphones who she'd never seen before, standing
in front of four colour video monitors lined up on top of the
chest-of-drawers. The first camera showed a shot of the
pavement in front of the hotel, headlights and a tram strea-
king through a corner of the frame. The second was looking
down across the reception hall. The third was very wide-
angled, almost fish-eye, watching from the ceiling down
onto the lobby in front of the lifts. The fourth camera was
obviously embedded somewhere in the plaster frieze just
outside Blake's room. Her eyes came away from the monitors when somebody else she didn't recognize came out of
the bathroom carrying a gun and lit a cigarette. Though she
couldn't know it, it was Addison, the man who had run
down the centre of the road shouting, just before Blake's car
had been blown up that morning.

'What have you done to Blake Hunter?' she asked the
room. Her heartbeat had begun to speed up and her mind
to race while she grappled with the conundrum of why these
people who she had herself been observing for weeks on end
were now in Blake's room observing her, bringing an air of
menace into what had been such a shared, private space.

'We were hoping *you* might be able to inform us of his
whereabouts, young lady,' Driscoll said. He stepped up to

her, his hands knitted characteristically together behind his back. Abigail sensed by the inquiring nature of his stare that he found her attractive. Her eyes left his and went back to the videoscreens. Figures were descending the steps outside the hotel entrance, but for a few seconds the reception hall seemed to be devoid of anybody at all, which had the curious effect of emphasising her feeling of vulnerability.

'Ah yes,' Driscoll said with an air of affected superiority, scrutinizing her even closer. He was mildly irritated by the fact that she was a little taller than he was. 'I knew that I recognized you. You're the woman who Hunter accosted in the corridor at Central Police Headquarters after the news conference the other day, aren't you?'

'What on earth's going on here, Chief Constable?' she asked calmly. If her tone gave an indication that she knew Driscoll was anything other than simply the head of Greater Manchester Police, she knew she would be in trouble. Her best hope of retaining her impartiality was to sound like a surprised member of the public who'd accidentally stumbled onto something she shouldn't.

Driscoll ignored her question and Stoneham lit a cigarette and blew the smoke across to join the cloud surrounding Addison's head. Abigail was disgusted at the stink. It had brutally despoiled what last night and first thing that morning had been such a clean, beautiful room.

'What relationship do you have to Blake Hunter, Mrs Sanders?' Driscoll asked.

'Professional acquaintance,' she said without hesitation.

'Really?'

He ripped open the velcro fastening her green leather coat down the left-hand side. Underneath she was wearing what appeared to be a very baggy russet-coloured pullover. It was not a pullover but a woolsilk dress. Though it had hung generously when she'd pulled it on after she'd showered at Copley Hall, the brown leather sash tied around her waist had the effect of causing the hem to ride up a good six inches above the knee. Driscoll's eyes went down her front, down the slender lycra-glittering legs, stopped at the pair of chocolate-brown Cuban-heeled suede court shoes at the bottom, then came back up to her face. 'And do professional acquaintances normally expose themselves so tantalizingly, when they arrive to discuss mere business matters? You'd no intention of being seen in public in that outfit, Mrs Sanders, had you? You're much too sophisticated.'

Abigail remained silent, unnerved by Driscoll's perceptiveness. He came close, and she felt his fingers touch her thigh, probing without looking down. She smelt his hideous hot breath, a compound stench somewhere between faeces and vomit. 'Stockings and suspenders, too,' he said, feeling the bumps of the studs. Then his hand moved across and she ground her teeth together and squirmed as he briefly lifted her dress. 'Hmm. You're not exactly covered up under here, either, are you?'

'Take your filthy hands off me,' she snarled, feeling dirty and exposed and struggling not to thump him in the stomach. She heard Addison titter in the background.

Driscoll took his hand away and smiled. 'I'm not going to hit you, Mrs Sanders. I'm not even going to snatch you roughly by the chin and bang your pretty head against the wall. But don't ever adopt that tone when you speak to me again. My hands are *never* filthy.'

Abigail was convinced she was in the presence of lunatics when she heard this and Driscoll stepped away from her and took a small foil sachet from a bowl on the coffee-table. It was a scented fingerwipe. He tore it open, then turned up his nose while he cleaned the hand that had been under her skirt, despite the fact that he'd only lightly brushed her pubic hair.

'That costume you are wearing is for bedroom use only,' he continued, flicking the whites of his eyes in her direction, folding the wipe into a square, and slipping it into his pocket. 'You've come here this evening for love, for sex, to go to bed with your man. Which means that a relationship of a rather more intimate nature has been established between yourself and Blake Hunter, since you had your little confrontation the other day.' He straightened. 'So where is he, Mrs Sanders? Your co-operation is likely to prove much less injurious to your continued good health.'

'Stop being so bloody illogical,' Abigail said. 'I don't know where the hell he is. Do you think I would have come on my own like this if I'd known he wasn't here?'

'You might have been coming to collect something on his behalf.' He picked up Blake's attaché case and emptied the contents noisily onto the floor. Abigail saw a colour photograph of two smiling little girls slide down the pyramid of papers and pens. Both of the faces had got Blake's eyes, and she felt her throat stiffen at the realization.

'How would I have got into the room?' she said. 'I haven't got his keycard, for God's sake. Here, look through my bag, search my pockets.'

Driscoll's eyes narrowed but ignored the handbag held out to him. 'No, you haven't got his keycard because we have. All the same, something isn't right here. Who are you, Mrs Sanders? What is your business? You have been present at several important news conferences recently, but you're no journalist.'

Abigail let out some breath to back up her nonpartisan demeanour, which now had to sound utterly convincing. 'No, I'm not a journalist, I'm a writer. Contrary to popular belief there is a difference, Mr Driscoll.'

'Indeed. So what are you writing about?'

'I'm writing a series about important real-life murder mysteries for an American magazine agency.'

Driscoll's eyebrows assumed a pattern that was suggestive of a question mark. 'Your identity card please.' He held out his hand, and for the second time in ten minutes Abigail took the piece of styrene from her handbag and passed it across.

Driscoll nodded at Stoneham and the two of them went to a laptop computer which was standing next to the video-screens on top of the drawers. Driscoll slotted the card into the machine, played with the keys, scrolled through the information, and read some basic biographical facts aloud, such as Abigail's date of birth, her height being five-feet seven inches, and so forth. He muttered most of the other things as a kind of tune to himself under his breath, which seemed to emphasise his devious intelligence. When he got to her artificial qualifications in History and Politics, and all the rest of the false information pertaining to her literary front, when he asked the computer to fill in the history of the American magazine agency, her heart was in her mouth. After a few moments he frowned, lifted his cellular phone to his ear, and asked somebody at police headquarters to use the station's computer link to Central Matrix to check the legitimacy of her American employers.

After another few moments the phone trilled, Driscoll answered, and it was confirmed that Abigail's identity seemed to be authentic. 'Has the other thing happened yet?' he asked, before he put down the phone. There was a brief pause and he muttered something in the affirmative, suggesting that the voice at the other end had said that it hadn't happened yet. 'Only five minutes?' Driscoll said, still not letting go. 'Excellent.' Then he cancelled the phone, removed the identity card, and handed it back. Abigail inwardly sighed. The false identity had worked at the one time it was likely to be needed more than any other.

Addison had come across to the computer and lowered his voice next to Driscoll. 'Sod her bloody ID, Derek. She's bullshitting. I've seen her type before. She's tough as old boots. I say we thump it out of her, or jab her with a needle. Get it out of her that way.'

'There's no need for truth drugs or violence at this stage. Look at her. She's a strong woman and she's in control of herself, but she's frightened. And she's frightened because she's on her own and she didn't expect to be on her own when she got here tonight. She knows nothing.'

'I'm still not convinced,' Addison said, sucking the life from his cigarette and reaching to stub it in an ashtray.

Outside, a babble of remote police sirens screamed through the city.

'Violence is your answer to everything, isn't it?' Driscoll said disapprovingly, still keeping his voice low. 'But there is another way.' He stepped across to Abigail and spoke up. 'Mrs Sanders, what would you say if I were to tell you that Blake Hunter is dead?'

Abigail drew in her breath sharply but remained composed.

'You don't believe me, do you?' Driscoll added.

'No I don't. Otherwise why would you be so anxious to know if I could tell you where he was? And why all this surveillance equipment? Your desire to ascertain Blake's whereabouts looks pretty authentic to me.'

'Very good, Mrs Sanders, that's very good indeed. But, you see, we might not actually be here to apprehend Blake Hunter. This set-up might be part of something far more elaborate than discovering the whereabouts of a humble TV journalist.' He looked at his watch while Abigail's eyebrows came together and he remembered that the remains of Blake's portable phone and his Newton had been found in the wreckage of the car, late in the afternoon. 'Let me suggest, young lady, that you have been trying to telephone Blake Hunter, but have been unable to make contact with him all day. Am I correct?'

Abigail's silence indicated that he was.

'In that case, let me show you something.'

He went across to the mahogany TV cabinet, opened the doors, picked up the remote-control, and brought the screen to life. Jon Snow was talking to camera from the studios of *Channel 4 News*. Driscoll looked at Abigail, who was now frowning confusedly. 'Come here,' he said, folding his arms. She came away from the wall and stepped up to the TV, her body silhouetted before the glare and flicker of the screen. 'By one of those remarkable coincidences that generally constitute the roulette-wheel of chance called human history, I'm going to reveal to you the sincerity of my words, Abigail

Sanders. And also the terrible helplessness of the predicament in which you now find yourself.'

They all stared at the screen and watched the last few minutes of a news report indicate that another trade disagreement was brewing between Britain and the Economic Alliance of Asiatic Nations; now that a couple of those nations were intending to manufacture some of the high-tech products they had agreed to buy exclusively from Britain, after Britain had shut down much of its own basic industry and depended for many of its low-tech components on them. Now the prices of those products were steadily rising as the wages and standards of living of Far Eastern workers rose; just as expectations rose for British workers throughout the late-nineteenth and the first half of the twentieth century, when the goods they produced were exported to hungry markets, and Britain shone bright upon the economic centre stage of the world.

The result of the latest disagreement between East and West, so a left-wing economic commentator said who appeared on the screen, would be that, in however ineffectual a way, the trade balance was going to plunge further into the red and living standards were going to deteriorate even more. He then referred to an article recently published in *New Socialist Today*. It claimed that the social unrest which the economic decline of the West was beginning to engender would, in conjunction with the rising of the economic giant of the East, lead ultimately to only one thing, and that was war. He finished by saying that some of Britain's leading City institutions, which that evening were uneasy about the stability of the pound, had built up their immense assets from the pension fund contributions paid to them over the years by millions of British industrial workers, as their own jobs were steadily eroded. What a cruel stroke of fate, he said, that some of these institutions had assisted in the death of our own industrial base at the same time as they had invested some of their industrial workers' funds in, for instance, Chinese manufacturing.

Then there was a piece linked to the same story about a former industrial city in the north of England. Some of the automotive components that had sparked off the trade row used to be manufactured in a suburb which that afternoon had been officially designated as the first high-risk AIDS area that the local constabulary were refusing to police any longer. They'd abandoned it because of the number of gang rapes being committed by groups of roaming feral youth against male officers. Two young policemen had been murdered on one of the city's old abandoned council estates only the previous evening. The two carcasses had been subjected to an orgy of brutal sodomy, the young manimals fighting amongst themselves like a pack of wild dogs gathered round a bitch on heat, in the frantic squabble to take their turn. Then the naked bodies had been tied to a stolen car and dragged at high speed through the centre of the city, finally to be dumped outside police headquarters, doused in petrol, and set on fire.

This latter item of information brought a barrage of foul-mouthed expletives from all the men present in the room, but confused Abigail even more as she wondered what on earth Driscoll was getting at and the blood started pounding in her throat. The news reporter said that, because of the murders, more national outrage was brewing, the hangman's noose was being dangled ever lower in cartoons above the Home Secretary's desk, and the government was still denying there was a connection between such barbarous behaviour and the systematic desensitizing of substantial chunks of the British urban population, as they were jettisoned from mainstream economic life, were thrown on the social scrapheap, and left to fend for themselves.

The report finished, then Jon Snow suddenly touched his earpiece and said they could now go back to the car-bomb explosion in Manchester, which they'd announced at the beginning of the programme. He informed viewers that since they'd gone on air, the Greater Manchester Police had released the identity of the single male victim, and the location of the attack as being at Prestwich. Though the body had yet to be formally identified, it was believed to be that of a BBC television journalist, Blake Hunter, who had been working on assignment in the city making a documentary for the new *Crime in Britain* series.

Driscoll smiled to himself as he wondered whether or not the information released to the media would smoke Blake out, or whether he might even be watching it.

As for Abigail, though she uttered an agonized sound somewhere between a gasp and a groan while the pictures on the screen played minutely across her lovely eyes, it would be something of an understatement to say that she was shocked to her very foundations by what she'd just heard. As the dreadful realization that Blake must be dead began to sink home, she felt her legs buckle and she actually swayed. She blinked rapidly and the tears spilt down her face, taking two black channels of mascara with them, and throwing the images before her into a kaleidoscopic frenzy of multicoloured lines shooting away in all directions. A nauseous pain was searching amongst her guts for a place to settle, her head shook slowly from side to side, and silently her mouth began pleading for clemency both to God and to the fates. Driscoll's observation about the roulette-wheel of chance and the fates had been clever. All day long she'd been in a meeting and hadn't seen the news. If any of her colleagues had been monitoring the day's events, they wouldn't have made the connection between the car bomb and Blake, because Jon Snow had implied that the police had kept the location of the explosion strictly *sub rosa* until now anyway. And bombs of one kind or another were going off in cities like this all the time.

Driscoll saw what was happening and looked across to Stoneham. 'Give Mrs Sanders a chair, Colin,' he said.

Stoneham dragged across an armchair and pushed it behind Abigail. She felt it touch the back of her knees and her reflexes obeyed and lowered her body to the upholstery. Her breath was coming in sharp gasps now, and a buzzing had started in her ears, but she remained remarkably composed. She saw a jerky telephoto image of a smouldering lump of metal, still recognizable as the remains of a red Ford Mondeo, filling the television screen, seen along a leaf-encrusted avenue and surrounded by the men in white suits. A colour photograph of Blake flashed up then was replaced by his head and shoulders speaking to camera, astonishingly clear because of the high-resolution screen. He was interspersed with archive footage showing Baroness Thatcher getting into a car and being bombarded by photo-flashes. Blake looked younger, thinner, and a voice was informing viewers that this was the first major incident Blake Hunter had reported for the BBC, as a young political journalist working in the provinces—that of Margaret Thatcher's resignation, for Manchester's very own *Northwest Tonight.*

Abigail lowered her head, her hair tumbling across her knees, more strands joining the rest with each successive heave as she grieved with immense dignity; with positively no sound except the quivering of breath in her throat. Then the news report was suddenly replaced by a set of jeering commercials. Driscoll stabbed at a bit of rubber button on the remote-control and sent the screen to oblivion. He stepped across to Abigail and took hold of her chin and lifted her face. Her eyes were riddled with tears and smudged with mascara.

'And those tears look pretty authentic to me, young lady,' he said, deliberately echoing her response to one of his earlier remarks. 'So you'll be pleased to hear that I believe you when you say that you have no idea of the whereabouts of Blake Hunter, seeing as all that remains of him are a few burnt scraps of meat arranged on a slab at the police mortuary.'

He watched her closely when he said this.

Abigail shook her head free and reached for her handbag. Instantly Addison snatched it from her, the harsh angularity of his features being brought out for a moment as he passed through the glow of the lamp.

'There's no need to be quite so jumpy,' Driscoll said to him. A helijet whined its descent onto Piccadilly in the background as the words came from his mouth. 'What did you want from your bag, Mrs Sanders?'

Abigail spoke slowly, her voice bulging with irritation. 'A handkerchief, please. I would like to wipe my eyes.'

'I admire your sense of composure, and your dignity,' Driscoll said, passing her the bag. 'Women of your professional calibre do not reach the positions that they do through being the kind of people who become gibbering emotional wrecks the moment some terrible personal catastrophe strikes them. That's something the soap operas and the films always get very wrong.' He walked back over to the computer and looked sharply at Addison on the way. 'You see how violence is not always the answer? One merely has to know how to appeal to a woman's softer instincts.'

Stoneham came alongside Driscoll again and lowered the tune of his voice. 'What are we going to do with her?'

Driscoll's voice assumed a similar frequency. 'We'll do what we said we would when we saw her coming up to Hunter's room.'

'But that involves violence, Derek,' Stoneham said, suppressing the sarcasm he was desperate to release.

'Then I refute my previous observations about the subject. If you recollect, I expressed the belief that violence was not necessary *at that stage*.' He smirked. 'Get it over with and let's get out of here.'

'Do I have to do it?'

'Yes, you do.'

With his back to Abigail and his face strangely puckered, Stoneham took a pistol from inside his coat, screwed on a short chrome silencer, then slid a cartridge into the handle. Keeping the pistol behind his back, he stepped into the centre of the room. Addison and the man in front of the videoscreens looked at one another sombrously. 'Would you please stand up, Abigail,' Stoneham said a little thickly. 'We have to leave now.'

Abigail felt oddly reassured by the way Stoneham used her Christian name. She blew her nose in that exquisitely quiet, unrepulsive manner that women have, crumpled the tissue into a ball, and pushed it up her sleeve. Then she stood up.

Driscoll stepped up to her.

'You were going to fall in love with Blake Hunter, weren't you?' He scrutinized her for a moment. 'In which case, I feel there is perhaps one final point that should be made.' Abigail looked at him: she didn't like the conclusive tone of Driscoll's words. 'If it's any consolation,' he went on, 'Blake Hunter *isn't* really dead. I had to find out whether or not you were telling the truth when you said you didn't know where he was.' He saw her brow knitting together as her mind ran through the information it had just absorbed from the TV. 'The news report was bogus, of course. It is being used to try and smoke him out. I am sorry that you have got mixed up in all of this, and for what we are about to do to you.'

Before Abigail could evaluate the words any further, she saw Driscoll nod once at Stoneham, she saw the silencer come out from behind Stoneham's back, she heard a muffled explosion, she felt her belly tear apart with a terrible impact that seemed to travel right through her and out the other side, and she felt a tremendous expanding numbness, almost sexual in its potency. She felt her legs and body crumple, felt the great numbness take over and the floor come up fast and slam against the back of her skull. She whimpered for a few moments and panicked, tried frantically to lift to her elbows; but her strength had instantly drained and she banged back down, her beautiful face contorting into a hideous pleading grimace. She saw Stoneham towering away into perspective, putting the pistol back into his overcoat pocket. She saw bluish-yellow reflections from the huge electronic billboard, fastened to the front of a tower block across from the hotel, flicking on and off against the gold light-fitting sprouting from the ceiling.

Then everything was swirling, and she was observing,

with a curious sense of detached objectivity as the blackness started to take hold, that suddenly nothing mattered. As her head fell against the carpet for the final time and those magnificent pupils stared lifeless and still, as a couple of tears ran away down either side of her face and Driscoll asked Stoneham to please bend down and close the lady's eyes, nothing mattered to Abigail Sanders any more.

Not even the knowledge that she was dead.

# PART TWO

*A Man for Hanging*

# *Twenty*

At the precise moment that Stoneham bent to close Abigail's
eyes, three floors beneath Blake's hotel room a naked Vanessa Aysgarth was opening a packet of Aristoc flesh-colour-
ed five denier tights, then was sitting on the edge of her bed
and carefully rolling them on.

After she'd recovered from the set-to with Max on the
telephone, she'd gone down to Sarah's room and they'd
apologized to each other profusely. It turned out that Sarah
had been under some stress herself, because she'd recently
learnt that her father, to whom she'd always been very close,
was seriously ill. She was so ashamed and embarrassed at
what had happened earlier that she'd feared she'd never be
able to face Vanessa again, and had more or less said farewell to her job. Vanessa told her not to talk such nonsense
and said that the incident was forgotten. They'd hugged and
made things up, and Vanessa had sensed that they would
probably be closer to each other now than they had been
before. If anything, she was grateful for what Sarah had
done, because the incident seemed to have had the effect of
releasing a tension in her. Things had a way of coming to a
head in the strangest and most obtuse of ways, and over the
intervening couple of hours she'd felt glad to be alive in a
way that she hadn't done for a very long time.

Because Blake seemed to have disappeared again and she
didn't want to spend the evening alone, she was getting
ready to go out for dinner with Sarah and cameraman Chris,

then on to a nightclub which the criminologist had recommended in the Chinese quarter of the city. Though she was still trying to suppress a feeling of unease that had been building ever since Blake had left the production meeting that morning, though she was trying not to think it unusual that his portable phone should have been switched off all day and it being some ten hours since they'd last spoken, the fact that he'd missed another afternoon's filming hadn't surprised her in the least. If she were concerned but not yet worried that he still hadn't contacted her, then that was because she was taking it for granted that he was with the beautiful dark-haired woman they'd seen in the underground car park the other morning. She was happy for him if he was with the woman because she wanted only to see him happy again, and for him to carry on being her most important friend on earth. But his failure to have phoned and apologized for his absence that afternoon was out of character to the point of being irresponsible.

As it happened, Vanessa was still isolated telecommunicationally herself. Since she'd smashed her cellular telephone, she'd plugged the phone at the side of her bed back in but had diverted it to her Newton memorizer when she'd gone into the shower some twenty minutes earlier. If Blake had tried to contact her, or if anyone had recently knocked at her door, she wouldn't have known. The consequence of this was that she had no idea that Blake's death had been announced on television shortly after she'd entered her bathroom, or that several people were trying to get through to her from BBC studios in Manchester and London, to see if she'd heard the dreadful news. She'd already glanced at the Newton's screen and scrolled through the list of numbers when she'd emerged from the shower. But because she'd recognized them and assumed the calls would be in connection with the making of the film, she'd decided to ignore them until after she'd got dressed.

Laid out on the bed next to her were some new clothes that she'd bought the previous morning, after she'd dropped

Blake off at the news conference and had gone on to do some shopping at the prestigious International Clothesdome, at Irlam on the outskirts of Manchester. The clothes were Italian made and designed, had been manufactured in identical colours of powder-blue, and were the most expensive that she'd ever possessed. There was a short leather skirt, a matching thigh-length leather jacket with a mandarin neck, cut rather in the style of a guardsman's tunic, a pair of leather Cuban-heeled bootees, and a polo-neck woolsilk sweater, glittering with silver lycra. Because the tone of her rather sallow skin leaned towards pink, and because her platinum-blonde mane was so fair as to be considered by some to be a pearliest white, she had to be careful about the colours that she chose to wear, and powder-blue was her favourite. She'd never needed the help of an image consultant to arrive at this conclusion, or to assist her in the co-ordination of her wardrobe, spartan though it was. Because she was an art school graduate—a degree in Fine Art Photography and Painting at Leeds Polytechnic, followed by a masters in Film and TV Production at the Royal College of Art—colour matching for her was more a question of second nature than a need to consult charts and graphs.

When she'd pulled on the pair of tights she tested the sheerness of the nylon with her fingers and raised her eyebrows in surprise. This was the first time she'd dressed like this in years, for she'd lived almost permanently in trousers since she was a student and rarely wore make-up. She felt strangely apprehensive, almost anxious, when she turned to examine the suit of garments laid on the bed. She ran her long fingers across the leather tunic, examined the closely-spaced blue glass buttons—rare in these days of velcro-this and velcro-that, but only serving to emphasise the jacket's air of expensive sophistication—and sighed. If it was out of character for her to have spent a morning indulging in her own vanity and to have bought such clothes, then she reassured herself with the understanding that the incident with Sarah needed to happen to clear the air and give her the courage to actually put them on, while the thought of how provocatively female she was going to look this evening only added to her growing feeling of revitalization.

To take her mind off herself, she opened the doors of the TV cabinet, aimed the remote-control handset, and brought the screen to life. A location report from Trafalgar Square, scene of the day's big public demonstration in favour of capital punishment, and part of the vigorous campaign being mounted by the Tory Right, was in the process of finishing as *Channel 4 News* drew to a close. She heard the commentator observe that the depth of concern felt nationally about the crimewave could be seen by the fact that the middle classes were becoming agitated and had been driven to make their voices heard on the streets. He referred to a similar expression of public outrage following the Pit Closure programme of the early Nineties (as Vanessa well remembered, from when she'd still been a young assistant producer of Current Affairs), but he wondered whether or not the moral atmosphere of society had substantially altered since then.

Then Jon Snow's face was filling the screen, his facial muscles were shaping his penultimate smile of the programme, and Vanessa was wondering if it was a figment of her imagination to think there was a similarity between the appearance of the newscaster's and Blake's rather sad-looking, but beautiful deep-blue eyes. Just as she was thinking how there seemed to be no escape from the confusion that had been creeping up on her these past few weeks, Jon Snow completed his smile and started running through the day's headlines, beginning with the Anglo-Asiatic trade row. When he came to repeat the details about the car-bomb killing in Manchester, however—and for no reason she would afterwards be able to explain—Vanessa picked up the remote-control handset again and switched to a cable channel before he'd started speaking.

There appeared a documentary concerning itself with the boom in home security services, as the siege outlook tightened its grip on the flavour of post-industrial British life. The film was being presented by a well-known middle-aged, middle-class male novelist who'd been travelling the country in a shiny blue suit, looking at how architectural and industrial design styles were being influenced by the need to keep the criminal underclass at bay.

He'd paused at a modern residential housing estate on the outskirts of Bracknell in Berkshire. Though the majority of people living on such estates now paid a monthly subscription to have their streets patrolled by private security firms, during the past couple of years an increasing number of developments were having fifteen-feet-high perimeter defence walls erected around them as they were built. What was unique about the estate at Bracknell was that it was the first such scheme in Britain where the wall had won an award for its design. There were shots of the buff-coloured wall when it was being built some twelve months previously; the developers having taken the trouble to record the construction with the aid of a video camera. The architect had utilized most effectively a quantity of glazed bricks and setts normally reserved for ground paving, applying them to the vertical surfaces instead. Bands of bright-blue and red ran down to the ground, formed borders along the paths running between the neat little Modernist Revival houses, then snaked out into the turning circles and crescents. There they formed stylish geometric patterns in the road, so that the defence wall seemed to work organically with the flow of the houses, and complemented the green plastic pantiles with which they were roofed.

A handful of residents were interviewed, intercut with shots of scurrying children, lolloping pet dogs, and a cat meditating on a bright-yellow uPVC windowsill. The residents were asked what they thought about the wall. Those whose homes were nearest to it seemed more interested in explaining that they didn't mind not having a view, and thought it a small price to pay for the increased feeling of security. The novelist looked noticeably uncomfortable within the confines of his own generous covering of skin, never mind his shiny deep-blue suit, when one of the residents suddenly made the penetrating observation that she thought that the bringing back of capital punishment wouldn't make much difference to the way ordinary people conducted their lives, but would probably make incidents of criminal violence more extreme than they already were. Once the State made the decision to take its gloves off in the relentless battle against crime, rather than getting to the root causes of it, because of the much-talked-about 'ratchet-effect' the criminal fraternity was likely to do the same. She believed that society would become more divided and dangerous than it already was.

The item about the Bracknell estate took some ten minutes to complete. During that time Vanessa finished applying her make-up and mascara, then deodorized her body and hooked a pale-blue silk brassière over her large, beautifully proportioned breasts. She paused for a moment when she realized that she hadn't put on her pants. She walked across to the bed, picked up a pair of silk briefs that matched the brassière, looked at them rather solemnly, then suddenly scrunched them between her fingers, as though she were fighting her emotions to the point of becoming distressed. She gritted her teeth, closed her eyes, took in a big gust of breath and let it slowly back out, quickly regained her composure, opened her eyes, let the pants slip over her distended forefinger, twirled them around a few times, then let them fly away into the shadows in a corner of the room. At the same time she ripped off the brassière, so that her breasts sprang free again. She lifted the blue skirt, which was simply a rectangle of leather that wrapped around the hips and velcro'd together down the right-hand side. She held it up, enclosed it around herself buttocks-first, and smoothed her hands down the seam to the hem, which finished exactly eight inches above the knee. She pulled on the sweater, which hugged her body like a second skin in its emphasis of those magnificent breasts, looked exhausted for a moment, picked up a gold brush from the dressing-table, went across to the cheval mirror, hung her head upside down, then began vigorously brushing her hair, the healthy sound of static crackling all about her.

When she came upright, she flicked her hair back with a horsy jerk of the head, so that it puffed out and fell girlishly across one eye, prompting her to stand for a moment and to admire herself quite self-consciously. She looked stunningly beautiful, the fine lines around her eyes only seeming to add to her voluptuousness. She'd not so much forgotten how attractive she could look, but how thoroughly female she could look, or indeed how good a pair of legs she possessed. Whether it would do her the least bit of good to parade in public like this remained to be seen, however, and she was half-repulsed at herself for even wondering. Again, a solemn, rather sad expression clutched at her features, as though a terrible conflict were raging and she was confused and dressing-up against her will. Then she resumed her position at the dressing-table, crossed her legs and gathered up her hair, and began fastening it into a pony-tail with an ivory-coloured silk scarf streaked with a blue-and-silver pattern. Her eyes went to the reflection of the documentary still playing on the TV screen, which had now cut to the scene of a notorious vigilante killing that had occurred a couple of months previously on a council estate in Bristol. But before she could digest any words there was a knocking sounded at her door.

Hoping that it would be Blake, she was on her feet and was aiming the remote-control and cancelling the screen almost before the knocking had finished. She stepped smiling into her blue bootees, her five-feet-seven inches raised now to Blake's five-feet-nine, and, suddenly proud of how good she looked, she went over and pulled open the slab of hinged pale-green uPVC. Sarah was standing there, dressed even more scantily than Vanessa, but in black leather and shiny gold-coloured tights. Chris the cameraman was behind her, resplendent in a pale-pink American sack suit but with his face as long as a wet fortnight. Sarah's face trembled for a moment then collapsed as she flung herself into Vanessa's arms and burst into tears, asking if she'd heard the news. Chris followed her into the room frowning, his fingers touching his beard nervously as his eyes went to Vanessa's legs, as Vanessa held Sarah, as the colour drained from Vanessa's face, as Vanessa asked what the hell was the matter, but knew, in a way that she couldn't explain, precisely what she was about to hear.

# Twenty-One

Blake had misjudged how long he thought it would take to get back into Manchester city centre.

When he'd been eating inside the café he'd felt sure that he couldn't have been more than a few miles away, but the bus he'd caught outside seemed to get nowhere fast as it crawled interminably through the dreary slums and suburbs. There had been roadworks delaying the traffic, and at one point a police helicopter had interrupted the journey giving chase to a stolen vehicle, causing the contraflow to grind to a halt as the beam of a searchlight arced across the carriageway.

Then there had been an argument about a foreign coin that the computerized ticket machine spat back out when a boarding passenger dropped it into the receptacle. It was many years since loose change had been carried by buses, and passengers either had to use prepaid tickets or offer the exact fare. The young black man who'd got on claimed that the coin had been given to him in a pile of change he'd just obtained from one of the bus company's own cashpoints (hideous armour-plated installations, looking like the one-man lottery booths that stand in grubby bus stations), and his distress indicated that he'd probably been telling the truth. But the driver wouldn't hear it, and had threatened to alert his company's security police unless he got off the bus straightaway.

As a result of which Blake had finally got to New Central

Square at precisely seven o'clock. He'd wanted to be back at the Great Northern for about six-thirty, so that he had plenty of time to blend into the shadows and wait for Abigail to arrive, to try to intercept her either when she parked up, or before she got to the hotel entrance. He knew he was taking a big risk by coming here, but he hadn't any choice. When he'd walked back from the heliport a few evenings ago, he'd noticed an area that was very dark where a street-lamp had failed, across from the conference centre and about five-hundred yards from the hotel. There was a recess set into the wall of an office building, beneath a row of marble cloisters that faced obliquely onto the huge cobbled square, where he could remain unobserved, and which offered an easy escape into a sidestreet if he saw anybody approaching.

He wasn't to know, of course, that he'd arrived at the hotel less than five minutes after Abigail had gone up the main steps, and less than two minutes after she'd been apprehended at the reception counter inside. It was now a little before five-minutes-to-nine. He'd stood in the bitter cold for two hours, watching the trams and traffic amble around the square. Although at one point the fog had threatened to obscure the lights of the tower blocks piled above him, his view across to the hotel entrance had remained clear. He was also fortunate in having in his pocket his pen-telescope. From his position he'd been able to see with it through the doors straight into the reception hall and up to the counter. There had been a steady flow of people going in and out of the building, but definitely no Abigail. If she'd gone into the hotel before he'd arrived, which he couldn't help but feel was unlikely, if she'd gone to his room and found he wasn't there, she would probably have enquired at reception and been told that he was still out because his keycard hadn't been collected from the desk. There was always the possibility that she could have been waiting in the lounge while he'd been shivering outside in the cold. But an hour ago he'd made his way slowly round the square, checked all the cars that were parked, and found that her Vauxhall Frontera was definitely nowhere to be seen. (It had been parked round by the side of the hotel, but had been removed by Stoneham, along with Abigail's body through a service entrance, when Blake had still been lurking under the cloisters.) Besides all this, there were so many car spaces free that there was no reason why she shouldn't park across from the hotel. So far as he'd been able to ascertain, Abigail hadn't been anywhere near.

Feeling like a dejected mangy dog, he was on the verge of walking away, having visions of booking into some seedy backstreet lodging-house for the night until he could decide what to do next, when he saw an attractive blonde-haired woman descend the steps of the hotel. It took him only a few seconds to realize to his relief, but also to his utter amazement, that it was actually Vanessa. The reason for his amazement was that she was still wearing the powder-blue leather outfit she'd put on over an hour earlier, and he'd never seen her dressed like that before in his life. Her hair was still gathered with the silk scarf into a stylish pony-tail, and, even from that distance, he could see that her face was made-up; something she hardly ever condescended to do. He reckoned that only once before had he seen her wearing a skirt, and that was shortly after he first got to know her, when she'd been presented with a BAFTA award at a ceremony five years ago.

She came across the road straight towards the cloisters beneath which he'd resumed standing. Thanking the fates for bringing her to him, as she came alongside he stepped out in front of her, making her jump.

'Vanessa.'

For a split second she didn't recognize him because of his spectacles and her hand was going to her bag to fetch her microstunner, her own round spectacles reflecting some light and looking oddly incongruous against the long legs and revealing clothes.

'Blake! Oh my God, you're alive!'

She seemed to sway, but he caught hold of her, pulled her beneath the cloisters, her heels scraping clumsily against the cobbles, and clung to her. She felt and smelt truly wonderful. Just to hold a woman at that moment, any woman, was the most important thing on earth. 'Please hold me, Vanessa,' he said, noting that she was rather red-rimmed, and that she seemed taller than usual in her new boots. 'For God's sake, please just hold me.'

They were overjoyed to see each other.

'Darling, what's happened?' she said, kissing him profusely on the cheeks and sounding more like a normal woman than he'd ever heard her sound before. 'They've been saying your car was blown up on the news. I was absolutely devastated when I found out. The phone hasn't stopped going since the announcement.' She pulled a handkerchief from her sleeve and wiped first his, then her own eyes, smearing her mascara in the process.

'It wasn't me. It was some poor kid who tried to steal my car. But it should have been me, Vanessa, it should have been me.' He shivered involuntarily, the tension of the day finally gushing out and heavily rooted in his disappointment about not having contacted Abigail; the desperate need to hold her suddenly welling in him like a kind of panic when he realized that if it had been revealed that it was him who was blown up in the car, she might have found out and not come to the hotel.

'I've been so fucking scared,' he said.

'So have I,' she replied, holding him to her so tightly that he noticed, not without alarm, that the nipples of her big breasts were rock hard, discernible through her coat.

'Why are you dressed up like this?' he asked. 'You look absolutely bloody gorgeous, but it isn't you.' He realized he was holding her against himself by her buttocks, and he could feel the nylon gusset of her tights sliding beneath the lining of her skirt.

She ignored the question because she seemed more interested in the location of his hands, pressing against him to show that she approved. 'What the hell's been going on, Blake? Why should anybody want to kill you?'

He gave her a brief résumé of the past couple of days' events, of the conspiracy surrounding the Michael Greenhalgh killing, what had happened since he'd got the forensic samples from Frank Wardle's shop, what was contained in the envelope inside his coat, the connection with the death penalty, and the news blackout since the car bomb. Something about the way they were caressing each other told him that it would perhaps be better not to mention Abigail just at the moment.

When he'd finished she let out some breath.

'Do you know what you should have done, love? You should have written me a note, then had a motorcycle courier bring it to me at the studios this afternoon. They're in and out all the time. It might have been that simple to communicate with your closest friend.'

'I know, but I've felt sort of brain-dead and disorientated ever since the explosion. I didn't know where I was going or what the hell I should do or who I could go to.' He wiped his eyes with the back of his hand and sniffed.

'You've been in shock, darling.'

He ran her pony-tail between his forefinger and thumb, relieved that someone who was such a crucial part of his universe was in his arms at last. 'I love you, Vanessa,' he said, deciding that her round spectacles didn't look out of place after all, but seemed to make her look more attractive than ever because of the studious contrast they created against the sexy leather clothes.

'I love you, too, Blake.'

Her own version of the phrase seemed to be coming at him from a distance. They'd said it to each other many times, it was essential to their friendship, but she'd never said it to him quite like this.

'What's the matter, Vanessa?'

Her face started to break up. 'What do you mean? I thought you were dead, and now you—'

'You know what I mean. Something about you is different. Why are you all dolled up? Where were you going?'

Still she ignored the thrust of his question.

'I was going to fetch your ex-wife's address and phone number from the glove compartment of the car over there, as it happened. Chris didn't put it under the hotel tonight.' She nodded beyond the cloisters at the cars parked in the centre of the square, then changed the tune of her voice. 'This is all too much for me to take in Blake. We've got to go somewhere and talk it through properly, until we can decide what to do next.'

'If we book into another hotel Central Matrix might be able to put out a trace.'

'In that case, we can go to Linda's flat down at Salford Quays. You asked me the other day why I never bother to use it, so now's the opportunity for us to go there together. Then you can tell me all about what's happened when you've had a shower and something to eat.'

'But they might be watching it. They might be watching us here, now, at this very moment.'

His eyes went to the square.

'Nobody knows I use the flat, Blake, not even Max. If we get a taxi down there and don't use the phone, how can anybody know? The readout on the alarm will tell us when someone last went in, and I know Linda hasn't been there since September.' She hugged him again and sighed. 'I just can't believe you're still alive, I really can't.'

He managed to put his finger on what was different about her. Apart from the way she was dressed, it was as though she'd lost the air of masculine assertiveness that was a normal component of her personality. Before he could think it out any further, she was kissing him on the mouth. Her tongue didn't go inside, but he could sense that it wanted to. He tried to roll his head away, but her lips felt their way back to his and she nuzzled him closely, stroking the side of his head and rocking him gently to and fro.

After a few minutes her pale-blue eyes, sparkling and

quite beautiful to contemplate, looked from behind her spectacles deep into his own, engaging him with an intimacy that left him slightly on edge.

'We're still here, darling. Nobody's jumped us.'

He smiled uneasily, and allowed her to lead him through the shadows. They deliberately walked arm-in-arm along a sidestreet like lovers, then climbed into a taxi at the rank at the end, behind City Hall.

# Twenty-Two

Blake was awakened by the beeping of a microwave oven. His eyes were not being assisted by lenses, and he couldn't see his surroundings very clearly beyond the first few feet. But he recognized the blurred blue shape of Vanessa come across from a galley kitchen and set down a couple of trays of steaming food onto the glass coffee-table in front of the sofa upon which he'd been sleeping.

Like the table, the sofa was transparent but made from inflatable plastic; the style in vogue again as national sentiment turned to the future for the seeds of aesthetic inspiration by once again digging up the past. It seemed to occupy most of the tiny lounge and it hawked rudely as he shifted his position and heard the creaking of central heating coming to life, taking the chill off the air. Then, as he blinked awake, astounded at how heavy his head felt, he regained his point of compass and placed himself as being inside Linda's flat at Salford Quays.

There was a chunk of plum-coloured glass on the table with nothing but two thin chromed strips of metal axled to a face that had been machined flat. He interpreted them as hands of a clock showing that about an-hour-and-a-half had passed since they'd come away from the hotel, and that it was now a little before half-past-ten. 'I feel as if I've been out for hours,' he said, blearily bringing himself upright.

'You've been out for about twenty minutes, love,' Vanessa said. She slipped off her boots, loosened her pony-tail, poured two glasses of red wine, joined him on the sofa, passed him his tray, lifted her own tray onto her lap, took a big gulp of wine, picked up a black perspex fork, and aimed her words at her food. 'I'm afraid this is vegetarian chilli, but it really is very good. Linda always keeps some microwave meals here in the freezer, but these are all that's left.'

The flat was small and neat enough, but had been contrived to suggest an air of convenience to disguise the fact that everything had been crammed into the tiniest available space. Blake had noticed when they arrived that the internal doors, even on the fitted units, opened in such a way that there was never more than a few millimetres to spare before they hit each other or the walls. Forming the centrepiece to the red-and-purple lounge was an ugly chrome sculpture which was actually an electric fire. (Its shape was echoed by the stylish chrome triangular motifs set into the simple red-and-black uPVC kitchen units.) The main front window became a small balcony that looked across the redeveloped quayside basin glittering in the darkness outside, while the other looked onto the courtyard where the tenants' cars were parked. Both windows were closed off by black venetian blinds. There was a hideous white tigerskin rug under the coffee-table; a preponderance of 'cocktail-cherry' ornaments and handkerchief vases old and new; a chrome spider lamp and a new daffodil lamp; and a photograph on the glass sideboard of a short-haired woman who he took to be Vanessa's friend Linda Summers, being presented with her degree on the day of her film school graduation in 1989.

The blue-and-green bathroom he'd showered in contained a plastic bath shorter than any he'd ever seen before; too short to be able to unfold his legs properly if he'd found himself sitting rather than standing in it. The single small bedroom where he'd changed into a white-towelling bathrobe and dried his hair was furnished in blue and red and orange, and a lot of white sheepskin, but had immediately unnerved him because it didn't have a window on any of the external walls. Everything in the flat was linked together organically by the white uPVC architraves, thin skirtings, and modular doors; all of which were inlaid with chrome beading, and of a standard size that could be slotted into an endless variety of housing permutations without cutting or waste, regardless of the arrangement the computer chose to offer the designer.

With its emphasis on heavy angular lines and wipe-easy surfaces, with its bold blending of primary colours, chrome, and transparent furniture, the flat was pure Modernist Revival: an ambiguous mixture somewhere between the machine-form inspiration of 1930s Art Deco and 1950s functional, with the bad-taste of early '70s kitsch thrown in for good measure.

They picked up the loose thread of the conversation they'd been having earlier, about the events of the previous few days, and then there was a silence where they seemed grateful just to be in each other's company. Blake cleared his plate and put it down on the table. Then, with a casualness that only close friends could adopt as a run-in line to a very serious observation, he suddenly asked: 'What's the matter, Vanessa?'

'What do you mean?'

'You know what I mean. I've just been through the worst day of my life, and I'm sitting alone with you in a flat feeling as though we should be talking about how the hell we get this conspiracy into the headlines, and keep me alive. There's an envelope over there that might hold the potential to bring down the government. There are things worrying me sick about which I haven't spoken yet'—he was meaning Abigail—'but I'm concerned more than anything because there's something wrong with you. I need your support now, love, but look at you.' He nodded at her thigh protruding generously from beneath the short skirt. 'You look positively stunning, but I'm not used to seeing you like this. I know you too well, and it's making me feel more disorientated than ever.'

He couldn't escape the uneasy conviction that whatever was the matter with her had something to do with why he was in this Salford Quays flat, and that in turn it must somehow be connected with the sequence of events in which he'd become embroiled.

A sly smile broke the corners of her mouth. 'Do you fancy me, Blake?'

He let out some breath. 'Please, Vanessa, this really is not the time to—'

'No, I'm not trying it on, love. I just want to know whether or not you find me attractive.'

'Of course I find you attractive. I'm not saying that I want to go to bed with you, but my body is responding to your presence, probably because of what I've just been through. You're turning me on. I can't take my eyes off your legs.'

'I know you can't. They're good legs, aren't they?'

'Yes they are. I've never understood why you don't make more of a show of them.'

She unfolded one and stretched it towards him across the sofa and wiggled her toes against his thigh, affectionately rather than suggestively. He took hold of her ankle. The nylon made it feel as smooth as glass yet as soft as velvet, and the fine lycra glimmered between the delicate threads of the five denier.

'You didn't find me attractive before, did you?'

'Before what, Vanessa?' He let go of her ankle, noticing that his heart was beginning to pick up speed and that he'd been lanced by a feeling of irritation.

'Before I bothered to put on clothes like these.'

She retracted her leg and moved across and leaned against him, holding his eyes all the way. She was ten years older than him, but at that moment, as he rested his heavily stubbled chin on top of her head, he felt ten years older than her. In the past couple of hours she'd become small and unassertive, vulnerable and utterly female—something which only presented another disruption to fit into the sphere of his already badly decomposing mental universe.

She pulled her head out from beneath his chin and looked into his eyes. 'I'm sorry. I shouldn't have said those things to you just then. I've absolutely no right after what you've been through.'

'What's happened?'

'Nothing's happened. It's just me. There are things about me that you don't understand yet, that's all. Things you've never remotely comprehended.'

Her words seemed strangely empty, working with the atmosphere of the flat, which now seemed uncomfortably quiet and alien and cool.

Far from feeling eased by what she'd just said he felt more unsettled than ever. 'Please, Vanessa, you're talking in riddles. I've been feeling for weeks as if I'm always on the verge of losing you, and I don't want to lose you. You're obviously under some strain, I can sense it. Something's on your mind. But I want you to stay just as you were.'

She sipped at her wine, swirling the liquid centrifugally in her hand and glowering at the glass. 'I know you do,' she said wearily. 'And I'm afraid that's been part of the problem for a very long time.'

She put down the wine and rested her head back against the sofa, her hair fanning onto the clear plastic. Locks of it started running across the surface of Blake's right hand, which was splayed close to her shoulder. It was a difficult moment, for although part of him was wondering where Abigail was, another part of him wanted nothing more than to lift Vanessa's beautiful hair to his face.

Her eyes were still on his and she seemed to be reading his thoughts. 'Why do you fight it?'

'Why do I fight what?'

'What you feel for me. You admitted a few minutes ago that I was turning you on. Or perhaps you didn't hear yourself?'

He swallowed with some difficulty and sensed the tension building again. Ever since he'd met her outside the hotel he'd had the uneasy feeling that Vanessa was going to try and manoeuvre him into a bed. It seemed that his suspicions were about to be proved right, and a curious feeling of apprehension came over him. He couldn't identify the source of the emotion. But the smell of clothes conditioner, warm leather, and clean female flesh surrounding her was as comforting as the aroma of summer washdays had been at home when he was a child.

Before he could say anything, she hooked her hair back behind her ear and started stroking the side of his face. 'Do you remember what I pointed out yesterday, about you preferring your women to be female? You *do* like them to be female, don't you? Not swaggering trousered types like Vanessa Aysgarth, always bossing people about and answering everybody back. Well, the Vanessa Aysgarth you knew has gone, Blake. This is the real me who was hiding behind the cocky attitude and the stupid masculine clothes. It's taken me a long time to find myself, but for the first time in my life I actually feel like I want to *be* a woman. I feel as though I've become myself, and I've absolutely no intention of going back.'

He was so confused by what she was saying that he could only assume the wine was going to her head. Before the observation could be fully processed, however, her hand was moving down to his neck, the long trembling fingers were going inside his bathrobe, caressing his shoulder, probing lower, her palm soft and very warm against his hardening nipple, her eyes searching his from behind the lenses of her spectacles. To his amazement, he found that the nipple was not the only part of his body that was hardening. Vanessa sensed this, crossed her legs, hooked the foot of one around the calf of the other, and drew up her knees—this was one of her characteristic postures, regardless of what she was wearing—the lycra effervescent as more of her thighs showed beneath the glow of the lamp.

And then her lips seemed to drift onto his.

His breath was shaking and his adrenalin was pumping when she moved into the kneeling position astride him and hooked the bathrobe from his shoulders. Automatically, his hands went to her own shoulders, which he'd always considered broad for a woman—they were almost as broad as his own—the arms joined onto them as strong and determined as any man's. The shoulders might have grown so wide to support the large breasts which he could now feel sagging against his chest, he reflected absently; but they also emphasised that durability about her which he found so vital to their relationship. As she busied herself sensuously cupping his face and whispered that she loved him, he began to perceive why they had such a unique understanding of one another; why it had fast been approaching an assured sexual conclusion. Vanessa was the strong older woman who needed the sensitive younger man. Perhaps she was the assertive older woman who haunted sensitive men's minds everywhere; men who respected the female and who didn't try to dominate her or compensate for their emotional inadequacies by trying to force her down into a passive rôle. Blake was emotionally mature enough to revere Vanessa because of this, and, though neither of them knew it at that moment, they were on the verge of fusing into a matchless couple. For they had each married the wrong person, and the reason they'd since left their partners behind was because they'd been in the process of growing together, their platonic companionship paving the way for a satiation of their unusual sexual needs. If they went to bed now, *she* would want to make love to *him*. There could be little doubt that, like Abigail had done the previous evening when they'd woken and made love the second time, Vanessa would want to assume the dominant rôle. That was how she would want to play it, and though the awareness left him feeling vaguely queasy, for a split second it was running through both their minds simultaneously; their hearts were beating in unison; their destiny together was nearly sealed.

She removed her spectacles and placed them on the coffee-table, then reared onto her knees and kissed him again with a most beautiful tenderness, her breath coming in short gasps when she sensed that he was allowing her to push him into the passive rôle. She waited for him to respond, sent her hands searching greedily down behind him, kneading the flesh, her fingers sliding underneath him as she tried to lift his buttocks away from the plastic, making strange petting noises of a kind he'd never heard her make before.

How or why he managed it he was never to know, but he didn't respond. Instead, he pulled his mouth away from hers, kept his voice deliberately neutral, and found that, for the second time in as many days, his words seemed to reverberate through his skull and he couldn't look her in the eye while he spoke. 'As I tried to suggest to you on Tuesday, I need you as a friend, Vanessa, not like this. If this carries on the way it's going, we'll never be able to relate to each other in the same way again. Our friendship will be finished. And you mean more to me than a quick fuck in this Salford Quays flat. Can't you understand that?' He didn't like using the four-letter word, but it seemed the only way to emphasise the sincerity of what he was saying.

'Have you ever wondered if we'd end up as lovers?'

'I admit it's crossed my mind . . .'

'You know that it's done far more than cross your mind, young man.' Her eyes narrowed, bringing out the crow's feet at either side, and to his surprise she took him roughly by the chin and turned his face back to hers. The movement unnerved him because there was aggression behind it, though an altogether more pleasurable emotion briefly ran through him as well. 'You don't want to go to bed with me, do you?'

He heard himself swallow again. 'No I don't. Even if I wanted to, I couldn't. You're married. You know my principles and you know that I can't stomach infidelity. It's the one thing that really cuts me up. No way could I do the dirty on Max either, not even if I hated his guts, which I don't. And you're doing the dirty on Max by trying to seduce me now, which bothers me a lot. Just as it bothers me that you're doing this when I've nearly been murdered today.' His eyes finally went to hers. 'In case you've forgotten about that minor episode, or about everything else I've told you.' He let out some more breath and rubbed his face with his hands. 'Christ, this all seems so bloody unreal . . .'

He was amazed at the hoarseness of his voice, but was more shocked at the intensity of anger he could feel welling at the thought of her being prepared to indulge in extramarital sex. It really struck a nerve with him. He'd thought she was stronger than that and had greater dignity and self-respect.

Then he wasn't quite so sure.

'My marriage is finished, Blake, and it has been for some time.'

He was stunned, feeling inexplicably, and not for the first time recently, that his world was on the verge of slipping away. 'You're just saying that. You would have told me. No way could you have kept something like that from me. No way would you have even wanted to.'

Vanessa moved away and slumped back against the sofa, a big silence erupting between them while a sense of futility suddenly drifted into the room. The moment of sexual intensity had passed. She looked at a point in space, her breasts rose and fell once, and he perceived a terrible loneliness in her just then; something that he'd never noticed before.

'Does it occur to you that I might not have said anything because I didn't want to exert any pressure on *you*? Sometimes you're just so bloody selfish, you know.'

'Why didn't you tell me?'

'It wouldn't have been fair, that's why.' This wasn't the absolute truth, of course, but now was not the time to tell him. 'Your own marriage was failing. How would you have felt if I'd have told you that mine was too? It would have been the last thing you'd have wanted to hear. A few months ago, you would have cracked. Remember that time when I found you on my bathroom floor, squatted in the corner? I was frightened that night, Blake. You were a hair's breadth from a nervous breakdown, and you needed me more than you've probably ever needed anybody else in your life. You held on to me so tightly you drew blood. I still have the scars on my back to prove it. I was your link with mainstream life and with your own sanity.' Her voice was starting to break now. 'What was it that Van Gogh once said? *I am a passionate man* . . . And so are you. You have a frightening intensity, but it's what makes you different to other men. It's what makes you desirable to women like me. And just remember this, too.' She hadn't blinked for several minutes. 'I've had nobody to talk to about *my* deteriorating domestic situation. And I haven't cracked.'

Though he was still mystified as to why on earth she'd never said anything to him, though he'd been consumed by a fierce sense of betrayal and a desire to get away from her, what had just happened on the sofa was so bizarre that he wondered if it was actually her way of cracking, and his respect for her returned.

There was another silence and his eyes went down to her thighs again. Her skirt had ridden up so much from when she'd knelt over him that he could clearly see that she wasn't wearing any pants underneath. The observation both shocked and aroused him. He could see, too, that the gusset of her tights was sheer throughout, the same as the legs, so that the brownish cast simply extended all the way up to her waist; something which generated a strangely erotic effect. She obviously didn't realize how she was exposing herself, or if she did, she didn't care.

Part of him was stepping back now, visualizing the inflatable sofa and the bright carpets and walls and the glass table and what was taking place in the flat as though it were a scene in a film. If it had been a scene in a film, in the background throughout the previous several minutes there would have been a barely audible but very menacing synthesizer sound. A finger depressing a single key somewhere at the bottom of the scale. Monotonous. Waiting for something to happen. Waiting for the tension to break . . .

In an obtuse way which he didn't want to begin to try

and analyse, he decided that the only way he could assuage his mounting sense of guilt was by breaking the tension himself and telling her the truth. It would hurt him to tell her. It was the very worst possible moment to tell her. But he hadn't any choice.

Hooking his bathrobe back onto himself he stood up.

'I'm afraid I've got a confession to make, love. You know when we were in the car park underneath Central Police Headquarters the other morning, and that tall woman with the legs came and stood outside the lift?'

'Yes.'

'Can you remember how I responded?'

'Yes.'

'Well, when I phoned you last night and asked you not to come up to my room, she was standing next to me. We spent the night together.'

'Blake, that's wonderful.'

'It was you who pushed me, Vanessa. You told me to go after her, so I did.'

'Isn't that what friends are for?'

Before they veered away he saw that her eyes had become slightly glazed. Then he heard a car pull up outside, felt not so much that he was panicky, but that the distraction would serve to punctuate an awkward few moments, went across to the window, and parted the slats of the venetian blind. He heard doors slam, heard a car alarm squeal into defence-mode, heard male and female laughter and the clacking of stiletto heels against herringbone setts, before a security-light registered the heat from the young couple's bodies and flicked a glow across the compound. 'Part of me can't help thinking that the bastards will probably have this place bugged,' he said, dropping the slats.

The noise of the slats had covered the fact that Vanessa had left the sofa and come up close behind him. He turned and almost knocked her over, his heart jumping into his mouth when he realized why she was there. She felt for the back of his head and kissed him again, but this time deeply and very open mouthed. This was the last thing that he wanted, but she had such an astonishing way of kissing, her lips tasted so unbelievably soft and moist, that to his horror he heard himself moan with arousal. Feeling an explosion of blood vessels between his legs his hands went to her thighs and lifted the skirt, despite the words, 'No, Vanessa . . . no,' choking his voice. 'Don't let's spoil what we already have. Please . . .'

He managed to take control of his hands and pulled himself away from what was undoubtedly the most difficult and confusing moment of his life; but Vanessa was already back in front of him with a very tenacious look in her eyes. She ripped the cord of his bathrobe loose, hooked the garment from his shoulders, dropped it to the floor so that he was naked, then sent her hand to his groin.

Blake groaned. 'No, Vanessa, you mustn't—'

He was remarkably unresilient when she turned him from the window, pushed him down onto his back, then came up and knelt astride him. All the time he was pleading with her not to do this and tried to squirm from beneath her. But she had him pinned, and he couldn't bring himself to apply the strength necessary to push her off because he didn't want to hurt her. He watched her lift her blue sweater over her head, her large breasts flubbering free, devoid of a brassière, he noted, the nipples almost obscenely thrusting and hard. She was backlit by a spotlight on the ceiling when she shook her platinum-blonde mane triumphantly, then released the velcro running down the seam of her skirt and threw the rectangle of leather aside. All that she had left on her body now was the pair of tights. With an extraordinary savagery, she actually ripped them from her legs, then pulled the elasticated waistband in shrivelled tatters angrily up her torso and over her head.

She, too, was naked now, and Blake looked down across the hair of his chest to see his erection twitching in time with his pounding heart and almost aiming itself towards her hand. She caressed it between her long fingers, then bent and began kissing it with the most incredible gentleness, until it disappeared into her mouth and her tongue began working wonders.

'Oh, God help me. . .' he wheezed, as blazing erotic fire started to burn between his legs. Determined not to succumb, he banged his hands down like a wrestler in a half-nelson, spread his fingers and scraped at the red carpet, felt fingernails bend back and break. 'Oh Jesus Christ, Vanessa . . . *no* . . .' he hyperventilated through teeth that were gritted so hard he expected them to split where they were sunk into gums. 'Please don't do this to me. You can't . . .'

The penis slid out of her mouth.

'Yes, Blake, I can, because you want to love me and you want me to dominate you. It's in your eyes.' The tears were streaming down her face when she took hold of his dithering wrists, thrust out his arms and pinned him to the carpet in the crucifix position, lifted to find her target, came down onto him, and writhed.

They both screamed at the moment of penetration, the fusing of their flesh trying to bend Blake double as the blazing erotic fire became a raging inferno that threatened to burn his entire body to a crisp. As Vanessa raped him and he made a feeble effort to fight free, he realized that, as usual, his priority was not his own feelings but those of somebody else. He didn't want to hurt her, either physically by throwing her off, or emotionally by rejecting her. She was his best friend. He loved her. But not like this, please God not like this.

'Abigail,' he snarled, 'I want Abigail . . .' The tears came to his own eyes as she brought her face to his, her hair and breasts draped against his flesh, his tongue reaching out to meet hers despite himself. 'Please, Vanessa, please . . .'

'Don't fight it, darling, love me,' she pleaded as she spread her legs wide and began grinding him into the carpet, fighting to keep his struggling hands at bay, her face aflame with red desire. 'For God's sake, please just love me . . .'

Though his erection showed how his body yearned to

respond, though he knew this situation was pushing him to the very edges of his personal morality, his emotional integrity was too powerful to allow him to compromise his feelings when his heart had already made its commitment. From out of the million confusions raging before his eyes there came a vision of Abigail telling him about her fifteen-year-old dream, and he snapped, snarled like a wild animal, then rolled over on top of Vanessa to pull himself free. But her hands had a grip of iron and her legs had locked across his buttocks and the blazing erotic fire wouldn't burn out. Every move sent its flames licking towards another part of his being; reminded him that, no matter what she was subjecting him to, this woman beneath him mattered to his life too.

Knowing that it was because his emotional barriers were down, knowing that somehow it was wrong, he embraced her and slowly started to fuck her, the big breasts flattened like balloons beneath him. Dark waters seemed to be closing over his head and for a moment they looked into each other's eyes and he was with her; saw how it might be if there wasn't somebody else already in the way.

'I love you, Vanessa,' he said, gulping on his lust as he saw her face framed by her hair on the carpet, then clutching that hair between his fingers as there came memories of erotic dreams about her; dreams which he'd never once recalled until this moment, but which channelled in him an emotional intensity that seemed to be backed up by the sexual desire of a lifetime. 'I want you,' he snarled greedily, now sliding her into the crucifix position and grinding her against the carpet instead, forcing her legs so far apart he decided that if he pushed them any wider everything would crack.

They rolled clumsily about, wrestling with one another in a furious passion of ecstasy, banging into furniture, sending ornaments and the spent plates from their meal flying.

Then, the moment having passed, the dark waters parting again like a mental Red Sea, his lips bearing back over grinding teeth, and his voice shrieking with rage: '*Oh God how I love you . . .*'

Already Vanessa was starting to come. Feeling emotionally drunk, seeing the events of the previous few days race before him again, he used the distraction of her orgasm to yank himself free. He stumbled on all-fours backwards across the carpet, then spun and banged head first into a wall, stunning himself from the impact. On the rebound he came up to his knees, screamed a single extended negative as he felt his loins beginning to heave, swung his fist angrily, and smashed it straight through the plasterboard, the flesh lost up to the elbow, his hand striking midair amidst an explosion of ceramic shards as it shot through to the kitchen at the other side.

Vanessa squirmed on the carpet then curled into a foetal position, her orgasm going on and on, until she opened out again and thrashed about like a fish tossed onto dry land. She uttered a barrage of ecstatic obscenities, reared shaking and gulping onto her elbows as though she were literally drowning from erotic pleasure. Then she screamed and gripped the leg of the coffee-table so hard Blake thought he heard her knuckles crack.

He dragged his arm from the wall and sat crumpled against the plastic skirting, trembling and panting so violently the shaking was nearly epileptic in its potency. His nervous system was shot to pieces and his body and mind were on fire.

'I can't believe you've done this,' he growled as he saw her go still, his voice savaged by emotion. 'I've nearly been killed and all you can do is think about yourself and dump this on me. You're supposed to be my friend, Vanessa . . . *my very, best, friend . . .*'

He'd always seen her as a kind of Mother figure. But even as he thought about it now he was assessing the difficulty of men and women being able to be just good friends, without Nature taking over; making a mockery of the guarded hugs at Christmas and birthdays; driving their bodies to consummate the friendship by fusing them together when the barriers finally came down.

They each remained where they were for what seemed like a very long time. The central heating went off and the room started to feel chilled and Vanessa moved a little and hugged her shoulders to try and keep warm, but she didn't get up. Though he resented her for assuming that his vulnerability after what he'd been through might present an opportunity for her to impale herself upon him, though he'd desperately needed her comfort, though he'd felt his body desiring hers with an increasing frequency over recent weeks and months, Blake didn't hate her. He only felt sorry for her; pitied her for the confusion she must be going through sexually.

Eventually, he walked over on his knees and touched her shoulders and felt her stiffen. When he managed to pull her reluctant body onto its back he was shocked at her expression. It wasn't so much that she looked sad, but that she looked dazed; all her facial muscles seemed to have collapsed and the colour to have drained away. She looked as though she were about to die. He took hold of her hand, brought it to his mouth, then suddenly lifted her and cradled her against his chest.

'I'm so sorry,' he said, meaning the words and fighting back the tears, 'I'm just so sorry.' His voice was muffled against her flesh and he noticed that his knuckles were bleeding. It seemed so pointless that he should have resisted her. 'Why does it have to be like this? *Why?*'

She remained limp in his arms and spoke softly and surprisingly hoarsely. 'Because you're human and honest and you've nothing to hide. You're never trying to be anything you're not. Not like me. Not like so much of the human race, living the big lie, fucking each other for profit, their prejudices shaped by an economic system that fucks them all.'

He reached for his bathrobe.

'I do love you, Vanessa, but not like this. Ours is a different type of emotional bond.'

The tears were glittering in her eyes.

Her voice was barely a whisper.

'I've always loved you, Blake. I managed to contain it while you were married, but not any longer. I'm overjoyed to see that you're alive, I feel as if my emotions have been banging around like a fly in a bottle all evening, and I just can't stand the frustration of wanting you and not being able to have you any more.' She gave him a long inquiring look. 'I need you, darling, I need you more than you'll ever be able to understand.' Her eyes closed and squeezed out the tears as she smiled from behind a thin escape of breath; then she pulled her hand free and rubbed its outstretched palm between her breasts. Blake realized now why she'd sounded curiously detached when she'd said she loved him outside the hotel earlier. It was because she'd been putting some feeling into it. She'd really meant it.

He had never felt so sorry for another human being in all his life, or felt that it was he who was directly responsible for its unhappiness. He looked at the closely-cropped platinum-blonde fur between her legs, felt ashamed for doing so, draped the bathrobe across her body, found himself picking her up in his arms, then carried her through into the bedroom and laid her gently on the double mattress. He slipped into the bathrobe, rolled back the red satin quilt, pulled it over her, and tucked her in as if she'd been one of his own daughters.

He kissed her on the forehead but as he straightened to go back and try to find some sleep in the lounge, she suddenly grabbed his sleeve.

'Stay with me. Please stay with me just this one night.'

'Vanessa, I can't—'

'I don't mean like that. Put your clothes on if you want to, but just stay with me, please just stay with me till morning.'

She was trembling like a frightened little girl.

He swallowed with some difficulty, being unable to suppress a hatred of both himself and his body. Feeling physically and mentally exhausted, but also horribly confused because he knew that deep down he wanted her, he sat on the edge of the bed and held the hair back from her moist forehead. After a few minutes, he sensed the tension beginning to ease, pulled back the quilt, got into bed with her, switched off the glass lamp, and laid facing the ceiling in the darkness, his head beginning to throb. In the distance he could hear the scream of police sirens, the vague thundering of helicopters, and just once, the chatter of machinegun-fire coming from one of the slums.

It wasn't long before he heard a category of breathing that indicated Vanessa was asleep. He turned over and put his arm round her, glad to have someone to hug. He closed his eyes, then, as he pressed himself tighter against her and wondered again where Abigail was at that moment, he was aware of an enormous sense of desolation washing over him as he wondered where the hell this nightmare was going to take him next.

# Twenty-Three

He seemed to hover at the brink of dark dreams throughout the night. Though he couldn't sleep, it was difficult for him to judge how quickly time was passing because there were no windows to the bedroom; no illuminated clocks to confirm how close was the yawning of the dawn. There was only Vanessa's quiet breathing, interfering with the hermetic silence of a strange ebony limbo in which he had somehow become stranded with his thoughts.

From time to time a childlike whimpering issued from the throat joined to the head laid on the pillow alongside, as Vanessa felt her way through her own private nightmare. The sounds started to become so forlorn that at one point he had to hold her close to himself and stroke her hair and whisper into her ear that he loved her. He'd spent so many happy times with this woman. He'd trusted her more than any other human being on earth, and now he wanted to protect her from the terrible harm that he felt he'd done by rejecting her. He wanted to send away the demons clawing at her troubled sleep and no doubt raking their talons through her ambivalent sexuality. It was absurd for him to blame himself, he knew, but there it was; and then his hand seemed to calm her, he heard her mutter his name, and his presence sent her quiet once again.

Eventually, he was aware that the swirling images had conquered the ache in his head and had carried him into a semblance of fitful slumber. He knew this because his mouth tasted of sleep when he vaguely remembered waking and being disturbed by Vanessa lifting his arm away as she got out of bed. From the darkness he heard a quiet letting loose of breath of the type that comes from someone whose mind is now walled-up by depression. It was followed by a rustle of clothing, then the sound of a door handle being turned, then the click of the uPVC panel meeting the frame again as she went into the lounge. A few minutes later came the flushing of a cistern, muffled through the wall. Straightaway the events of the previous evening bulged back into his mind and a sick feeling began clutching at his entrails, as he grappled again with the guilt that he couldn't seem to escape. He heard the rattle of the blinds being opened in the lounge, then the oddly reassuring sound of water hissing into a kettle; seemed to sense the rumble of traffic through the framework of the bed. Then he was falling back into sleep, hugely grateful for the warm place where Vanessa had been laid, and into which he had a sudden compunction to roll, while he inhaled the smell of her hair where it had been pressed against the pillow.

Sometime later he was aware that she was coming back into the bedroom; that a wedge of brilliant daylight was slanting through the door; that his forearm was going up to his eyes to cancel the dazzle. She got something out of a drawer, then the door closed and the bedroom went black again. He heard her cough and the sound of a teaspoon clattering into a mug; felt oddly reassured by a smell of toast seeping through the darkness; remembered the loaf of bread he'd seen her take out of the freezer the night before.

Then, after what might have been a minute or an hour, he heard the door open and his arm went up to his eyes again. She came across and he sensed her bending down as she took hold of his arm and lifted it away from his face. He squinted through the dazzle . . . only it wasn't Vanessa who was standing there, it was Chief Constable Driscoll, and Blake yelped and jumped up and banged his head against the plastic shelf which blended with the top of the bed.

'Woke you up, did we Hunter?' Driscoll said, chuckling while he knotted his hands together behind his back. He was in uniform and smelt of bad breath and the frosty outside. 'I won't waste time informing you about your rights because you no longer have any, I'm afraid. Not that you've done anything technically unlawful, though in my opinion the existence of liberal-minded persons such as you is a crime in itself.'

'How the hell did you find us, you bastard?'

He looked past Driscoll and shouted for Vanessa, worried only about what they might have done to her.

'We have our little ways.'

Driscoll smirked and turned to contemplate a human silhouette that was framed in the doorway behind him, its shadow now breaking the rhombus of light sloping into the room. Though the figure appeared blurred to Blake because he wasn't wearing his lenses, and despite it being backlit, he knew that it was Vanessa. The resigned way she was standing there said everything, and his body seemed to turn to ice as a horrible realization began to sink home.

'Oh Christ no . . .' he said, slowly shaking his head. 'Not you Vanessa . . . anybody but you . . .'

'The proverbial catch in the story,' Driscoll said. 'But then, let's face it Hunter, as with all the best stories, the drama evolves from the personal interrelationships of the characters and not the other way around.' He tut-tutted theatrically. 'And here you are, fast approaching a most unpleasant conclusion in a story of constitutional importance, and all because you resisted the sexual advances of a beautiful woman.'

Vanessa stepped into the room and switched on the light. Her voice sounded lifeless and flat. 'Could I have a few minutes alone with him, please.'

'You've got five minutes, Vanessa,' Driscoll said, heading back to the lounge obediently and closing the bedroom door behind him.

Blake dropped his head back against the shelf, mom-

entarily dazzled by the light. Because of his disabled eye-
sight, everything had become a mass of blurred colours
identifiable only by its shape. As the shape that he loved
called Vanessa separated from a purple-and-white blob that
he remembered to be an authentic Saarinen tulip chair, circa
1956, then passed before a plain white wall studded with
orange Penguins, it was as if she'd become a stranger and he
found that he had a compunction to laugh; to laugh and
allow himself to descend into what seemed like a very
inviting abyss called madness. He wanted to shut himself
away from the world and forget that he'd ever been born.

'Please don't let it be Vanessa,' he kept pleading to the
room, scrunching the quilt between his fists. '*Please don't let
it be Vanessa* . . .'

She sat on the edge of the bed but was unable to look him
in the eye. She was wearing blue jeans and a red polo-neck
sweater, presumably Linda's clothes which she'd taken from
the drawers earlier on. Curiously she was barefoot. But now
that she was close up and he could focus he noticed that the
skin on her feet seemed wonderfully smooth and unblem-
ished in contrast to the faded jeans, almost like that of a
child, though she was forty-one years old.

His head was spinning and his mouth was becoming
gagged with the sticky mucus of fear. He managed to aim
his eyes at her, but his nostrils flared from the effort of
choking back emotion through clenched teeth.

'You asked me to sleep with you, Vanessa,' he said
slowly, overcome by a feeling of humiliation when he realized how his integrity must have been manipulated; when
he remembered how he'd wanted so much to comfort her
when she'd been asleep. 'How could you do that when you
were going to bring them here?' Suddenly he was struck
dumb by another realization that was so obvious it sent him
even colder. 'It's because of Abigail, isn't it?' He thanked
God that he hadn't had the chance to tell her anything
about Abigail's involvement, beyond the night they'd spent
together in bed.

'No it isn't,' she said quietly, 'and I didn't bring them here. They'd have got you anyway. One of the other tenants heard us screaming last night, thought there was a murder or something going on, and reported the disturbance to the police. Driscoll says the tenant knows I occasionally come here, so it was only a matter of time before they put two and two together when they realized I'd slipped out of the hotel. I swear to you that I would never have brought them here. They've been outside the flat all night.'

'But you're obviously involved with them, Vanessa,' he said accusingly.

She looked at the floor and played with her breath for a few moments while she tried to gather some words. 'No, I'm not involved. Max has had something to do with a company that's been building the new execution facilities at the prisons. I don't know what exactly he's been up to, I've only been able to make vague assumptions, but it started when he did some PR work for one of the shareholders. I got roped in because I accidentally found out who the bastard was mixed up with. That's why my marriage is finished. My position with the BBC became of some use to them because they wanted me to keep an eye on you.' She managed a sad smile. 'They couldn't decide whether or not to regard you as a dangerous influence. Max once heard me talking about you in my sleep and so they blackmailed me emotionally. They said that if I didn't comply they'd kill you, or that they'd kill me and then kill you. They'll kill me now anyway, because I brought you here without informing them, and I never would have told them where you were, I promise you that. I'd have gone on the run with you if I had to. I'd no idea they were going to try and kill you with a car bomb. If only you'd told me that you went out to the IFI the other afternoon, and why, I might have been able to warn you about what you were getting involved with. But you wouldn't tell me, Blake, *you wouldn't tell me.*'

'What do you mean "new execution facilities"?'

She let out a bit more breath.

'Unofficially, capital punishment has been reintroduced. The legislation was completed months ago and the prisons are already gearing up for a culling of the underclass. I've even heard Driscoll talking this morning about them having built incinerators. It's like what Hitler did to the Jews, Blake. There's the same cold reasoning behind it. The debate in Parliament and the furore about Greenhalgh's Bill, the endless discussions on TV . . . they're just formalities.' She paused. 'There's so much that we don't know about. There's so much that everybody doesn't know about—'

'What about the film we've been making?'

'It was a diversionary tactic and would probably never have been transmitted. I suppose it was just easier to let it get made. Britain has already entered its new Dark Age and there's nothing we can do to change that now.'

'But you aren't like they are, I know you're not.' He looked at the ceiling. 'Jesus. To think there was a moment last night when I looked into your eyes and—'

'I know, I was there. And it was the most wonderful moment of my life. I've seen that expression so much in your eyes recently, but you didn't seem to be aware of it yourself.' The tears came to her eyes. 'You're just too decent for a lousy, rotten bitch like me. That's why I've always held myself back. I didn't want to risk losing you as a friend by making a clumsy pass. I wanted you to come to me if and when you were ready. And then, when I found out about Max and they threatened to kill you . . .' Her face looked to be draining of colour as she spoke, so that the pressure points created by the bone seemed to be turning her a pearliest white.

Blake felt to be choking, the room now on the verge of joining in with the spinning of his mind. 'How could you manage to keep this from me when you spend so much time with me? It must have been driving you insane . . .'

Though his initial reaction was to think that she'd been deceitful, he realized why he'd sensed for the past several weeks that she'd been under pressure. He knew from the look in her eyes, too, that she was telling the truth, and because he needed her now as much as she needed him, he had no choice but to offer his affection and take hold of her hand. She used the linking of flesh to pull herself towards him and more or less collapsed onto his shoulders, while he held her head, and stroked her hair, and kissed her cheek, and felt the blood pumping in her neck, and heard her whisper so pitifully into his ear that she was sorry, that he felt himself beginning to panic.

'Don't you see what this is all about?' she went on, her face back in front of his. She had started to look and sound very tired. 'I've felt like this about you for such a long time, Blake, but I've always had to chew on my emotion, on my frustration, on my desire. I've had to bottle everything up. Think what you think about me now, but I never even so much as implied what I felt about you when you were still with Vicky, not even when your marriage was breaking apart. I *couldn't* take advantage of you when you needed my support. I was at least being honest when I said that to you last night.' Her eyes searched his face. 'What we have is so rare between men and women outside the sheets of the same bed. But when you said you'd spent the night with somebody else, I don't know, I think I realized that the moment had passed. And after that morning in the car park before the news conference . . . I thought you were coming to me, love . . . I had to try and . . . I'm so sorry, Blake. I truly didn't know what I was doing.' It was now her turn to choke back emotion, her body also gripped by a kind of panic. She dropped her head and let Blake go, then stood up. 'I think I'm going to be sick.'

He pulled her back down and held onto her tightly, tasted the salt of tears against her cheek. The feeling of panic was intensifying now, and there was a buzzing in his ears, although he suddenly felt closer to her than he'd ever felt before in his life. 'Why the hell didn't you say something when we got here last night? *Why?* We might have been miles from the flat by now, together, safe.'

'I was going to tell you, but I didn't know how to tell you or what to tell you first. I was so happy when I saw you outside the hotel, and found that you were still alive, that all I wanted was to hold you, really hold you. But by the time you said you'd slept with Abigail I was so close to the edge my head was reeling, and I just flipped. I can hardly remember what happened after that; it's as if I were drunk. You see I can't crack, Blake, not in the conventional sense. I'm too bloody tough. My psychometric counsellor told me years ago that I'm so strong I could never have a breakdown. Sometimes I wish I could. At least then the tension would be released. I suppose my frustration has just been building and twisting against itself, distorting my sense of priorities, until finally I caved in and tried to rape you.' She paused. 'And I can see now that it all goes back to when I was a girl . . .'

Again he perceived a terrible loneliness in her; then he remembered what she'd said the previous evening, about there being things about her which he couldn't begin to comprehend.

'What happened when you were a girl?'

'Do you know why I'm the way I am, Blake? Do you know why I'm so brusque and strong and bloody "assertive"? Because when I was a girl I was sexually abused.'

'Oh no . . .'

He interlocked their fingers, found that his breath was filtering noisily from his nose, found that the panic was becoming a physical rather than a psychological sensation. What she was saying was hurting him, causing him actual physical pain. He wanted nothing more than to comfort her, to turn back the clock several hours and override his own stupidity and his ridiculous moral decency and make love to her beautifully and very slowly when she'd tried to seduce him on the sofa.

'Throughout my childhood and into my teens, growing up in that rectory in that quiet little Yorkshire village, I was abused . . . by my eldest step-sister Mary. She tried to seduce me regularly from when I was about ten. She'd have been fourteen at the time. She'd climb into my bed in the middle of the night and kiss and cuddle and caress me; send her hand where it had no business to be.' The tears were running down her face now, the memories gouging at her tortured subconscious, distorting her words with a hideous muscular contraction that was frightening to hear. 'At first, the hand was a comfort, when I was still too young to understand. But as I grew older and began to notice boys, I started to resist her. I found that I could keep her from coming into my room at night by putting on a tough exterior during the day, by wearing jeans instead of skirts, by adopting a brazen masculine charm, by finally socking her on the jaw one snowy Christmas Eve and breaking three of her teeth.

'That's where it's rooted, Blake. The experience didn't warp my sexuality, thank goodness, but it certainly left its mark. It meant I was always on my guard, being pushy to stop people from dominating me because the feeling made me insecure. It steered me away from taking on the rôle of a "traditional" passive woman, though I'm sure half the feminists I know would applaud what Mary did. I've never found it easy to adopt the guise of a subservient female, not because I didn't want to, but because I was shaped by my circumstances when I was young, marooned in that big old house. We're all shaped by them. We can't help it. All I attract half the time are the amorous advances of predatory lesbians, who can't seem to resist my domineering "masculine" charms. They seem to get a kick out of making a pass at an assertive heterosexual female. But I'm not interested in going to bed with members of my own sex, and never have been, though I do wonder sometimes if it's the rejection that's part of their thrill . . .

'And then the strains I've been going through just lately and the knowledge that you were in danger. One minute you being dead, then you being alive. Being told that the moment I said anything to you or showed the merest hint of being involved with you that I would be killed. Being interrogated by double-barrelled voices from Whitehall, discussing whether or not I should be allowed to live and how much of a danger I was to the "operation." Knowing there was no escape because of ID cards. Not knowing if my head was going to be blown off each night when I got home. I just wanted to die, Blake, but I had to stay alive to protect you. I can see now that I revolted against myself, got dressed up in the leather clothes because I wanted to break free. I wanted you to notice me, that's all. At least I've now found myself, even if I am about to die. Please forgive me for what I've done.'

The tears were running down Blake's face. He knew now why he'd resisted her for so long when his body had been trying to respond. Because he'd lost so much when his marriage broke up, he'd been clinging to the one thing that represented for him a form of absolute stability. He'd been fighting to keep hold of Vanessa, struggling to keep his relationship with her intact, forcing *her* to stay the same for his benefit and nobody else's. And what she'd said was true. Everyone was shaped mentally by their personal circumstances. Schools of self-justifying intellectual thought existed which had yet to realize this about themselves. He knew that strong women found him fascinating because he wasn't in the least bit chauvinistic. This was why he regarded the female as his equal and offered her only the greatest veneration and respect. This was why he'd been blacklisted mentally by a number of his critics who couldn't understand people like him because it was beyond the range of their limited social experience. This was why he was prepared to rest his head on the female shoulder as well as encourage her to place hers upon his. There was nothing peculiar about this. It had merely been the way his father had related to his mother, as millions of fathers related to millions of mothers in households up and down the land. He'd been brought up in a balanced emotional environment; as an attitude of mind it had been inculcated into him from an early age.

But look where his preoccupations had brought him. Nothing ever stayed the same.

One was forever rising to a different mental plane.

'I'm going to marry you, Vanessa,' he said suddenly, the panic returning when he heard the trill of a cellular phone and self-satisfied laughter coming from the lounge. 'If we get out of this alive—'

'No, you're not going to marry me. It was never meant to be. You needed me to help you find Abigail, for you to reach the next stage of your development. She's strong, Blake, far stronger than me. And her strength isn't a product of unpleasant things that happened in her past. She's right for you. She has dignity.'

Considering the nature of the present circumstances and what was going to happen to Blake and herself, Vanessa wondered if she ought to be referring to Abigail in the past tense, though of course she hadn't any idea that Stoneham had shot her.

She stood up again and started walking towards the door, still unable to believe that her love for Blake, which she'd suppressed for so long it had almost become part of the natural landscape of her mind, could have manipulated her so cruelly as to cause her to bring this dreadful catastrophe upon them both. She was too emotionally numbed to see yet that her recent behaviour was not a reflection of weakness but of her formidable strength. She desperately wanted to hear Blake's voice behind her but he said nothing. More guilt was rising to blank out his mind and cancel his voice; preventing a logical coupling of words and thoughts; stopping him from articulating the devastating realization that love had been for so long staring him in the face, while his emotional integrity had always held him back.

Vanessa stopped and clenched her fists with her back to the bed. 'I'm just so tired, Blake. I'm tired of trying not to love you, I'm tired of trying to live with what my husband has been doing to me. I'm tired of everything.'

Driscoll timed the opening of the door so perfectly she

took it for granted that he'd been stood behind it listening to them.

The same realization brought Blake to his senses and caused him finally to call out.

'Vanessa.'

She stopped and still didn't turn, but the sound of his voice seemed to send a shockwave through her body.

'You knew I wasn't dead before you met me outside the hotel last night, didn't you?' He was thinking how she'd somehow seemed less upset by everything than she should have been; it was as though she hadn't been truly grieving before she'd emerged from the hotel. How else could she have become so instantly preoccupied with sex?

Driscoll spoke for her.

'She thought you were dead for about five minutes after some of your compatriots told her about the announcement made on the news, Hunter. And you were in a proper state, weren't you, Vanessa darling? Until you phoned me and found out that everything was hunky-dory.'

Vanessa still didn't turn but closed her eyes to shut off Driscoll's hideous staring face; then she picked up the thread of Blake's previous words. Driscoll perceptibly winced when he heard her say: 'I did not use you last night, Blake. I swear to you that I have never used you and I never would. I was just overjoyed to see you were alive, and I made a fool of myself and subjected you to a humiliating ordeal that was an affront to human decency.'

'I love you, Vanessa,' Blake said. He noticed that the tone of the words bore a startling resemblance to the way she'd used them outside the hotel the previous evening; that tone having since bothered him so much. 'I won't forget our moment together, love. Ever.'

She started to say something too, but her voice broke and she had to walk quickly out of the room.

Driscoll shook his head despondently. 'I think if I hear much more of this sententious crap I shall have to sit down and have a good old cry.'

Blake's voice was as hard as ice.

'The trouble with your kind, Driscoll, is that you just stick people in at one end and shit them out at the other, but you fail to observe the resemblance between yourself and the waste matter as it makes its way down.' He couldn't be bothered to use up breath expounding the psychological basis of Driscoll's philosophy upon life any further.

'An interesting choice of metaphor, Hunter, but quite pointless and immature really for a man of your intelligence, don't you think?'

He came into the room with Stoneham and a tall bony man who was carrying a small blue plastic case and a black body-bag. Stoneham was leafing through the lasergraphs and ruffling his ginger eyebrows.

Driscoll looked at Blake pitifully.

'You don't seem to have had much luck with women, do you, you poor bastard?' He grinned with an air of self-satisfaction that instantly put Blake on edge. Before he could work out what the words were getting at, Driscoll was speaking again: 'This is Dr Morton from Strangeways Prison. He's going to give you a nice little injection, though you needn't be alarmed by the body-bag. Its purpose is to prevent any spectators outside from seeing who you are. The drug won't kill you.'

Blake sat up on the bed and Morton smiled as though he were some kind of mad scientist and placed the case on the dressing-table and opened the lid. Inside were a number of small bottles and a stainless-steel hypodermic gun set into contour sponge-foam. He lifted an ampoule, withdrew some clear liquid into a syringe vessel that formed the barrel of the gun, then clipped a small compressed-air cylinder into place and released a catch at the back of the handle.

'Please don't harm her, Driscoll,' Blake said. 'Whatever you do to me, please don't hurt Vanessa.' He felt the futility of the words even as he heard them come out.

'Whatever you say, Hunter.'

Morton looked at Driscoll and waited for his cue.

Driscoll nodded and Morton stepped across and swabbed the side of Blake's neck.

As the smell of antiseptic filled his nostrils, Blake could only wonder if the events of the past several days had been part of a process of cruel inevitability; that they had really been leading up to this scene in the flat. He realized that the nagging sense of fear that had come into his mind repeatedly since the murder of David Kowalski had not been born of a horror of dying but of simply not knowing what was going to happen next. Now he knew exactly what was going to happen next, and, far from being afraid, he was overcome by a curious feeling of relief. There was nothing left to anticipate but the end. He couldn't help Vanessa now. He sincerely hoped that both he and she would be killed together. Above all, he was confident in the knowledge that Abigail must be safe; a realization which, as he searched for something positive to which he could attach a bit of hope, meant more to him just then than anything else in the world.

'What are you thinking about?' Driscoll asked.

'I was just thinking how things can't get much worse,' Blake said before he could prevent his mouth from opening.

'Oh yes they can, young man. They can get very much worse than this.'

He nodded again at Morton.

Blake's eyes went to Driscoll but he was already hearing a hiss of compressed air below his ear and feeling a cold liquid entering his neck that rapidly became an expanding warmth. Driscoll said something else, but his voice seemed strangely isolated from the rest of his face. Then it was submerged beneath a cushion of sound rising from somewhere inside Blake's head that made the room seem very remote.

Then everything went black.

When Blake had slumped into unconsciousness and they'd lowered him back on the bed, Driscoll turned to Stoneham. 'Go downstairs and put the blue flashing light on, will you Colin? We might as well make this look authentic.' He squinted through the door at Vanessa sitting in front of a policeman in the sun-drenched lounge and lowered his voice. 'Then, when we've got Hunter into the car, come back upstairs and kill Vanessa, there's a good chap. Her husband has already given his compliance.'

'Not me, Derek. I'm not shooting any more women.'

'Well then, tell Addison to come over and do it, but just get it sorted out.' Driscoll took his cellular phone from his jacket pocket and walked through to the lounge, stabbing at the rubber buttons on the way. He stood by the window and looked out across Salford Quays; at the ambitious ramble of post-Modern and the more brutal Modernist Revival architecture, stretching away above lapping water into the frosty early-morning sunshine.

The phone was answered.

'Howard? It's Derek. Yes I know it's early, but would you care to put the kettle on before we arrive?' He turned as Stoneham and Morton carried Blake's unconscious body between them inside the black zip-bag out into the lounge. 'I think we have our prototype at last.'

When he cancelled the phone, he looked disapprovingly at Vanessa, who was seated behind him on the transparent sofa, staring at a point in space. He told the young policeman to watch her, lifted his eyebrows once, then walked out of the room.

# Twenty-Four

Blake was stranded in a dense limbo much like that in which he'd been caught when he'd slept in the bedroom with Vanessa. Though everything was black, utterly black, though still he had no grasp of time, he knew that if only he could slip his hands between the liquid darkness and find an ebony split, then, and only then, might he find Abigail somewhere at the other side.

But no matter how hard he struggled to part the material he could not feel a pair of hands in front of himself with which to reach out and try. He could not register his own body. All he could feel was a sensation of weightlessness and of floating, backed up by the knowledge that somewhere terrifically remote, yet somehow part of the fabric of the blackness, there were voices, and that those voices were directing their attention towards him.

Now he knew that he was drifting away from the curtain of blackness and the sound of dull voices; that he'd failed in his attempt to try and break through. Instead he was twisting head over heels, despite the fact that the laws of gravity no longer applied and he was invisible and did not in theory exist and could not see himself at all. He knew that he was moving into a place of bright unlight. The unlight took on the form of the flat at Salford Quays, and he saw Vanessa spread naked beneath him on the floor in the lounge. They were laughing and joking about all the happy times they'd spent together. They were recalling all those Sunday afternoon drives in her Range Rover looking for places to film, even though they both knew that in reality they'd been searching for places where to fuck. He knew that his erect penis was digging amongst her platinum-blonde fur and was deep inside her body in the flat now; knew that somehow he'd always wanted it to be there. But there was no feeling of eroticism, no burning of fire and desire going on between his legs, for he was not actually fucking her. What was taking place was a necessary fusing of the flesh that was part of the bonding of their minds, because they were just good friends, even if they happened to be in love.

Then Vanessa was smiling and looking beyond his shoulder and pointing to his birthmark and saying *hello* as Abigail came up naked alongside. She laid next to them, and, still inside Vanessa, he leaned over and kissed the dark fur between Abigail's legs. He looked at the soft curve of flesh sloping down from her thighs, one leg slightly proud of the other, with the inviting tuft smudging the soft tissue in the middle. In the place where he was now he felt what he always felt when he was awake: that this arrangement of female flesh, this special place between the combined legs of femininity, was the most beautiful and important composition in the entire universe. An appreciation of that view was his very reason for existence. No single aesthetic panorama on any part of the earth, no picture that had ever been artificially created by humankind, could compare with Nature's sculpting of this part of the body of woman. There were no words to describe the fulfilling effect this sight had upon him, nor for the excitement the animal scent excreted by glands between those legs was capable of having upon him, once he'd started its generation with his fingers and tongue; once he'd inhaled the smell and tasted the taste and drunk the potent drink.

For a contemplation of that part of female produced in him a sensation of ultimate peace and solitude. The only way he could express his gratitude to the forces of creation for having enabled that composition to colour the horizon of his life was to blend his own fur with that fur; to place his hardened self between it and gyrate until the feeling of ecstasy that took over his body made him think of the exploding centre of the sun; of an atomic fusion of flesh between himself and that special female place for which he knew ultimately he would be quite prepared to die.

But now Vanessa was pushing him aside and talking about how she, too, had always been conscious of the importance of this composition, despite their sweet-smelling drives in the country. She was speaking of how crucial was the smell of female and the taste of woman to the fire stoking her own spirit and groin. He felt himself slide out of Vanessa and was conscious of her wonderful musky scent smearing his flesh and soaking his fur. He was conscious that he was wiping it onto his fingers and reaching across and smearing it between Abigail's legs, to lubricate her ready to receive him. He was aware that he was rubbing Vanessa's juices across that magnificent curving of flesh, then was sinking himself between Abigail's opening instead. And then after a period of time, and as soon as he started to fuck Abigail—because this time the blazing erotic fire had set him alight almost instantly—to his horror Vanessa pulled him aside and was placing her head between Abigail's legs and gulping up what she found there, as greedily as a puppy gobbling up a bowlful of food. He was screaming negatives as he watched them make love, as he saw their limbs intertwine, as he saw them gasp with desire and slaver at the sight of each other's projecting breasts glistening in the unlight; as he saw their thumbs depress the big shiny nipples; as he saw their tongues seek out the tiny hardened triggers that would fire the bullet of their combined erotic rage.

And then he was conscious that he was Vanessa, but conscious that he was Abigail, too. He could feel the breasts sprouting from his own chest and he was trying to pull them to his mouth as he arched and the juices were being sucked from between his legs by each other woman. And then he was screaming more negatives and was back in front of the wall of blackness because he wanted his penis back, only this time there was a massive fist on the end of a forearm between his legs, and somewhere in the background the incessant laughing of his ex-wife Victoria, who was standing above the writhing tangle of flesh that represented the two women he knew he now loved, and who were slowly, inextricably fusing into one.

And Vicky was aiming a gun at both their heads and pulling the trigger and asking *who was it to be?* and exploding the two womens' skulls and turning to point the barrel accusingly at him for fucking the two of them both, before she turned the gun on their children. And as he heard the bullet leave the gun and begin to crack apart his own skull, he called out the names of the two women he knew he now loved. He couldn't remember whose name he called first. But he knew that whoever's name he did call first was the most important sound in the universe.

Almost as important as the beauty of the composition arranged between her legs.

# Twenty-Five

Dazzling sunlight was breaking between the blanket of blackness at last, coupled to a blurred view through a window, and the fist on the arm between his legs had grown again and was smashing a hole through to the other side. But as the landscape beyond pulled itself into focus, Blake saw that the sunlight was not sunlight, but a strip of fluorescent light placed behind frosted glass set into an artificial pale-green ceiling panel about ten feet above his head. There was a smell of new paint and plastic overlaid with the odour of rubber—above all rubber—afflicting his nostrils; and he could hear the muffled voices from before. They were clearer this time, sharper; and the sharper they became the stronger became a familiar feeling of apprehensiveness gnawing at the pit of his stomach, when an awareness of the cruel process of inevitability crept in to haunt his mind again.

As he blinked back into consciousness and the abstractions began to clear, he recognized a blurred shape standing over him and identified it as Chief Constable Driscoll, still in uniform. There were two other blue-uniformed men frowning alongside him, whom he took to be prison warders. He didn't grasp the shape of Driscoll's words to begin with, but was aware that he was asking Driscoll where he was and that, judging by the sounds being directed back at him, he was being welcomed back to the land of the living. Then he saw a plastic pair of something that he recognized coming towards him on the end of a bony hand. 'I must confess that I'm tempted to say that you are wherever you want to be, young man,' Driscoll said. 'But why don't you put on your spectacles and try to work it out for yourself?'

Finding that he was coming round surprisingly quickly, Blake did as he was asked and lifted to his elbows and looked around the windowless room. It was quite obviously a prison cell and was sparsely furnished and surprisingly airy, but also ultra-modern, almost hi-tech, and like nothing he had ever seen before. His first reaction was to think that it had something of the quality of being part of a submarine, or perhaps a crewman's cabin aboard a realistic spacecraft in a film of the future. The walls were made from steel panels that had been powder-coated with a toughened light-green enamel. There were three stainless-steel automatic sliding doors, with finger panels to either side. The floor was finished with dark-green studded-rubber matting, which explained the smell assailing his nostrils. Each article of furniture had been fabricated from metal, then powder-coated in a warm apple-green and bolted down. There was the single bed upon which he was laid on a light-blue quilt and pillow. There was a table, and four chairs. There were yellow triangular shelves fitted into the four corners of the room, upon each of which was positioned an artificial plant. On a rack of metal shelves embedded in the wall alongside what he took to be the door leading to a corridor, he could see a number of popular board games, some packs of cards, and a box of dominoes. He could sense by the even atmosphere that he was in the presence of air conditioning; that it was probably being fed through the border of stainless-steel grilles running at dado height around the room; and that the grilles were connected to the muffled rumbling of a generator he could hear coming from somewhere beyond the walls. The fluorescent lights shining from behind the overhead transparent casings, which had greeted him as he'd struggled to break free of his dream, bathed the space with a curiously ambivalent cast of bluish-yellow light.

He slumped back onto the bed, not giving a damn about his surroundings, not caring about the buzzing in his ears, or the dull ache in his neck where it had been pumped full of tranquillizer, or that he was still only wearing the bathrobe and that his bare feet were very cold.

'Where's Vanessa?' he asked, anticipating the reply.

Driscoll spoke without hesitation.

'You needn't concern yourself about Vanessa Aysgarth any longer, Hunter, because she's dead. Her hired Mazda Stingray will be found burned out, along with her body and that of a young male prostitute, in one of the city slums later this morning. And her charming husband really will be so upset.'

'Damn you to hell, Driscoll.'

'Yes, damn me to hell, though I'm sorry to inform you that you will be going there long before I do.'

Though Blake was still conscious of somehow having gone beyond grief, he closed his eyes tightly and found his body ejecting some breath as he made a passionate mental farewell to Vanessa. He was not a religious man, but the words that ran through his mind at that moment were the closest he would ever get to making a prayer.

Driscoll knitted his hands together behind his back and paced once around the room. 'Before we proceed, I perhaps ought to explain to you something about the place in which you are now unfortunate enough to find yourself incarcerated.' He glanced approvingly at the walls and smirked. 'You are inside the condemned-prisoner's cell of the recently-completed Execution and Disposal Block at Strangeways Prison, Greater Manchester. It is largely the existence of this underground prototype complex that has enabled the government to legislate, for it is the first fully operational execution facility of its type in the country, and the most advanced in the world. It was planned some five years ago, and its construction over the past two has been one of the most closely-guarded Official Secrets of recent times. Hence the decision to build it away from London.

'You will see that there are three doors opening onto the chamber. That door over there'—he lifted a finger towards the rack of metal shelves—'leads to the main corridor and to what could be politely termed Manchester's very own death row. The door to your left leads to our weighing, toilet, and medical facilities, each equipped with the very latest technology. The door to your right leads through to the execution chamber proper.' Now he stretched fingers and palm towards the furniture in the centre of the room. 'Four chairs, one being for the inmate, two for the warders, and the other for the prison chaplain. Please observe that everything is bolted down to prevent it from being used to assault the warders.

'Your nostrils will also have registered the brand-new studded-rubber matting which has been adopted as a floor covering throughout the facility. The idea behind this is that it will help to deaden the approach of the secondary warders, as they come along the corridor in the mornings to assist an inmate through to the gallows. In the old days they did precisely the same thing with coconut matting, of course. But things have advanced somewhat since then, haven't they? And, let us face it, rubber matting is a lot easier to hose down, and it offers the warders a better grip with their feet if they find themselves struggling with a distressed inmate. You see, Hunter, apart from such obvious practical considerations, despite the purposes for which this facility has been built—and despite what you will be thinking about us morally—we are still obliged to ensure that the surroundings remain as unintimidating as possible for the inmate, and help keep him at ease as he awaits disposal.' He smirked again. 'You will not, however, be surprised to hear that we nicknamed this chamber Room 101 whilst it was being built.'

Blake was still shaking his head cynically from hearing another mention of the word *disposal*.

Driscoll read the expression.

'Yes, I rather like the term "disposal" myself, though

technically it is a plagiarizing of White Paper speak. And there really is no need to look quite so surprised about everything, Hunter, because there is an awful lot goes on in this country that you liberal journalist bastards, and the poor unsuspecting masses, know nothing about.'

'Nothing surprises me any more, Driscoll, but let me articulate something so that I can bring together a number of loose threads and put myself in the picture.' He paused. 'Question: Why would a black criminal gang, whose violent behaviour is ostensibly a product of the depoliticization of the underclass due to economic decline, turn its attention towards the rather civilized subject of political kidnapping and murder? Answer: Because it is not a criminal gang at all, but a number of bent policemen masquerading as West Indians, who are in the process of gerrymandering public events to ensure that a wave of national moral hysteria continues unabated, so that the death penalty can be reintroduced. Their clandestine directives, along with the killing of David Kowalski, scenes of televised inner-city anarchy, and lynched policemen being shot by snipers in the leg before being shot to bits by rioters, having been issued from very much on Whitehall high.'

'Your analysis is absolutely correct, Hunter, though it would perhaps be more accurate to say that a little public relations assistance became necessary, to ensure the new legislation gets its Royal Assent. As for our motives, the reintroduction of capital punishment has long been a foregone conclusion. Our economic-cum-industrial decline was bound to ensure that, as was the fact that our society is disintegrating very much in line with the American model. I'm sure I needn't bore you with talk about flows of history, or shrinking industrial capacity piling up the unemployed, or the social transformations that have been taking place as a result of economic decline, or the importance our various industrial revolutions have played in effecting society's complexion over the years. I know that you've been explaining all about it to a camera during the making of your engaging little film about the advance toward a new social order, with our late, lamented Vanessa.'

Driscoll folded his arms, joined his buttocks to the edge of the table, and glanced around the cell again. 'You have to look at this execution facility not in a moral, but in an economic context, Hunter. The British prison system has been successfully privatized, and the bringing back of capital punishment is merely one of the "productivity improvements" that market incentives were bound to introduce, once the transformation from public to private ownership took place, but within a rapidly deteriorating economic climate. We cannot go on stockpiling the murderous elements of the underclass in our penal institutions forever. The keeping alive of these people serves no constructive purpose whatsoever. Would a factory continue to maintain a piece of machinery from which it could no longer extract a reasonable profit? It would not. It would have it sent to the knacker's yard. And so it should be with human life within an efficiently-run penal system. What works against this is that it is very much in the interests of privately-owned prisons that they do *not* reform offenders, but that new buildings go on being constructed and more prisoners are convicted. What must be maintained is a steady flow of inmates, because we are allocated a proportionate amount of funding from the government to use in the most cost-effective way that we think possible.

'But with restrictions on public spending becoming more prohibitive by the day, heavy cutbacks are now taking place within the prison-building programme. The result is that existing facilities are in danger of being overwhelmed, to say the least, so that profits are being undermined because the number of convicted serious offenders is rising all the time. They receive lengthy prison sentences and occupy cells that might be better utilized in a rapid turnover of less chronically brutalized members of the criminal fraternity. Obviously, the greater our turnover of prisoners, the greater the remuneration we receive from central government. Though it was never officially-stated policy, before privatization it was assumed that serious offenders would be returned to the community, where they would quickly re-offend and pass again through the prison system, enabling ourselves and the courts to retain a steady profitability.'

He smiled and combined a shrug of his shoulders with a somewhat perspicacious release of breath. 'Unfortunately, we have a Home Secretary and a governing administration, who, for reasons of political expediency and plain moral dunderheadedness, desire to placate public unease by threatening tougher sentences for offenders.

'So, the reintroduction of capital punishment not only placates public anger and ensures party political popularity in the run-up to a General Election, it makes sound economic sense, too. For it eliminates waste from the system. As their offences become more serious, criminals will move up the inmate hierarchy until they do something that results in them being hanged. That way the prison population should remain fairly constant. It ensures crime works to the prison system's, rather than to the criminal fraternity's, advantage. It is less of a burden on the national exchequer and the taxpayer. It tackles a social problem efficiently through an application of the rigid disciplines of the market. And because Britain has nurtured a large, brutalized male underclass, by systematically ridding society of its more unruly elements we can expect a fairly steady flow of—how shall I put it?—"disposable income" for some time to come. Meanwhile, we are attacking the crime problem, with the result that society will eventually stabilize, once the bad elements are weaned away.' His brow adjusted to indicate something along the lines of a three-dimensional full stop.

Blake had to admire the cold logic of the man's mind. 'Jesus,' he said. 'A steady profit, not from tackling the socio-economic causes of crime, but from putting institutionalized murder back onto the statute books . . .'

'You could put it like that, yes, though I prefer to see it as a form of eugenics; a systematic stamping out of the slum class in an increasingly criminogenic society. And you have to admit, Hunter, that it benefits society at large. Of course, as more prisons complete their own execution facilities, and once competition increases, we can expect our profitability to come under pressure. But the shareholders of Strangeways can expect a reasonable monopoly for some time to come. And, because the whole of the Western world is going into economic decline, and what with there now being some twenty million people unemployed in the European Union alone, it will only be a matter of time before we can sell the service to customers from abroad.'

Blake snorted derisively.

'Human disposal turned into profit. The crimewave turned to the advantage of market forces, despite the problem being largely a product of market forces to begin with. Jesus Christ. Do you know what you ought to do, Driscoll? You ought to build railway lines to the prison from the city slums, then marshall the unlawful elements living there, put them in cattle wagons and fool them into believing you're going to transport them to a better life. Just think. You could get rid of West Indians and Asians—all the "semi-apes", as I'm sure you term them in your quaint White Paper speak—and then you could move onto fat people, spastics, and people who are mentally ill, not to mention useless geriatrics. And, when you've eliminated those, you could move on to homosexuals, old-age pensioners, and the working class as a whole. You could even set up a little sideline in the manufacture of lamp-shades and bars of soap, and get into a bit of upholstery-stuffing with all that human hair. And why not go the whole way, and start producing your own variant of good old, bad old Soylent Green? Why not turn the disposal of human carcasses into profit as well, grind them down, mix them with a few vitamins, and transform them into protein-rich food chips? That's the eventual aim of such fucking fascist madness, isn't it?'

'Perhaps it is Hunter. But that is only because the developed world is becoming ever more "fascist", as you insist on describing it, because there is less wealth and fewer jobs to go round.' His throat issued a sound somewhere between a laugh and a melodic tune and he gazed thoughtfully at a point in space, somewhere near the ceiling. 'If only Britain could have remained in the 1950s forever. Full employment, steam trains, no motorways, no redeveloped inner cities, fewer machines doing the jobs of men and women, hardly any immigrants, a youth still largely under the thumb of deference, everything still picturesque, everything still on a human scale. A patrician society where everyone knew their place. The stability of work keeping its arm around the shoulders of all those disgusting working-class neighbour-hoods; keeping their moth-eaten spirit alive even as they slept; fitting them all into the cosy economic scheme of things; giving them a stake in life.' He smacked his lips theatrically. 'It was perfect in a world of low technology, big distances between places, and poorish communications.'

He turned away from the point in space and brought his eyes back to Blake. 'But surely you must accept that the situation society now finds itself facing has arisen because of historical cause-and-effect. Surely you agree, Hunter, that an economic constricting process is taking place and that an ever-advancing technology is working against a huge pop-ulation conditioned to think in terms of aggressive self-interest. Our society is guided along so fundamentally by the lure of—how did the learned professor once put it?—*imm-ature emotional satisfactions?*

'So why deny this? Why fight against it, when covetous desire is such an essential and rewarding component of human emotional make-up? We are simply ensuring that the balance is retained, along with the stability of our proud British institutions, and the divine rule of our ancient social order. If you want to find the roots of social breakdown, Hunter, look at the shops, don't look at the ruling class. Look at clothes, cars, vanity, popular culture, a vigorous self-aggrandizement controlled by the will of the market. Everybody desperate to protect what they own. Everybody struggling to stay at the top of the pile. Analyse your appreciation of a pretty woman embellishing her femininity through the things she chooses to wear, as she struts upon her heels proudly along a street, or by the way she cuts her hair. Think of the way Vanessa Aysgarth was dressed last night, right down to the pale-pink lipstick that she had painted onto her lips. Your heterosexual instincts *feed* on a display of such naked female plumage, and the female *feeds* on the market to preen that plumage.

'Think of the continuous striving of the individual to gain admiration socially through an aggressive projection of personal sexual display. Think how vital these emotions are to the survival of our species. Then ask yourself why "socialism" was such a miserable failure, when the hypocrites who devised it couldn't let go of the very emotional values they deplored, but which capitalist culture had actually bred into them.

'We *depend* emotionally upon social prestige to generate in ourselves a feeling of self-worth; to ensure there is a sense of order to society. Even *you* get a kick out of knowing when you've said something good to a camera; when you know that you've made a penetrating observation, struck an audience's nerve, sensed that your intelligence will be put on a pedestal and admired. Vanessa was quite right, you young bastard. Our prejudices are shaped by an economic system that fucks us all, though I would prefer to define it more accurately as a raping instead of a shaping.'

'What the hell do you mean by that?'

Driscoll lifted something from the table which Blake had been unable to see because he'd been too low on the bed. It was a small red tape recorder, about the size of a cigarette packet. A button was thumbed and Blake's tinny voice filled the room from the previous evening, surprisingly loudly. It was a recording made after Vanessa had raped him in the Salford Quays flat and they'd laid recovering for a good hour afterwards, before he'd picked her up and carried her into the bedroom.

'*I do love you, Vanessa,*' he heard himself saying again, '*but not like this. Ours is a different type of emotional bond.*'

'We were outside aiming our very sophisticated microphones, while you two lovebirds were, I take it, recovering from something of an explosive sexual *tête-à-tête.*'

Blake's head dropped back against the pillow and he laughed half-deliriously. 'You rotten sadistic bastard, Driscoll. Why do people like you consistently revel in the humiliation of others?'

'Because we are honest enough to acknowledge that certain human beings have a divine right to be superior to others, that is why. I accept that. I articulate the thought. I do not suppress the urges common to my human nature.' He switched off the tape recorder when Vanessa started speaking, then came away from the table. 'I thought you might be amused by that little playback. However, time is stealing away from us, and we really must be moving along.' He stepped across to an intercom on the wall and held down a button. 'Come downstairs now, will you Colin? We're nearly ready.'

He let go of the button and stepped back up to the bed. 'You know, Hunter, there has long been a widespread belief that if capital punishment were ever to be reintroduced, it wouldn't involve hanging but would probably be administered by intravenous injection. Perhaps an injection is perceived to be rather more humane; more in keeping with the sophisticated clinical environ of a modern, highly technologicized world. The belief is quite misguided, of course, because as long ago as 1953 the Royal Commission on Capital Punishment concluded that hanging was the most reliable and humane method of execution yet known. It also concluded it to be the quickest and least messy in terms of actual damage caused to the body of the subject. Provided that a number of precautions were taken into consideration beforehand, as I am sure you are aware.' He grinned. 'The dark musty surfaces and antiquated Victorian atmosphere might be things of the past. What you see around you might represent the hi-tech execution facility of the future. But the views from 1953 still hold, and they are expected to be re-affirmed once the new Commission being set up to monitor the reintroduction of capital punishment reports in five years' time.' The smile Driscoll's face now moulded upon itself could have been transformed into yet another smirk without much difficulty. 'Meanwhile, we have to test out the new gallows apparatus, break it in so as to speak, which is where your very good self comes in.'

They heard a muffled pneumatic whine and the sound of lift doors sliding open in the corridor outside. Then Stone-ham came in and Blake's head nearly exploded because Stoneham was helping a drained and very weak, almost bedraggled-looking *Abigail* into the cell with him . . .

Instantly, Blake snarled and leaped from the bed and tried to lunge towards her. The slight stickiness of his bare feet enabled him to get a grip on the rubber matting. But the two warders had him and there was such a scuffle that the three of them fell into a heap, grappling with each other amongst a knot of groping limbs. Blake thrashed and blew off a ferocious stream of obscenities, and wondered if he felt a tooth split as his jaw gnashed against his upper skull. Never in all his life had he wanted anything more than to touch Abigail at that moment.

'Let me touch her, for Christ's sake you bastards, *let me touch her!*' The veins stood out on his forehead as he heaved with all his might, the emotion finally breaking when he realized that not only had he lost Vanessa, he was almost certainly going to lose Abigail. He shrieked her name and exploded into a rage of angry growls and felt his cranium bang against the floor; then strong fingers locked onto his chin and rucked up the flesh and he closed his eyes so tight-ly the muscles began to ache at the back of the sockets into which the eyes were slotted.

Driscoll smiled at the pleading Abigail, watching the fracas as though he were a cricket umpire calmly monitoring play. 'Well now, he certainly has his moments, doesn't he my dear?'

Abigail was overjoyed to see that Driscoll hadn't been lying, and that Blake was indeed still alive. But she was panting slightly, her eyelids were very heavy, and her mascara was still smeared from the previous evening's shock and tears. She'd made a feeble attempt to go to Blake as well, but Stoneham easily restrained her and stood her against the table. The two warders lifted Blake back up and pinned him to the bed. The younger, balder of the two addressed Driscoll. 'Will it be necessary to tranquillize him, sir?'

'No it won't. I don't want to placate his adrenalin, I want to make him suffer.' Blake's spectacles had come away from his face during the scuffle and Driscoll now bent and picked them up. 'You won't be needing these again, young man,' he said, and he dropped them back onto the floor and stood on them.

Blake managed to open his eyes and direct them at Abigail. Because she'd been carrying some spare clothes in her Frontera, after Driscoll's people had abducted her and the vehicle from the hotel, they'd allowed her to change into the pair of rust-coloured leather trousers, the beige angora sweater, and the brown ankle-boots she was wearing now. Blake recognized the smell of her clothes conditioner and her clean hair filling the room—realized for the first time—and felt a curious wave of somewhat guilty confusion as he did so—that it was not at all dissimilar to Vanessa's.

Abigail looked at him and smiled weakly, the translucency of her eyes being only slightly dulled, the rims glistening. She mouthed his name silently, then her eyes closed, and her head fell forward. In conjunction with a pain that was expanding from the centre of his chest, Blake's brain seemed to be hurting as he grappled with the question of how on earth they'd managed to establish a connection between himself and Abigail.

'What have you done to her?' he asked of the room. '*What the hell have you been doing to her . . .*'

'Don't worry, Hunter,' Driscoll said, 'it's not as bad as it looks. She was shot in the stomach with a tranquillizer dart that we tried out for the first time last evening, in your hotel room as a matter of fact. The darts are contained in a cartridge that snaps into the handle of a normal automatic pistol, and can be fired like conventional bullets. And a most unusual drug it is too. It knocks out the victim but leaves their eyes open as though they were dead. She's still very weak, of course, and she does have a rather unpleasant ache and a quite nasty bruise in her belly. But beyond that she's perfectly all right.'

'You went to the hotel?' Blake asked her incredulously.

'Yes . . .' she managed to croak, without lifting her face, her voice now so husky it was almost belch-like in quality. 'I thought I was dead when I'd been shot . . . they made me think that you were . . .'

'She arrived just before seven, to be precise,' Driscoll said, 'only she bumped into us.' He scrutinized Abigail. 'And of course, Abigail, that you were able to *think* you were dead only serves to underline the fact that you weren't, doesn't it?'

Blake dropped his head when he realized that he must actually just have missed her after all. He had a vision of himself standing unsuspecting outside in the cold beneath the cloisters; had a picture of her being shot in the room; saw the rape scene at the Salford Quays flat; and had never felt such a stab of angry futility in all his life.

Driscoll walked once around the table, still scrutinizing Abigail as though he were a customer contemplating a purchase. 'You know, Hunter, I cannot understand why you wasted time worrying about such a worthless human specimen as Vanessa Aysgarth—'

'Vanessa wasn't weak, you bastard. She'd got more strength and dignity than you will ever know. She was just like—' He almost said *Abigail*. But the shock of what he was thinking stopped the word dead in its tracks, despite the deadliness of the situation in which he now found himself.

'Oh yes, we're not supposed to speak ill of the dead, are we? But this female here'—he nodded approvingly at Abigail—'is of a type I have never encountered before.'

'That's because you don't mix amongst intelligent circles, Driscoll,' Blake said. 'You don't come into contact with real human beings.'

Driscoll smiled, said nothing, then reached out and lifted Abigail by the chin. 'Stand up, young lady. Come away from the table. I want to look at you.'

Abigail pushed herself upright and glowered weakly. She stood a couple of inches taller than Driscoll, though she was being assisted by her squat Cuban heels.

'Do you know,' Driscoll said to her, 'Hunter hasn't broken until now, and I doubt if he would have done, had he not seen you. And I must confess that I can understand why. For I don't mind saying that I feel as intimidated by you as I might do if I were standing in front of a man. You have a quite extraordinary stage presence. And those strange, glowing eyes. There's a force hidden inside you that I cannot accurately define. It isn't so much an assertiveness as a sort of controlled reading of the mind. You know exactly what people are thinking whenever they come anywhere near you, don't you? You know exactly what I'm thinking now.'

'That doesn't take a lot of doing, Chief Constable,' she said thinly. Though the tone of her words was flat, and the breath carrying them out was straining from the effort, it was as if she were a teacher addressing a small troublesome boy.

Driscoll closed his eyes once and nodded curtly. Then he pushed the dark hair back over her ear and allowed his eyes to traverse her body.

'I wonder what I might do with you once we've disposed of Prince Charming here,' he said. He inspected her closely and ran a finger along her trembling eyelids, then examined the tip. 'Hmm. You don't need all that much make-up, do you? Dark-haired women never do. Their faces don't need paint and powder to pull them into focus.'

'I told you before to keep your filthy hands off me.'

Driscoll turned away from her.

'Yes you did, and I told you not to adopt that tone of voice with me, young lady.'

He took another half-step away then spun round and smashed his clenched fist straight into Abigail's solar-plexus. There was such a terrific blast of air blown from her lungs that Blake felt a drop of spittle strike his forehead. As she crumpled to the green floor and squirmed, she managed to shoot out her hand and grabbed Blake's ankle. For a second they looked at each other and her eyes sparkled and he felt a momentary sensation of utter calm as his body responded to her touch, before she was choking and gasping, her hand had been kicked away, and he was stifling a scream of anguish and struggling to fight free from the warders again, but they still had him pinned.

Then, with his face completely expressionless, without taking his eyes away from Blake or aiming them at the body on the floor, and with his hands still knitted together behind his back, Driscoll kicked Abigail in the stomach, hard. The brutality of the assault surprised even Stoneham and the guards. Blake saw one of her ankle-boots fly off and go skating like a boomerang across the floor and clatter against the metal wall. He dropped his head and tried to pull forward but felt the guards push him back. He looked for mercy to Driscoll's staring eyes. 'Please let me go to her,' he pleaded, his voice a broken croak. 'Please just let me go to her . . .'

'No,' Driscoll said nonchalantly.

Then he kicked Abigail in the kidneys so violently that his hands shot out from behind his back to steady himself, and his hair became dishevelled.

Blake knew that Driscoll was kicking Abigail again and again. He tried to shut everything off, but his eyes split once and he saw her trying to lift to her elbows, her hair fanned and flying, her mouth gaping, as the foot drove cruelly into the soft flesh of her body. Though the sound of her suffering was truly the most frightening thing he'd ever heard, he could no longer actually hear, because he'd wished to God that he couldn't hear, because his body had begun to heave and convulse, because the guards were straining to keep him down, because his mouth opened, and because he screamed and screamed and screamed and screamed and screamed and screamed and screamed. The shriek was banshee-like in its intensity and was carried out into the chamber by such an unbridled release of repressed emotional energy that it seemed to split the skulls of everybody standing in the room. Had this been another scene in a film, it would have been the moment when there was a rapid succession of shots showing different parts of the prison—the empty landings above the suspended nets, men reading in their cells and staring at television screens in recreation rooms, the warders about to slide open or close metal doors, a crowd of diners suddenly falling silent as the terrific scream ripped through the babble and clatter of the canteen: everything finished off by an establishment shot showing the outside of the building, with the superimposed scream relentlessly tearing the fabric of the air.

But it wasn't a film, it was real, and Blake found himself thinking, as his lungs finally emptied themselves, that the cliché about wanting to wake and find it was all a bad dream was entirely accurate. As his eyes opened, as his throat began to burn, as the scream died away and the metal furniture sang like a tuning-fork from the echo before everything turned to a piercing silence, he saw Driscoll step across to the foetal-positioned shape that was his almost-unconscious—his beautiful beloved—Abigail. With an agility that was quite horrible to contemplate, Driscoll grabbed her by the scruff of the neck, and, his teeth angrily gritted, manhandled her roughly across the floor and dumped her at the feet of a rather pale-looking Stoneham, who he demanded get the fucking bitch out of the room.

As Stoneham hooked her arm over his shoulder, touched the finger-panel to slide back the door, and helped her stumble out of the cell, her free hand was groping at the air. 'Blake . . .' she groaned, 'please don't leave me . . .'

It was the most desperately pitiful moment, and Blake would have swapped his own life for hers without hesitation if it meant that only she could live. Then her words were trailing into a bronchial-sounding cough, the door was sliding closed, and he knew that she had almost certainly gone forever.

Everything seemed to have given way since Abigail had been brought into the cell. The curious feeling of relief he'd experienced before he'd been drugged back in the Salford Quays flat, which he'd hoped would sustain him as he anticipated nothing but the end, had completely evaporated. A sensation of ice-cold fear had consumed him so powerfully that his genitals had started to constrict. Though his position was still contained by the two obtuse and silent warders, he closed his eyes, squeezing the tears down his face, then opened them and spoke coldly and very methodically, staring at the space between his knees.

'I am going to kill you, Driscoll,' he said, amazed at the passion in his voice. His shoulders were rising and falling as he struggled to keep the lid on his rage. But already he'd assessed the futility of the words, because his emotions felt as though they were going numb and the room seemed to be on the verge of floating away.

'No you're not going to kill me Hunter,' Driscoll said, coming back to stand in front of the bed, 'because if you did you would never sleep decently again. Quite apart from the fact that in a few minutes' time I shall kill you, your type is too weak. Tough, cardboard heroes in the films and novels can kill as the finale approaches, then walk away and feel no remorse. But not real, sensitive, three-dimensional human beings like you. Oh no. This is the real world, Blake Hunter. The reality of this condemned cell, the reality of this entire facility, the reality of the events in which you find yourself embroiled, is the reality of a boot stamping on a human face forever.'

He retrieved Abigail's ankle-boot from the floor, slipped his hand inside it, flexed his fingers and caressed the heel, and seemed to chew over a quiet, erotic sigh. Then suddenly he turned and snarled and threw the boot as hard as he could against the wall. It bounced from the metal surface, ricochetted from the tabletop, and skidded into a corner of the room. His hair became dishevelled again, but as he brought himself upright to straighten it, the door to the corridor slid open and Stoneham came back in, looked once around the cell, picked up Abigail's boot, threw Driscoll a quick desultory glance, then walked back out, stabbing the finger-panel behind him.

Driscoll finished straightening his hair, then was back in front of Blake, his face contorted with rage as he tried to cancel the atmosphere that Stoneham had just brought into the room.

'Do you know something, Hunter? When I was at university I actually toyed with the idea of becoming a Communist. But do you know why I became what I am now? Do you know why it was so easy for an extreme left-winger to transpose his emotional outlook to that of somebody who is extreme-Right? Because we are each motivated by the same authoritarian instinct! By the desire to impose, through force, our idea of conformity onto others! Doesn't it frighten you to think that I'm intelligent enough to analyse my own motives? *Doesn't it?*'

Blake shook his head indifferently.

'Perhaps it explains your fucking sexual inadequacy, then, Chief Constable. Because to truly appreciate love you've got to know how to give, how to share, how to co-operate. People like you just love themselves, hence the hopeless frigidity of your desperate, degraded emotions. You can't form fulfilling relationships, so you compensate for what you lack emotionally by being attracted to the idea of tyranny.'

Driscoll couldn't believe that he'd been penetrated so deeply so quickly. He lashed out and slapped Blake across the face with the back of his hand. Blake felt the back of his head bang against the metal wall, and the nerves of several of his teeth jumped in their sockets from the impact. But still he spluttered stubbornly, his voice hoarse. 'What you lack in compassion you make up for with violence. You react, I proact. *And the two shall battle for supremacy of the Earth.*' He laughed mechanically before Driscoll's fist sent him silent again, and the coppery taste of blood lanced the interior of his mouth.

Driscoll's breath was shaking as he pulled himself away from the bed and touched the finger-panel to slide back the door leading to the execution chamber. He nodded at the two warders and mopped his face with a handkerchief while they brought Blake roughly to his feet. One of them began tightening the belt of the bathrobe but Driscoll intervened. 'No,' he said. 'I think it would be more touchingly symbolic if we were to hang Blake Hunter naked.' He pushed the warder aside and tore at the bathrobe, the sleeves snagging for a moment at Blake's wrists; then he threw it to the floor leaving the body before him completely exposed. He stepped away, and, in true penal tradition, the warders pinioned the prisoner's arms to prevent him from struggling.

Driscoll allowed the silence to linger while he scrutinized the hairy torso and finished getting back his breath. 'We shall now take Blake Hunter through to the gallows,' he managed to say calmly. 'It is time for the investigative journalist to die.'

And with that they frogmarched him through.

# Twenty-Six

When Stoneham brought Abigail into the darkened execution chamber to watch Blake die, her first reaction was to think that the room was so sparsely furnished as to be almost abstract in its simplicity.

Dominating the space was the executioner's elevated control podium, growing from the rubber matting alongside the centreboards like a futuristic grey plastic pulpit. Driscoll was standing self-importantly behind it, still in uniform, but with his tunic unfastened and the sleeves rolled up trendily to the elbows, his bony features picked out like those of a death's-head mask by the blue glow of a computer screen embedded in the console. There was no other source of illumination in the room except for a shaft of intense white light, shining down from the ceiling above the gallows. Apart from the podium, the only objects Abigail could see were the orange nylon noose hooked around Blake's neck, an intercom that was part of the finger-panel by the door on the wall, and a stainless-steel rack to which were attached a hood and several pairs of velcro arm- and leg-straps. The textures of the powder-coated metal and studded-rubber surfaces looked to be the same as those of the condemned cell, except that through here everything was finished in a neutral mid-grey. There was a narrow black-and-yellow hazardline describing the position of the centreboards, which were about the size of a pair of domestic doors laid flat. (The shiny studs of the rubber matting covering them being of a slightly different

texture to the rest.) Similar markings described the outline
to a flight of metal steps disappearing through a hole in the
floor at the back. She knew these would lead to the secondary chamber underneath, remembering from her A Level
History lessons that executed prisoners needed to be left
suspended for about an hour, to allow any waste matter to
be expelled once muscular contractions had ceased.

Though she was overjoyed to find that Blake was still
alive, though her heart and her love went out to him now,
she didn't know where to put her face when she saw him
standing stark naked with the noose around his neck, his
hands and feet bound, positioned beneath the spotlight over
the centreboards ready to drop. She didn't get the chance to
meet his eyes properly because Driscoll was in the process of
more or less torturing him. He was manipulating the computer keypad moulded into the podium, watching some rot-
ating figures on the blue screen, and revelling in Blake's
suffering as maliciously as a cat toying with a wounded
mouse. As he touched the keys, the rope to which Blake was
attached was being tightened by an electric motor hidden
inside the ceiling, his body having been hoisted by his neck
to the point just before it would swing away from the floor,
leaving him straining on tiptoe to prevent himself from
pirouetting. He was snuffling and snorting noisily, there was
spittle hanging in front of his face against the bright light,
and the whites of his eyes were showing as he stared down
his nose to try and look at Abigail as she came in. But the
pressures against his throat were causing him to fight for
breath so savagely that his face was flitting rapidly between
light and shadow, and he couldn't fasten his eyes properly
onto hers.

When he was satisfied that Blake had been immobilized
verbally, Driscoll stepped down from the podium, and, keeping the whites of his eyes on Abigail's all the way, knitted
his hands together behind his back and stood to the right of
the centreboards. Before he started speaking, he aimed a
forefinger at Stoneham, then at Abigail, then at the rubber

matting a couple of yards in front of Blake. Stoneham slotted his cigarette into his mouth and moved Abigail forward, positioning her so close to Blake that she could smell his musky masculine scent, and even the sweat in his hair. She was puzzled when Stoneham brushed her own hair back from her shoulders and smoothed it gently with his hand, before he stepped away. It was the kind of gesture she would have expected from another woman, not a rather brutish man.

'Bind her ankles only please, Colin,' Driscoll said, his bony features slipping in and out of shadow, 'then you can go.'

Blake was suspended on the end of the rope as if he were hanging from a meat hook, and a mess of veins were embossed against his forehead and neck. He gurgled angrily when Stoneham went up to the stainless-steel rack and unhooked a velcro strap, came back across to Abigail, and, with his cigarette still protruding from his mouth and the smoke smarting his eye, knelt and bound her ankles, smoothing her brown leather trousers to finish the job off in the same way that he'd smoothed her hair. Then he stood up and noisily blew out a lungful of foul-smelling smoke, lifted his eyebrows at Driscoll, walked over and touched the finger-panel to the side of the door, and went out through the condemned cell looking bewildered, if not actually relieved. Only Abigail, Blake, and Driscoll remained in the chamber, poised like actors ready to go into action upon a stage.

The door to the condemned cell slid closed and Abigail brought her eyes back to Driscoll's, bracing herself for the monumental task she knew lay ahead of her, if she were going to get Blake and herself out if this vile predicament alive and keep her appointment with a beautiful fifteen-year-old dream. She knew now why they'd allowed time for the lingering effects of the tranquillizer dart to wear off, why they'd given her the chance to recover in her cell after Driscoll had beaten her up, why they'd frogmarched her so dramatically into the execution chamber, and why Driscoll had deliberately checked Blake's ability to speak.

It was because the Chief Constable's personal vendetta was against her more than it was against Blake. Driscoll didn't know it, of course, but because she'd been shadowing him and delving into his background for the better part of a year, she knew more about him than probably he knew about himself. She knew that he harboured a deep hatred of strong, intelligent women such as her. She knew that between the ages of nine and eleven at boarding school he'd been a housemaster's boy, and that great pains had been taken to conceal this from the media over the years. Her sources indicated that the housemaster had also sadistically beaten him, because that was how he became sexually excited during the taking of young boys. Driscoll was not, and so far as she'd been able to ascertain, never had been, truly homosexual. But the lasting damage to his emotions was that from an early age he had learned to equate violence with a certain amount of sexual satisfaction, prompting an emotional inadequacy, and an inability to form satisfying relationships with women, that had accompanied him into adulthood. She suspected that his brutal assault against her earlier had been part of a perverted process of sexual arousal. It was almost certainly his way of showing that he was attracted to her, but also a sign that his subconscious mind was still struggling to come to terms with how his body had been so horribly defiled when he was a boy. When faced with a woman who would not respond to his advances, he probably reacted aggressively because he'd been beaten when he'd resisted his housemaster all those years ago. He'd been so disturbed by what had been done to him that his anger manifested itself by incorporating violence into his own sexual psychology, so that beating up a woman to try and make her submit actually turned him on.

Abigail experienced a small feeling of triumph to think that Driscoll had no idea that she held a veritable psychometric file about him in her mind, when he narrowed his eyes and started to speak, savouring grittily the texture of his own words, picking them up as though he were starting a new paragraph halfway through a lecture, determined slowly to break her.

'You are probably wondering, Abigail, why on earth there should be the need for computer technology in an execution chamber nowadays. You are probably wondering why there should be standing alongside these gallows a control podium which looks like a prop from a science-fiction film, where once a cast-iron lever, like something from an old railway signal box, was sufficient to control the operation of the trapdoors and to send a human body to its death.'

Without unfolding his hands from behind his back, he started pacing slowly around the centreboards, during which time the shadows kept leaving his eye sockets and coming back to fill them in again.

'Well, to understand why, you need to remember that there has long been a number of popular misconceptions about the carrying out of a judicial sentence of hanging. You need to remember that the most common of these is the belief that when a human being is hanged it is simply stood upon the gallows, a hood and noose are placed over its head and neck, the trapdoors are dropped out of the way, the body is allowed to fall through, and that this is a straight-forward procedure which does not vary from one execution to the next.

'You need to remember that nothing could be further from the truth, and that the very technology which is now helping to destroy the economic prospects of the people whom this chamber has been designed to annihilate, is also being utilized to ensure that their efficient disposal becomes as painless an operation as possible. You need to remember, in other words, that this is the future, Abigail, not the antiquated atmosphere of the past, and that, as obvious a statement as it might sound, we do now live in a highly technologicized world.

'To see what I mean, please direct your pretty, translucent

eyes to the rope that is coiled around your lover's neck.'
Abigail's eyes did as they were asked, though they barely
needed to swivel in their sockets. 'Once a prisoner has been
weighed and brought through to the gallows,' Driscoll went
on, 'once the noose has been positioned around his neck, the
computer in that podium over there—which is itself linked
to weighing and medical facilities elsewhere in this building—is programmed to adjust the length of the rope to within thousandths of an inch, by use of the electric motor you
will have heard hidden inside the ceiling.

'And that is because the working out of the length of the
drop via mathematical calculation is, and always has been,
the single most important detail of a gallows execution. So
much so that in the old days a bag of sand was hanged first,
to stretch the rope to eliminate any potential for error. And
the reason really is quite simple. When Blake Hunter's body
falls through, at the moment of impact his cervical cord will
be dislocated at the base of his neck, his spinal column will
be ripped apart about halfway along, and a strong concus-
sion will instantly sever consciousness from his brain, never
to be resumed.' He smirked. 'Or at any rate, that is what
would happen, had we taken the precaution of weighing him
to establish the amount of rope necessary first.

'For you see, Abigail Sanders, if a length of rope proportionate to the subject's body-weight has not been worked
out beforehand, one of two things will happen when the
centreboards disappear. Either the rope will be too short,
meaning that Blake Hunter will die of asphyxiation, because
his body will not jerk against his head violently enough to
ensure a clean breaking of his neck. Or it will be too long,
meaning that his body will achieve such a velocity that at
the moment of impact he will actually be *decapitated*.' He
smirked again and scraped a forefinger against the side of
his face, deliberately trying to stretch out the tension,
searching for an indication in Abigail's beautiful eyes that
she might be starting to break. 'More accurately, as Blake
Hunter feels himself plummet and hears the air whistle past

his face and perhaps snatches a final glimpse of the rectangle of light as it recedes above him—and bearing in mind that we shall not use the hood—his body will be torn from his head, possibly dragging out with it much of the interior of his wretched skull.'

He had made his way round to the back of the centre-boards, and had paused to scrutinize Blake, who was now snuffling and gargling so painfully on the end of the rope he was being racked by a series of violent muscular contractions. 'But why, you may also ask, bother with an activity so barbaric as hanging in the first place? Surely a method of execution could be devised that is more in keeping with this aerodynamic, highly technologicized world upon which we find ourselves standing.' He took his eyes away from Blake's naked buttocks, aimed them back at Abigail, raised a couple of fingers, imbued his voice with something of an insane evangelical strain, and started pacing again.

'Popular misconception number two, and it connects to what I was telling your lover earlier, about how I've lost count of the number of people I've met who are staunchly pro-capital punishment, whose consciences would still feel troubled at the prospect of somebody having their neck snapped by a length of rope, but who could rest easy in the knowledge that a criminal was to be "put to sleep" with the aid of a nice clean needle and drug.' He glanced at Blake again and appealed to Abigail with a titter. 'But as you can see, when under extreme duress the human metabolism is capable of the most extraordinary resilience, and of course physiological characteristics vary from person to person. Indeed, there have been instances in the United States where prisoners under sentence of death by the electric chair have simply refused to die.' He tittered again, the shaft of light still playing with the hollows of his face. 'They were burned to a crisp, of course, but they did not die. And they did not die until several further attempts had been made, and they had endured excruciating physical cruelty along the way.

'Similarly, the use of an intravenous injection might be

effective in a good number, perhaps even in a majority of cases, but there would be a minority where it would not prove reliable enough. As you can imagine, Abigail, the insertion of a needle into a human body not only requires skill on the part of a doctor, but also the co-operation of the subject. Unfortunately, the emotional trauma experienced by a prisoner facing capital punishment means that neither of these things can always be guaranteed. The object of the disposal procedure is to get the thing over with as quickly as possible. But the actual speed of death, once a drug has been administered, cannot be guaranteed either, because the subject has to wait for it to act. He has to wait for his body to cease functioning. *He has to wait for himself to die.* Meanwhile, his adrenalin can build up a small resistance, which can delay the reaction time and prolong the suffering still further.' The shadows left his face, the smirk broadened and arranged itself into a smile. 'I hope that goes some way to answering the questions you have been thinking, Abigail, but have not yet managed to ask, about why it is that we should find ourselves confronting one another in such an ultra-modern execution facility as this.'

'Oh but you're quite wrong, Chief Constable,' Abigail said, her husky voice breaking her long silence at last. She noted that Driscoll did indeed consider this to be a confrontation. 'I'm well aware of the things you are saying because I watched Blake Hunter present a television documentary about the history of capital punishment, not long after the present controversy began. I just thought I'd let you carry on with your little self-indulgent soliloquy, so that I can better prepare myself to carry him out of this chamber alive.

'Meanwhile, I'm tempted to refer to what some poet or other said a long time ago, when wittering on about a remote political cause, no doubt from the comfort of a warm drawing-room while sipping a glass of very good sherry, about Spain and the *necessary murder*. But I shan't, because I doubt if you would appreciate its relevance. Instead, I shall remind *you*, Derek George Driscoll, that you've neglected to mention the traumas suffered by the warders, doctors, lawyers, and chaplains, who were involved in this perverted procedure of systemized State killing the last time round. People are needed to do these things, and they do tend to be drawn from the sensitive middle classes, don't they? And they're bound to question the morality of what it is they are doing, while the really nasty higher-ups who are giving them their orders needn't bother to dirty their hands.'

Although his head was ringing and the curtains of his consciousness were at last beginning to close, Blake gargled and tried to look at Abigail, as if to plead with her not to aggravate Driscoll, whose eyes had just come back onto hers before they pushed up his narrow brow in response to the impertinence of her words. But all that came out of Blake's mouth was a hideous moaning rasp. Abigail felt the agony as much as he did. Despite her apparent cool-headedness, she'd sought resolve in the belief that it was unlikely Driscoll would have strung Blake up how he had done, if he thought it was going to deny him the pleasure of seeing the live body hanged. But as Blake began to wheeze and she saw water run down his leg and form a puddle on the centreboards, she wasn't quite so sure. A couple of tears finally departed from her eyes and hurried away down her cheeks.

Driscoll had completed his little circuit, had arrived back in front of the centreboards, and was stood facing Abigail. He hooked his chin over his shoulder and scrunched his eyebrows distastefully when he saw the puddle flowing through the join in the rubber matting, and heard it splash against ceramic tiles in the chamber underneath. Then he smiled and flexed his shoulders contentedly when he turned back to see the moisture shining on Abigail's cheeks. Using the tears as his cue, and ignoring the things she'd just said, he reached out and ran his fingers through her silky hair, lifted it carefully behind her shoulder, and buffed one of her gold button earstuds with the ball of his thumb. Then he lowered the hand and explored her elegant neck sensuously with the tips of his thin dry fingers.

Abigail was looking straight into his eyes, but she was looking through him, she was absolutely motionless. Though her heart was beating so powerfully the blood was singing in her ears, though she felt sure that Driscoll would be able to see the jugular actually throbbing against the side of her neck, her head didn't so much as crick. If her ankles hadn't been bound she would have brought up her knee and crippled him there and then, knowing that it would have created enough of a distraction for her to be able to damn the consequences and pull the noose from Blake's head. But that was why Driscoll had authorized the use of a leg-strap before sending Stoneham away. He was frightened of her. The realization prompted her to finally allow herself the beginnings of a wry smile. She knew that she was in charge.

Driscoll's probing fingers had found the pumping jugular. 'You're not going to break are you, you bitch?' he whispered, twirling a lock of her hair around his forefinger in the simulation of a hangman's noose, then tugging at it gently so that it brought her face towards his own.

It wasn't what Driscoll was doing or saying that was Abigail's immediate concern, but the unbelievably foul stench of his bad breath staining the air between their faces. It was so powerful she could practically taste it.

'No, Chief Constable, I'm not going to break. Not because of the sounds your words are forming, anyway.' Her unblinking eyes were still on his, the perfectly-formed nose above it was trying not to breathe in the hideous stink. Driscoll was too vain and too sexually aroused to pick up the cryptic inference of what she'd just said. She realized this and broadened her smile another few degrees, then added: 'I'm afraid you'll have to do to me what you did back in the condemned cell, if you want to make me buckle. Which I think would better serve to illustrate where intellectually either of us stands, wouldn't you say?'

'We shall see, young lady,' Driscoll said, 'we shall see.' The thin colourless lips framing the orifice that was releasing the bad breath lubricated themselves with a rather bluish tongue. Then the head over which the thin covering of pale flesh was stretched intercepted another sequence of gargling sounds via its ears, swivelled on its neck again, and noted that the whites of Blake's eyes were finally beginning to roll.

To compensate for the feelings of inadequacy that he experienced whenever he was near assertive women such as Abigail, and to cancel his constant sense of irritation at not being just as tall as she was, Driscoll brought his hand away from her neck and dragged the fingers slowly between her breasts. He bent down and unwrapped the velcro strap securing her ankles (approaching her from behind, she noted, for the same reason a dog always yaps at somebody's heels), then hummed a tune while he marched across and mounted the podium, before she had the chance to grab him.

To distract her, he stabbed at the computer keypad and instantly cancelled the tightness of the rope supporting Blake. Blake yelped and slammed onto his back on the rubber matting, almost as fast as he would had he been attached to an elastic-band that had been stretched to its limit then suddenly snapped. He began squirming and coughing as he fought to regain his breath. But because he'd landed on his back, because his feet and hands were still bound, because his energy was almost completely depleted, he couldn't turn onto his side, and he started choking on a fountain of his own bile.

Now that her ankles were free, Abigail tensed as though she were about to lunge; but Driscoll was already speaking from behind her. 'Don't even think about it, Abigail. My finger is over the button. The moment you move, Blake Hunter will drop before the blood has finished pumping through your heart to form the beginning of the next beat.'

She had to stand no more than her own body-length away from Blake and watch him suffer. Though she remained extraordinarily composed, though she was rooted to the spot for fear that Driscoll might think that she was moving and cause the floor to disappear, the tears streamed down her face despite herself, as much a product of rage as of her desperate need to go to her man. Blake's eyes were just about meeting hers through the blur of moisture. She could see the sweat shining on his brow and she mouthed encouragement silently, knowing that Driscoll would be unable to see what she was doing. Blake choked when he saw her lips moving; when he saw that her beautiful eyes were catching the light and seemed to be glowing like luminous gemstones against the darkness; willing him to turn over; willing him to live; willing him to love. The emotion channelled in him a massive burst of energy and he snarled and lurched at last onto his side, his cheek skidding through the pool of frothy bile. He was twisted into an obscene contortion, he'd started panting violently, his throat was burning from a succession of angry coughs, there was a tremendous carbonated-water sensation assailing his nostrils; but he was managing to get his breath back, and for the moment he was safe.

Then Abigail realized that he might not have been in as much distress as she thought. She saw that he'd been using his position to cover the fact that he'd been loosening the velcro strap binding his wrists, while he was laid on his back, and that, because of his new sideways attitude, Driscoll still wouldn't be able to tell.

Driscoll allowed a generous length of rope to feed from the ceiling, then spread his hands upon the podium as though he were preaching from a pulpit, the whites of his eyes faintly manic set against the darkness.

'Now that I've freed your legs, Abigail,' he said, thoroughly turned-on as his eyes fastened onto her leather-trousered buttocks and he geared himself up for what he was going to do to her after he'd killed Blake, 'if you're quick, when I make the floor disappear, you might just be able to reach out in the nick of time before your lover drops. I want you to think about that during these closing few moments, young lady. I want you to think about what you've got to do when the floor gives way, because I am going to break you if I have to snap your fucking spine over my knee first.

'I want you to think of your man, naked and shrivelled and pathetic as he is. I want you to think of Blake Hunter, forever chipping away from the comfort of his *Panorama* pulpit, undermining the laws of natural human evolution, but with the programme of his own life story drawing to a close. I want you to imagine how the two of you might have settled down together. I want you to imagine how you might have begotten him another child. I want you to inhale his musky smell. I want you to picture yourself wrapping your slender naked limbs around his. Look at him Abigail, look at him now. Think of how you long to cradle him to your naked bosom, to run your fingers through his hair, to nurse him back to life. It's rare for a man to be able to identify with strong women like he does, isn't it? Think of that now. Think of how you yearn to feel Blake Hunter pushing himself deep inside you and fusing to your own marvellous body; expressing to you his tender, undying love.

'I want you to think of all these things before I finally take away the floor, Abigail Sanders. I want you to look at the urine-stained hairline split where the rubber matting will part to send Blake Hunter to his decapitation. *Look at the floor you bitch.* Can you grab him as it opens up, perhaps breaking your pretty, clear-varnished fingernails as you scramble with him against the edge of the hole?

'I hope for entertainment's sake that you can, young lady, for it would be a great shame if there were only one attempt made at this liberal-minded journalist's execution. Think of Blake Hunter scrabbling against that shiny rubber matting upon which your shiny brown ankle-boots stand, the studs of that matting as yet untarnished from being witness to a hundred-thousand useless working-class deaths.'

He paused, during which time a helicopter thundered above the underground complex, muffled somewhere outside.

'Well?' he demanded. 'What is it to be, Abigail Sanders? Is it to be death, or is it to be life?'

The blood was pounding in Abigail's ears so fiercely now

that Driscoll's words were oscillating and she was beginning to hyperventilate. She knew how close she was to the end and braced herself ready to spring, her fists clenched so tightly that her fingernails were digging crescents in her palms and her eyes were drilling into Blake's. Though she had her back to Driscoll, she tried to decide when his eyes were likely to flash for a split-second away from her shoulders and fasten onto Blake.

'I'm going to save you, Blake,' she said, to try and prompt Driscoll, surprised to hear the words that she was thinking emerge from her mouth, not surprised to hear that they were trembling, but suddenly shivering as she came to terms with what was about to happen. 'I promise I'm going to save you.'

Blake's thoughts were at last starting to clear and he, too, braced himself for what was coming, his teeth gritted, his eyes flitting between Abigail's and Driscoll's, his fingers grappling with the velcro strap, groaning to disguise the noise of the tearing, heartbeat pounding, snarling and trying to say something but wheezing hoarsely, voice temporarily obliterated after his strangulatory ordeal.

'You're scared,' Driscoll said. 'By God, the two of you are scared!' He was beginning to mutter erotically between sentences now, but still Abigail remained rooted to the spot, her feet together, her hands by her sides, her body silhouetted against the shaft of light, her adrenalin pumping so powerfully that a pain was intensifying in her stomach where Driscoll's opening punch had set the wound from the tranquillizer dart throbbing again, after he'd thumped her back in the cell.

'Break, you bitch,' Driscoll shrieked, fighting for breath himself now, his hand trembling above the button, determined to see Abigail move before he touched it, determined to stay in the ascendency, then screaming for all he was worth: *'For Christ's sake break, Abigail Sanders, break!'*

When Driscoll smashed his clenched fist onto the keypad and obliterated half the console rather than depressed merely a single button upon it, Abigail sprang. She saw the centre-boards split and sag as they were raped of their definition of the horizontal, and Blake's body began to fall. At the same time, Blake's hands flew out from behind his back, the velcro strap spinning free like a discarded ribbon and skidding towards the podium as he dived towards her. Abigail slammed full-length onto the rubber matting, heard Driscoll squealing like a wild pig in the background, winced as her breasts were flattened from the impact, and reached for Blake's hands, the smell of new rubber suddenly close to her face.

Blake's hands slapped onto the floor in front of hers, and he managed to lunge and hook himself by his belly against the edge of the hole, his fingers clawing and scrabbling desperately. But with nothing to grip and with nothing but empty space beneath him, the weight of his body was already pulling him backwards, and he felt his palms ripple away from her across the bumps of the rubber studs, his mouth opening as he fell. Abigail felt her own hands briefly encircle his wrists. Their eyes met, said silently to each other the only thing that mattered; but before she could fasten onto him properly the force of him falling had yanked them apart, and to her horror he was gone.

He screamed the first two syllables of her name as he fell. She saw the rope feeding itself crazily into the rectangular chasm, during which time she was horrified to note that she was waiting for his scream to finish. And then there came the impact. She heard a sort of muffled snap and a bark as Blake was decapitated, then a second later heard his body slam against the floor, before everything was brought to a violently sudden, all-consuming, terribly deafening silence.

Abigail's chin was resting against the rubber matting, the saliva was stretched between her mouth and the studs, her face was angled towards the hole, and a gargled moan was sounding out at the back of her throat. She saw the orange rope kink as it snapped up from the recoil, almost as though it were moving in slow-motion. Then it came back down and swayed loosely, devoid now of tautness and of the heavy weight at the end. When she realized she'd failed to save Blake, despite knowing that if she had done Driscoll would have hanged him again and done the job properly, she screamed and screamed and screamed and screamed and screamed and screamed and screamed. It wasn't a hysterical female scream, for Abigail was not that kind of woman. Now that the worst had happened, it was a release of repressed animal rage, much like that which Blake had let out in the condemned cell when Driscoll had beaten her up.

When the scream finished and she knew that Blake was dead, when she heard Driscoll step down from the podium and contemplated the horrors that awaited her now, she began to wheeze violently, her eyes glued to the rope swinging in the hole, her trembling hands still outstretched, her fingers frozen in claw-holds at midair, her entire body consumed by a sort of queasy numbness that somehow seemed to originate from her sphincter.

Driscoll was breathing heavily, almost like an exhausted animal, when he came up alongside her and tittered. 'Oh dear, Abigail, you didn't manage to save him. And now I'm afraid that I have to fuck you. Perhaps we could stand Blake Hunter's head on the table in the condemned cell while we do it. Would you like to go down and fetch it, please? I shall break your fingers if you don't.'

He was about to step over and look down between the open centreboards when a spontaneous concentration of angry energy exploded in Abigail's body, and she snarled and sprang to her feet and smashed her clenched fist straight into his mouth, her dark hair flying. The blow was delivered with such a ferocity that most of Driscoll's front teeth were obliterated, and Abigail felt them give way. The teeth were not actually real. All the originals in his mouth had long since been removed, then replaced, at a cost of many thousands of pounds, with a set of perfect vitrified-porcelain replicas; the new teeth sunk in the holes and cemented to the bloody gums before the flesh had contracted and healed.

Now the thin colourless lips covering the place where the front teeth had been glued were splitting, as the throat at the base of the cavity from which an angry snarl was rolling felt broken fragments clog it up, and the blue-uniformed body staggered backwards and crumpled like a rag-doll against the podium. Abigail yelped from the pain of punching him, her hand suddenly sizzling as though it were on fire. But the yelp instantly became another snarl and she rushed forward, grabbed him, then smashed her fist into his face again and again, lashing out with her hand, every other swing a vicious backhander, sending him careering across the chamber, shrieking obscenities at him all the way, her dark pupils mere dots against the furious whites of her eyes.

After several blows, Driscoll overbalanced and started pedalling away from her. But she caught hold of him before he fell over and swung him round again, so that he ricochetted against the side of the podium for a second time, then stumbled clumsily onto all-fours. He shook his head and frowned while he tried to find his senses, her attack having caught him completely unawares. Then he growled and lifted himself from the rubber matting, garbling threats to kill her. But as he came at her, Abigail ran up to meet him and smashed her fist into his face yet again, so hard that this time she felt his nose break, and he careered full length onto his back, his tie thrashing like a snake, his body dragging beneath it a bloody skidmark across the sea of grey rubber-studs.

He rolled over and scrambled upright and coughed blood and fragments of broken teeth out onto his palm, clearing his throat at last. His fingers went feverishly to his mouth, panic flashing across his face when he pushed the flaps of skin backwards and realized there was nothing substantial left behind them. He snarled again and launched himself towards Abigail, who was in the process of launching herself at him. But before she could move out of the way, Driscoll levered up his leg like a pole-vaulter's stick, caught her in the stomach, then hoisted her so that she somersaulted through the vertical above him and slammed full-length onto her back.

She was momentarily stunned, and her body wouldn't respond. This gave Driscoll the time to crawl up and roll onto her and pin her and start trying to strangle her, his eyes wild, a hysterical laugh screeching from between his rapidly-swelling lips. Abigail spluttered and coughed, her brilliant teeth grinding, her hair splayed onto the rubber matting, blood splashing from Driscoll's mouth down onto her contorting face. She took hold of his hairy wrists then scratched his face and tried to kick up her legs. But he was too heavy. As his thumbs started depressing her larynx she felt his body thrusting while he moaned and simulated trying to fuck her, the damage to his face only serving to heighten his depraved sexual excitement.

Abigail was beginning to cry. Mucus was clogging the back of her nose. The shapes around her were distorting as there swelled behind her eyes the pressure that becomes an unpressure that then becomes sleep. But suddenly she clenched her fists together and brought them up as hard as she could against the sides of Driscoll's head, as though she were clapping together a pair of cymbals. He barked and his tongue shot out, then he went limp as he felt his eardrums pop and wondered if his skull had cracked and saw a stream of light flash crazily before his eyes. Before he slumped onto her Abigail shoved him aside and scrambled away on her haunches, one of her ankle-boots coming off as she pulled her foot out from beneath him. She was horrified at what was happening; was appalled at how she was indulging in such a disgusting orgy of physical violence. But there was absolutely no other way she could expect to stay alive, and all she could see was Blake's pleading eyes as he'd slipped away from her; as he'd disappeared and screamed her name as he fell through the hole.

Driscoll had managed to find his feet again and was staggering towards her, but his eyes were not focusing properly. Abigail stood up to face him. He swayed, the blood actually frothing at the base of his nostrils as he panted and wheezed, the bottom part of his face a soaking cherry-red mess with tiny fragments of broken teeth sliding down all the time, dripping onto the slimy red bib that formed the front of his white shirt. There was a moment when the now-bloated lips suggested they might be trying to form a grin, the flesh being manipulated by a broken cackle that had started rattling in his throat. Then he coughed and tried to mutter something obscene and his hands were lifting weakly towards her throat.

It was the final punch that disgusted Abigail most of all. It seemed to drive home the true horror of what had taken place in this execution chamber; emphasised how these events and the memory of this environment would be coming between her and sleep for the rest of her life—assuming she managed to alert somebody with the phone attached to the intercom on the wall, and escaped from the building alive. Before she hit him, she wondered if she saw something like respect flash through Driscoll's black, rat-like eyes. Then she growled, her nostrils flared characteristically, and she lashed out with the back of her other hand, not as strongly as before, and he fountained a spray of blood and pirouetted and crashed again into the podium.

As he did so, his distended fingers accidentally brushed what remained of the computer keypad, the electric motor sounded in the ceiling, and the rope began to rise slowly from between the hanging centreboards. Abigail dragged him away from the podium by the scruff of the neck, her own strength rapidly dwindling. Driscoll was now trying to cover his face with his hands and was begging her to leave him alone. But it was as though she were possessed, and she swung him round and let him go and watched him flail head first against the stainless-steel door leading back to the condemned cell.

Then she dropped exhausted to her knees.

There was a sickening thud as Driscoll impacted against the metal; then his flattened face dragged a bloody smudge down the shiny surface as he plunged to the matting. He moved slightly and made a sound that might have been a belch or a groan, while Abigail crawled across and grabbed the collar of his tunic, lifted him with both her hands, and slammed his face against the door. She experienced a terrible feeling of pathos as she bludgeoned him repeatedly against the metal, knowing that what she was doing was wrong, knowing that she'd somehow lowered herself to the emotional level of a brutal reactionary, crying all the way, her emotion intensifying but her teeth gnashing harder with each successive swing.

Then suddenly, when she was aiming his face at the metal for the fourth or fifth time, noting that he'd gone limp and that it was time to be merciful and let him go, to her amazement the steel panel slid out of the way. Just at the point when Driscoll's face would have hit the metal she had to release him and let the body flop across the threshold, to prevent herself from falling on top of him from behind.

Then several Airborne Policemen were jumping over them into the execution chamber, gazing in amazement at what they'd stumbled upon, wielding machineguns and wearing visored helmets and telling everybody to freeze. Abigail ignored the order, scrambled aside, and brought her back up against the steel wall to the right of the door, as the policemen spread out. She started to moan when the fluorescent lights flickered on and she realized how messily her beige angora sweater, her face, and her hands were spattered with Driscoll's blood; that her knuckles were also bloodied and torn; and that the pain in her hand was now really beginning to burn.

The policemen danced around the chamber and assumed absurd commando-type crouches; then they relaxed and straightened. Three of them hooked their guns onto their shoulders and came over and picked up the mumbling Driscoll, then carried him through to the condemned cell as if they were soldiers picking up a corpse and dragging it from the field of battle.

The fourth policeman rested his machinegun against his shoulder and walked across to the open centreboards, arriving just as the rope finished coming up through the hole and automatically drew to a halt. Abigail saw that the noose had been ripped completely away by the force of Blake's fall, and she could have sworn there was blood staining the fray at the end.

The policeman squinted at the rope, then stood at the edge of the hole and looked down between the centreboards and frowned. He muttered something into the radio-mouthpiece that was clamped to the side of his head, and which linked him to the Operations Controller back in the helicopter; then he was called through to the condemned cell by the others. He glanced at Abigail along the way, made a quick assessment of what she had obviously done to Driscoll, and felt that it would probably be better if he left her alone for the next few minutes.

Abigail put her hand over her eyes, drew up her knees, tried to gather some breath and decide if her nightmare was real, and struggled not to imagine the scene that must be spread beneath the gallows. She was also wondering what had suddenly happened; why the policemen had burst into the chamber at all. She was wondering whether she'd caught a glimpse of Stoneham in the corridor beyond the condemned cell, just before Driscoll had slumped away from her when the steel door had parted. She was remembering the way Stoneham had smoothed her hair, the expression on his face when he'd left the chamber, and her suspicion that he was probably a homosexual. She was remembering, too, the muffled sound of the helicopter she'd heard outside the building, moments before Blake had dropped.

But she was thinking, above everything else, that if the policemen had got there only a few minutes sooner, then they would almost certainly have saved Blake's life.

Then she was conscious that a pair of legs were standing alongside her, and she glanced up sharply to see . . .

Vanessa looming over her . . .

Abigail recognized her as Blake's producer, having seen them together on a number of occasions in the past. Vanessa was still wearing the blue jeans, red pullover, and her blue leather jacket, having come straight from the Salford Quays flat. She was also wearing her rimless round spectacles. The pale-blue eyes behind them were moist and her face was rapidly losing colour when she dropped to her knees, hooked her hair behind her ear, and reached out for Abigail. Both women were shocked to find each other in the death chamber but at that moment Abigail didn't care. All she knew was that Vanessa represented her only living link with Blake. She clung to Vanessa and started trembling violently, the shock of what she'd been through finally beginning to sink in; her crying muffled against the older woman's shoulder; both of them thankful that at last they'd each got someone to hold.

There was no need for Vanessa to say anything because she could see by looking at the torn rope, and by guessing at what had happened to Driscoll, that Blake must be dead. And she was so preoccupied with blaming herself that having managed to escape from the flat alive was already becoming an insignificant blur. She recalled a lot of grunting and swearing after she'd kicked the young policeman who'd been left guarding her square between the legs, when he'd finally stepped too close just as they were about to leave. She remembered several shotgun blasts when Addison leapt into the room, and, several minutes later, the screeching of car tyres as she'd fled at what seemed like a hundred miles an hour in her car across the herringbone sets. She remembered phoning Sarah and desperately telling her to alert David Kowalski's unit of Airborne Police, having more or less lip-read Driscoll when he'd whispered to the young policeman where they were taking Blake before they'd left. Because of the late-sergeant's connection with the film, she'd managed eventually to convince the policemen about what was probably taking place at Strangeways Prison. Only they'd arrived too late, and as far as she was concerned it was because she'd tried to seduce Blake, when he'd already given his heart to this poor trembling young woman in her arms, that he was now dead.

Vanessa pulled a handkerchief from her sleeve and began wiping the blood from Abigail's face, then looked up when the young policeman came back through from the condemned cell. She watched him step over the bloody skidmarks covering the floor and resume his position by the open centreboards. He examined the broken end of the rope, then glanced down into the hole again, supporting his body on one knee as he bent to look over the edge, frowning as he had done earlier while he contemplated what was obviously laid on the floor of the chamber underneath.

Abigail sniffed and looked up too. She'd been enormously reassured by Vanessa's presence, but was suddenly gripped by a terrible fear that she might have become a killer herself. 'I didn't kill him, did I?' she asked the chamber hoarsely.

Vanessa was surprised at how husky Abigail's voice sounded, now that she'd broken her silence.

The policeman turned to face them and lifted off his helmet, revealing a rather narrow head surmounted by very tightly-cropped bristly blonde hair. 'Did you kill who?' he asked in a light Mancunian accent, feeling a pang of guilt when his body registered how attractive both the women were, despite it being such a distressing moment.

'Chief Constable Driscoll,' Abigail said.

'No, I don't think so. But I think it would be fair to say that you gave him a bloody nose.'

He could see that Abigail was relieved, and he attempted a smile. He felt an urge to say that Driscoll had merely got what he deserved, and that plenty of people in the force would be raising their glasses that evening; but he thought better of it under the circumstances. Then he noticed that one of Abigail's ankle-boots was missing, saw it alongside the podium, picked it up, and passed it to Vanessa. Vanessa straightened Abigail's sock for her and slipped the boot back onto her foot.

The policeman was still frowning. He was confused about what the environment represented, though because of the fantastic story Vanessa had told them as they'd flown up to the prison, he could imagine easily enough. He was a little nervous yet of asking any questions, but he cleared his throat and decided to give it a try. He wiped his fingers across his forehead and aimed his words at Abigail. 'My name is Air Constable Winstanley. Forgive me if I sound like I'm stating the obvious, but what exactly happened in here? Was the Chief Constable going to hang you first?'

Vanessa started to say something, but Abigail let out some breath and cut in. 'It's pretty obvious what's happened isn't it? You've stood and looked down through the hole twice since you've been in.'

Winstanley frowned again and looked as though he were a stock character about to scratch his head. 'I'm sorry, but I don't understand what you mean.' One of the other policemen appeared in the doorway with his mouth open, but Winstanley waved him away.

Abigail swallowed. Her mouth felt terrifically dry, and the bruises caused by Driscoll beating her earlier in the condemned cell had started to complain all over her body. 'But you've looked down through the hole, officer,' she said firmly. 'Blake Hunter has been hanged. Don't tell me you can't use your own eyes, even if you don't know who Blake Hunter is.'

Winstanley looked genuinely puzzled.

'But there's nobody there, Miss.'

'What do you mean there isn't anybody there?'

She was already levering herself up the steel wall, her heart beginning to pound again, her breath coming in short gasps.

Vanessa was alongside her, holding her hand.

'There's nothing there,' Winstanley repeated. 'That's what I can't fathom out. The end of the rope looks like it's been snapped, yet I can't see a noose.'

Abigail let go of Vanessa's hand and went up to the hole,

closing her eyes and taking in a lot of breath before she looked over the edge. She knelt down and opened her eyes. There was nothing but white ceramic covering the floor a couple of storeys beneath, with a number of black drainage grates set into the surface. There was no blood, no Blake, no severed head, nothing; just a faint wet shine catching the light, where the urine had spattered the tiles.

She pulled herself away, a sensation of vertigo briefly numbing her mind. 'But Driscoll hanged him . . .' she croaked, her eyes appealing to the others for support. 'I saw him fall away from me. He was screaming my name . . .'

Utterly confused, she laid down but this time leaned right over the rim, looking past the hanging centreboards, her dark hair dangling, the blood pounding in her ears as it rushed towards her head. She could see most of the chamber beneath her now and there was definitely nobody there. The white tiles covered the floor and extended all the way up the walls to meet the underside of the floor upon which she was laid, which formed the ceiling of the secondary chamber. She felt sick when she saw a mains-hosepipe, some mops and shovels, a waste-disposal socket set into the wall, and a pair of steel doors that were identified by an embossed legend as leading to an adjacent crematorium.

Then her eyes went to the flight of metal access steps, which came up through the hole in the floor of the upper chamber, across to her left. From her position she could only see the foot of the staircase before it disappeared behind a tiled wall that enclosed it downstairs, and which created a blind-spot. She lifted her head away from the hole and saw a huge expanse of grey rubber-studs, sweeping towards the hazardline framing the place where the steps arrived through the floor by the wall.

'Oh my God . . .' she moaned, as the realization sunk home. She jumped to her feet and bolted across to the top of the steps and froze. Blake was about a third of the way up, crumpled full-length, dead or alive she couldn't tell, but with a single clawed hand outstretched. She scrambled down the steps, almost slipping on the embossed metal treadplate, with Vanessa and Winstanley close behind her. Winstanley was startled to see that Blake was naked, and said something about not moving him. But Blake was already coming round as Abigail cradled his head and brought their mouths together. She knew what had happened now, when she saw the orange noose actually looped around Blake's chest. As he'd fallen, his subconscious reflexes had obviously sent up his hands, parted the rope from around his neck, and wrenched it down beneath his armpits, all in the couple of seconds of weightlessness prior to impact. If such an escape wasn't a physical impossibility, then it was because it was probably a miracle. Vanessa was lowering her buttocks to one of the metal steps and thanking God and deciding that it was definitely a miracle.

Abigail laid next to Blake and hugged him and also thanked God that he was still alive. He was shivering from a combination of fear, exultation, and cold. But he smiled and lifted his hand and touched the tears running down her cheeks, then brought the fingers back to his mouth and tasted salt against his tongue. Then he was muttering something about the quantity of dried blood smeared across her face and staining her clothes.

'Don't worry about me,' she said. 'Can you still feel your legs?'

She was afraid that he might have broken his back.

'Yes,' he winced, and lifted one to prove it. 'But I feel as if I've slipped half my discs, and I think I've broken one of my calf-bones.'

Abigail saw a bulge beneath the surface of the skin on the lower part of his left leg. She saw, too, that the flesh was grazed raw from friction where the noose had jerked against the sides of his chest, before the rope had snapped. She tested the noose to check that it wasn't cutting into him. 'How the hell did you manage to do that, Blake?' she asked, still not believing such an escape was feasible, shuddering at the thought of how close she'd come to losing him.

'I don't know. But I know that the rope didn't break for about half-a-second when I hit the bottom, that it seemed to slow me down, and that I blacked out. When I woke up there was a terrific commotion going on upstairs as I crawled across to the steps. I thought Driscoll was killing you. I had to bite back the pain'—he pulled out his other hand from beneath him: there were teeth marks gouged into the flesh—'and then I passed out again until now.' He grimaced then coughed, then grimaced from the cough. 'God, my leg hurts, and my rib-cage feels like it's been crushed.'

Abigail realized that neither herself nor Driscoll had heard Blake moving because of the noise of them fighting. Suddenly she knew that what she'd done to Driscoll wasn't going to stain her life as badly as she'd expected. If Driscoll had made it to the open centreboards before she'd jumped up and attacked him, because of the condition that he'd been in after his fall, Blake would probably now have been dead.

Then Vanessa was saying something about the steps being cold against Blake's body and was holding out her blue leather jacket. Abigail accepted it and laid it gently over his shoulders. Blake recognized the voice and the coat, but more especially he recognized its wonderful lavender-like smell. He looked up and saw Vanessa. 'Vanessa,' he croaked, his tongue clogging his throat, 'but I thought they'd killed you. I thought they'd killed my best friend. But you're alive . . .' He noticed that she was wearing her spectacles, and that this morning they had the effect not of making her look studious and scholarly, but of somehow bringing out her femininity more naturally than ever.

'Oh thank God, *you're alive* . . .'

'Yes, Blake, and so are you. The nation is hardly going to believe it, but so are you.'

She had to put her hand over her mouth and drew in emotion as well as air between her fingers, when she saw the look in his eyes . . .

Abigail scrutinized Blake lovingly, but she was hopelessly

confused when he clung to her yet seemed to be trying to push himself away from her at one and the same time, pressing his face so powerfully between her breasts it were as though he were trying to shut out the light. Obviously delirious, he told her that he needed her but that he was suddenly hurting more than he'd ever hurt before in his life. He started saying something about losing control of a car again. He said that this time he'd hit the verge and had cartwheeled into the field beyond; that he'd exploded amidst a great curtain of flame spreading against the blackness of the night.

Then he moaned somebody's name and passed out.

A voice in Winstanley's ear told him that the media had arrived outside. He clumped back up the steps and pulled the radio-mouthpiece to his face, asking the Operations Controller aboard the helicopter to call for an Airborne Ambulance then to send down a stretcher. But when he got to the top he was surprised to see that Abigail was following him up. He waited for her and looked down at Vanessa, who was still sitting on the step above Blake, her already pale face turning even whiter, her hands literally shaking against her lap.

When she reached the top of the steps, Abigail turned and Vanessa saw that she was looking rather pale, too. Blake was stirring again, trying to lift to his elbows, trying to focus his eyes, still muttering somebody's name.

The two women looked at each other, and smiled.